KARMA IS A WITCH

Deadlights Cove, Book 5

B. PERKINS

AIMEE VANCE

Revel Books

Revel Books
Paperback ISBN: 979-8-9882650-4-7

www.aimeevancebooks.com

For our Covies:
You know who you are.

Chapter One

DEVANNA

"STUPID SHITTY-ASS HOUSE," I muttered as I shoved my back against the front door unsuccessfully, trying to push it closed. More than likely it was stuck on one of thousands of uneven floorboards I had yet to address. Old houses — or in this case, churches — were stubborn and full of quirks, but I could out-stubborn and out-quirk even this damn building I'd so foolishly bought earlier this spring.

I tended to do this thing where I bit off more than I could chew, then refused to admit I might have been wrong. Purchasing this church was at the top of my "stupid decisions" list, right up there with the time I'd decided to cut my own bangs. I still hadn't forgiven my best friend Nimue for not talking me out of that, though I had enough self-awareness to know that if she'd told me no, I'd only have wanted to do it *more*. But that was besides the point.

Two weeks ago, I'd sat in my bell tower and watched Lysander, a fellow witch from my Coven I considered a brother, go through the Linking ceremony with Maisie, his gorgeous sea nymph princess girlfriend. The spell would allow them to access each other's magic, so now Lys could turn into any one of the various sea-nymph forms, and Maisie could work witch spells. At least, once they practiced. Happiness surrounded them like a bubble as they stood on the steps of Deadlights Cove Town Hall, even after the horrid turn of events only days before that had left Lys tied to the bottom of a pier, awaiting a watery grave.

Several days later, Kit and Nimue had followed in their footsteps, Linking their powers in a lifelong bond, then Selene and Ryker, and even Petra and Blaze. I still couldn't believe the Linking had worked, passing magic to Petra, a *human*. No one knew the extent of her powers yet, but Blaze had fallen to his knees in a weeping pile of emotion as he clung to her, laughing uncontrollably when she accidentally set fire to his shirt.

It wasn't often I felt left out — and I had *no* desire to Link myself forever to anyone — but seeing all of my friends start a new chapter of their lives had left me feeling… feelings.

I hated feelings.

And despite knowing *why* I felt the way I did, it didn't make the feelings go away, or any less real. After years of therapy, I was able to identify that having my parents abandon me at a young age had left scars I wasn't sure I'd ever outgrow. I knew *rationally* Nimue and the others wouldn't abandon me as their lives changed, that this quirky town was more my family than I'd ever had with my flighty, hippie parents, but there were no TSA guidelines for the size of emotional baggage one could carry. Mine might as well have had a large neon orange *HEAVY* sticker on it.

But that was the nice thing about baggage. It could be zipped up, shoved in the dark, and never seen until you needed it again.

I'd need mine never.

So I did what I did best and stuffed those swirling *feelings* from seeing all of my friends pair off into the metaphorical luggage and threw it in the basement, where it could gather cobwebs with the rest of my issues.

What I needed was a distraction, something to do with my hands so my mind didn't have time to wander to the forgotten *luggage*. For a month, I'd thrown myself into renovating the ancient church I was making into my home, pushing all thoughts of changing friendships far from my mind.

The moment Orion, our town mayor, had said it would be impossible to refinish the church to "acceptable standards" before the Summit, I was determined to prove him wrong. Though, that could be said of almost everything our obnoxious angel overlord had said to me in the last ten years. Why he, of all people, got under my skin so easily was a mystery to me, but I loathed him with every fiber of my being.

Orion had one fatal flaw in his argument — he'd never specified *whose* acceptable standards it had to meet.

His stuffy standards and mine were vastly different, and the only opinion I ever cared about was my own.

So, the week before the Summit, I'd focused my energy on the *outside*.

Or, at least, had attempted it.

I'd used every drop of my witchy knowledge to paint the outside in shades of the deepest black. I'd banished every weed among the many tombstones decorating my front yard. I'd even refinished the walkway from the sidewalk to the church, planting peonies all along the front of the building, and trimmed back the overgrown oak trees. Gothic, scary, with a splash of charm, just like me.

Except for the windows.

The bane of my existence.

Maybe I should have tackled them before I'd exhausted myself getting the peonies to bloom just right, an eruption of purple against the black background. By the time I got to the windows the night before the Summit, I watched window after window explode with each spell I cast.

Should I have asked for help?

Probably.

Did I?

Abso-fucking-lutely not.

I'd been on my own for a long time and done just fine. Asking for help was one tiny step away from admitting defeat, and there was no way in hell I would do that, no matter how desperate my desire was to shove Orion's words in his face.

Again and again, I kept trying. Glass shards had rained down on me long into the night, until I finally slid to the ground in defeat, slumping against Willa Rosewood's tombstone and whispering quietly that I'd sacrifice my first child in her honor if she came back from the dead long enough to fix the damn windows. At least I knew she'd keep the fact that I'd asked for help a secret.

I didn't plan on having children, but the ghost of Blaze's mother didn't need to know that.

I'd closed my eyes for a moment to take a breather and, exhausted from a long day of physical and magical labor, had drifted off. I still wasn't sure how long I'd been out, but I'd awoken to shiny new windows, crystal clear panes with the same leaded detail the originals had.

Almost a month had passed since then and light shone through those same windows now, highlighting how dusty and awful the inside of the church was despite weeks of tireless work clearing out the inside. But I was determined to fix this old piece of shit up, now more than ever.

I refused to abandon this house the way I'd been left behind. Difficult. Unlovable. Not worth the time.

"You can't get rid of me that easy," I hissed at the door as I leaned in, gathering whatever strength I could find as I assigned emotions to inanimate objects — a habit I'd always had. The front door had sat ajar for decades, and before I started spending money on the interior fixtures, I needed to get this thing closed. "Now *move.*"

Wood creaked as I heaved on the door again, sweat beading on my brow as a strand of bright blue hair fell in front of my thick-framed glasses. I let out a shout of victory as the door inched closed, leaving a sliver of space between it and the jamb. Before I could push it any further, a black cat streaked through the opening, scampering into the church.

I stopped, spinning to look into the mostly dark space, staring out over the vast room that used to be the chapel but now stood barren of any furniture — totally gutted.

"Bagheera?" I called, squinting into the darkness. Silence lingered, but unlike the witchy TV shows humans loved so much, this black cat didn't talk — which was probably a good thing. Bagheera was meaner than me, but who could blame him after living with Mrs. Farrington for so long? The kooky old witch from my Coven had a penchant for dressing the cat up against his will, forcing him to take walks around town. Anyone would go a bit feral in that situation. "Kill some of the mice in here and I'll let you hide out for a bit. We'll keep it a secret."

Just as I moved to step into the room, sirens wailed in the distance, moving closer. Spinning back to the door, I peered through the gap, debating if I should pry the door back open and then inevitably start all over as I tried to close it again later.

A sheriff's car, three Spring Harbor Police Department cars, and two black SUVs barreled through town, circling the gazebo before flying past Immortali-Tea and down the street where Morgaine and Lysander lived.

Deadlights Cove never called for outside police.

"Uh oh," I said, throwing my weight into the door to haul it open. I hurried down the steps and onto the sidewalk as Blaze emerged from Scallywags, his bar a few buildings over from the church. Spotting me, he flickered to my side in an instant, disappearing and then reappearing the way demons could.

"Are those *human* cops?" Blaze said, running a hand through his dark, messy hair as we both stared after the cars. His white tee stood out against his olive skin, and his ripped jeans and black Chucks, not to mention his appearance, which looked like a human in their mid-thirties, gave no indication to his true age. Demons were all but immortal, and Blaze was considered a fairly young one at 147 years old.

"They have to be, right? And maybe don't flicker, just in case."

"Smart. Orion is going to have a coronary." Pausing on that thought, Blaze's brow scrunched. "Can angels have heart attacks? O's blood pressure has got to be through the roof."

"Pretty sure you have to have a heart to have a coronary, so Orion is safe."

Blaze chuckled, then remembered the cop cars. Their sirens had turned off, but the silence was almost more ominous. We stood there, listening to the waves in the cove and the sound of the harbor bell buoy clanging in the distance.

"We shouldn't go check it out, should we?" I asked, chewing on my lip. Meddling with human affairs could be dangerous for supernaturals, and Deadlights Cove was supposed to be glamoured, repelling humans from the town hidden along the coast of Maine.

"Curiosity killed the cat," Blaze said as he crossed his arms, still staring where the cops had turned onto Morgaine's street. With a mischievous grin, he raised one eyebrow. "Good thing we're not cats, right?"

I shrugged. "I'm very anti-hairball."

"Ditto. So messy. Nothing against cats personally."

"Obviously."

"Wonderful creatures."

"The best."

"Except Bags. Not him."

"He's just misunderstood," I said, a touch of defensiveness in my tone I didn't quite understand. The cat and I were *not* friends.

"Aren't we all?"

I hummed in agreement, and together, we stepped off the sidewalk and past the gazebo, working our way across the green. Blaze whistled, hands in his pockets, the picture of innocence — unless you knew him — as we walked towards whatever drama was happening.

As we passed Immortali-Tea, the door opened, and a pale hand shot out, yanking my arm until I was inside, Blaze right behind me. Nimue stared at me, hand still wrapped around my arm as she squeezed it.

"There's a dead body," Nimue whispered, her black eyes wide as she glanced between her cousin Blaze and I. "I think it's Mrs. Farrington. The house next to Lysander's."

"Why are the human cops here?" I whispered back. "And why are we whispering?"

Nimue shrugged, her long brown hair tied up in a high ponytail swishing with the movement. Her freckles stood out against her pale skin in the summer, painting an intriguing combination of innocence and mischief that was purely Nimue. "Kit's on the roof, seeing if he can hear what they're saying. He already called Orion."

Kit, Nimue's mate, was a fox shifter, and shifters had impeccable hearing. "Why aren't we up there with him?"

Nimue opened her mouth to answer when the door above us opened and closed, and Kit came down the steps. As was typical for the male, he wore an unbuttoned flannel over an Immortali-Tea shirt, sleeves rolled up to show off his rich bronze skin painted with swirling skulk tattoos.

"They're saying this matches the pattern of a serial killer. Looks like a ritual killing."

"Shit," I muttered, moving to the window to peer down the street. I couldn't see anything but the taillights of the cars parked there, but unease rippled through me at the implications.

That wasn't just the cops, then.

That was the FBI.

"This is really bad," Nimue said, leaning over my shoulder to look with me. "Really, really bad."

"Swear, Nimmie," Blaze said from my other side, speaking to his cousin, a fellow demon, though surely the sweetest one in existence. "Just do it. I know you want to."

"Well, now I can't, just to spite you."

"Shut it, both of you," I said, waving my hand in the air.

Just then, Orion walked by, his white angel wings glamoured from view as he moved towards the humans taping off the scene ahead. Unlike the rest of us dressed down for a summer day in mid-coast Maine, Orion wore a full suit — grey, to match his hair and eyes, with a pale blue tie that was annoyingly flattering to his coloring.

As he passed the window we were all plastered against, he shot us each a deeply reproachful look, and I couldn't help but push my glasses up my nose with my middle finger.

Orion didn't bother responding, only tugging on the cuffs of his button-down shirt that was as uptight as he was. With an exaggerated eyeroll, I turned away from the window and moved behind the counter, helping myself to a croissant.

"Put it on my tab," I said as I slid into a chair at one of the tables towards the back of the room.

Blaze chuckled as he joined me at the table. "Are you ever going to settle those tabs of yours?"

I shrugged, pulling apart the flaky pastry and shoving it in my mouth. "The fact that I haven't hexed either of you yet should be payment enough." I smiled sweetly at him. "You're welcome."

Chapter Two

ORION

EVERY TIME I thought we'd hit rock bottom over the last year in Deadlights Cove, a new level of hell opened up at my feet. Like they had so many times over the last three weeks, my eyes cut to the TV I had muted on the far wall of my office, sandwiched between my walls of bookcases, and watched the ticker scroll across the bottom. Shifters had been all the human news could talk about since the disastrous Summit and Lysander's kidnapping by Inessa, an evil sea nymph in league with Errakal and Nergal, Blaze's demon family.

Today's report was another protest in Washington, D.C. Humans held up picket signs saying hateful, vile things about shifters. At best, they called to treat shifters "like the animals they are" and corral them into zoos or pounds, others insisted shifters should wear collars or some other way to identify them. And at worst? Well, more than one sign insisted the only way humanity would be safe was if shifters were eradicated completely.

None of it was new — the footage was on a never ending loop as the same protests and riots took place all over the world. Yet, I couldn't make myself switch it off, no matter how depressing.

Somehow, the Paranormal Relations and Interspecies Council — the governing body of angels over all supernatural law that was not-so-affectionately dubbed the PRICs by most supes — had managed to condense the news to stories of wolves and legendary sea creatures, explaining Ronan's sudden appearance as a kraken in the waters. Humans seemed more amenable to the idea of wolf shifters due to werewolf lore and the ocean was full of unfathomable and terrifying creatures, both real *and* legendary, so the decision had been made to out shifters — including sea nymphs under that umbrella — and hide the other species, a verdict not many shifters were happy with.

When the footage switched from the protests outside the Capitol building to an interview, I unmuted the TV. One-half of the TV was blurred out, the face of the shifter hidden for privacy as he called in remotely for the interview, but I sat taller, recognizing that office.

"Thank you for joining us today, Padfoot," the reporter said, tapping the papers on the desk in front of her. "And where are you joining us from?"

"Happy to be here," the shifter answered, sitting in a wingback chair in his own office some thousand miles away from New York City in the heart of the Rocky Mountains. I'd recognize West Larkin's voice anywhere, even hidden behind a pixelated screen. "For the safety of my family during these times, I will not be answering that question, but I am a law-abiding American citizen just like you. Many of us have… concerns about what might happen if our locations were exposed to the public. And before any of you get any ideas, don't bother trying to trace my IP address. My sister is a genius — you'll never find us."

I chuckled at his words, full of warning and yet somehow still friendly — an ability I could never quite master. Larkin was the wolf Alpha in Timber Creek and one of the best males I knew. The Council's choice to use him as a liaison between the human world and the supernaturals was a good one. It was practically impossible to ruffle his fur.

"Perhaps rightly so," the reporter said. "News of supernatural beings have shaken the world for the last month, unveiling creatures that defy everything we know about science, including werewolves and what we'd all considered mythological sea creatures. There have been reports of things like krakens and even mermaids. From what we're seeing online," — the screen brought up a handful of tweets — "half the country is ready to go out and hunt down the supernatural community they've just learned exists, and the other half wants to study you in one way or another. Anti-Super-23 wrote, *'Let's go put these monsters down like the animals they are.'*" The reporter leaned towards the camera, "What goes through your mind when you read things like that?"

Larkin's ability not to react to her calling him a *werewolf* was impressive, but he didn't so much as flinch as he replied amiably, "Actually, Miranda, the correct term is wolf shifter."

"Apologies," the reporter said, a saccharine smile that convinced no one she didn't want to side with the picketers in D.C. "Can you explain the difference?"

"Of course," Larkin answered. "Common werewolf lore

requires a bite from a werewolf and a full moon to shift, neither of which applies to wolf shifters. It's a genetic trait passed down from our parents, no different than eye color. Yours are green, aren't they Miranda?"

The reporter was quiet for a moment, her eyes shifting between cameras before she answered, "Yes."

Larkin nodded, confident as ever. "Green eyes are an extremely rare recessive gene. Only about 2% of the population has green eyes. The gene required to shift is far more rare than that."

I'd seen dozens of news reports broadcasting sit-down interviews with Council-approved shifters calmly explaining the magic behind their powers and that no, they were no more dangerous to humans than they were before they'd been outed.

Regardless, almost every interview was followed immediately by falsified footage of wolf attacks on humans that had nothing to do with shifters, blood dripping from their teeth for effect, then real footage of the riots and protests.

My faith in humanity dwindled with each report, discouraged by how quickly they turned on us, even though their reactions weren't shocking. Just disappointing.

I glanced at the back of my phone case — a Tardis image I usually kept glamoured to appear black to anyone but me — and sighed. I didn't know how the Doctor kept up his relentless optimism sometimes.

My phone rang, pulling my attention away from the TV. I muted it again as I flipped it over to see Kit's name on the screen.

After Kit's text, I'd made some calls to gauge how bad this was.

Really. Fucking. Bad.

Early this morning, the glamour around Deadlights Cove that protected us from the human world had somehow developed a tear and humans had entered town, driving right over the border that should have kept them out like it had for the last 25 years I'd overseen it.

Lots of humans. *Law enforcement* humans.

I breathed deeply through my nose, fighting back the urge to scream in frustration as I stared at the phone on my desk, knowing what I needed to do.

"Fuck," I muttered to myself, dropping my head as I scrubbed a hand across my face, a tension headache forming behind my eyes, but still didn't reach for the phone.

Protocol said I needed to message the Council the second an anomaly occurred, but I couldn't make my hand cooperate, couldn't pick up the phone. No matter how much I was dreading this, I knew I needed to make the call.

Protocol also said that I had to await direction from Headquarters before approaching human officials, but before I could do that, I had to tell them it had happened. To admit my own failure.

With a sigh, I picked up the phone, entered the code to

submit the message to Headquarters, then put it back down as quickly as I could as if it would burn me the longer I held it. Someone would call back shortly, so all I could do was wait.

I pushed back from the large walnut desk, restless energy coursing through my body as my heart pounded with anxiety. I flexed my white wings, wishing I could go for a flight to relieve some tension, but settled for rolling up the sleeves of my light grey button down to give myself something to do while I waited.

This was going to be a headache.

I moved around my leather chair to stand at the office window, and watched two more SUVs barrel through the town square, swinging around the gazebo and heading off the main street to stop in front of Mrs. Farrington's house.

Who had called them? Who would alert *human* law enforcement of a murder in *our* town?

Kit continued to update me with what he'd overheard from the cops, which was the only reason I knew what was going on out there.

While I was more than concerned that Mrs. Farrington had been murdered right under our noses, not understanding how the odd witch had gotten involved with anyone sinister enough to wind up a murder victim, my mind reeled over the very real possibility that her death was connected to the destruction of the glamour magic. I'd bet my left wing this was part of Nergal's plans, whatever they were. The question was, had she been a willing participant, or not? And would she be the last town resident to be involved, or merely the first?

Since they'd broken free of the Iron Keep, it had

become more and more obvious that Nergal was the true mastermind here. Only a centuries-old ancient demon could wield the power and influence it took to orchestrate a global attack like what was happening. The level of destructive chaos was at an all-time high in our world. Unfortunately for me, the ancient demon had a vendetta against my town and wanted to shine the spotlight on us here in the Cove, and I was sick of it.

My phone chimed, a call coming in, and I swiped it to answer immediately.

"Care to explain how your glamour failed, Officer?"

I recoiled slightly, not expecting to hear from Ezra, the *Chancellor* of the Paranormal Relations and Interspecies Council and, thus, second only to Premier Malachi Russo.

Not one for pleasantries, my dear brother.

My grip tightened where my hand rested on the back of my chair. "I'm still working on that, Ezra. What should I do about the humans?"

"A murder, yes?"

"That's correct. A low-power green witch from the local Coven. I haven't approached the FBI yet, but shifters near the scene overheard the police force talking about ritualistic killings, so evidence of witchcraft may be present at the crime scene."

A deep sigh came down the line. "In case you haven't noticed, we're facing a bit of a shit show up here. Everyone is overworked doing damage control. Shifters are all over the media, and we're watching every channel to see if this is about to turn ugly. You have to deal with the humans on your own for now."

My eyebrows rose at his words. "Deal with them?" From

the Council — especially *Ezra* — that could mean a lot of things.

"Just play along, don't provoke them," he clarified, tone clipped. "Don't give them any reason to look further into the town than they already will and dismiss all notions of witchcraft, however you can."

I silenced my groan. Looked like I'd be spending the day talking to humans.

"What about the glamour?" I asked. "If I fix it now —"

"Don't be a fool," Ezra snapped. "You have to leave it how it is. Humans might be stupid, but even they might notice if they keep getting lost on the way to their *documented* crime scene."

I grimaced. Great. So any number more humans might start stumbling upon our town, especially as we were entering the height of vacation season here in mid-coast Maine.

I made a mental note to check if the Last Resort showed up on any internet maps or search engines. The last thing we needed was to become known as a diamond in the rough for tourists.

"And Orion?" There was a weighty pause. I imagined Ezra petting a white cat in his lap in a high-backed leather chair like a Bond villain, which was ridiculous. Angels never owned cats; they couldn't keep their scratchy little claws out of our feathers.

"Yes?"

"We'll be looking into this glamour issue. If we find any fault on your end, you know what will happen."

I'd already been given my one and only Official Warning. One more strike, and I'd be removed from my post as mayor.

My stomach turned over at the mere thought. Ezra was probably cackling with glee.

"I do."

Ezra hung up without so much as a *Talk soon.*

The prick.

Chapter Three

ORION

"RECORDS SHOW there was another murder last year in Deadlights Cove," Special Agent Garcia said, glancing up at me from over her glasses as she checked the folder of notes she'd perched on the hood of an SUV. I'd been standing on the sidewalk in front of Mrs. Farrington's house for the last hour as they questioned me, my headache growing worse by the minute.

I studied the FBI agent, bright yellow letters standing out on her navy blue jacket. Garcia looked to be in her early forties, a few gray strands mixed into her dark brown hair, slight wrinkles at the corners of her eyes. She wasn't a smiler — no laugh lines yet — but that wasn't surprising for a woman who dedicated her life to hunting serial killers. I'd spent so little time around actual humans, I forgot how quickly they aged.

"Yes, a John Doe. No one local that we knew," I answered, resisting the urge to pinch the bridge of my nose. "The body was found in the old schoolhouse."

She hummed, scratching something on the notepad in

her hands. "That crime scene also had ritualistic symbolism, is that correct?"

I nodded, taking a deep breath as I answered Garcia's thirty-sixth question. That wasn't an exaggeration — I was keeping track. "Correct. I turned all evidence over to the state once the investigation was concluded. The murderer was found and arrested."

"Right," she said, glancing down at her notes. "An Errakal Rosewood?"

Thirty-seven. "Correct."

"Unique name. In fact, it's so unique that the US government has the only listed Errakal Rosewood as being born in 1845. You were aware of this?"

Thirty-eight. "I was not." Technically, not a lie. I didn't know what year Kal was born.

"I see," Garcia said, closing her notebook and adjusting her glasses. "We'll need all of your local department's records on that."

"Of course," I said, forcing a polite smile. "Any way I can help. Mrs. Farrington was an upstanding citizen in our community. Everyone here will be eager to help however we can."

Garcia studied me, turning her head to the side as she squinted slightly, her dark brown eyes boring a hole right through my head. But I didn't react. Didn't flinch. Didn't so much as move a muscle.

"Garcia," someone called from behind us, and the woman spun. I blinked slowly, closing my eyes as I fought to remain calm. "Come take a look at this."

Special Agent Garcia looked over her shoulder at me

and nodded her head. "Thanks for your assistance, Mayor. We'll be in touch."

Without waiting for an answer, she ducked under the crime scene tape and up the stairs into Mrs. Farrington's house, snapping gloves onto her hands.

My shoulders sagged, feeling the weight of my angel wings even though they were glamoured and hidden from sight around the humans.

Shit.

Darius, the wolf Alpha and head of our police force in town, showed up a few minutes later, offering me a nod as he approached the cops gathered to the side of the yard. His dark coiled hair was neatly trimmed, and paired with his black pants and a crisp short-sleeve button-down with a shiny gold badge I'd certainly never seen him wear before, he looked the part of the *actual* police. He usually dressed in a much more relaxed style, but I was glad to see he under-stood the severity of the situation at hand. Under no circumstances could the FBI find out that a *wolf shifter* was our chief of police, or that hundreds of other supernaturals lived within our town borders.

Darius and Garcia spoke in low voices, and I took the opportunity to leave. Word must have spread to meet at Immortali-Tea as at least a dozen faces peered out at me as I walked by for the second time today, but I didn't stop in.

"Hey, *Mayor Orion*," a voice called as the bell on the door jangled, the speaker pointedly using my title in earshot of the humans, and I stopped but didn't turn to meet her eyes.

My blood pressure rose just as it always did at the mere sound of her grating voice. "Not even going to tell us what happened?"

"I'm sure Kit already told you everything," I said, closing my eyes and fighting the sigh that threatened to escape without my permission. "Or any of the other fifteen of you up on the roof watching and listening."

"Can you blame them?" Devanna said, stepping out into the street and circling to face me. Like always, the stunningly beautiful witch was wearing all black from head to toe, even in the summer sun. Her black tank top showed off her ample curves, but I couldn't look away from where it said *Big Witch Energy* in bright, shimmery blue letters. It was the exact same shade as her hair, which was currently tied in a knot with a few tendrils loose against her dark skin. Her deep brown eyes focused on the scene behind me, jaw working as she added in an undertone, "I'm shocked you didn't just blast all of them with your powers and steal their memories."

"This crime has already been entered into their system and logged as a serial killer, so how *exactly* do you think tampering with six people's memories would fix anything?"

She scowled at me. "Good to know no matter what other shit goes down around here, I can always count on you to be an asshole."

I clenched my teeth at the insult, trying not to rise to her bait. Every word that came out of Devanna's mouth aimed at me was barbed, always ready to make me the villain, but I was too tired to fight her on it today. "As much as I love to stand around and listen to insults thrown at me, I need to get back to work. That church won't fix itself, so maybe you should do the same. Also, please refrain from wearing your witchy merchandise while there are humans in town." I waved a hand towards her shirt. "No one but you thinks it's funny and we don't need any other questions aimed our way."

I could have sworn she growled at me then, but Nimue exited, pulling Devanna's arm before she could say anything else. Nimue, the sweetest demon I'd ever met and yet, somehow, best friends with this hellcat, smiled at me, her face full of freckles in the summer sun. "Hello, Orion. How are you enjoying our first FBI guests?"

I shrugged with a grimace, but Nimue was already tugging Devanna back towards the tea shop. "So, Dev, I'm trying to convince Kit that black is a perfectly acceptable color to paint our new front door. Nobody argues like you do. Help me convince him. Bye for now, O."

Devanna's murderous gaze softened as she turned to her best friend and scrunched her brow. "Can't you just promise sexual favors and get your way? That sounds like a debate that could be settled with a good BJ and you're done."

I stepped away with a shake of my head, my mind conjuring images I did not need to see.

Swiping open my phone, I searched through my contacts before pressing the call icon.

"Ostara, we need to meet. I'll be at your place in ten."

A half hour later, Ostara was tapping her perfectly manicured nails against the arm of her chair after I'd shared all the information I had so far about Mrs. Farrington's death. While Ostara and I didn't often interact socially, I'd always respected the Coven leader's professionalism. Dressed in a conservative plum dress and blazer with her white hair styled neatly against her deep brown skin, Ostara looked as put together as ever. She was a fellow believer in rules and understood the importance of maintaining respectability — the finest qualities one could have in my book.

While investigating the murder wasn't in my job description — technically this was Darius's job — the thought of waiting for others to handle this first was impossible to consider. If I was going to protect my town *and* my reputation, I'd have to do it myself.

Mrs. Farrington had been a member of Ostara's Coven, so if anyone would have more information about her actions and whereabouts over the past few days, it would be her.

"Did you see the scene?" she asked, brow raised.

I shook my head. "Not yet. We'll have to wait until they clear out for the night, then I'm hoping your Coven can cast an imprint reading for us. But the police did imply there were similarities to the schoolhouse killing last fall, suggesting ritualistic signs."

She gave me a flat stare. "Errakal again."

"Perhaps." I lifted a shoulder, fighting back my eightieth sigh of the day, tension creeping in at my temples. "You have no idea as to why he would target Mrs. Farrington, if indeed he was responsible? Had she been acting odd or going anywhere out of the ordinary?"

"She was always acting odd," Ostara scoffed. "If she wasn't walking her cat in a rainbow light-up collar or carrying him around in a backpack, she was singing to her plants in the worst operatic coloratura soprano I've ever heard. Windows shattered and the plants withered around her, but nothing could deter that woman. No one can say she wasn't determined." Ostara shuddered slightly at the memory and I couldn't say I blamed her. Deadlights Cove was full of some of the strangest supernaturals I'd ever met in my long life, and Mrs. Farrington would give them all a run for their money. "As for her comings and goings, she wasn't under house arrest. My witches can move around as they please. Perhaps you can hack her phone's GPS records?"

It was already on my list of things to do, but I nodded. Apparently, any further answers would have to wait for dark.

Safe in the comfort of my own home later that afternoon, I finally let the glamour slip off my wings, rolling my neck with a sigh of relief as the tension of holding the magic dissolved. While the magic was near effortless to use, keeping it in place for long stretches of time was a strain on my body. This was going to be tedious to keep up until the humans cleared out of town.

Setting my keys in the dish on the kitchen counter, I took off my watch and laid it there as well, then washed my hands, needing to distract myself.

Technically, the house belonged to Blaze, but given that the 9,000-square-foot *Cottage* could house a dozen people without a hitch, we shared it easily enough. I had my own wing he'd let me renovate to my style, as he had his own, and between them were some common rooms, such as this kitchen.

However, despite the kitchen being shared, it was my domain. Blaze couldn't be trusted not to set the place on fire — mostly by accident — and as I had no desire to eat charcoal every night and enjoyed cooking, I'd taken it over.

Professional grade appliances, white marble countertops, and huge banks of cabinets made this the chef's kitchen of my dreams. French doors took up most of the exterior walls leading to the outdoor kitchen on the patio.

Garlic and mushrooms sizzled in a pan not long later as I turned the burner on under the cast iron skillet and waited for it to warm up. I added a pat of butter, then grabbed a beer from the fridge and took a long swig.

I glanced down at the beer's ABV, low even by human standards for alcohol. *Might need something stronger.*

"Murder and marsala, always an excellent pairing for a summer evening," Blaze said as he wandered into the kitchen and pulled open the pantry door.

"Don't eat now. I'm making enough for you and Petra too if she's here."

Blaze shoved six cookies into his mouth like a chipmunk packing for winter, then closed the pantry door. I rolled my eyes, stirring the pan as I added the wine.

"How is it that you've lived with me for almost 20 years and you *still* expect me to follow instructions?"

"Wishful thinking, I suppose."

"What a wasted wish," Blaze said as he dropped onto a barstool at the counter, leaning on his elbow and getting cookie crumbs all over the surface. "If I could wish for something, I'd wish for the Nile."

I looked up from the pan, turning to him slightly and saw the far-off look in his eyes. "The Nile?"

"Yeah." Blaze nodded. "Ever since the Genie mentioned it in *Aladdin,* I haven't stopped thinking about it. How exactly would one acquire a river? And then what would I *do* with it? Also, does it come with the crocodiles? I hope so. Though I hear it's the hippos you should really be concerned about. Who do you think would win in a race, a croc or a hippo?"

"How your mind works baffles me," I said, turning back to the pan. "That this is what you spend your time thinking about."

"I'd bet on the hippo. And it's better than whatever boring shit you think about, like what kind of fabric wrinkles the least."

Polyester, but I didn't bother answering, used to his badgering after all these years together. For the millionth time I wondered why I'd ever moved in with the male. Once the chicken was done, I slid it onto a plate and passed it across the island.

"Petra?" I nodded towards Blaze's wing of our shared home, but he shook his head.

"Petey's here, but she's got her *Do Not Disturb* face on, practically buried herself under a pile of books Lance gave her on witch history. I'll bring her a plate when she comes up for air." Blaze beamed, like the idea of his girlfriend needing hours alone to read was the hottest thing in the universe, and dug into his meal as I plated up my own. Lance was Lance Morgaine, our own Morgaine's brother who'd come up to town for the Summit a few weeks ago. We hadn't interacted much, but he'd been lingering in town, getting to know his son Lysander, and helping Mo and Petra with research.

Blaze shoved a bite of chicken into his mouth, then mumbled his approval. I pulled out a bar stool to sit next to him, not sure whether his distracting company made the heaviness of my thoughts better or worse.

Still, something made me look up from my plate and ask, "The *hippo*?"

Sure enough, Blaze launched right into a long-winded and surprisingly thought-out explanation, and as I stifled a chuckle, some of the tension in my forehead eased.

Chapter Four

DEVANNA

CRICKETS CHIRPED as peach light flooded the forest at sundown, a normal Maine summer evening. But nothing about today had been normal.

I'd eventually left Immortali-Tea to head back to the church, trying to work on the door again but my phone vibrating incessantly in my pocket was hard to ignore. No matter how many times I removed myself from the town-wide group text, Morgaine always added me back. Then there were the half-dozen or so various groups Blaze had going. One with him, me, Kit and Nadir, Endymion, Nox and Aurora, and Val and Caedmon for the local business owners. Another that was him, me, Nimue, Maisie, Val, and Ryker that was just full of Blaze's "Sandy B Multiverse Theories" as he called them. Some days, I regretted ever giving him my phone number.

I pulled my phone out, ready to chuck myself out of all of his group texts once more when I noticed the emergency Coven meeting notice from Ostara.

With a sigh, I put my tools away and headed for the door that still wouldn't close.

A cacophony of voices reached me as I climbed the steps of Ostara's Victorian house. While I was used to the sound of the full Coven assembled here, tonight felt different. Sure, Mrs. Farrington had been a member of our Coven for well over a hundred years, but her death should have left our Coven feeling subdued, somber, reflective. The raised voices coming from inside meant something was off.

"No!" someone cried, "I refuse to believe it."

"I don't know how much more evidence you need, Peg," Morgaine's voice carried from the meeting room out into the foyer, and I made my way through the house quickly to join the meeting. "What if she was working with him?"

The room was packed — a contrast to our usual meetings. Like me, many of the witches in our Coven found excuses to skip Ostara's many meetings as often as we could. I didn't have time for this shit. The only reason I was even a part of the Coven was because it was less hassle than being on my own. The number of regulations the PRICs assigned to witches not part of a Coven was ridiculous, one of the many bones I had to pick with the angels.

Chairs lined the walls, every one occupied in the large space, and Ostara was stationed right in the middle, holding court as usual.

"She was *murdered*, Morgaine," Peg answered, her voice shrill and her purple coiffed pouf of hair shaking with her hysteria while Mo patted her shoulder where they sat side-by-side. While Mo and Peg both looked to be in their 80s, they couldn't have been more different. Mo dressed for shock value, pairing clashing patterns and colors with her oversized teal glasses in a unique style that was all her own. "You don't know that she was working for him. She couldn't tell you herself. She didn't have a moment to explain her reasoning."

"Everyone needs to calm down," Ostara's voice cut through the rest, and the room silenced. "Peg, rest assured I will have an imprint reading done. We will not let Mrs. Farrington's name be dragged through the mud unnecessarily. She was a part of this Coven and I have to hope her loyalty was true, but *someone* has been leaking information only our Coven knows to Errakal. We've known that for a while."

I shuffled closer to where Lysander, Dillon, and Aurora sat on the outskirts of the meeting, then leaned down to whisper, "What's going on?"

"Mrs. Farrington's body was mutilated," Lysander answered. His tan, tattooed arms were crossed over his chest, looking his usual brand of effortlessly cool in a black t-shirt and ripped jeans. "Her magic had been siphoned out of her, and then her neck snapped."

My brows shot up, and I met his light green eyes. "Completely drained?"

Lys nodded, then leaned back as we returned our attention to Ostara.

"In an effort to dispel any extra rumors, here are the facts so far." All whispers ceased immediately as Ostara addressed the Coven. "One, her magic was drained. That, in itself, is troubling, but we'll return to that later. Two, her neck was snapped. And three, several incriminating papers were found in her house, including a map of all our local nexus points."

"Last fall," Eva Watford spoke up, her words slow like she was processing as she spoke. One of the older witches in town, she was co-head of the town's Historical Society with Peg Fernsby. "That's how Errakal and his group knew the precise spot for the nexus point in the Haunted Meadow. No one but Coven members know those exact coordinates."

Ostara inclined her head. "That's my thought as well. At this point, we don't know how or why she became involved with him — *if* she did at all — or how much she told him about our local practice."

"With Errakal out of prison now, why would his people kill her, if she was on their side?" Peg asked, dabbing at the corners of her eyes with a handkerchief.

"We can only speculate until we learn more. Perhaps his followers sought to tie up loose ends in the Cove before they move on to larger operations."

"I'd like to volunteer to do the imprint reading," Lys said, standing up so Ostara could see him over the crowd of people in the room.

His mother nodded at him as a few others spoke up to volunteer as well, including myself "I'll help, too. The moon is high tonight — my power should be strong."

The sky had turned to inky black by the time we arrived at Mrs. Farrington's house for the reading. The police and FBI had cleared out, but crime scene tape still wrapped around the yard and was taped over the door. Casting a spell so we wouldn't tamper with any human evidence, Lys led us into her house. Watching him effortlessly tap into his magic with little to no use of the witchy accoutrements the rest of us would have needed was a reminder of just how much had changed recently. Lys had not only Linked with Maisie, a powerful sea nymph, but had also learned he carried a hint of demon blood, which explained the ease with which he could access his magic.

Dillon, Lys's roommate and bandmate, had volunteered as well, along with Castor, another younger witch from the Coven, and Morgaine. For most intricate spell work like this, it was best to have five witches.

Mrs. Farrington's body had already been removed from the house, but the outline of her body was still chalked on the floor, and the magical symbols that had been painted on the walls and floor remained as well.

"Do you feel that?" Castor looked over his shoulder at the rest of us as we approached the chalk outline.

With each step closer, the air grew heavier, like a weight on my shoulders, in my bones, on my soul —

"A dark aura," Mo put in. We formed a circle around the outline, the ocean air drifting through the open door behind me but having no effect on the heavy feeling. "I'd say either Mrs. Farrington or her murderer were quite angry at her time of death."

"I'd be pissed if a demon was trying to kill me, too," I muttered, pulling a few bundles of herbs from my bag, along with a handful of crystals and a bag of salt.

"This feels like more than that, but I suppose it's hard to feel the subtler differences if you're not an Aura witch."

I finished putting out the items and knelt on the floor to adjust their arrangement more carefully, mapping a pentagram of twigs between the objects. If there was one thing I was a stickler for, it was proper spellwork. Ostara had overseen most of my training after my parents left town, and I'd had alignments and object orientation and spacing drilled into me until I could set up spells with my eyes closed, could see or feel if something was even a millimeter out of place. For the typical spell, it might not make much of a difference, but for something like this, it could be the difference between being able to see 70 or 72 hours into the past, and those two hours could be crucial to finding out the truth.

When I was satisfied with the arrangement, I stood, and the five of us moved into position around them. Lys snapped his fingers, and the bundle of twigs caught fire. As smoke started to trail up in the middle, I passed everyone a borage leaf to strengthen the spell, and we each held it over the flames, then dropped them simultaneously.

We synchronized our breathing as the leaves burned, the smoke increasing from a single tendril into a billowing funnel like a small tornado, even from the small bundle of twigs. Now, it was fueled by both magic and wood.

Our senses to the natural world began to dull as our inner eyes grew sharper. The sounds of ocean waves and the calls of seagulls all started to dampen, seeming farther and farther away, and the world lost its saturation, turning monochrome.

With our next breath, we were in the imprint. Distantly, I was still aware of my physical body standing in the circle before a column of smoke, but I now had a secondary layer of awareness as though I was watching a movie.

In this layer, at first, there was nothing. Just the greyed out vision of the house as it usually was. Time was sped up in an imprint, so before long, it changed, the light and shadows shifting quickly as a day passed. Night fell again, and a beam of headlights shone through the windows at the front of the house.

Several beings — at least one demon, if I had to guess, as well as several witches, none of whom I recognized — piled out of the black SUV, stepped onto the porch, and blasted the door open. A spitting mad Mrs. Farrington stood in the front room, bearing an uncanny resemblance to her cat in that moment. Quickly, her hands were bound, and they dragged her over to the spot where we all stood in the present.

"Slow it down, Mo," I said. Mo nodded, raising her hands as the vision slowed to real-time. Although imprints didn't allow us to hear sounds, Mrs. Farrington was clearly yelling, screaming out words as they moved her.

"Did she just say, '*I gave him the coordinates, just like he asked*'?" Lys said from my left, reading her lips. I nodded in agreement, bitterness taking over any sadness I had at watching her demise. Harmless, odd Mrs. Farrington apparently wasn't so harmless after all.

She was the reason Errakal had known exactly where to murder one victim to gain power from the ley lines, and why he'd attempted several more times here in Deadlights Cove.

"I think she just said, '*Leave her alone, you don't need another witch,*'" Castor said, frowning. "Who is she talking about?"

"I didn't catch it," Lys murmured.

"'*We have another use for you,*'" Morgaine said, reading their lips.

I turned away when I saw the demon reach for her throat, knowing what would come next. Just outside the imprint's reach, a shadow moved along the porch, but it was too hard to tell if it was happening in the past or present. With a start, I rushed to the door, leaving the others to see if there was anything else to learn from the imprint.

But when I swung the front door open, nothing awaited me but Bagheera's glowing yellow eyes, his tail swishing where he sat on the porch rail.

Chapter Five

DEVANNA

IMPRINT READINGS TOOK an excessive amount of power, and I left the house just before midnight feeling depleted, both in body and spirit. Mrs. Farrington had always been exceptionally annoying, but no one deserved the end she'd had.

Nevertheless, what we'd seen in the imprint reading confirmed the idea that she'd betrayed us by working with Errakal. At a minimum, by giving him the nexus coordinates, but who knew what else she'd done? I still wasn't sure what her motives would have been for helping him. And who had she been trying to protect?

I stepped off the porch, ready to head home when a strangled sob caught my attention, and I peered into the night in search of the sound. Moonlight mixed with the one lamp post further down the street, casting a warm glow.

"Ruby?" Lys whispered, staring in the same direction, watching a figure run away from us into the darkness. I hadn't been able to tell who it was, but Linking with Maisie must have given him enhanced senses. The knowledge that he'd kept a lot of secrets from me over the years still annoyed me, but he was like the brother I'd never had. Since neither of us had any actual siblings, I couldn't say for sure, but maybe this was just what siblings did.

"I'll go after her," I said, and Lys looked visibly relieved. I controlled my eyeroll — barely. He was probably desperate to get back to Maisie, since they were newly married. Well, not married — Linked. Whatever they wanted to call it. She'd moved into his house right after their ceremony, her days now split between the watery world below and her home here with Lys. As much as I personally thought romance was a waste of energy, they were happy together, and after all the shit Lys had dealt with from Ostara over the years, he deserved it.

He knocked my shoulder with a quick, "Night, Dev," before heading towards his house.

I strode after Ruby, hearing Morgaine's door open and slam closed several houses down. Not bothering to knock, I pushed the door open, walking through the dark house like I'd done so many times before.

Following the sound of choked sobs, I turned into the living room and flipped on the light, immediately assaulted by the bright, obnoxious floral patterns that covered nearly every surface in the room.

"Ruby?" I sank down on the couch where she'd thrown herself, arms over her head, her back shuddering with her sobs. Over the few months Ruby had been in town, I'd come to admire her quirky punk-floral sense of style, like a young Latina Gwen Stefani. Her long dark hair dyed red at the ends covered most of her face, but seeing her so upset had me feeling like I should do… something.

I hated crying. It was weakness leaking out of the body, which I never did, considering I had no weaknesses. Physically uncomfortable, I rested a hand on her back, giving her a soft *pat pat* I recognized as a weak attempt at consoling the distraught girl, and wondered what was taking Mo so long.

I stopped myself right as I was about to ask if I needed to kill someone for her — my go-to for comforting distraught friends — remembering she might be sad over Mrs. Farrington's passing. I'd seen them together a time or two around town in the last few months.

"Are you okay?" I tried instead, hearing how dumb the question sounded. *Of course she's not okay, Dev. She's crying.*

Thankfully, Mo entered the house shortly after me, lights turning on with the flick of her hand as she sank to the floor in front of Ruby, her neon pink and blue kimono flaring around her. Mo's hand settled on Ruby's back, and I pulled mine away as if I'd been burned. Her other hand settled on my wrist, circling it as she spoke in a whisper to Ruby. I felt the sizzle of Mo's aura magic, the unease coursing through me moments before dispelled until I wrenched my arm free and moved to the chair across the room.

"It's m-my f-fault," Ruby stuttered as her tears ebbed under Mo's soothing touch.

"What's your fault, dear?" Mo asked, her tone calm even though the look she cast my way was anything but. "Everything's all right. You can tell me what's wrong."

"I keep blacking out," Ruby said between gasping breaths, "waking up in places I don't remember being."

I leaned forward in my chair, concern rippling through me at her words. "What do you mean, blacking out? When did this start?"

Ruby's red-rimmed eyes met mine as her breathing evened out. "A few weeks ago," Ruby answered, wiping the tears on her cheeks. "At first, I didn't realize what was happening, because it was right when Lys helped me out with my hex."

"Wait," I said, brows dropping, "what hex? Who the hell put a hex on you? Why didn't I hear about this?"

"Lysander and I took care of it," Mo said, rising to sit on the couch next to Ruby now that the younger witch had recovered from the worst of her meltdown. "He was looking into her magic before the Summit, and then, of course, we all got a little sidetracked when You Know Who arrived."

"Her name is Inessa, not Voldemort," I deadpanned. "Let's not give her more power over us than necessary."

Mo patted Ruby's leg. "Now, tell us what you think is your fault, dear."

"I can't remember," Ruby said, shaking her head. "And it's driving me crazy. But I just," the girl swallowed, her eyes meeting mine again, "I can't get rid of this feeling that I had something to do with the humans all arriving in town. Goddess, I can't stop wondering if *I* killed her and can't remember. What if I did, then woke up somewhere else, not even realizing I'd done it?"

Tears welled in Ruby's eyes again, but I held up a hand as if I had the power to dam up the emotions overflowing her. "Let that one go. Mo and I were part of the imprint casting, and I can promise you, I never even saw you enter her house in the 72 hours we rewatched."

Ruby sagged in relief, her hands covering her face, and I couldn't help but feel for the girl. She was young, and relatively on her own, though Mo had adopted her in the few months she'd been in town. Something I could relate to.

I didn't know the dynamics behind her arrival, but something was a little off about the girl, and Mo happened to do exceptionally well with the oddball children, as shown by Blaze and Nimue.

"It wasn't me?" I shook my head in confirmation, and Ruby repeated the words for her own reassurance. "I didn't kill her."

"Where have you been waking up?" I asked, not wanting to skip over that fact.

"I haven't written it down or anything," Ruby said, her eyes meeting Mo's with a hint of hesitancy in them.

"Sweet child, nothing you could say would make me dismiss you or send you away. You're safe here." Mo cupped Ruby's cheek lovingly, and Ruby nodded, tears welling once more.

I was pretty sure this girl had cried more in the last 15 minutes than I had in 15 years, but that was beside the point. Teenage hormones and small-town dramas could bring it out in someone, I guessed. And, shit, Mo's words had me rubbing a hand across my chest, remembering how often she'd shown me that her words were true, not just for Ruby but for all of us.

"All over town," Ruby said with a sigh. "Mostly on the outskirts. Near the road, down by the lighthouse, out by pack lands."

"That's odd." I frowned, unable to dismiss that this was connected even though I couldn't see how yet. "Are they places you've been lately, other than when you've woken up there?"

"We've been all over town in the last month, Mo and I," Ruby said, wringing her hands in her lap. "She's been teaching me about the differences in powers when I'm working away from the ley lines, versus in direct contact with them. Lys took me to help with the glamour magic at the border before the Summit, too. Mrs. Farrington was there that day, actually."

Mo sat up straighter, turning to me with her eyes wide. "Lysander."

Not following her train of thought, I waited for her to elaborate. She pushed to her feet, and I followed her into the hallway before she pulled the front door open, peering out into the night.

"He went home," I said from the end of the hall, half an eye still on Ruby, crumpled on the living room sofa, while I waited for the pieces of the puzzle to reveal themselves.

"He keeps asking me about Ruby's Aura," she said as she shut the door, coming back towards me but not returning to the living room. Her voice dropped low enough that Ruby wouldn't hear in the next room. "Mentioning something still isn't right, even with the hex now gone. He said it looks like there's a split in her magic, letting it seep into the in-between. I've never heard of anything like it before, so I dismissed it as a peculiarity of Ruby's history."

"What history?"

"Irrelevant right now. Text Lys and Ostara. Orion too. Whatever that hex was on Ruby — I'm afraid they were using her to tear open the glamour. Errakal must know. He *has* to."

"Know *what?*" Frustration crept into my tone, tired of

Mo speaking in riddles I didn't understand. "Spit it out, Morgaine."

Mo chewed on her lip, turning to look out the window towards town where the bell tower of my church-house rose in the distance. "There was more magic on the border than just keeping the humans out," she whispered, her words still solving none of the questions she brought to mind. "If they were using her… if Ruby was somehow able to dismantle the barrier magic — that keeps both humans and *him* out — with whatever added power they might have given her…" Mo trailed off, her hands shaking in an uncommon sign of worry.

"What *kind* of 'more magic'?" I asked, pulling my phone out and texting Lys, tapping the screen a little too aggressively as I fought the need to shake the answers out of Mo. "And who the hell is 'him', Mo?"

Mo lowered her voice, and I stepped closer, putting more distance between us and Ruby in the living room. "Over a century ago, some of us came together to keep Nergal — Blaze and Kal's father — out of town," she said, my eyes widening. "If she was able to dispel that magic, he'd be able to come back."

"*How* would Ruby have done that though? I hate to be blunt, but Ruby seems… a little inconsistent, even for a young witch. To take down the barrier magic would require an extreme wealth of power."

"That's just it. Mrs. Farrington kept showing up, wanting to help with Ruby's magic. I should have questioned her more, should have suspected something was strange, but that woman always had a screw loose." I bit my tongue, keeping my thoughts to myself as I eyed the woman wearing the neon kimono and clashing plaid pants. Now was not the time for sass. "I dismissed it as wanting to help, to feel a sense of accomplishment since the only thing she was good at was driving that damn cat of hers nuts and growing a decent tomato now and again."

I hummed in agreement, but still wasn't sure I followed Mo's leap in logic. "So you think Mrs. Farrington was working with Errakal this whole time, revealing Coven secrets to help him, then somehow hexed Ruby?"

Mo took a breath, before dropping a bigger bomb on me. "Given what we just saw, it would be more likely that she simply knew of the hex and maybe wanted to, I don't know, make sure no one else noticed. Or maybe she wanted to protect her, who knows. But there's more to it than that. I think the hex was a decoy or a first step for a deeper demon possession spell."

"Demon possession?" I blurted, before Mo's flapping hands reminded me to lower my voice. But, honestly, *possessed?* That was the stuff of Puritanical fairy tales, just a myth conjured up to excuse the wrongful murder of countless innocent women. "Is that even possible? And how did *you* not notice?"

Mo sighed, gesturing for me to follow her into the kitchen as we waited to hear back from Lys, Ostara, and Orion — the last of which I'd texted only a begrudging, brusque *Mo's. Now.* Already more words than I ever wanted to exchange with him.

"Ruby's only half witch," she said as we sat in the multi-colored chairs in her rainbow kitchen, but Mo immediately popped back up out of her seat and started a pot of water for tea.

"And the other half?"

"Wolf." She leaned back against the counter. "All this time, any oddness in her magic, I just attributed to her exp—ertly odd wolfy senses, or to the hex, once Lys had worked that part out."

My phone buzzed, and I flipped it over on the table, expecting to see Lys's name confirming he was on his way, but instead finding a text from Orion, though that wasn't how I had him labeled in my phone.

HEAVEN'S REJECT

I am on my way, since you asked so sweetly, Devanna. - Orion, Mayor

My jaw tightened. What sort of absolute goody-two-shoes signed their texts? And why did it make me so irrationally angry?

"Orion?" Mo said, and I glanced up to see her eyes twinkling, the woman reveling in my discomfort even in this moment of crisis.

I turned my phone back over with a *crack*. "He's on his way."

Chapter Six

ORION

I HAD JUST STEPPED into my bathroom to brush my teeth before bed when my phone chimed with a text.

HELL'S MERCENARY

Mo's. Now.

Of course Devanna couldn't write complete sentences. Frankly, I was surprised she'd even bothered with punctuation. Still, if she was at Morgaine's, then chances were it was because they'd learned something at the imprint reading and wanted to share it with me, so I texted back I was on my way and hopped in my car.

I knocked three times on Morgaine's yellow door when I arrived and only had to wait a moment before it was flung open, Morgaine gesturing me in hurriedly.

In the kitchen, Devanna sat at the table with Ostara, who was thoughtfully swirling a spoon in a mug of tea, and Lys leaned on the counter.

"What did the imprint reading show?" I asked.

Morgaine held out a selection of teas, but I lifted a hand to decline.

Lys crossed his arms, then recounted what they had discovered at the reading, my lips pursing with each detail he revealed about Mrs. Farrington, then he gestured to Devanna to continue the story. She gave him a sharp glare for seemingly no reason, then turned to Ostara, speaking directly to her.

Only what she had to say wasn't about Mrs. Farrington, but Ruby.

I rubbed my forehead, trying not to let the absolute clusterfuck this day had turned out to be to send me into an angry tailspin. "And Ruby hadn't told anyone about blacking out?"

"She was scared, Orion," Mo said, her pale arms crossed over her chest in a *don't mess with my children* gesture I knew well. "Ostara and Lys checked Ruby when they got here, and we all agree that a demon possession is most likely, though all but unheard of. Lance is going to come by in the morning to see if he can't help us perform the exorcism."

Ostara shifted in her seat at the mention of Lance, Lys's father, but I didn't have time to deal with everyone else's personal drama.

"I'd like to be present for that," I said, and Morgaine nodded. "In case there is anything Ruby remembers during the process or afterwards that might be useful."

"The *how* isn't what I'm most concerned about though," Morgaine said, drawing in a deep breath. "It's *why*."

"Any day now, Mo," Dev said with an eyeroll I couldn't help but agree with.

"Many years ago," Mo began, and I sensed this was the beginning of a long tale, so I took a seat at the table. "Willa and Nergal lived in what is now Turkey, where Blaze and Kal were born. I don't know the exact circumstances, but shortly after Blaze was born, Willa turned up here with him to live with her mother, Althea. Errakal was already grown, stopping in only from time to time, but Blaze was just a child. I myself didn't yet live here full-time — I was a bit of a free spirit, actually," Morgaine got a far-away, devious glint in her eye. After seeing her lengthy rap sheet, calling herself a free spirit was an understatement, but I wasn't about to drag this story out any more than Morgaine would on her own. "Anyway, it was clear Willa was running from something. Whenever I stopped in town, I'd stay with Althea and do whatever I could to help with her daughter and possibly the *most* destructive toddler known to humanity. Like a Saint Bernard puppy on cocaine, whose tail would randomly burst into flames and who would suddenly disappear and then reappear stuck in a cabinet or on the roof or upside down in a tree. In fact, I remember this one hat in particular that I *swear* he chewed the lace off of on one visit." Mo tapped her chin, frowning. "I was quite fond of that hat. But, I digress.

"Eventually, Althea was able to get out of Willa that something she'd learned about Nergal had spooked her, and that was why she'd fled. Something about Nergal... and Blaze."

I sat forward, instantly feeling protective of my best friend as I waited for her to go on.

"Apparently, Nergal had never gotten over the angels putting down demons and the other supernaturals in the last demon uprisings in the 1500s. He'd been researching how to claim ultimate power for himself ever since, and Willa found Nergal's notes on a ritual to ensure just that. A spell that, in exchange for the life of the caster's child, would grant them the power of a thousand angels. It would essentially make Nergal a god.

"It appeared, from the notes Willa could put together, that Nergal had stumbled upon this spell… about a year before Blaze's birth." Lys whistled, and Mo nodded grimly. "Kal was nearing thirty at that point and was too old for the spell's requirements, so he needed another child."

"Does he know?" Dev demanded, a bite to her voice that mimicked my own feelings. Not that I'd ever had any doubts that Nergal needed to be taken down, but after hearing this, I had difficulty keeping myself rooted to my chair, needing to take action *immediately*.

"He knows Nergal has ambitions for great power," Mo hedged. "But Willa made us promise to never tell him what Nergal truly wanted with him. And Nergal basically disappeared for decades after Willa's death, so it hasn't been relevant."

"And now? He's too old for the spell, right? Like Kal was."

Mo lifted a shoulder at Dev's words. "Unless he found a way around that. But Willa did more than just bring Blaze here to make sure Nergal stayed down. She did her own research, along with Althea, for several years. When she was ready, she lured Nergal to a meeting point just outside of town. With her Coven at her back, she ripped Nergal of all the power she could. Using the power of the same spell, she banished Nergal from the town, tying his banishment to the border.

"Unfortunately, Willa used every ounce of power, of energy that she had to work that spell. Even with the Coven assisting her, she never recovered."

"Shit," Dev said, breaking the silence as we all absorbed this tragic story. "And I thought my parents were terrible."

I couldn't resist looking in her direction at her words, wondering for the first time what her story was. I'd met her parents a few times in passing when they'd visited and could never quite combine the image of their nomad lifestyle with the woman sitting across from me.

"Can you feel if the magic is still in place, keeping him out?" I asked, forcing myself to look away from Dev as she chewed on her bottom lip.

"I'll have to go out to the border with the others," Mo explained. "We can't sense it from this distance. But, Orion," she caught my eye meaningfully, "It may already be too late."

"What do you mean?" Ostara asked.

"Assuming Ruby was possessed, which I'd say seems a safe bet at this point," Morgaine continued, "Then it's likely whatever demon was using her has been watching her closely. Waiting for the moment when the spell was undone."

"To alert Nergal," Devanna said, catching on quickly.

Morgaine nodded. "If it wasn't Nergal himself, then, yes, I'd assume he was alerted immediately. He may be here already."

"Why?" Lys said. "What does he care about Deadlights Cove if Blaze is too old to use for the spell now?"

"No one knows what Willa bound his power to. After she died, Althea and I looked for a talisman or something she might have left behind, but neither of us ever found anything. Then Althea died a few years later and I was raising a hellion on my own. I haven't thought much about it in the last several decades." Mo took a sip of her tea, sighing as she set it back on the saucer. "I think he wants to try to undo Willa's spell, to retain the power she pulled from him, and, if he can, perform the spell he planned for all those years ago. With the way he's been orchestrating Kal's movements for the last year, I'm afraid he's found a way around the age limitation. How many times has Kal tried to lure Blaze to come with him? To leave the protection of Deadlights Cove willingly? If Nergal completes the ritual, then he could finally overthrow the angels, and demons could wreak havoc once again."

"Lovely," Devanna deadpanned.

"If it's even remotely possible that Nergal will come here, we need to inform the town to be on the alert," I said, Morgaine and Ostara nodding. "Morgaine, gather whoever you need to head to the border and check if the magic is still in place. If it's down, do what you can."

"I'll call Ryker, see if he can find any trail of where Nergal's been," Morgaine added.

I pulled out my phone, preparing a town-wide text alert about the extra precautions everyone should take until we could get a better handle on the situation. Mo slipped out of the room, her phone to her ear, though I could hear her perfectly well as she addressed Eva Watford on the other end of the line.

"I strongly recommend no one goes anywhere alone."

My comment earned a snort from Satan's Spawn, and my jaw ticked, though my eyes never left my phone. I pressed Enter, alerting every supernatural within the town's borders that there was the possibility Nergal, if not others, might pay us a visit, and everyone should be careful.

ORION

RAIN PATTERED against the window in my office the next morning, low-hanging clouds blurring my view of the town. Everything was dark, including my mood.

Until I'd received Mo's text reassuring me the barrier against Nergal was still in place, I hadn't been sure I'd ever sleep again.

Now, even with that modicum of safety, I still couldn't relax. Namely because I'd been on a conference call with Ezra and two other Council officers for an hour already.

"Our contacts within the FBI are hitting roadblocks," Ezra said, and I leaned my head back against the chair, holding back a sigh. "I don't have a way to stop this investigation for you."

Of course he didn't. That would be too easy.

"So what do you suggest?" I asked, trying to keep my tone even, despite wanting to scream in frustration.

"We need to lead them away from town," one of the other officers suggested, and I glanced down at my watch for the tenth time this morning. The exorcism was scheduled to start half an hour ago, and I was stuck here dealing with red tape. "I'll see if I can't find a way to lure them out of Deadlights Cove. Maybe we can plant a false evidence trail in a non-supe town nearby?"

Ezra sighed, sounding frustrated, but what right did he have to feel that way? It was *me* that had to deal with this headache, not him from his high and mighty seat in Headquarters. It wasn't *his* friends who would be investigated for murder and taken by the government for experimentation if I messed this up. He had no skin in the game.

"I'll look into it, but I can't make any promises. With how sophisticated human technology has become, there might be a limit to how much we can interfere. I can't just make this go away by mind-wiping everyone like in the good old days." Ezra chuckled bitterly, but neither me nor the other officers joined him.

After another agonizing few minutes of administrative bullshit, the call finally ended.

The urge to fly to Ostara's to get there faster was almost unbearable, but I walked down to my car and drove there — *like a human* — knowing the FBI was still here investigating, one street over.

"They're just finishing up," Lysander said in a low tone when he answered the door, leading me into Ostara's living room.

The coffee table had been moved against the couch so Ruby could lay on the rug in the middle of the room. Lance and Morgaine knelt on either side of her.

The siblings' resemblance was easy to see — same pale skin, same white, almost blond hair, same laugh lines that showed they'd both spent a lifetime being mischievous.

Many witches could control the aging process, using spells to keep themselves appearing young for longer. Mo had looked to be in her mid-70s for the entire time I'd known her, but Lance seemed younger, the same as Ostara's late 50s. How old either sibling truly was was a mystery unto itself — though I knew for a fact Mo's rap sheet went back at least as far as the 1850s.

As always, Mo dressed to blind in her orange citrus-print kimono, standing out like a neon light in the dark room. Lance, on the other hand, had a Western vibe — dark jeans with a white button-down under a brown suede vest, complete with boots and a bolo tie. His outfit choice in midcoast Maine stood out nearly as much as his sister's.

"Ruby?" Mo placed a gentle hand on the girl's shoulder as she blinked awake, coming out of a trance.

Ruby slowly sat up. "Is it over?"

"Yes, dear. All over now."

"You were in the early stages of demon possession, which is why you only lost patches of time, but were aware at other times," Lance explained. He sat back on his heels and looked between Ostara and me. "We've removed all trace of demonic magic now."

The trio on the floor rose to their feet and took seats around the room. Ruby was still shaken up, but if there was any chance for answers, the sooner we got them, the better.

"Do you remember anything else, dear? Any recollection of what else they might have coaxed you to do for them?"

A butler brought a tray, setting it down on the coffee table as Ostara thanked him and poured Ruby a mug herself. Ruby took it, clasping the porcelain with both hands, as she struggled to think back.

"I remember Mrs. Farrington leading me out into the woods one night, I think — or, leading me back?" Ruby shook her head and took a sip of her tea. "It's hard to remember."

"Close your eyes." Lys took a seat on Ruby's other side. "It might make it easier to remember images."

Ruby nodded and closed her eyes, sinking back into the couch and taking a long, even breath.

"Wings."

I straightened up, exchanging a glance with Mo.

"White wings?"

"It — it was so dark. Maybe they were white, or grey?"

"An angel?" Ostara prompted.

"I don't know." Ruby shook her head. "I don't see a face or anything else, just... just the wings. And — I think they brought me to the Hanging Tree."

"Thank you, dear," Mo said as she brushed a strand of Ruby's brown and red hair behind her ear. "You did great."

My jaw tightened as I walked towards the door, Lance following not far behind.

"Do you think someone's turned against the Council?" Lance asked as soon as the door shut behind us.

"Seraphina was found dead at the Iron Keep after the prisoners were set free. I don't know how deep they dug into why she would have gone back for Nergal, but I guess it's not impossible it was more than just her that betrayed us."

Lance nodded, his expression thoughtful, but I didn't know the male well enough to guess what he was thinking.

"I got a call from Heath this morning."

"Heath Larkin?" I frowned, not following his train of thought. "West's dad?"

Lance nodded. "With West in the news lately, he's worried about his family. He's asked if I can come out and help with their own town border in case there are any more attempts on the wellspring. I can't stand the thought of leaving my family, but I know you'll look after them like you always have. Mo knows how to find me if you need me."

"Of course," I said, swallowing the anxious feeling clawing up my throat at losing another powerful witch who could have helped us.

Lance clapped me on the back, squeezing my shoulder. "I'm proud of you, son. This town is in capable hands."

I stood frozen as Lance walked down the sidewalk and into town, shocked by his words. Lance didn't even know me, so why did his approval mean so much?

I sat in the dark, wishing we'd learned more from Ruby after her exorcism, and the idea of an angel betraying the Council weighing on me. Slumped on the couch I'd picked for the music room, I knew I should go try to get some rest, but couldn't quiet my mind. This was the one room that brought me peace when anxiety crept up on me, and Blaze knew it. He'd let me be in charge of the remodeling and finishing touches in here, so I'd picked a pale, almost white, blue. Windows stretched from floor to ceiling facing the water — the best view in the house — and my baby grand piano sat directly in front of them.

This place was my solace. I came here often, the sound and rhythm of the keys bringing order to my life when I desperately needed it. After several centuries of practice, I'd mastered the piano, and loved the way a song could carry me away.

Tonight, though, I couldn't even bring myself to touch the cool ivory keys. My head pounded as it had every day lately, thinking through all of the disasters this town had been through already, and all the ones that were sure to come.

Everything was spinning out of control, and I was grasping at straws, foolishly hoping I could rein it in. With each passing moment, doom settled on my shoulders, waiting for the final blow, for my life to crumble around me.

Yet, despite the shambles of my own life, I had to admit Blaze's family was even more messed up than mine. That Blaze had turned out so happy and carefree, even after having such a terrible beginning, made me admire him more.

I was lost to my thoughts, the room only illuminated by the moonlight sifting through the windows just after sundown. Home alone. Pilsner glass dangling loosely from my fingertips. I'd forgotten to bring a coaster in from the kitchen, so I couldn't bring myself to put it down, and the thought of a ring on the wood coffee table only made my anxiety creep higher.

The front door opened, and Blaze and Petra's happy laughter drifted down the hallway towards me as they returned home after Scallywags closed. I sank lower on the couch, hoping they'd just walk straight by me without stopping to chat. But of course, that was too much to wish for.

"What are you doing in the dark, O?" Blaze's voice came from right behind me, and I fought not to jump. I didn't bother with an answer, hoping he'd catch my drift that I'd rather be left alone, but this was Blaze. "Scallywags was *hopping*, my male. You should've been there. I had to kick everybody out or they probably would've stayed up all night gossiping and taking bets about the FBI. Bunch of busybodies."

"I'm pretty sure the busiest body there was you, Blaze," came Petra's voice, and Blaze laughed.

A light flicked on overhead — a simple but stunning pewter chandelier I'd picked to hang over the piano, gorgeous from both inside the house and out — and I sat up as Petra stepped into the room.

"Oh, sorry," she said, probably in response to my scowl. A pink blush crept up her pale cheeks, made all the more prominent by her bright red hair. Tonight she wore a Scallywags t-shirt tied at the waist over a long, flowy skirt with brown sandals, looking as casual and at ease here in town as I'd ever seen her. "I can turn them back off."

"I know what will make him feel better," Blaze said as he stilled her hand where it reached for the lights. Blaze circled the couch, heading for my piano, and I groaned.

"You play?" Petra asked, her voice rising in question to her boyfriend.

"I have many hidden talents, Petey," he replied with a wink, and I shook my head.

"This is not one of them, though," I grumbled.

The bench scraped across the polished wood floors, and I flinched. Blaze dramatically cracked his fingers, lifting them high into the air before delicately laying them on the keys. The opening notes of Bette Midler's *Wind Beneath My Wings* lifted into the air, and I pulled my back from the couch.

Petra chuckled as Blaze attempted to croon, making pointed eye contact as he sang the first verse.

I stood to leave, shaking my head. "Unbelievable," I muttered. "Did you learn this song purely to annoy me?"

As always, my annoyance only fueled Blaze's metaphorical flames. But I couldn't sit there, listening to my closest friend laughing like he didn't have a care in the world, all while his evil demon father was probably about to break down the barrier and try to sacrifice him. Shit, I was probably two beers away from telling him the whole story myself, and then what? I'd ruin his life?

"I'm not listening!" I tossed back over my shoulder as I entered the hallway towards my wing, needing to put distance between us.

Uncaring, Blaze sang the chorus louder, and I slammed the door shut behind me as I entered my room, barely holding myself together.

Chapter Eight

DEVANNA

"ERROR 404?" I scrunched my nose, pushing my glasses up my face as I leaned closer to my computer the next afternoon. Between the late night meeting at Mo's and all the drama yesterday had contained, I'd slept in until noon and was just now getting started for the day. I hadn't been able to fall asleep until Mo had texted us the all-clear that the Nergal barrier was still up, and even then, I'd tossed and turned for what felt like hours as the storm rolled in off the ocean. Now, even the scent of orange and bergamot burning in my diffuser couldn't calm my nerves — both the simmering worry in the back of my mind for the future of our town and supernaturals as a whole, as well as fury at the computer in front of me. "What do you mean, *not found*?"

The bell to my shop, Carpe Noctem, chimed, but I was too busy trying to decipher lines of cyber-speak to look up. I'd been trying to set up an online storefront for a while now, but every time I made a change and went to publish it, error codes kicked back. First my images weren't the right file type, then I'd converted them and lost all the quality, so I'd had to retake them. No one in their right mind would spend hundreds of dollars on crystals for witchcraft with grainy photos. I'd finally fixed the photo problem last week and had spent hours today working on the descriptions for each listing, only to have the whole page *not found* once I hit live.

I wiggled the mouse, clicking the back button to refresh and… nothing. "You've got to be kidding me."

"Everything all right, there?"

I looked up to find Maisie eyeing me with concern. Now that the sea nymph princess didn't need to hide her identity, she no longer covered herself in giant hoodies and sweats. Today, she had on a bright blue romper that made her eyes glow, her platinum hair in loose waves around her shoulders, standing out as a bright beacon in the dim light of my store.

Throwing one last scowl at the offending screen, I decided to give the whole thing a rest. "Not at all, but it's not your problem." I squinted at her while she trailed a suntanned finger over a display of crystals in the middle of the shop. Shelves of spell ingredients covered the walls behind her ranging from salts to frog spawn (dried). "Do you need something?"

"Well, now you mention it, yes, actually." She plucked up an amethyst, holding it up to the light and twirling it. "It's the witch stuff."

"Which stuff?"

"No, I mean, the *witch* stuff. Powers. Magic, et cetera," she waved a hand in the air that I took to encompass *everything*. "From the Linking spell?"

Ah. That.

"I'm having some trouble learning how to use all my powers and focus everything and —"

I held up a hand. "Um, hello? This is what Lys does. As a Harmonic witch, this is, quite literally, what he's best at."

Maisie gave an exasperated sigh, and threw herself — or possibly tripped — onto one of the deep plum velvet poufs set to the side of the checkout counter.

"Okay, yes. First of all, the male is obnoxiously good at *everything* and that's more than a little intimidating. The first time he tried to shift into a mer form, he had gills within seconds, like he'd been born to the powers same as me. Do you know what happened the first time I tried to cast a spell?" Her eyes expanded, leaning forward to emphasize the importance of this rhetorical question. "He wanted me to conjure a flame, which considering I inherited both his demon and witch powers through the Linking, should have been easy right?"

I stared at her, waiting for her to elaborate, but held back a grin at the deadpan expression she wore.

"Wrong. I cast the spell, said the words, held my hand out just how he'd showed me to and absolutely nothing happened. Not even one little twitch of magic, not the hint of smoke. Zero. Zilch. Nada. I. Was. Mortified."

I understood her frustration even if it was a little funny. I'd grown up with and trained with Lys my whole life — I was more than a little aware of the frustration of comparing yourself to him. "Well, you know how the saying goes: If at first you don't succeed…"

Maisie sighed, her eyes rolling as she finished, "Try —"

But I cut her off. "Destroy any evidence you ever tried until you're positive you can kick some ass."

She laughed, head snapping back up towards me. "See? You get me."

I did smile at that. The more I'd gotten to know Maisie over the last few weeks, the more I liked her. That had kept happening to me over the past year for some reason, letting more people into my circle — maybe I was coming down with something. Maisie was quirky and clumsy, but the depth of loyalty she had for her family, for Lys, was something I couldn't help but admire. If ever I needed someone to help me bury a body, Maisie would be my girl. "Have you talked to Lys about it yet? Explained why you're frustrated?"

Her eyes met mine in a pointed stare. "Here's the thing, and remember that I love him when I say this. I'm sure he's a great teacher for *other* witches. But he's too in love with me to tell me when I'm doing something wrong, or *what* I'm doing wrong! He keeps being infuriatingly positive and anytime we try to work on a spell, he gets his star-crossed heart-eye face on and we never get anywhere! I mess every single one up and all he says is, '*That was a great try, Maze, you'll get it next time.*'" Maisie made a choked sound of annoyance. "Next time?!"

"Okay, so he's a lovesick puppy and it makes him a terrible teacher." I shrugged. "Why are you *here*?"

She sat forward, an eager grin taking over her face, and I shook my head, sensing where this was going.

"Oh, no. Trust me, you don't want me as your tutor."

"Please?"

I gave her a flat stare. "That word doesn't work on me, Maisie. Believe me, if I try to teach you, you'll end up in tears. I don't know the meaning of the word *sugarcoat*." I waved a hand, dismissing her. "And then Lys will come barging in here to yell at me about making his girl cry. So beat it, find somebody else."

Maisie snorted, and I shot her a look. "You think Ronan ever went easy on me, on any of us?" She raised an eyebrow. It was a fair point. "I need someone who will tell me, point blank, what I'm doing wrong and how to fix it. I need to learn this, to actually get better, not have my self-esteem stroked. With everything going on, I need every tool in my arsenal to protect and defend my people, if it comes to that, Poseidon forbid. If I wanted sugarcoating, I'd be with Lys right now."

She held my stare.

My eyes narrowed.

The antique grandfather clock ticked ominously from the back of the room.

Finally, I threw up my hands. "Fine! But don't say I didn't warn you. And we're not practicing here in the shop where you could break all my merch. That amethyst you're holding sells for over a hundred bucks." Maisie blinked and cautiously set it on the coffee table in front of her, raising her empty hands. "Meet me at the house."

Maisie leapt off the pouf with a smile, then promptly tripped over it, though that didn't dampen her excitement. "Thank you! Tomorrow night work?"

I agreed, then rolled my eyes at her retreating back as she left the shop, already wondering why I'd agreed to this.

Right as I looked back to my computer, the bell over the door rang again. I took a steadying breath to rein in my flaring temper at yet another intrusion on the off chance it was a customer. Home renovations were expensive — I needed the business.

At the sight of the yellow *FBI* label on the woman's navy blue raincoat, alarm bells started going off in my head.

"Ms. Bailey?" the agent asked, and as she moved closer, I recognized her from the crime scene yesterday.

"That's me. You can call me Devanna, or Dev," I said, proud of the fact that my hand didn't tremble in the slightest as I stood and stuck my hand out over the counter for the woman to shake. "How can I help you today?"

Her handshake was brief and firm; to the point. I liked her already. "I'm Special Agent Garcia, overseeing the murder investigation of Mrs. Primrose Farrington."

I nodded, feeling like it was weird to smile, but everything about having a human investigator in my store was off-putting, especially as I looked around my shop and noticed just how much merchandise I sold that was similar to what I'd seen in Mrs. Farrington's house last night. Fuck.

"Of course," I said, my voice taking on a higher pitch I hardly recognized as I fought to do my best impression of Nimue. While a demon, my best friend was far less scary than me, and scaring this woman — a very *human* woman — would not bode well for me right now. "Is there something you need from me?"

"Just a few questions for you, if you're not busy." Garcia's dark eyebrows lifted as she looked over the shop, noticing there weren't any customers in the store to give me an out. I was well and truly cornered.

"Please, have a seat." I waved a hand at the sitting area Maisie had just vacated and circled the counter to join her, my heart racing in my chest. While I often left Deadlights Cove to head into the human towns around us, I didn't frequently interact with humans, especially law enforcement, and prayed to the Goddess I could think quickly on my feet.

"What do you know about the murder that happened last September?"

My brows raised, thinking back to the schoolhouse murder when Petra had first arrived in town. "Deadlights Cove is a small town, so I've heard some of the rumors about it, but I wasn't directly involved in any of it, so nothing concrete. Was the victim ever identified?"

"A John Doe." Garcia shook her head, then rose to walk towards the wall of salts displayed on the back wall. "What are these for?"

I followed her, staring at where she pointed. "Salts are used for a wide range of things. Pink Himalayan salt is great for healing headaches. That's what I focus on here at Carpe Noctem — holistic healing, self-care, that sort of thing. Some people say it's all nonsense, but modern medicine can't explain everything, right? And some people just like the aesthetic, the scents — so I sell a variety of crystals, oils, and such."

"And what about this black salt? What is it used for?"

I swallowed, trying to think of a reason that a human would ever use black salts.

"It's sourced from volcanoes," I explained. "Some people use it as bath salt, and there are some studies that show greater detoxification with it, though it's possible that may be placebo effect." I hoped she wouldn't ask for my sources. I was pulling this out of my ass. "But really, I think people just like the symbolism of volcanic salt in their self-care. Rejuvenation through fire." I nodded towards the phoenix statue on the top of the shelf. "Same idea as our fascination with phoenixes."

Garcia jotted something down in her notebook, and it

took everything in my power not to look over her shoulder. She moved slowly around the shop, looking over my displays and shelves, until she stopped in front of my bookcase. I cringed, but joined her over there. Suddenly Orion's aversion to having humans in town made a lot of sense, and I hated to admit that male was ever right about anything.

"Are these spell books?"

Crap. "Some of them," I admitted, because, well, the woman could read. The cover facing out front and center literally read *A Modern's Witch's Guide to Spellcraft*. "Some are cookbooks" — if you were cooking in a cauldron — "others are gardening books." I tried to adopt Nimue's open, friendly, thoughtful expression as I continued. "I think people like the little rituals, you know? Putting together a little bundle of herbs to drink for good luck or fertility — even if it doesn't medically work, if it helps someone mentally or emotionally, they enjoy it." Who was I right now? But Garcia was nodding along, so hopefully she was buying this. I shrugged, forcing a little grin and glad I couldn't see my own face right now. "Again, self-care, little treats — whatever keeps people going through long days, right?" I hesitated only a moment before adding, "Have you ever considered carrying quartz? It's said to be good for intuition."

Garcia shot me an unreadable look, but didn't answer that, instead asking, "And most of your customers — are they local?"

Okay, I might have pushed it with the quartz. "Some are local, but I also get a lot from the surrounding areas — Spring Harbor, for example. Some of my repeat customers call and I'll mail their orders."

"Do you have a website?"

"No." *Not yet*, I added internally. "But I do have a social media account for the store, so out of towners can also find me that way and message me for orders."

"I see." Garcia jotted something else into her notebook before flipping it closed. "Would you be willing to provide your customer list?"

I hesitated, but I knew my rights. "I value my customers' privacy, Agent Garcia. I'm sure you understand." No one needed to know how often Val and Caedmon came in to buy patchouli (an aid for *passion*), and it would only cause drama if Peg and Eva learned they'd both been trying to sabotage the other's garden for years, even if I'd long since sold them placebos instead.

"Right. Well, I'm sure I don't have to tell you, but with a murder investigation, we *will* need that list to make sure we leave no stone unturned. And until I come back with a warrant," she met my eye pointedly, "don't leave town, Ms. Bailey."

I shook her hand again as she left, my heart racing as the bells jingled over the door once more. As much as it pained me to do so, I reached across the counter for my phone and texted the last person I wanted to talk to. Just looking at his name on the screen had annoyance taking over some of the panic clawing at me. This was going to be painful to say.

DEVANNA

I might need your help.

I hit send, then slid my phone into my pocket, trying to erase this moment of weakness from my memory.

Between Garcia's visit and my frustrating website, I decided to close the store for the day, unable to concentrate. Orion had said he'd stop by later tonight, so I had time to kill. Luckily, my church was right next door and needed all the attention I could spare. Next up, the bell tower.

With a clatter, the pieces of the old church bell crashed down several stories to the ground floor below. Luckily, I'd spelled it earlier, so the heavy pieces hung suspended several feet off the ground and didn't ruin the floors. I finished sweeping them over the ledge, then turned my attention to hacking through all the old rope cords that had held it up. The bell itself had been in pieces and unusable long before I'd purchased the old church, and after coming up here a few times to enjoy the view, I'd decided to repurpose the space. Once I had everything cleared out, I'd have supports, French doors, and flooring installed over the expanse, then turn it into a little den. Somewhere with a comfy chair where I could curl up with a whiskey and watch the town and the ocean in the distance.

I followed the winding staircase down to the ground floor, preparing to collect the bigger pieces into a dumpster and sweep up the rest, when rapid-fire knocking came from my front door.

"What now?" I muttered to myself, dusting off my hands and heading over. But before I even reached for the handle, the door swung open and Blaze, Nox, and a bunch of other guys I'd never seen before swept into my house.

"Ah, Devvie! Excellent." Blaze clapped his hands

together as the other guys let themselves into my future living room. "Listen, I had to close Scallywags for today — too much, ah —" he waved his fingers, where sparks danced between them, "— with too many humans around, and then Petey kicked me out of the house when one of her books caught on fire, so — surprise! We're here to redo your floors. And possibly your whole house, depending on how long this murder investigation lasts."

I pointed at the other guys. "And they are?"

"Oh, don't worry about them. Just some other demons — I mean," he cleared his throat, then continued in an exaggerated, loud voice, "— normal, human guys that I know." I rolled my eyes. "They're great. They're from that demon — dammit, that *normal* town outside of Vegas. They helped me redo the carriage house for Nimmie once upon a time."

The carriage house was beautiful, so I shrugged my mouth and nodded to Nox. "And you? Cops seem like they'd like popcorn."

Blaze threw an arm around the kid, chuckling. "Orion's asked him to stay out of sight until the humans leave, too. You know."

Nox grimaced, but didn't deny anything. More than likely, he'd also been accidentally setting fire to one too many things for humans to ignore completely.

The other guys were already starting to bring in tools to prep the floors, so it seemed like this was happening whether I wanted to or not. And hell, free floors?

"Why not?" I threw my hands up. "I'm sending you my design though, and it had better look exactly like my pictures when you're done."

After the guys started working, it quickly became evident I was no longer needed here. I still hadn't heard back from Orion, so I headed back to my apartment above the shop, poured myself a whiskey, and drew a bath. I hadn't *totally* been lying to Garcia about the self-care stuff — I enjoyed a little pampering from time to time.

I was just getting to the good part of my book when my phone buzzed from the stool beside the tub. I set my glass down and picked it up.

HEAVEN'S REJECT

Bit busy here at the office. What is it? - Orion, Mayor

I scowled at him through the phone and swiped it open to reply.

DEVANNA

FBI wants my customer list. Getting a warrant.

I waited, comforting myself with the image of the uptight angel freaking out about yet another thing. The dots to indicate he was typing appeared, then disappeared, then appeared again, and I was struck with the uncomfortable sensation of… was this anticipation?

I snorted. No. I did not care one iota about getting a text from *Orion*. As if.

HEAVEN'S REJECT

I'll take care of it. - Orion, Mayor

"That's it?" I grumbled, tossing my phone onto a towel on the floor. "*'I'm Orion and I have to do everything by myself and keep everyone else in the dark.'* What a control freak." I took a healthy sip of my whiskey before calling out as if he could hear me, "This is why you always look like you have a stick up your ass, Orion comma Mayor!"

Chapter Nine

DEVANNA

THE NEXT MORNING, I was too on-edge to open the store, worried about the incoming warrant. The thought of Orion's *take care of it* didn't offer much relief, especially since he hadn't shared how that was going to happen.

Apparently, it wasn't just me that was feeling the tension in town. Blaze and his demon crew showed up at the church again earlier than I would have anticipated. Last night they'd somehow finished my floors. Over the course of the day, they overhauled the vestry, turning it into a luxurious bathroom, complete with a soaker tub and rainfall showerhead, and had started mapping out my kitchen. Blaze had also moved all of my bedroom furniture over to the house, flickering back and forth with each load like the most efficient moving team I'd ever seen. It was amazing what a little magic and the nervous energy of demons could accomplish.

I planned to keep the lay-out open, except for the bedroom, which I was putting in the already closed-off room behind the now removed pulpit. It was the farthest from the road, so it would be the quietest spot, and the surrounding woods offered a peaceful view through the windows. Blaze said they'd probably have it done in a few days, and, at their current pace, I believed him. They didn't even look tired, and since they'd finished the floors in one night, they must have been here pretty late.

I was clarifying the kitchen layout with Nox — I wasn't a huge cook, but I did like nice things — when a knock on the front door drew my attention. Leaving the demons to it, I stepped over to the large, arched front window, looking out to see Maisie standing between the drooping purple peonies around my front door.

Only, she wasn't alone.

I grimaced as I dusted off my hands and cracked open the front door — even though it swung open easily now over the fixed floorboards — just enough to squint one accusatory eye out at her.

"You said *you* wanted help." I glared at her, barring the entrance.

Maisie and Petra exchanged a glance. "Okay, so I might have mentioned something earlier when I stopped into Immortali-Tea about you helping me. Petra was there and mentioned she *also* needs help, so I thought, maybe you could help both of us at the same time."

"Demon magic is completely different from witch magic."

"But the principles are probably the same, and you know Orion said no one should wander around alone," Petra countered. Quick with that one, she was. Almost like she'd been anticipating my refusal and came up with counter-arguments before she got here.

I ignored the reference to Lucifer, choosing to take the high road.

"Why can't Blaze help you?"

A flush rose up over Petra's pale, freckled skin, and I rolled my eyes.

"Fucking hell, that horndog," I muttered, begrudgingly stepping back just enough to let them in.

"He just gets so excited to see me using magic —"

"For the love of the Goddess, I do not want details. If you want to avoid him, we need to go hide. He's finishing up the tile in the bathroom.

Petra pressed her lips together as Maisie laughed, and the two of them followed me through the entryway. I led them to the basement, which I planned to turn into a home gym, and spun to face them.

"All right. Show me what you got."

After two hours, it was clear that Lys and Blaze should both be ashamed of themselves. They were *abysmal* teachers. Whether I was any better, only time would tell, but at least both Maisie and Petra had managed marginally better magic by the time I called it for the day. I could tell they were getting worn out.

"One of the most important things in using magic is knowing when to stop," I said as they sat back against the wall, exhausted. "If you used up all your power today, it could be days before it replenished enough for you to use it. It always takes longer to refill the well if you let it empty completely; better to leave a little gas in the tank. Though, honestly, no one really knows what to expect from the Linking spell transfers, so you guys are guinea pigs here."

They nodded, flushed from the exertion, Petra's pale skin in particular turned as red as a ripe tomato.

"You should exercise more," I told her with a frown. As a nymph, Maisie already had a leg up, since the physical exertion from magic wouldn't be as hard on her — she was used to being active. The wheezing academic had no such advantage.

"Right. I'll get right on that." Petra wiped the sweat from her brow, and I shrugged.

"You asked for my help. A little cardiovascular health can go a long way in magic."

Petra gave me a once-over, taking in my black sneakers, black shorts overalls, and the deep violet *Big Witch Energy* shirt I wore under it. Not my usual attire — at least the shoes and overalls — but a necessity during my DIY projects.

"*You* exercise?"

I considered telling her one reason I'd bought this church was to transform this basement into my own personal dojo, so I'd have more space to train and spar with my punching bags and assorted weapons. Not many people in town knew how much I trained, but it wasn't really any of her business. If she stuck around for my training sessions, she'd find out soon enough. I lifted a shoulder. "Sure."

By the time they left, it was late evening and my stomach grumbled loudly as I stared at my not-yet-kitchen, hands on my hips. I could head back to my apartment, but knew there wouldn't be any decent options to put a meal together.

I frowned at the little microwave and meager pickings of

food, none of which looked remotely appetizing. The door to the bathroom opened and Blaze walked out, covered in dust from tiling all day. With one look at me standing in my soon-to-be-kitchen staring at my microwave, he put his tools in the orange bucket and waved me towards the door.

"Let's go to Scallywags and I'll get us some food."

I frowned. "Isn't it closed?"

"I'm on good terms with the owner. Great guy. I think we can work something out." Blaze winked, then opened the front door and waited for me to follow.

Rosemary fries were better than cup-o-noodles every day of the week.

Chapter Ten

ORION

MY NERVES WERE STRUNG like a livewire, and this was going on six days. I kept jumping and twitching at every unexpected sound, any shadowy movement, expecting it to be Nergal or Errakal plowing into town in attack, or the FBI ready to arrest us all. I kept having nightmares about Agent Garcia popping up behind me when I hadn't remembered to glamour my wings and thus exposing angels to the world too, letting down my entire species.

I hadn't been sleeping much.

The witches had tried to reinforce the enchantment to keep Nergal out, but the last time they had set it up, they'd had access to him to do so, keying it into his magical signature. Without him showing up again, they could only make it so secure.

We also hadn't been able to resurrect my full glamour on the town yet, since Mrs. Farrington's death was still under investigation. So now, on top of worrying about Nergal, we'd started getting other humans sniffing around town.

And not just any humans. Tourists. The worst kind.

This was a harbor town in Maine in the middle of summer, and we'd idiotically tidied up the Last Resort for the Summit. We were in danger of quickly becoming a Vacationland destination, and we just couldn't have that.

Ferron, the demon who technically owned the Last Resort but was rarely in town to run it — hence its usual dilapidated state — was beside himself. He'd never had so many reservations in all the time he'd owned the motel, and to say he was out of his depth would have been an understatement.

The third day after he'd started receiving bookings, he'd called me in a panic, asking me to send out an SOS for help from anyone who could offer some time. From my understanding, Castor had taken pity on him, and had become his de facto manager until we could sort all this out and send the humans on their way.

The way the humans flocked around the lighthouse was alarming, but Zaphiel had instated himself as keeper, barking at tourists to follow the rules posted on the sign if they wanted to climb up to the galley deck and ruthlessly turning them away if they did not. His internet reviews were abysmal, but the tourists kept coming.

Needless to say, I was in contact with someone from Headquarters every day, and every day, they told me to sit tight, not draw any additional attention to the town, and not provoke the humans. When Devanna had asked for help, I'd pulled her sales records and adjusted some of the numbers, making sure to include the sales of the items used in Mrs. Farrington's and the school house murder's rituals under false names from Vermont. Agent Garcia and her team had left, chasing down that lead, and for the moment, we were in the clear.

If my hair wasn't already silver by birth, it'd be turning grey.

"No, something stronger," I waved away the beer Blaze had started to put down as I slumped into a stool at Scally-wags. He raised his brows in surprise, but quickly spun away to get me something else, for once thinking better of opening his big mouth.

Much as it would have been better for supernaturals if Scallywags stayed closed, it was too suspicious for the only bar in town to keep shutting down with tourists flooding in. As a compromise, Blaze had set up what he had named *the Poop Deck* — a new seating area on the roof that he kept ushering the humans up to. It let the humans think we were offering them the best view in the bar, while simultaneously getting them out of our hair.

A glass of whiskey appeared in front of me, and I took a long sip, closing my eyes and taking a breath.

Unfortunately, one of the drawbacks to being an angel was that it would take a *lot* of human alcohol to make the tiniest impact on my nerves.

The bell above the door jingled, but I could tell just by the way she walked it was Devanna. The light jasmine scent that reached me as the air eddied around would have been my next clue.

"I have never heard a single person who walks as heavy as you do," I commented as she sat in the barstool farthest from me. "It's like the running of the bulls in Pamplona, except it's just you stomping around angrily for no reason."

"I like to imagine your face on the floor," she said,

reaching across the bar to grab a glass. "Couldn't help but stomp extra hard, just for you."

I rolled my eyes, sipping at the whiskey in my glass as I avoided looking at her. Blaze snorted, taking Devanna's dinner order, then moved through the swinging saloon doors to the kitchen beyond.

The minute Blaze was out of sight, Devanna circled the bar as I'd seen her do so many times before, standing on her toes to reach for the Knob Creek whiskey. I watched as her hand patted blindly along the shelf, those damn black overalls riding up to show every spare inch of smooth skin on her legs, calves flexing. The outfit was casual for her, far different from the tight leather pants or pencil skirts that hugged her curves, but she was no less attractive with dust in her bright blue hair tied high up on her head.

She sank down to her heels, and I pried my eyes away from her ass, swirling the whiskey in my glass. She spun, a deep frown forming creases between her eyebrows, searching for the missing bottle.

Her brown eyes rose, spotting the brown liquid splashing around in my glass. "What are you drinking?"

"I wasn't aware you were buying or I would have gone for the Glenfiddich."

She reached over the bar, chest resting on the counter as she yanked the glass out of my hand, brought it to her mouth, and took a small sip.

"You son of a kumquat," she said the moment the whiskey hit her lips, eyes alight with passionate rage. "You drank my Knob Creek! Where is it?"

"My stomach, I think." I plucked the glass back from her hand, ignoring the frisson of charge that shot down my hand as our fingers brushed, and downed the remaining liquid. "Would you like me to baby-bird it back to you? Glenfiddich sounds better anyway."

"You'd think someone who grew up in the Dark Ages would know the difference between Scotch and whiskey. Should I paint a diagram of the differences onto a cave wall for you?"

"Cave paintings would be from the Paleolithic Age, not the Dark Age, but, please, tell me more about my ignorance."

She glowered at me for a long breath before she lunged across the bartop, hands extended.

"Hey!" Blaze said as he pushed through the door and seized her around the waist, pulling her back. "No fries if you strangle him."

Steam practically billowed from Devanna's ears as she twisted out of Blaze's hold, walking back around the bar to her seat and shoved several fries in her mouth, dramatically biting into each one as if she pictured it was my head.

I tapped the counter, pushing my glass across the bar to Blaze and stood to leave as my phone vibrated in my pocket. I pulled it free, worry coursing through me instantly when I saw Zaphiel's name on the screen.

"What's wrong?"

"Lighthouse," Zaphiel's voice cracked, spoken in a low whisper. "Now."

The line went dead, but not before I heard a piercing scream in the background.

"Blaze, flicker me to the lighthouse *now*," I said, and luckily, the demon was smart enough to follow my command. First time for everything. Angels could travel through dimensions to reach Headquarters and back, but flickering within one realm would be a bit like trying to separate individual grains of sand using a bulldozer. With the amount of humans currently on the roof, I couldn't fly either.

Blaze appeared directly in front of me, grabbed my hand, and we disappeared into the in-between.

"Oh shit," Blaze gasped as we reappeared in front of the lighthouse seconds later. Standing out against the dark water, flames licked up the sides of the lighthouse, screaming humans trapped on the galley deck above.

"I don't know what happened," Zaphiel said as he ran to us, eyes wide with panic as he frantically shook his head. "The flames aren't reacting to water, and the only way I can get the humans down is to fly, which, I figured you wouldn't be okay with."

"A seagull-man appearing would be a little alarming, yes," Blaze said, eyeing the flames. As if summoned to the fire, Blaze moved forward mechanically, eyes glazed in a trance as he watched the flickering light.

"Help us!" someone screamed from above, and I glanced up, counting five humans through the thick smoke, including two small children, trapped on the galley deck on the ocean-side of the lighthouse. "Get the fire department!"

Blaze's fingers flexed, pulling on the fire with his magic while I watched cautiously. Between the smoke, the setting sun, and his position, the humans wouldn't be able to see him working magic openly, but still, the thought was enough to make bile rise in my throat. The flames moved as he pulled, dancing in the wind, dwindling slightly, then seemed to suck Blaze forward, toward the fire. He released his hold as he slumped, and instantly, the flames inched higher. "Get Nimue," he said through labored breaths, hands on his knees as sweat beaded on his forehead from exertion. "Endymion. Nox. Anyone. I can't do this on my own."

I pulled my phone from my pocket, dialing all of the demons in town, ordering them to join us here now. We didn't have a fire engine — had never needed one since the few demons in town were more than capable of handling fires on their own.

Seconds ticked by while we waited for everyone to arrive, and my wings itched at my back demanding I rescue the humans, consequences be damned.

But not yet.

Nimue arrived first, Devanna and Maisie at her side. Without a word, the girls moved into action — Nimue held her hands outstretched, pulling on the fire at the same time as Blaze. Together, the two demons wrangled the flames, pulling them down and away from the humans above as Maisie called up water from the ocean, sending it crashing onto the rocks and over the fire near the base of the tower. Devanna worked fast, sprinkling something at her feet, then held her hands up to the third-quarter moon, chanting something I couldn't understand, but the water at Maisie's disposal seemed to double with a rising tide.

Endymion and Nox arrived next, taking up positions near Nimue and Blaze as they fought to control the raging fire out of sight of the humans above. I watched as the flames licked higher, eating the ancient wood with a power only magical fire could. Even the combined power of four demons wouldn't be fast enough.

"Zaphiel," I said, electricity zapping along my skin as I let my glamour go, white wings appearing on my back against the dark night. "Time to go."

The other angel's grey eyes studied me, knowing what doing this meant. I'd have to wipe the memory of every human on that deck, and report it to Headquarters. There was no way to cover up the amount of magic we'd used in front of them, but their lives mattered more than my future.

Without waiting for him, I pushed off the ground, flying into the air as I circled the lighthouse. Heat washed off the fire, burning against my skin as I hovered above the deck and reached forward to grab the two small children first. As my hand grasped the small girl's wrist, her mother shrieked, pulling the girl into her arms, away from me.

"I'm taking her to safety," I said calmly, but the mother spun in front of the little girl, hiding her from me. Frustration coursed through me as I looked to the flames licking up from below then back to the woman. To the girl coughing and sputtering from smoke inhalation. "Please, I promise to take her to safety and come back for you."

"You're one of those *shifters* from the news," the man spat at me, putting both the woman and the little girl behind him. "It's not just wolves — I knew it wasn't. Don't touch my family."

Anger took over, and lightning streaked the sky in the background. "Your judgments will be the death of you if you do not come with me *right now.* Those flames are uncontrollable and have destroyed the stairs to this deck, so come with me or die. Those are your options."

"I'll go first," a teenage girl said, voice shaking as she stepped forward. "Lucy, you come with me. We'll go together."

The little girl peeked out from behind her mother, moving to the side as she reached forward to take the teen's hand. Together, they stepped towards the edge, and I landed lightly on the deck while I wrapped an arm around both of the girls' waists.

"I promise I'll keep them safe," I said, looking directly into their father's eyes.

"I'll fucking kill you if you don't," the man snarled.

Not bothering to answer, I pushed off, soaring over the lighthouse and landing gently next to Devanna, who helped the two girls move back from the fire towards the beach a safe distance away. Zaphiel was right behind me, carrying the girls' mother, and I rose into the sky once more, grabbing the boy who waited with his father. Noticing the murder still in the man's eyes, I flew to Zaphiel, handed off the boy, then came back for the father.

"Don't think I won't be calling the police on you the minute I get away from this damned town," the man said while I carried him away from certain death. "There needs to be some sort of registration for your kind, whatever you are. You're unnatural, un-American, and a danger to society."

Gritting my teeth against the man's hurled insults as I saved his family's life, I resisted the temptation to drop the man in the ocean rather than on the beach next to the others.

The moment they were all together, I closed my eyes, letting my magic pool in my fingers, prepared to wipe their memories. A strong gust of ocean air swept over us, Maisie sucking the smoke from their lungs as I glamoured my wings once more.

With a burst of light, all five humans' eyes blew wide, blinking rapidly. The teen recovered first, her head swiveling to look around the beach. Then she noticed the flames behind us, pulled her phone free from her pocket, and started recording.

"I'm sorry, but as you can see, the lighthouse is closed tonight," I said, forcing a smile on my face as I held my hands out to the sides, pushing the humans back down the beach, away from the fire beyond. "Unfortunately, it's closed indefinitely."

"Good thing we didn't go on that stupid sunset light-house tour, right Dad?" the teen said with an uneasy laugh, having already forgotten that she was *in* the burning light-house mere moments ago.

The father didn't answer, his eyes settling on me in a way that had every hair on my body standing on end. I gritted my teeth against whatever he was going to say next, but was saved when Devanna pushed in front of me, shoving the humans back away from the flames.

"Get," she said, shoving at the man well over a foot taller than her. "Stop gawking. How dumb can you be to stand this close to a raging fire?"

The mother snapped out of her stupor next, grabbing her three children and pulling them down the beach away from us. The man eyed me a moment longer, then finally turned and walked after his children.

"Are you going to just stand there, or are you going to help?" Devanna said, and I whipped my gaze to her, watching as she ran across the rocks back to where the demons still fought to control the flames out of sight of the beach.

Suddenly, a burst of magic shoved all of us back, flying through the air and stunning my power. I landed hard on my side as my head snapped back on the rocky beach beneath me.

Whatever work Blaze and the other demons had done to control the flames was pointless as it slithered up the lighthouse, circling like a snake as it ate at the ancient landmark.

"Touching," a deep, masculine voice said, his words ringing in my ears as if he stood just behind me. I rolled, rising to my hands and knees on the beach as I looked around. "When Kal said all of the species were working together, I hardly believed him. But look at you — an angel working with demons, a sea nymph, and a witch."

I stood, searching for the source of the words, but there was no one here I didn't recognize.

"Show yourself," I barked, whirling around, willing my magic to return more quickly.

"You should know better than to order a demon to do anything, Orion," the voice said, amusement heavy in his tone. "After all, you've lived with my son for how long?"

"Nergal," I said, confirming what I'd already suspected, still spinning as my magic slowly started to return to me, humming along my skin once more. "What do you want?"

"The same thing I've always wanted," Nergal answered, still nowhere to be seen. "Power."

Judging by the flames licking dozens of feet in the air, and the supernaturals struggling to pull themselves back together after his magical attack, Nergal had *plenty* of power already.

"I'm tired of hiding," Nergal said, appearing before me. I stepped back on reflex, putting another foot between us. Like Blaze and Kal, Nergal had olive skin and wild black hair, but everything about him was a shade darker, even his voice. Where Blaze was the embodiment of mischief, his father was the picture of malice. Flames blazed in his black pupils that weren't just a mirror of the fire behind me, but that came from his own internal magic. "You see, I've been around for nearly a millennia. People used to worship me. To lay sacrifices in temples dedicated to me. They feared me, and sought to please me to protect themselves. But then that changed once the cursed angels took over. Don't you think it's time humans learned what lurks in the dark once more?"

"We'll be hunted," I said, the human's words as he'd rather face death than come with me ringing in my ears. My hands clenched as I willed the electricity to pool, waiting for enough to take on the demon in front of me, but I was outmatched and I knew it, so I kept him talking. "Shoved into laboratories for studying. Treated as animals."

"Some of us, maybe. Shifters, sure, but they hardly count as supernaturals if they don't even have enough magic to escape capture." Nergal shrugged as if this didn't matter to him in the slightest. If I hadn't hated the male before, I did now. "But not me. No one can stop me, not even the angels who thought they could keep me in an iron cell. And certainly not my wife who thought she could trap my powers."

Before I could answer, Blaze stepped forward. "Nergal, never a pleasure."

"Likewise," his father said, a small smile playing at his lips as he studied his son. Knowing the secrets I did, the way Nergal had planned to use Blaze, I moved, putting myself in front of Blaze. "When your brother said you'd taken up with a human, I thought it couldn't be true. But then, you always spent too much time with your mother and Althea, and that damned Morgaine, didn't you? They softened you into a blunt weapon, useless to all."

"Just what every child loves to hear," Blaze said with a contented sigh full of sarcasm. "I liked this lighthouse, by the way. Not happy with you at the moment."

Stomping sounded from behind me, and panic rose quickly in my chest. Without thinking, my magic flared with my wings, using the little power I could access to lock Devanna behind me and out of sight. Winding its way around her mouth and legs, I trapped her in place, mute. Whatever she planned on saying to Nergal would only ignite his wrath, and fear coursed through me at the thought of what Nergal would do as her poisoned barbs sank in. While Devanna was the most powerful Cosmic witch in Deadlights Cove, her powers didn't hold a candle to Nergal's.

"Your brother failed at his attempts to pull from the ley lines, both here and in Timber Creek, to undo whatever your mother did to keep me at bay when she locked my powers. I wasn't sure she would have kept the spell-lock object here, but given that even destroying this nexus isn't enough to break down the barrier she installed, I'd bet someone's life that it's hidden in town somewhere. I'll be back, and if you don't change your minds and side with me,

I won't be taking it easy on you," Nergal said, eyes focused on Blaze. "I *will* remove this barrier and find the object she spell-locked my powers to. Then I'll destroy it, along with everyone in this town for hiding it for this long."

Without another word, Nergal disappeared. Blaze deflated with an exhale, falling to his knees as he sank to the pebbles below. I let Devanna go, feeling her ire as she rounded on me.

"Did you *bind* me?" Devanna said in a low whisper that was somehow more intimidating than if she'd yelled.

"You're welcome," I said, letting go of a deep sigh.

"Wrong response," Blaze coughed, then heaved himself back to his feet. "We're just gonna go… back there."

"Do what you can for the lighthouse," I said, rubbing the bridge of my nose as the tension built in my head. "Just contain the fire. Let it burn out. I don't know."

"Pretty positive that fire can't be contained, and it's not going to burn out."

I opened my eyes in confusion, but Blaze wasn't pointing at the lighthouse. He was pointing at Devanna in front of me, practically vibrating with anger.

Chapter Eleven

DEVANNA

ORION SIDE-STEPPED around me on the beach, heading back towards town as I flexed and fisted my hands in frustration. *No one* made my decisions for me. I'd been on my own for a long damn time, and didn't need anyone holding me back or doing anything "for my own good." Because that was exactly the type of thinking this male would use. The *audacity*.

"Don't walk away from me," I spat as I rushed to catch up with him, already at the sidewalk.

Orion stopped, and, even though his wings were glamoured, I could see the faint way they bunched at his shoulder blades, pulling every muscle taut in his back. He spun around, jaw tight. The look on his face held more anger than I'd ever seen on the male, but rather than back down, I walked forward, slapping him across the face with as much strength as I could muster.

Orion's head whipped to the side as the sound seemed to echo, a sonic boom through the night. Shock momentarily coursed through me that I'd actually hit him — I'd never hit anyone outside of a fight before and hated myself for this weak moment, for the temper he brought out in me. Regret threatened to pull me under, but then his head slowly swiveled back towards me, seething in anger.

"Are you done?" he said, the words damn near growled. And shit, why was that sexy?

No. Nothing this male did was sexy.

Equal parts mad at myself and him, I hissed, "How dare you hold me back after I'd helped save those people without a second thought. You didn't even try to stop Nergal, even though you know what he wants to do with Blaze."

Orion took a step forward, the lamp post behind me shining on the glowing red handprint evident on his face. "I saved your life before you could act like a bratty child in the face of the strongest demon I've ever encountered. One who claims his powers are currently bound and *weakened,* yet he took all seven of us out like it was nothing. So yes, how dare I. Go ahead. Blame me like you always do, Devanna. I am the problem here, even though I will undoubtedly lose my job over this shitshow that just happened."

His words stung as if he'd slapped me in return, but I refused to back down, focusing on the last part instead.

"This town is falling apart, and, like always, you're only worried about yourself," I spat, fury coursing through my veins as I clenched my fists, barely holding myself back from hitting him again. But I was better than this, stronger than the rage I contained. No matter how angry he made me, I had to control myself.

A gamut of emotions rolled across Orion's face so fast I

couldn't track them before he leaned down, nose practically touching mine.

"You think I don't *care?*" Orion said through gritted teeth as he moved closer.

Involuntarily, I stepped back, bumping into the lamp post behind me. Orion towered over me, but I craned my neck, never breaking his stare. He'd never stood this close to me before, and for the first time, I noted a subtle sandalwood scent coming off him, and fought not to take a deeper inhale. I struggled to keep my breathing steady, well aware that the rise and fall of my chest nearly skimmed against his own.

"Yeah." I pushed on his chest, needing to put some distance between us, but Orion didn't budge, leering over me as his face contorted into some unknown expression I couldn't read. "I think you're the most selfish asshole I've ever met. You're so concerned with following the rules, seeing everything as black and white, that you never stop to consider there's more to it than that. Those humans almost died tonight, and rather than checking to see if they had damage from smoke inhalation or warning the rest of our town that a crazy-powerful demon is ready to destroy us all after he sacrifices your best friend, you're worried about your *job.*"

"And then you stomp in to my black-and-white world like a rainbow explosion of color," Orion said, slamming his hand on the post above my head, the heat of his body warming me as the motion brought him even closer. I didn't flinch, baring my teeth in a snarl as I waited for his insults, knowing they were coming. "Like a live wire, electrocuting me every time you open that damn mouth of yours so I can't see *anything* clearly." Orion closed his eyes as his jaw worked, fighting to maintain his composure when he so clearly wanted to unleash. I braced myself, ready for whatever he said, ready to dish it right back out. "You are the most—"

"Overwhelming. Obnoxious. Bitchy. Controlling. Demanding. Take your pick. I've heard them all before," I interrupted him.

Maybe if I said it first, whatever word he threw at me wouldn't hurt.

Orion's eyes snapped open, the grey in them almost white as his gaze raked over my face before settling on my mouth. "Do you *ever* shut up?"

I snapped my mouth shut, teeth creaking with the force as I shoved on his chest again, harder this time, needing to get away from him.

His hand snagged my wrist before I could pull it back, holding it against his chest as he leaned down, gaze level with mine. *"Alive."* My eyes expanded in shock, not following his train of thought as he hovered mere inches from my face. "You care so deeply about *everything*. You are more passionate than anyone I've ever met, and it's —" he cut himself off, shaking his head as if at a loss for words.

As if he just realized the way his body trapped mine against the post, Orion stood, then stepped back, running a hand through his silver hair as a deep sigh escaped him. He closed his eyes, tipping his head up to the moon above as he regrouped, locking down all of his thoughts once more, then walked away into the night alone.

My chest heaved with a wild torrent of emotion,

swinging so quickly from anger to… I didn't even know what to name this.

Dazed, I turned to where the demons and Maisie worked to contain the fire, the smoke stinging my eyes. The flames were pulling back from the lighthouse, leaving behind the burnt structure that hopefully could be repaired.

By the time I looked back to where Orion had been before, he was gone, and my brow scrunched in confusion, not understanding why I felt this need to go after him. To let him scream at me just to get him to let go of some of the tension that held him so tightly.

But we weren't friends.

I hated that male more than any I'd ever met.

I let my head fall back to rest on the metal post, a sigh that sounded very much like the Mayor escaping me.

"Fuck this shit, and fuck you," I whispered into the night, aimed at everyone and no one as I kicked a stray rock back towards the beach.

"You going to help?" Blaze said as I strode away from the fire with my middle finger in the air.

Maisie eyed me as I passed, but I glared at her, pushing her away like I did everyone else, and walked through the dark streets back to the church.

Shoving my shoulder into the door, it flew open, banging against the wall. Leave it to me to accidentally put a hole in the wall — at least I could add it to the list of reasons I hated myself right now. It was dark, but I didn't bother to turn on the lights, moving through the kitchen construction to grab a bottle of whiskey off the counter.

Behind the kitchen was a set of rickety stairs leading up to the bell tower. I gripped the handrail so tight the wood broke under my grip, and I tossed it to the side, pounding up the stairs. Throwing myself down on the floor, I let my legs dangle over the side as I sipped straight from the bottle.

A soft purr came from my right, and I watched as Bagheera climbed the stairs, sitting on the far side of the bell tower from me, several feet out of reach.

"I'm not even going to try to pet you," I said, staring at the cat who apparently lived here now. "There are no leashes, no constricting outfits, no *backpacks* in your future here, bud. Enjoy the all-you-can-eat mouse buffet that is my home."

Bagheera stretched, his green eyes shining in the moonlight as he moved an inch closer to me. The two of us watched each other, and I could have sworn the cat nodded.

I put the bottle that was at my lips down, twisting the cap back on. Apparently, I was hallucinating now, seeing a cat respond to my words.

Closing my eyes, I breathed in the ocean summer air as I let the tension out of my body, soaking in the power of the moon as I numbed myself to the emotions rolling through my system.

Bagheera let out a loud *ra-ow* and I opened my eyes, following the cat's gaze as the doors to Town Hall opened and closed, lights inside framing the male I loathed.

"Me too, Bags," I said, watching Orion move down the street, shoulders nearly touching his ears, emotions returning too quickly for my liking as I watched him move nearer.

Just as he was about to pass by the graveyard that was my front yard, he looked up to the bell tower. Indecision racked me momentarily, not sure whether I should hide in the shadows or lean forward into the moonlight. But I wasn't one to back down from anything.

I leaned forward, elbows on my knees, and flipped him off. Orion shook his head, but didn't give any other response as he continued past.

And why did that make me feel the least bit disappointed?

Chapter Twelve

ORION

FOLLOWING PROTOCOL, I returned to my office after leaving the lighthouse, and filed the reports about what the humans could have seen, and why I'd wiped their memories. The moment I hit send, a clock started ticking in my mind.

My time here in Deadlights Cove was coming to an end, and there was nothing I could do to stop it.

Walking home from Town Hall, I paused, noticing how bright the roses were this summer, almost fluorescent in the moonlight against the gazebo. So many new businesses had started since I'd been mayor, and I couldn't help but feel a sense of pride in each one's success. Knowing I'd helped these people, even for a little time, filled me with a sense of deep satisfaction.

Feeling it all slip through my fingers, hopelessness settled in my bones, pulling at me just as the moon pulled at the tide.

I shook my head as Devanna flipped me off from her bell tower, ignoring her attempts to antagonize me. I didn't want to acknowledge, even to myself, how much it had affected me to be so close to her earlier. How my blood had pounded when I crowded her against the lamp post, when her eyes flared as I caged her in. No, I did not have the time to deal with either of our reactions to each other.

Scallywags was closed with Blaze at the lighthouse, so I walked past, listening to the ocean waves, smelling the smoke in the air, the scent of all of my hopes and dreams up in flames.

The cottage was quiet when I entered, moving through the dark to grab a beer from the kitchen before heading to the living room. Grabbing the remote, I turned on the TV to the evening news as I'd done every night lately, listening for any reports of supernatural activity and hoping for none.

The moment my phone lit up with a new calendar appointment, I knew my luck had already run out.

My hands were practically shaking, I was brimming with so much energy as I clicked on the invitation. Ezra had scheduled a meeting in a few days, probably to give me time to panic, *in person.*

Nothing good could come of an in-person meeting with the Chancellor. Ezra and I had never gotten along, and after my first Warning, I dreaded anything my brother had to say.

He'd been waiting for the opportunity to rob me of my dreams for decades, and no doubt he finally found his chance.

Desperate for a distraction, an outlet, my eyes snagged on a paper on the edge of the counter. An infraction I'd been in the midst of filling out earlier this week.

How many had I written against Devanna? And yet, she

continued to try to push her luck, to bend the rules. In the time I'd been the official mayor of this town, she'd always acted like she was above the law, like none of the regulations should apply to her.

They were there for a reason. They were there to keep us safe. *All* of us. So we could all fly under the radar and get away with living right under the humans' noses.

It didn't matter that this particular infraction was, admittedly, slight. It was the *principle* of the thing. It was the fact that she'd pushed her luck one time too many. My cheek tingled, remembering the feel of her hand connecting with my face. The exchange still felt surreal, but I'd had enough.

The straw that broke the camel's back.

I swept the paper off the table, gripping it so tightly it crinkled as I strode out the door, marching right back towards downtown again.

Despite the thickness of the wooden door of the church, it rattled on its hinges when I knocked, using the full power of my angelic magic behind it.

I wanted her to know who was coming.

I waited, blood pulsing in my ears, and glanced up once at the offending bell tower, wondering if she was still up there, watching me. Toying with me like that damned cat she'd apparently adopted.

After several long moments, I finally heard her all-too-familiar stomping coming from within, and then the door cracked open.

I pushed through before she even had a chance to open the door, slamming it closed behind me. She'd showered since I'd seen her earlier, the scent of her fresh, clean soap in the air as she barked some complaint at me. Her crop tank top and shorts barely covered her curves, and I fought to keep my eyes above her shoulders.

Devanna's brown eyes flared with anger, but I didn't give her the chance to spew her usual vitriol at me, and shoved the paper in her face.

"What now, Lucifer?" she groaned, snatching the paper from me. "Do you live to write these up against me?"

I barked a bitter laugh. "Yes, that's it. I spend my days staring out my office window, watching your every move, just hoping I can nail you." Her eyes widened and I realized my error, but tried to stop my own face from reacting. The flush from creeping up my neck at the images those words conjured in my mind. I cleared my throat and tried again. "Hoping I can catch you."

A tiny, unwelcome voice in the back of my mind commented that my sarcasm was only partially a lie, but I shoved that away.

Devanna ignored me, scanning the paper instead, then glared at me. "The *bell*?"

"It was historical. You destroyed it."

She threw her hands up. "Had you ever even seen that old piece of shit? It was already destroyed! Had been in pieces for decades, probably. What did you want me to do, spell it back into condition?"

"Spell it, smelt it, whatever it took." I shrugged. "It was a part of this town's history."

"This is the stupidest thing I've ever heard. You want to fix the bell? Fix it your damn self."

She crumpled my carefully written paper and threw it in my face. Then looked me dead in the eye and, with a snap of her fingers and probably a pinch of salt or whatever witches needed to do magic, set it on fire at my feet.

My tether snapped.

I lurched forward, pinning her against the wall in the blink of an eye, and she hissed up at me, beating a fist against my chest. I let my wings snap out, caging her further.

"Back *off!*"

But I didn't. I couldn't make myself step away from her, couldn't stop my knee from sliding between hers as I held her tight, couldn't get my heart to stop pounding in my chest. I'd gotten one tiny taste of being in her space earlier, of pushing her limits, and suddenly, I realized I wanted more. I wanted *her.*

Didn't that just take the damn cake.

"Why do you insist on making my life here a living hell? You've gone out of your way for *years* to flout every rule, to go around every single directive I've ever given in this town. What is the point in fighting every little thing? You've always sought to make everything so damn *difficult.*" I was seething, out of breath with rage as I forced myself to remember why I was here, tamping down every emotion but those caused by her breaking the rules yet again. Forcing every filthy image flitting through my mind to the way back recesses.

"*You're* the one who makes everything difficult! You wrap red tape around every little thing and blow a gasket if anyone dares to take *any* sort of initiative!" She put her shoulders back, her chin jutting out. The movement lengthened her neck, and my gaze zeroed in on the juncture of her neck and shoulders, a spot I knew would be sensitive and so soft to the touch. To my teeth. My wings twitched at the thought. "And I'm a *fighter*. I'll always be a fighter. You should be used to that by now."

She glared daggers at me, but I couldn't help but notice how dilated her pupils were, how she was pressing herself back against the wall. Holding herself back, maybe? From what?

Her words rang in my ears, and I took in the petite female who always threw a tantrum when she didn't get her way. I leaned down, lowering my voice as I said, "A fighter, huh? That's funny, because all I see is a spoiled little brat."

Just like I knew it would, her hand moved before the words finished leaving my lips, but I caught her wrist in my hand with a *snap* and a crackle of my magic before she could land the hit.

Eyes widening again. And damn if that wasn't satisfying.

She tried to wrench her hand away, but I tightened my grip as I growled, "I let you land that one on the beach, but believe me when I tell you, that was the last time. If you hit me again, I will bend you over my knee and repay you in kind."

With that, I threw her wrist from me, taking a step back, though it took all of my considerable self-control to pull away.

The air was thick between us as we breathed heavily, emotions still running high, my magic on alert and swirling through the air between us like static.

Finally I forced my feet to move me towards the door before I gave in to the desire coursing through me.

Before I let myself acknowledge the new scent permeating the air that signaled exactly what she thought of my supposed *threat*.

As I reached the front door, I shot over my shoulder, "It was part of your sales contract to maintain the historical integrity of the building when you bought it, so either fix that bell, or find a good replacement. But there *will* be a bell in that tower."

Chapter Thirteen

DEVANNA

THE DOOR swung shut behind Orion as I let out a hiss of rage that had Bagheera's ears flattening in alarm. I narrowed my eyes at him.

"You're going to have to be better than that at attacking pests to earn your keep around here," I scolded him as he skittered behind the cabinets waiting to be hung in the kitchen, pointedly ignoring my reproach. "You let that pigeon waltz right in."

I stomped down the stairs to the basement, looking at the space that would be my gym when I finished renovating it.

Fury coursed through me as I flicked on the single naked lightbulb, eyeing the boxing gloves and punching bag I'd already hung up in the corner. I pulled my phone out and set up my playlist, switching on the speaker currently sitting on a cardboard box. Blindly, I strapped myself into my gloves, adjusted my stance, and unleashed on the bag, settling into a rhythm to *Breakin' Dishes*. I could never tell whether Rihanna made me feel better or worse, but damn, I felt seen in her words.

Punch after punch landed, the bag swinging wildly as I took out all of my aggression on the inanimate object, keeping my temper in check. Or at least, healthily directed.

Why did I always let Orion get under my skin like this? While I'd always had a short fuse, only with him did I feel this unending, passionate *loathing*.

He thought he was so perfect with his dress shirts and fitted chinos, his silver hair and grey eyes, chiseled jaw, huge white wings and lean frame, and I hated him for it. And the way he'd been rolling up his sleeves lately was obscene. *That* was what should be getting a damn write-up around here.

Then he'd threatened to take me over his knee, my body had betrayed me in the *worst* way. When he'd backed me into the lamp post earlier, I'd attributed my reaction to the adrenaline of the scene, or maybe just a visceral response to the proximity of a male — I could admit to myself that it had been a while. But then he'd showed up here, and my body had reacted *again*, and even I had to admit the truth to myself. The fact that I could be so physically attracted to such a vile being was probably my biggest personality flaw. And to his 'threat'? If he so much as tried, I'd kick him where it counts so hard, he wouldn't walk for a month.

While I was wallowing in my flaws, I could admit I'd always been attracted to him, even when I was a stupid teenager with a crush on the much older male when I saw him around town. As my fists hit the bag harder, the vision of the first day we'd truly spoken surfaced. I'd been 22, climbed the steps to Town Hall, and headed to his office with my business permits to open Carpe Noctem.

I'd clutched the papers in my hand, having spent half the night awake with Nimue, planning out all the minutiae of my shop and how it would look. The building I'd planned on renting was a pretty white brick, and I wanted to add purple awnings, and paint the door black with brass fixtures. The logo we'd spent hours drawing was a cauldron, magicked to stir itself as "Carpe Noctem" floated above in rising smoke. It was going to be the perfect little local apothecary. My dream come true.

Foolishly, I'd introduced myself to Orion wearing a black pencil skirt and a purple silk top, standing on the other side of his desk, trying my best to look older and responsible so he would know how serious I was about this. I'd taken business classes online so I'd know all the financial, administrative, and marketing sides of things, and had been schlepping myself up to Spring Harbor, odious as that was, to work in a retail clothing store for experience ever since I'd scraped enough money to buy my old Bronco. I'd followed all of the protocols in our town code, making sure to dot all my i's and cross all my t's. I even had the financing lined up to get the business off the ground.

I'd stepped one foot into his office when the crackle of his magic in the air, his perfectly chiseled face, had set my heart racing.

How naive I was to be attracted to that asshole. Then again, that was before he'd opened his mouth, so how was I to know?

My first lesson in the deception of appearances.

I'd pulled down the front of my blouse slightly, exposing an extra inch of cleavage as I'd walked towards his desk, hoping he'd notice me.

The sound of my fists thumping against the bag sounded an awful lot like his giant red *DENIED* stamp, smacking down on the paperwork he hardly even looked over. Me, he'd given a cursory glance, his storm grey eyes lingering only for a moment on my chest, his face impassive, before he returned his attention to his paperwork. A clear rejection if ever there was one.

My blood had turned to ice as he handed me back my paperwork, saying the logo violated the PRIC's code against magic use in public spaces. He couldn't have asked me to change just that, rather than denying the whole thing?

But no. I'd opened my mouth, ready to explain how I could make it look like the cauldron was electrically wired, but he'd abruptly dismissed me.

Orion didn't care about me, or anyone but himself.

Rage had built in me as I walked out of Town Hall that day, pounding down the steps and out into the town. Even without his approval, I rented the building, and instead of keeping it the original white brick, I'd painted the building jet black. It stood out like a sore thumb in the otherwise bright, colorful town, and I loved it. Like a giant middle finger every time Orion looked out his office window. A nice reminder that I didn't care about him or his opinion, not even a little.

Then I'd gone behind his back, with a little help from Blaze, and convinced the secretary at the time that I had full approval from Orion for a business license for my shop.

Orion hadn't been happy about that, but what was done was done.

For the last decade, I'd skirted his rules, toeing the line at every available opportunity. Never were my infractions enough that he could actually close my business, but I was determined to annoy him at every turn for trying to stand in my way.

I hadn't been lying when I'd told him I was a fighter.

Teeth clenched, I spun, swinging my leg high as I kicked the bag so hard it creaked loudly on the chains it was suspended from. Placing my hand out to stop its movement, my chest heaved with the exertion.

The song had changed to *Rude Boy* while I was in the zone, and I sighed, undoing my gloves to change it. My phone rang as I picked it up, my mother's name scrolling across the screen. I debated letting it ring through to voicemail like I so often did, but I'd ignored her the last three times she'd called, and I didn't want her to suddenly pop by like she sometimes did when she hadn't heard from me in a while.

Swiping my finger across the screen, I hit the speakerphone and dropped to the mat to stretch. With how sore my muscles were, I glanced back at the punching bag, wondering how long I'd been at it. It had definitely been longer than two songs.

"Hi Mom."

"Oh, you actually answered this time, chickadee. What a nice change." Wind chimes sounded in the background on her end, and I wondered what kind of hippie-yurt-earth-dome nonsense they'd found to stay in this time.

"Sorry, I've been busy lately. Town has been insane since the Summit."

"Yes, I heard all about that. We have the Daily Discord's e-subscription now to stay up to date," my mother said, her tone full of questions I had no intention of answering, as well as a guilt-trip to the tune of *Since you never talk to us, we'll read your town newspaper*. "I'm glad you weren't involved with that business. This is why your father and I have never settled in one place for long. Too much drama."

I gritted my teeth, not bothering to address the subtle judgment in her words. My parents were both powerful Cosmic witches and had traveled for decades, long before I was born. They insisted every nexus — the point where ley lines crossed — was slightly different, and liked to travel around to experience them. But we'd always spent every summer in Deadlights Cove, so it became the closest place I had to home before we hit the road again to some other commune, or other remote supe town. By the time I was thirteen, I'd convinced them to leave me in Deadlights Cove, bouncing between several of the Coven's homes.

My childhood had forced me to grow up too fast, being by far the most responsible of the three of us, and I'd be lying if I said I didn't resent my parents for it. I was the one balancing our checkbook at age ten and finding coupons; offering to do odd jobs for the other supe families when we needed a little extra cash to get to the next weigh-point. Meanwhile, my parents were basking under the moonlight and insisting I didn't need to worry about how much school I was missing — it was the school of *life* that mattered.

"Are you still there, chickadee?" my mother said, drawing me back from my thoughts. "The connection is horrible here in New Mexico. You'd think we could fix that with magic, but no."

"I'm here," I said, inwardly breathing a sigh of relief at the continent that divided us at the moment. No surprise visits anytime soon, then, since my parents refused to travel by airplane. They didn't trust human reflexes by a long shot, and said the recycled air was bad for their chakras.

"Good," she said, then paused with a half intake of breath that I recognized for the calm before the torrential downpour that it was. I braced. "Now, your father and I hear through the grapevine that you've gone and bought yourself a *church*?"

I pictured all the nosy, big-mouthed witches in town, mentally marking each of their faces with a thick red *X* for going behind my back to talk to my parents. No one was a meddling gossip like a witch, and those old bitties better be ready to pay.

"Yes, Mom, but don't worry, I won't be holding any religious services. I'm converting it into a house."

"A *house*? For whom?"

"Me."

Cue the guilt trip —

"*You*? You and what family, baby?" A mock gasp sounded down the line, and I rolled my eyes as I reached for my water bottle, taking a long sip before flopping onto my back on the mat as my mother continued. "Or is this your way of telling me you've finally found yourself a good male and are going to make me the happiest grandmama in the world?"

"Nope," I cut her off, popping the P and staring at the ceiling. Damn, lot of cobwebs up there. Then again, maybe they added to the aesthetic. "Just little old me and a vestry full of ghosts. Oh, I guess that's not true. I do have a cat now."

Silence for a long moment. "*You* adopted a cat?"

"Not exactly. He belonged to a witch who was recently

murdered and he sort of just showed up. But if he helps with the mice, he can stay."

"Eugene!" I pulled the phone away from my ear as she shouted for my father, completely ignoring the whole *my neighbor was just murdered,* thing. "Our baby got herself a familiar at *last!*"

"He's not a *familiar,*" I snapped. "He's just a cat." This was why I never told them anything. Said cat was currently sitting in the empty cardboard box that my exercise mat had come in, his green eyes just above the rim and staring at me, unblinking. I gave half a shrug at my unintentional insult, but he didn't seem bothered.

My mother ignored me — typical — as she and my father gushed to each other about me taking this witchy step, even though I hadn't. Using a familiar was an old practice in witch society, allowing the witch an extra well of magic from the familiar they were linked to. But the fact that a familiar's *lifeforce* was the source of the magic always sat wrong with me. I'd never subject an animal to that, not even a hissing, spitting Bagheera.

Finally their murmuring died down, and my mom was back. "When can you come visit? You'd just *love* this place. We're staying in this community of earthdomes —" *Called it.* "— and it's so sustainable. There's an exercise bike in the kitchen to power the blender, we grow all our own food right here in our little greenhouse, and we recycle *everything!*"

"And we mean *everything,*" my dad chimed in. Apparently I was on speaker on their end now. "Even our urine and feces go to water and fertilize the landscaping! Ain't that something?"

I grimaced at the mere thought. "I don't think I'll be able to get away anytime soon."

I could practically see their crest-fallen expressions, but I pushed that feeling of guilt aside.

"We'll come to you, then! It's been ages since we spent a summer in the Cove."

"Uh, actually, this summer may not be the best time. We're kind of under a lot of scrutiny, and I think Orion might actually combust if anything else happens around here he can't micromanage to within an inch of its life."

"Oh, Orion!" My mother's wistfully reminiscent tone brought on another eye-roll. She always conveniently forgot what a total asshole he was to me. "He's always such a hoot! Angels and their silly little rules. How is that adorably prickly young male?"

"Mom, he's older than the two of you put together, you realize that, right?"

"Age is just a number, chickadee. In angel years, he's maybe only a smidge older than you are now." I gritted my teeth, counting backwards from ten to calm myself before I responded, but my mom continued before I could say anything. "The poor male must be under a lot of stress at the moment. How is he holding up?"

How is he *holding up?* She hadn't asked me how *I* was *once* in this conversation, but the angel who could do no wrong, sure. *Him,* she asked about.

"How do you think? He's being a total control freak, treating all of us, especially me, worse than the dirt beneath his perfectly shined shoes, and as usual, caring only about himself."

"You sound upset."

You almost sound like you care.

"Yeah, I'm upset. He hit me with another fine tonight for taking down the already broken old bell in my house!"

A pause. "Tonight? You mean, he came by your place personally? After business hours?"

Ugh, of course she would go *there* immediately. She always focused on the wrong pieces of information. "Oh, my Goddess, it wasn't like *that*. He did it just to provoke me. Because I'm his favorite punching bag."

"Hmm."

I closed my eyes as steam billowed out of my ears. Only my mother could imbue such a simple sound with such powerful *subtext*.

"Was there anything else you needed?" I asked, glancing back at the punching bag. Sore muscles be damned, I needed to pummel something again.

"What, a mother can't just want to hear her only daughter's voice?" my mother said, and I could picture the way she'd be holding her hand over her chest, acting like my words had wounded her. The sad downturn of her eyes that told me I'd yet again disappointed her. "We just wanted to check in. I do wish you'd leave that town. I keep having premonitions that something worse is coming."

"Deadlights Cove is my home," I bit out, my voice as defensive as I felt. "I'm not leaving. My friends are here, and I won't abandon them."

"I see," my mother whispered, and I ground my teeth together. "It always circles back to this, doesn't it? You still think we left you all those years ago." I didn't bother to answer, because, yeah Mom, that stung. "You were happy in Deadlights Cove. Happier than you ever were with us. It was the right choice for you — your idea, even. It was time for the streams of our life paths to diverge, for you to forge your own rivulet and carve it into your future river."

Right, because every child wants to be completely and totally forgettable at thirteen, forging their own *rivulet*.

"Sorry to cut this short, but I'm getting another call," I lied, needing to end this conversation as soon as possible.

"Before you go, sweetie, just remember this. There's only one reason a male goes out of his way to... *provoke*."

Okay, at that I scoffed. It actually made me feel better, how utterly wrong and ridiculous that statement was. "Believe me, Mom. That douchecanoe has no other interest in me than to make my life miserable. Talklaterbye."

I clicked off my phone, flinging my arms to the side as I stared up at the ceiling. Tomorrow, I'd call Blaze and figure out a way to get his demons back in here to help.

Suddenly, I felt like the gym was a higher priority than the kitchen. Pushing to my feet, I trudged up the stairs and into the foyer where the pieces of the broken bell rested on an old rug, not having decided what to do with the broken fragments. How exactly did one dispose of this much bronze?

As Bagheera batted at one of the ropes laying across the floor, an idea formed in my head, and I smirked.

Orion wanted a repaired bell? Fine. I'd give him a repaired, *functional* bell.

Chapter Fourteen

ORION

I TOSSED AND TURNED, unable to sleep even a wink as worry twisted my stomach. The moon had set hours ago, leaving the town in the darkest part of the night as I stared at the shadows on my walls for the second night in a row.

My wing in Blaze's cottage was minimalistic and modern, the way I liked it. A dresser, a chair, a rug, a bed. Wall sconces instead of lamps to keep clutter from accumulating on my nightstand. But it felt like home, and I'd miss it terribly.

While no one had said anything official yet, I was almost positive this would be my last day in Deadlights Cove, that my time would be up once I met with Ezra tomorrow. I'd spent almost 30 years in this town, and what had I actually done? What mark was I leaving here, if any?

While angels lived centuries, I couldn't help but feel like I'd wasted my time, never pursuing anything for myself. With most angels working in a position of power, it was relatively uncommon for us to form friendships outside of our species, let alone relationships, but I couldn't help but feel like I had *nothing* to show for my time on Earth. Even after all these years, I still felt like the outsider here.

I'd worked hard to earn my position as mayor in my eagerness to live on Earth. I'd been fascinated by this realm since I'd first learned about it, had wanted to help supernaturals live among humans peacefully for as long as I could remember. I'd wanted to study and interact with humans themselves — their lives, history, and world so different than what I'd known growing up — but of course, that was off the table, so this was as close as I could get.

And now it was all going down the drain.

I was one box of hair dye away from a midlife crisis, and I knew it. But now was far from the right time to make rash decisions like stopping at Devanna's house two days ago. That had been stupid.

Sure, the bell actually *was* a historical feature of the church and needed to be replaced, but did I need to handle it right then? Personally deliver the notice? No.

I'd gone over there because I wanted to. Because I hadn't been able to stop my feet from taking me there.

I'd wanted to provoke her, to see the way flames lit in her expression, murder written across her gorgeous features. I'd wanted her to hit me again so I could follow up on my promise, because I'd meant every word.

The image of bending her over my knee now lived rent-free in my head, making for two damn uncomfortable nights.

And why did I get the feeling that Devanna *would* try to slap me again, just to test me?

Because I knew her, that was why.

As I closed my eyes, hoping for even ten minutes of sleep at this point, a loud clanging sounded in the distance.

Bong. Bong-Bong. Bong.

Over and over it rang, louder than the harbor bell. Sitting up, I dropped my feet to the floor, brow scrunched in confusion. What the hell was that?

Then the pieces slid into place.

"You've got to be kidding me," I muttered as I yanked on a pair of khaki shorts and a t-shirt and slid my feet into a pair of boat shoes. I never left the house like this, but the sun wasn't up yet, and that witch was already pushing every button I had. Grabbing my keys off the table by the door, I hopped in my electric car and headed into town.

I barged through her front door faster than I could form rational thoughts to consider what I was going to say to her, her meager lock no match for my magic. *Not* my usual M.O., but Devanna knew exactly how to throw me off-kilter.

"Do I seriously have to specify for you not to ring the bell in the middle of the goddamn night?" I called out into the dark foyer. "I'd have thought even *you* could handle the bare minimum courtesy to the people of this town."

Glancing around the space, I didn't see Devanna anywhere, and wandered over to the base of the tower. I climbed the spiraling steps all the way to the top, only to find a scowling black cat in the center. Bagheera's green eyes gleamed in the scant light from the open-air windows, his claw suspiciously stuck in the rough twine of the rope.

The hooligan bell-ringer, apparently.

I pointed an accusatory finger at him. "You know better than this, Bagheera."

He hissed, trying to wrench his paw down, but as his

claw was still stuck, he only succeeded at ringing it several more times. How such a small cat could pull hard enough to ring a bell that was a hundred times his size was a mystery only solved by magic, which the owner of said bell had in spades.

My gaze caught on the end of the rope, and I narrowed my eyes as I realized a feather — a *white* feather — had been threaded through the end of it. In all likelihood, to make it more enticing for Bagheera to play with. And if I wasn't very much mistaken, it was one of *my* feathers.

"For the love of —" I bent down, meeting his eyes before telling him sternly, "If you claw at me, this is the last time I help you out of a scrape." Gripping the scruff of his neck, I gently plucked his paw free. But the hellion knew not one moment of freedom before he ruined it, scampering up my arm and over my back — claws *fully* distended — and pulling out quite a few more of my feathers on his frantic journey to the floor.

"What the hell is going on here?" A light switch clicked a second before soft light filtered in from the stairwell.

I sighed, picked up my scattered feathers, including the one in the rope — no way was I leaving anything that could be used against me in a spell anywhere near this witch — and stuffed them in my pocket, then turned around.

Holy shit.

All the blood rushed right out of my brain and some-where *else* as I took in Devanna wearing a pale purple tank top and matching shorts that were so tiny, they were practically underwear. Lace trimmed the edges against her deep brown skin as it hugged her ample curves, showing off the fact that she wasn't wearing a bra. Her hair was tucked up into an adorably ridiculous satiny cap, showing off the sleek column of her neck. Her black-rimmed glasses were gone, brown eyes squinted sleepily. Back-lit by the soft sconces, she almost looked delicate.

I swallowed, trying to still my body's reaction to her. Blaze's haphazard paint jobs. Morgaine's hideous mismatched floral living room. Caedmon sunbathing in a Speedo on my front lawn. The water ring now permanently set on my coffee table from the last time Blaze had forgotten a coaster. My future, going up in flames literally any moment.

I took a slow breath as I ran through every non-sexual thought I could conjure, trying and nearly failing to pull my eyes up from her chest.

"Breaking and entering is legal now?" Devanna said, crossing her arms, which only accentuated her chest even more. "Or is there a fine for that? Citizen's arrest is a thing, you know."

Blinking rapidly, I forcibly turned my head to the side, clearing my throat. "Well, if you weren't ringing the bell at 3:27 in the morning, this wouldn't be an issue."

"*I* wasn't ringing the bell," she said, leaning back against the door frame as she yawned and stretched her arms over her head, letting several inches of skin show between her low-slung shorts and her incredibly thin top. *Fuck.* "I was asleep."

Devanna turned back to me, then leaned forward, eyes focused heavily on my biceps. "Is that—"

"Tattoos, yes," I said, barely fighting the urge to tug the

sleeve further down my arm to hide the ink there. "You fixed the bell in two days?"

Devanna still stared, eyes flicking up to the neckline of my t-shirt as if she had x-ray vision and was inspecting the rest of my body for more ink. "Hm?"

"The bell," I deadpanned. "My eyes are up here."

"Funny coming from a man who bore a hole through my cleavage less than a minute ago."

"Considering the fact that your top covers almost nothing —"

"Oh, so by dressing this way, at night, when I'm alone, in my locked house, again, I repeat, *alone*, I'm inviting your leering gaze? Is that correct?"

"That's not what I meant," I sighed, shaking my head. "And no. Of course not."

Devanna paused, taken aback that I didn't argue further. "What are your tattoos of? You know they usually have meaning, right? Which means you'd have to have felt an emotion at some point in your life, and I'm pretty sure you're incapable."

That gave me pause. "You think I'm incapable of emotion?"

"I'm actually pretty positive on that one. Other than moderate to severe annoyance. Maybe that's what your tattoos are — a log of everything you detest. That tracks, actually."

"I guess you wouldn't believe me if I told you what I was feeling right now, then."

She barked a laugh, then waved a hand through the air. "Try me."

Taking a step toward her, I lowered my voice, barely

above a whisper. "I'm feeling like this little outfit of yours is the damn sexiest thing I've ever seen, and it's begging me to rip it to shreds."

Devanna's eyes snapped to mine, surprise written across her features before her eyes squinted. "Again with blaming me and my outfit for your own inability to control your sexual desires. What a typical *male*."

I dismissed her comment, moving closer still. "Now I'm feeling like I need you to shut your damn mouth or I'll do it for you."

She pressed back against the door frame as I boxed her in, eyes blazing that passionate fire she so often carried as her chest heaved.

"You are the most arrogant alpha-hole that's ever walked on the earth, anyone ever tell you that?" she sniped back. I didn't miss the way her voice took on a breathy quality, the way her pupils dilated as heat spread between us.

"Alpha." I smirked.

"Of course that's the only word you heard in that sentence," she said, her eyes rolling as she started to shake her head.

I grabbed her chin, holding her in place, electricity charging through me at feeling her skin against mine. She let out a gasp, her eyes flicking down to my hand then back up, shock written across her face that I'd touch her like this. But unlike the last time I'd caged her in, she didn't push me away. Didn't make any move to shake off my grasp.

The air crackled with the static of my magic, and Devanna shivered as a whisper of it ghosted through her. "Eyes on me, hellcat."

Her tongue darted out, running across her full bottom

lip, so plush. The need to bite it, to mark her was almost overwhelming in its intensity. Those rich eyes of hers darted between mine, then to my lips as I hovered, holding control over her. Over both of us.

"Here's what's going to happen," I said, my voice barely above a growl, I was so close to snapping. I so rarely touched *anyone*, and it had been years since I'd felt so emotionally charged by a physical connection. "You walk away right now, down these stairs to your bedroom, shut the door behind you, and I'll go right out the front door, forgetting this whole night even happened."

She held her breath, waiting for the other shoe to drop. For the other option on the tip of my tongue. My hand on her chin started shaking, the other one at my side clenched tight into a fist in my attempt to hold myself back. My wings flared with my tension, casting shadows around us, cocooning us in this private world all our own.

I could hardly believe the words I was about to say; the forbidden desires I was about to voice, but all of my emotions were too close to the surface these days. Images raced through my mind, blocking out access to coherent speech as I saw Devanna beneath me, Devanna on her hands and knees, Devanna's dark eyes full of seduction as she rode me. *Fucking hell.*

She grew impatient with me, giving me a bratty cock of her head and prompting with a sing-songy, "Or…"

My nostrils flared, my fingers tightening on her chin as I tipped her face up further, craning her neck, my lips now mere millimeters from hers as she panted heavily. "Or I'll spin you around right here in this bell tower, rip this sad excuse for pajamas from your body, and fuck you until you're screaming louder than that damn bell."

Her pupils dilated, and for a long moment, nothing happened, the only sounds our increasingly labored breathing. Then her hand landed softly on my chest, and I felt actual pain at the restraint it took not to lean into her touch. She tilted forward slightly, angling her mouth to my ear to whisper, "You're so much *talk*, aren't you?"

Her breath skating across my ear, the side of my neck nearly made my eyes roll back in my head, but I knew a challenge when I heard one.

"Not as much talk as you. Do you ever shut up?" In one movement, I ripped her tank top down the middle, my vision tunneling. All I could see were her perfect breasts. She opened her mouth to retort — of course — so I took one nipple into my mouth, cutting off her words for a startled whimper of pleasure instead as my teeth scraped her skin.

Better.

With my head bent towards her chest, her hands were at the perfect height to land right where my wings met my shoulders, and a shudder ran through me at the sensation of her soft touch on such a sensitive area. But she had a history with my feathers I had no interest in repeating, so that had to stop *right* now.

Needing to stay in control of this situation, I gripped her hips, fingers digging into her skin as I forcibly spun her, slamming her front against the cool stone of the tower wall. She gasped as I ripped the scraps of her tank top off, tossing them aside, and grabbed her wrists, pinning them behind her. "I didn't say you could touch me, did I?"

"And I did?" she pushed back against me, yanking hard

enough against my hold that her cap fell off, her blue hair falling around her dark skin in a shimmering cascade, but I didn't let her go. In fact, the more she struggled against me, the tighter my grip became, and the increasing scent of her arousal in the air told me she got off on me taking control as much as I did. I knocked her feet out wider so I could slide my thigh between them, giving her my weight.

"I gave you your chance to leave, to walk away, and you didn't take it," I said, running my nose along the sensitive skin of her neck, feeling the way she trembled beneath me. Trailing my teeth along her shoulder, I resisted the temptation to clamp down on her. "Besides, you should know your scent will give you away every time."

"You're such a dick." She pulled on her hands again, but the attempt to free herself was so weak, I knew she wanted this as badly as I did. Felt this same desperation as I did.

"Tell me no right now, and I'll let you go," I said, letting my free hand skim across the top of her shorts, sliding along her hip bone, loving the contrast in our skin tones. I forced myself to pull back, allowing the cool night air to drift between us, and if I wasn't much mistaken, a sound of disappointment left her as my body did. "I'd never force you to do anything, no matter what you think of me. But I don't think you want me to go, do you?"

Her chest heaved as I continued to move my hand across her hip, dipping just below the waistband, teasing.

"Tell me what you want, hellcat," I said, lips trailing across her neck, feeling the erratic pulse of her racing heart. Moving my hand up, I cupped her breast, feeling the weight of it in my palm as I held onto the last scrap of my control. Her hips ground back against me, rubbing against my hardness, every synapse in my brain screaming for more. "Let me hear you say it."

"I always wondered if angels even know how to have sex, so yes, I want it. Fuck me."

"Say my name, Devanna. Say *who* you want to fuck you." I bit down on her earlobe, tugging gently, eliciting a delightful whimper she tried to hide from me.

Her breath caught as she hesitated, like she couldn't bear to taste my name on her lips. Then she gave in to what we both wanted when she practically spat at me, "Just because I want your dick doesn't mean I don't still hate you, *Orion*."

I smirked, loving the sound of my name on her lips as she all but begged for me. As she forced herself to submit to me. "Good girl."

"Oh my Goddess, I hate you right now —" Her words cut off on another gasp when I pulled down her shorts, under which she wore absolutely nothing. I left them around her legs, restricting her movements further, and went for my zipper.

"I should have brought something for that mouth," I muttered, then instantly grew harder at the picture of my tie wrapped around her head, gagging her. Next time.

No.

No next time.

This would be a one-and-done, get it out of our systems, singular time. A momentary lapse in judgment never to be repeated.

Better make it count, then.

Grabbing her ass, I lifted her leg up, resting it on the windowsill to her right, raising her a few inches to make up for our height difference. I gripped myself, lining up with her, not at all surprised to feel how wet she was already.

"Do you get this horny for all your enemies?"

"I'm not horny, I'm angry —"

I scoffed as I slammed into her, shoving her hard against the wall, a sharp exhale leaving her as I filled her. "Keep telling yourself that."

Letting go of her wrists, I let my hands roam across her body, loving the way she arched back into me, thrusting herself back on me just as hard as I moved. "Apparently there is one part of you that isn't terrible."

"You have the stupidest haircut I've ever seen. What are you, a Mormon choir boy?" she hissed, her hand rising above her, winding its way around my neck, pulling on the hair at my nape. "I hate your khaki shorts, and your boat shoes are the worst fashion crime in town. They're an instant boner-killer."

"I can tell."

"Stop talking, you're ruining it."

"*I'm* ruining it? The sound of your voice makes me want to cut my ears off," I growled, biting her ear as I said it, wrapping my hand around her mouth. She bit my palm, and I chuckled, not even bothering to move it. "Or find some other way to shut you up."

Suddenly, she shoved hard back against me, nearly sending me flying as she spun, throwing her weight into me as she pushed me to the floor, straddled my lap, and sank right back down onto me.

"*Fuck.*"

I wasn't sure which of us said it, but damn. Her hips moved as pressure built, my breath becoming ragged.

"Make yourself good for something," Devanna said between gritted teeth, grinding hard against me, her eyes filled with lust like the image I'd played in my head moments before, only this was far better than any imagined scenario.

Wrapping my hands around her waist, I took control right back from her, slamming up into her, her body jolting forward with the force of my movements. She locked eyes with me as she trailed her hands over her body, teasing me as much as herself.

Then she dropped her hands to my chest, pulling off my shirt that moved around my wings with a dose of magic, and her mouth dropped into a perfect O as she took in my body.

More specifically, my chest covered in ink, usually well-hidden under my button-downs, as tattoos weren't exactly Council approved for angels.

She swore, running first her fingertips, and then her nails, over the lines of ink on me. Somehow, she picked up the pace, moving even harder, even faster on top of me, until I slammed into her once more, and drew a satisfying cry from her lips. We both peaked, shuddering wildly as her fingernails carved crescent moons into my shoulders. She slumped back, panting heavily.

"You tell *anyone* about this, and I'll kill you myself, Lucifer."

"You think *I* want anyone to know about this? As far as I'm concerned, this never happened. You're the one screaming from the bell tower."

Without ceremony, she rose off me, swiping my shirt where I'd tossed it and throwing it on.

Some primal switch flicked in me seeing her in it, the way it reached the middle of her thighs. The way it covered her in my scent.

"Coming down for more, or is that all you got?" She cocked her head, raising a brow.

I growled as I lurched to my feet.

Chapter Fifteen

ORLON

MY HEAD JOLTED off the pillow at the sound of a phone vibrating. Groggily, I rolled over, sitting up to stare around the unfamiliar room. Morning light shone through the windows, draped in soft white sheer curtains. The deep plum comforter was shoved to the floor at the foot of the bed, strewn across the wood floors along with my clothes and a few of Devanna's.

Slowly, I turned my head to the side, seeing Devanna on the other side of the bed. She faced away from me, sprawled on her stomach, but the way her arms were under her pillow showed off her plush curves from head to toe. And dammit, that ass.

Scrubbing a hand across my face, I marveled at how far I'd fallen to end up here. The phone vibrated again, and I rose, reaching for my shorts. Pulling my phone free, I tapped the screen and frowned at seeing two missed calls from Blaze. While we lived together and he was my closest friend, demons were notoriously late sleepers, and it was still early.

Alarm bells rang in my head as I swiped the screen, calling him back.

I tugged on my shorts while it rang, turning in a circle to look for my t-shirt.

"Where the hell are you?" Blaze said when he finally picked up.

"In town, why?"

"Well, get back here. There are two angry angels standing in my kitchen, wondering why you weren't in your office when they showed up this morning."

My stomach plummeted, breath leaving me in a whoosh. "Ezra is already here?"

"And Pascar, the scary bitchy one."

"We can hear you, Sabazios," came Pascar's slightly muffled voice from the other end.

"Shit," I muttered, throwing the comforter to the side as I looked for my shirt. "Okay, I'll be right there." I clicked off the call.

"What's going on?" Devanna mumbled, sitting up. We'd kicked all of the bedding off in our fuckfest last night, but the brazen witch didn't even attempt to cover herself as she rubbed her eyes.

"I have to go right now and I can't find my damn shirt you stole from me last night," I said through gritted teeth, a headache already forming at my temples. "Though it hardly matters considering the rest of my wardrobe right now."

"Chill out." Devanna stooped to the floor on her side of the bed and threw me a black shirt. I pulled it on, storming out of the room without a glance behind me.

We both knew this had been an epic slip in judgment. There was nothing left to say.

I threw myself in my car, speeding through town as I thought through any and everything I could say in my defense, but what was the point? I'd missed my meeting and was showing up wearing *shorts*. Plus, the way Devanna had pulled on my hair, I was sure I looked like the trainwreck I was. While I could magic my hair back in shape, there was nothing I could do for the fact that I smelled like everything we'd done all morning, or my outfit. If I was meeting with humans, I could have glamoured myself, but that wouldn't work against fellow angels.

I parked in the garage, feeling like I was willingly walking in front of a firing squad, and squeezed my eyes shut for a minute to myself, my vision nearly blacking out. Then I forced myself to trudge through the yard to the house. My hand settled on the French doors to the kitchen, and I paused long enough to pull in a deep breath, exhaling slowly to calm my racing heart before I opened it.

"How nice of you to —"

"What the *hell* are you wearing?" Pascar's voice interrupted Ezra, who shot her an angry glare.

Ezra didn't even attempt to hide the smirk as his eyes settled on me. "Well, if I wasn't planning on arresting you today, I would be now. You know the rules about graphic tees, Orion. Truly, how far you've fallen."

Confused, I glanced down at my shirt, expecting him to comment on the shorts, or the boat shoes, or my hair, but then I saw what shirt I'd pulled on.

That little witch hadn't handed me my plain tee. No. She'd thrown one of *hers* at me, and it said in big, bold letters *Karma is a Witch.*

"This has been a long time coming. You've always been

such a scoff-law," Ezra said. My brother stood several inches taller than me, his silver hair parted to the side as he wore a crisp grey suit over a white button-down, the picture of angelic perfection.

Pascar pulled her phone out, snapping a picture as she cackled. "No one will believe me if I don't document this."

I ground my teeth together, humiliation warring with utter rage at Devanna, but I'd earned this punishment all on my own. Even if I wanted to blame her for the shirt, I couldn't blame every other mistake I'd made on her.

Pascar brushed a stray silver hair behind her ear, long black nails standing out starkly against her pale skin. While Pascar had always pushed the rules of the angel's strict dress code — today she paired a form-fitting black sheath dress with a pair of her typical motorcycle boots — even she looked far more put-together than I did.

Of course, Blaze turned the corner into the kitchen right at that moment, adding to my humiliation as his eyes expanded in shock, reading my shirt, then a laugh bubbled out of him. "You didn't."

"Leave, Sabazios," I said, eyes mere slits in my face. It figured this was how my best friend would see me for the last time, at an all-time low. But, of course, he didn't leave. It was too much to hope that he'd listen to me, even once.

Ezra leaned on the counter ignoring Blaze as he crossed his arms and ankles, the picture of ease as my life crumbled under his shiny loafers. "Here's how this is going to work. As of 8 a.m. this morning, you have been removed from duty here in Deadlights Cove. Pascar will be staying on in your place, acting as interim mayor until an acceptable, permanent replacement can be identified. She will oversee all activity with the human infestation you have. Meanwhile, you're going to come with me to Headquarters, and await your hearing from a nice little cell where you can think about all of the many ways you royally screwed yourself here."

I grimaced. "May I change first?" I gestured to my ensemble, and Pascar laughed once more.

Ezra tilted his head, eyes alight with cold glee. "Absolutely not. This is exactly how the rest of the Council should see you. As the human-loving disaster you are."

Blaze made an indignant sound on my behalf, yet there was nothing left for me to do but nod.

"Excellent." Ezra pushed off the counter and moved towards the doors, Pascar following on his heels.

My head dropped, chin resting on my chest as I heaved a sigh, trying to steel myself for what was to come.

"O," Blaze said, moving over to me, his black eyes wide as he searched my face. "This is bad, isn't it?"

I closed my eyes, pulling in a deep breath. "You are by far the most annoying person I have ever met, Blaze."

"Well, that's one way to say goodbye."

"I'm not finished," I said through clenched teeth, and Blaze tilted his head. "Begrudgingly befriending you has been the best decision I've ever made. No matter how this ends, it has been an honor being your friend and roommate. Thank you for everything. For making me feel alive."

Without waiting for him to respond, I turned on my heel and moved through the door, chin held high.

"Ready?" Ezra said, hands in his pockets as he looked

over me, laughing yet again at my outfit. But I didn't rise to the bait, letting his reaction roll off me as I numbed myself to any and all emotion. Just as I'd always been taught.

"Let's go."

With a nod, Ezra moved to my side, gripped my arm, and we disappeared.

Chapter Sixteen

DEVANNA

I GOT UP SHORTLY after Orion left, moving into the bathroom and under the hottest stream of water I could handle. With the way Orion had used my body, every part of me was sore.

Shit. I hadn't expected that.

And how the hell had it gotten so wildly out of control so fast? I moaned as the hot water beat against my sore muscles, remembering the many times I'd made the same sound hours before.

I should have known Orion would be dominant and demanding in bed, but I hadn't known how much I'd love it. Hadn't known he'd wring more pleasure from my body in one night than most other males could have managed in months. When he'd pinned me to the wall, holding my hands behind my back, I was shocked I didn't combust at the move alone.

And *good girl?* I hated myself for loving his praise. I knew my own worth without a male's validation, and I wasn't a damn dog.

So why had it made my knees so weak?

Never again.

Even if that had been the best sex of my life, the male that came with it was insufferable. It wasn't worth the headache.

By the time I dried off, pulled on a pair of black cut-off shorts and a black tank top, a knock sounded on my door, quickly turning into pounding.

"I'm coming, hold your broomsticks," I shouted as I twisted my hair up into a bun, throwing on my glasses.

Blaze stood, fist raised to pound again, when I opened the door. His eyes raked over my body, a small smirk spreading until he visibly shook himself. "We have a huge problem."

Within twenty minutes, several other townsfolk had arrived, all sitting and standing around my foyer as I sipped a giant black coffee. Thanks to Blaze's demon squad, I now had a fully furnished and finished living room and kitchen.

"Explain this to me again," Mo said, leaning forward on the chair she'd dragged over from the kitchen.

"He was wearing —"

"Not that part, dear. We all know what he was wearing. Hard to get that image out of your head." She gave me a *very* pointed look, which I returned with my signature scowl.

"Right." Blaze nodded, fighting a grin. "So, Ezra said Orion was officially removed from office, and they arrested him, taking him to Headquarters until his hearing."

"Did they let him change?" I asked, suddenly feeling a

twinge of guilt for my last jab at him this morning. When I'd seen one of my new merchandise shirts laying on the floor, temptation had been too strong. But when I'd thrown it at him, I hadn't known he was off to face Ezra and the whole Council.

"No." Blaze shook his head. "He went to Headquarters in *shorts*. I need to find a way to be arrested too so I can witness him over there in that t-shirt."

"Let's not get anyone else arrested right now," Petra said, the voice of reason, as always, and Blaze sighed. "Is this the same Pascar who came to interrogate Kal's witches last fall and came to the Summit? Is this going to be a problem?"

"Not for you, dear," Mo said, reaching out a hand and squeezing Petra's gently. "Since the Linking, I can feel your magical signature. You're no longer fully human."

Petra's shoulders dropped slightly, her relief palpable as Blaze circled his arms around her waist, pulling her snugly to his chest. I could begrudgingly admit the two were perfect together.

"So Pascar is now working as mayor," Kit said, glancing around the room. "Do we need to be concerned about that?"

"Orion was terrible," I scoffed, sipping my coffee again. "How much worse can she be?"

Famous last words.

The first few days with Pascar in office were pretty normal, as far as Deadlights Cove went. Winston, our local moose, chased the coffee van down the street, one of the goats got loose from Zaphiel's yoga class and was found on Peg Fernsby's roof three hours later, and a couple young wolf-shifters got caught in a harmless snare when they dared each other to step foot into fox territory. A regular old week in the Cove.

While no one had forgotten the threat Nergal posed, the spell to keep him out of town was still in place. Even the FBI weren't around much, whether that was the Council's doing or not, I wasn't sure.

Between my own work, Blaze's demon crew, and even Nadir and some of his buddies, the major renovations on my church-house were quickly finished. I was left with this constant excess of energy, and put all of it into perfecting my house. Since I wasn't the only one who needed the distraction, it had worked out, and now the place was practically perfect, down to my state of the art basement gym.

The fifth day, shit hit the fan.

After all my hard work on the house, I decided to treat myself to Scallywags for lunch. Things were looking pretty great for me: warm sun on my skin, the breeze drifting off the ocean, FBI not trying to pin a murder on me, house just the way I wanted it. It was a beautiful summer day in Maine, and I was in a great mood. Orion was out of my hair. Casey, one of the foxes who'd shown up with Nadir but who was actually a programmer, had fixed the issue with my website, and I already had orders rolling in.

I walked down the sidewalk, damn near whistling in contentment until I came to a halt in front of Scallywags, seeing the large sign taped over the door, a lockbox on the handle.

Closed Indefinitely for Health Code Violations

"What the hell?" I muttered, squinting to read the sign. Under the big block letters were 81 infractions, one of which was letting patrons behind the bar to serve themselves.

Oops. That one might have been referring to me.

"You can't do this," someone cried between muffled sobs. Down the beach, Val and Caedmon stood outside the coffee van, arguing with Pascar. I started making my way over to them. If she was about to shut down our coffee source, we were about to have a problem.

"I very much can," Pascar said, not bothering to look at the two whimpering males as she signed the paper in her hand with a flourish and held it out to them. "Orion had documented thirty-seven instances of public indecency between the two of you. *Thirty-seven.* Not to mention a plethora of other infractions. Explain to me why your former mayor never closed you sooner? Were you bribing him?"

"What?" Val shook his head violently. "No! How could you even suggest a thing? Once you've tried our coffee, maybe you'll understand how important we are to this community."

"Don't think I haven't noticed the magic laced into those donuts you sell." Her black talon nail pointed at the two males.

"It's only for the moose!" Caedmon stepped in front of his now openly sobbing partner. "Donuts are actually terrible for Winston. We magic some of the donuts so they're more nutritious for him, even though he's duped into thinking they're just regular donuts."

"And since neither of you are witches — which, by the way, your files are pointedly blank where your species should be listed, another thing I have every intent to remedy — who exactly is spelling these donuts for you?"

"I am," I said, barely recognizing the sound of my own voice as I strode down the beach towards the angel, anger coursing through me. "Blame me, not them. Pick on someone your own size."

I was not, in fact, Pascar's size. The female was tall and leggy like all female angels and stood nearly a foot taller than me, but I was scrappy. This bitch was going down, and I would be the one to do it.

Pascar looked down her nose at me, eyes raking me from head to toe. "Devanna, is that right?"

"Bailey," I said, chin held high, shoulders back. "Devanna Bailey. Leave them out of this donut debacle. It's my fault."

"Your file is exceptionally thick." Pascar tapped her chin, the black claw fitting for this bird of prey ready to devour anyone in her path. "Interestingly enough, your business license isn't even official. Signed by a secretary, not the mayor himself. I feel like you're lying, just stepping in to defend these two perverts, but the list of your offenses is so long, I wouldn't put it past you."

I smiled, taking her comment as a compliment, though I was pretty positive my expression was more of a sneer as I never broke her stare.

Pascar clucked, looking down first as she scratched something on the pad in her hand, then ripped the paper, slapping it to my chest. "Consider yourself closed for business, Ms. Bailey. The time for leniency is over."

I flipped her off behind her back as she marched away, then turned back to Val and Caedmon, who were consoling each other.

"Thanks for jumping in there for us," Caedmon said, arm around his husband who was wiping his eyes with a handkerchief. "You didn't have to do that."

"Pascar can go to hell." I waved a hand in the direction she'd gone. "And your secrets are your own; it's nobody's business what type of supes you are if you don't want to share it." I shrugged, turning to go, when I caught the two of them exchanging a loaded glance. "What?"

"Well, of all the people in town, we know we could trust you with a secret," Val said as Caedmon nodded. "*If* you want to know, that is."

Oh my Goddess, did I want to know? Of course I wanted to know! I tried to keep the building anticipation off my face. This was a mystery that had haunted everyone in town ever since the guys had arrived, but of course, like I'd said, it was nobody's business if they didn't want to share it.

Was it weird that no one could tell what they were? Hell yeah, it was weird. Even shifters couldn't scent their species, and they could scent just about anything. But it was possible the pair had spell-locked it — it was rare, but not unheard of — so we'd all left them in peace.

I cleared my throat as I took a half-step forward, aiming for my best nonchalant tone as I said, "I'd be honored, if you want to share it, but don't feel like you have to."

Yeah right. No, *now* they had to, or I'd riot. But I could play it cool.

"Is this really happening?" Caedmon said, meeting Val's eyes like the lovesick romantics they were. "Someone will finally *know*?"

"I think it's time," Val said, and Caedmon nodded right before they shared what was, for them, a relatively chaste kiss.

There was clear open-mouth and ass-grabbing, so I cleared my throat again.

"Right." They broke apart, and Val met my gaze, his eyes still red from his tears. "Well, Devanna. You're the first on this continent, in this century, to know… we're vampires."

Val let out a heavy breath, then grinned, looking at me expectantly.

"Ha," I said unenthusiastically, rolling my eyes. "No, what are you really?"

They frowned. "No, really. Vampires."

I scoffed. "Guys, that's ridiculous. Everybody knows vampires aren't real. Come on, what are you?" I eyed them up and down, "Panda shifters? Sloths? No, I know — some kind of reptile, right? That's why you like the sun so much?"

They turned to each other. "How do we convince her?" Val asked.

Caedmon shrugged. "Show her?"

"You mean — here?" Val looked around the empty beach, then to the van. "Get inside." He waved me over, and I rolled my eyes as I followed the two "vampires" into the van.

"All right, we're inside." The back door slammed shut. "Let's see these supposed *fangs* and — oh my *Goddess*!"

My palm covered my mouth with a *slap* as I turned to,

indeed, see fangs protruding from both of their mouths. Val's eyes flashed a deep red, the exact shade of the Hawaiian shirt they both wore. Like it was nothing, Caedmon grabbed Val's wrist and bit it, taking a gentle pull of his blood before pulling away. The two fang marks healed almost immediately, but my worldview never would.

"*What?!*" My voice cracked into an unflattering screech. Not in fear, but at the realization that vampires were actually *real*, after we'd all been told our whole lives they were fantasy. "Are you freaking kidding me? All these years, you guys never said?" They put their fangs away, shrugging innocently. "Oh, my Goddess. The Twilight obsession. It all makes sense now."

"For the record, almost nothing about those films is accurate," Caedmon interjected, and Val nodded. "Much to my chagrin, we do not glitter. But even we enjoy a little escapism sometimes."

"And eye-candy."

"Mm. Yes. That Taylor Lautner fellow. I can never get enough."

I stared at them as they waxed on about their favorite characters until they turned their attention back to me. "How do you expect me to keep this a secret?! This is the biggest news, possibly ever."

"Our kind are very secretive," Val said. "We usually only reveal ourselves on a need-to-know basis."

"Consider yourself one of the privileged few!"

I held up a hand. "I have so many questions, but the most important one is this." I paused to make sure I had their full focus. "How can you help us get back at that chicken-wing Umbridge?"

Caedmon tilted his head. "Are you asking what sorts of powers we might have to… Peeves it up?"

"Yes." I pointed a finger at him. "Exactly that. What have you got?"

They shared a look that was all mischief, and I knew they wouldn't let me down.

Chapter Seventeen

ORION

WE LANDED in the lobby of Headquarters, my boat shoes touching down on the pristine white floors. Angels had an obsession with white: the floors, walls, furniture… everything was white. Or, on a stretch, light grey. All that was missing was a row of straight jackets waiting for visitors to give the space an asylum vibe. But a classy asylum, to be sure.

After spending the last 30 years in Deadlights Cove, I couldn't help but think everything here felt sterile, bordering on boring. Were these blasphemous thoughts for an angel? Absolutely. I couldn't help but think how Headquarters didn't feel like home anymore.

Ezra strode under the giant LOBBY sign without a backwards glance, knowing I'd follow like the obedient dog I was. I crossed my arms over my chest, trying to cover the scrolling *Karma is a Witch* logo, but it was no use. So I did the only thing I could — I walked in, chin held high.

I'd earned my position on Earth, whatever my brother thought, and, whether they were willing to recognize it or not, I'd done the job to the best of my abilities. The more time I'd spent among the other supernaturals, the more obvious it was that not every rule needed to be followed to a T.

Were Val and Caedmon's 37 instances of public indecency against the law? Yes. But were they hurting anyone? Only our retinas, permanently seared with the image unless I did one the favor of erasing the memory. If only my powers worked on myself.

Angels stopped as I walked by, whispering and laughing quietly, some even outright pointing. I gritted my teeth, trying to think of the number of times I'd seen Morgaine walk with confidence in her intentionally outrageous outfits. The beauty of Earth was in the imperfect, and the more I looked around Headquarters, noticing how every angel looked exactly the same, the more I was sure of it. I had a lot to learn from my neighbors in Deadlights Cove, public indecency aside.

Faking Morgaine's confidence, I smiled, never saying a word as I followed Ezra to a landing, and we took off for a lower level. My wings expanded, snapping out as we floated to the ground floor, then moved to an elevator blending in with a wall. The door slid open, and we entered.

My breath caught as Ezra leaned forward, pushing the button for Omega Level. Silently, the elevator dropped quickly as we sank. Headquarters wasn't on Earth — it was on a separate, parallel realm — so we weren't underground, per se, but I'd heard of Omega before.

Shit.

The doors slid open, and Ezra led the way silently, hands in his pockets. The floor was empty, bright lights overhead illuminating a long hallway with doors on either side. A scream pierced the air from behind one of the doors, followed by a loud *thunk*, then pounding fists.

"Please! Anything but this!" a muffled voice cried, and I stared at the door, wondering what sort of torture lay behind it.

My heart raced as we moved down the hallway, Ezra still silent. "How long will I be here?" I asked, hating the way my voice cracked. "When is my sentencing?"

"As long as it takes," Ezra said, stopping at a door several rooms down on the left. He laid his palm flat on the wall, and the door opened, revealing a room beyond. It was minimally furnished like a long-term hotel: couch, TV, bed, small kitchenette, and bathroom beyond. Nothing seemed particularly torturous about the space. I frowned as I moved inside, turning in a circle to understand what was so bad about these quarters.

Maybe the rumors about Omega Level were exaggerated?

"Enjoy your stay, brother," Ezra said from the hallway, a sinister smile on his face, and I knew I was missing something. But what?

The door snicked shut, and a crackle of magic zapped through the room. With a jump, I grimaced as my magic was sucked from me. I lifted my hands, examining them as I tried to pull on my powers, but nothing.

Maybe this wasn't just an involuntary vacation. But not having access to my powers wouldn't kill me.

I took a deep breath, moving through the space as I tried to figure out what I was missing. Placing my hand on the bathroom door, I pushed it aside, then gasped, clutching my chest as I took in the scene from one of my worst nightmares.

Large toothpaste globs filled the sink, bright blue as they stuck up like braille on the white porcelain. Two towels were on the floor, stinking of mildew. The toilet paper roll was empty, but still on the holder. Trash overflowed from the small wastebasket, littering the floor around it. And then I saw the shower door, covered in soap scum and brown stains better left unidentified.

Pulling in a shaky breath, I yanked open the cabinet under the sink, breathing a sigh of relief at the sight of the cleaning supplies there. I sank to my knees and got to work.

What must have been hours passed as sweat beaded on my brow, but the bathroom was as clean as it would ever get. I pushed to my feet, stretching as I turned back to the rest of the room, headed to get a glass of water from the kitchenette.

My breath caught as I turned the corner. What had been tidy when I entered now looked like a scene from *Hoarders*. The room was covered in trash and rotting food, smelling so awful I couldn't help but gag. Suddenly the screaming voices in the hallway made more sense.

This wasn't just a holding cell.

This was angel hell.

Chapter Eighteen

DEVANNA

JUST BECAUSE PASCAR had forced me to shut down Carpe Noctem's brick and mortar store — for now — didn't mean business had to stop. I'd gotten the word out over social media — something I suspected Pascar wouldn't be familiar with — that my physical shop was down, and had asked all my regular customers to consider supporting my business online or by phone in the meantime.

On the off chance Pascar knew about websites, I had Casey monitor it for me. Since this was my last avenue of business at the moment, I put all my efforts into making it fantastic.

In the last two days, I'd gotten all my merch listed online, except the ones that would be ludicrously annoying to ship, like the salts or cauldrons. I also decided to leave out the ones that could be potentially dangerous, or less FBI-friendly in case they came sniffing around again, like some of the more toxic herbs or the gunpowder. Some witches used it for added flair in their spells.

Apparel, decor, books, and most of my spell ingredients were good to go, and, even in the short time the website had been live, I was pleased with my sales numbers. I had a loyal client base, being the best witch shop on the East Coast. Even if customers might not have liked me personally, they knew I had the best stuff around.

Done for the day, I powered down my laptop, ready for a long bath to soak the knot out of my shoulder I always earned from too much computer work.

I went to my room to strip down and pull on a black robe, but my eyes caught on the black shirt I'd stolen from Orion a week ago.

Had he had his hearing yet? Would we know what happened?

Did I care?

I picked up his shirt, my hands acting of their own accord as I brought it to my nose, inhaling his sea salt and sandalwood scent that haunted every dream I'd had since our night of madness. I could try to convince myself I'd stolen his shirt just to mess with him, just to make him walk out of my house wearing that *Karma is a Witch* one instead, but a tiny, annoying voice in the back of my mind told me that was a lie.

That the truth was I'd wanted to be able to do this. To smell it, smell him, and remember that night, since it would never, ever happen again.

Scoffing at myself, I tossed it to the floor, then wandered back to the bathroom, started the water, then threw in a bath bomb and watched it fizz as steam filled the room.

As the tub finished filling, I hesitated only a moment

before popping back into my bedroom, returning with a little *helper* in hand. Just because that night would never be repeated didn't mean it couldn't be re-lived in my mind from time to time.

Feeling much more relaxed after my bath, I pulled on sweats and headed to the kitchen, nodding at Bagheera perched on the counter. I lifted my hand to pet him, then thought better of it. He knew how to find me if he decided he was ready to snuggle. Not that I wanted that.

I reached for the almost empty bottle of Knob Creek to pour myself one last sip when Bagheera tilted his head, his ears swiveling as he gave a chirp of curiosity.

"Mouse?" I asked, as if he could answer. Was this a thing now — me talking to a cat? Then I heard what he'd heard before me — a subtle bass line sounding through the house. "What the —"

I set my drink down, walking towards the basement steps. Had someone broken into my house, and decided to… host a party? Deadlights Cove was a weird town, but that was a little intrusive, even for the Cove.

I picked up a hammer from when I'd been hanging pictures earlier and stomped over to the basement stairs. The music grew louder when I opened the door but it wasn't the bass line of club music as I'd originally thought. It was the rolling bass guitar of swing music.

I wasn't even a little surprised to see Blaze in the middle of the room, having made himself at home along with what looked like half the town. "Have you lost your mind?" I shouted over the music.

Blaze waved, a broad smile on his face as he poured a drink for Mo. My jaw couldn't decide if it should hang slack or clench tighter than a fist at what I saw in my basement. How he'd done all this in the span of my bath, I had no idea, but somehow, Blaze had built a mini bar on the left side of the basement opposite my gym. The exposed brick walls were refinished beautifully, giving the room a speakeasy vibe I didn't hate. Scattered throughout the rest of the space were a mismatch of chairs and tables. He'd even installed a neon sign behind the bar. Ever proud of himself, Blaze grinned and placed a chilled bottle of Knob Creek on his mini-bar counter, black velvet bow tied around the top.

"Welcome to Mini-Wags, Devvie —"

"First of all, no to the nickname. You know better."

"— Where your drinks are free all night long in exchange for giving the townsfolk a safe watering hole far from the prying eyes of our new evil overlord. Well, Overlady."

I narrowed my eyes, sliding onto a stool that looked suspiciously like it had come straight from Scallywags itself. "Keep talking."

"Oh, more?" Blaze leaned forward over the bar. "I was hoping the whiskey would be enough. What else do you want? Let us stay, pretty please? We all need a break from Miranda Priestly up there." He jerked a thumb skywards, indicating Pascar.

"Hmm." I drew out my contemplation, knowing I had

him right where I wanted him, as he hastily poured me a healthy glass. Looking around the room, Val and Caedmon were talking quietly with Mo, more subdued than I'd ever seen them, and I was mad at Pascar all over again. Decision made, I swung my gaze back on Blaze, taking a sip of my whiskey bribe. "I'll tell you what I want. I want Pascar gone. I want you unleashed, Sabazios. This is your time to shine." I gave him a stern glare. "Do you have what it takes to make this happen?"

Literal fire danced in his eyes, at his fingertips, as he cackled with glee. "Oh, Devanna Rainbow Bailey —"

"I told you that in *confidence* —"

"— I thought you'd never ask."

It wasn't long before word got out to the rest of town about "Mini-Wags." The next night, our newest speakeasy was filled with grumbling townsfolk. In a different century, they'd be grabbing their pitchforks and heating vats of tar.

"She crashed Wine and Wade Wednesday!" Eva Watson cried to a chorus of outrage. "She said it wasn't *safe* for 'the elderly' — yes, she called us *elderly!* — to drink and wade, and that it wasn't something 'real humans' would do. She confiscated our wine and sent us all home! The tide was going out and everything. It was going to be our best wading of the month."

"She shut down yoga!" Zaph added, and his boyfriend Archie gripped his shoulder sympathetically. "She said goats were a hazard to the town image after what they'd done before the Summit, eating everything in the square, and if she saw them there again, she'd send them to a Mediterranean restaurant."

Peg gasped, her hand over her mouth as her eyes went wide.

"My bad." Lys raised a guilty hand, and Maisie patted his arm as Zaph shot him a flat stare.

"She ordered me to release Belphie," Endymion put in, tears shining in his eyes. "She said a goblin shark wouldn't be able to survive in a regular human tank, so it was a dead giveaway his tank is spelled. Now I have him at home where no one else can enjoy his company! But my poor Belphie is a social butterfly — he *needs* the attention. So now he's depressed and keeps floating upside down, refusing to eat his shrimpies!"

"Yeah, that's a damned shame," I muttered into my glass, catching Blaze's eye as he pressed his lips together. Endymion's pet goblin shark was the most horrifying creature I'd ever seen, and that was saying something considering I'd seen Peg Fernsby in her slutty Puritan outfit more times than I cared to recall.

"Justice for Belphie!" Blaze raised a fist in solidarity. I couldn't tell whether he was serious or not, but either way, the statement was ridiculous. Google a goblin shark and tell me I'm wrong.

"She made the skulk put glamours up around our kit enclosures, so humans wouldn't drive by our houses — *way up off the main roads* — and wonder why so many of us own 'pet foxes'," Kit scoffed, and several members of the skulk murmured in confirmation. "It cost a fortune."

"Same thing happened with the pack houses," Darius

agreed. "That's all our pack savings, gone. We were going to use that money to build a new pack house."

"Look, I love a good airing of grievances as much as the next person," I called out over the crowd, and they quieted down. "But this isn't Festivus. We need to focus and come up with a plan to run her out of town."

"About that." Blaze wheeled out a white board— where had that even come from? — and flipped it over, revealing a web of images and bullet points intricate enough to make a serial killer proud. "There's nothing angels hate more than chaos," his eyes gleamed, and his entire body shivered in excitement, "the unexpected, the impulsive. The downright dangerous and stupid. Needless to say, I have a plan."

After a planning session that lasted well into the wee hours of the night, we disbanded, scattering to get some rest before we started Phase One early the next morning. Blaze, Endymion, Nox, and Nimue worked all night to set it up.

Nothing made a demon work harder than the promise of inciting total chaos. Even Nimue, who was practically an anti-demon, was all but glowing with how hot the fire in her veins was running.

Morning dawned like a Disney cartoon, blue skies, a cool breeze off the ocean, bird calls and the faint *ding* of the harbor bell a beacon to town residents, broken only by the random *bong* as Bagheera attacked the church bell once more.

I pulled on my favorite — well, easiest to put on — sports bra, my *Not All Witches Live in Salem* shirt for good measure, and capri leggings that made my ass look fantastic, before grabbing my yoga mat and heading out the door.

Had I ever attended Zaph's yoga class before? No. But none of us wanted to miss today.

Yoga mats of all colors covered the square from end to end, and I found a spot by Nimue, Aurora, and Petra to set mine up. Zaph walked around, barking orders in his drill-sergeant fashion for people to rearrange and make more room. Blaze was in his best imitation of an 80s exercise video outfit — a bright orange headband and matching leotard that left little to the imagination over black leggings with flames up the sides. Where he'd even found that get-up, I didn't want to know.

I nudged Petra and nodded towards her demon. "Really? That? What do you call the male version of a camel toe, because he has it."

"A moose knuckle," Nimue said, then gagged at the sight of her cousin. "I wish I didn't know that."

Petra chuckled. "Confidence can make any outfit work."

"I beg to *strongly* disagree."

Well over half the men here were shirtless like there'd been a mass rebellion against clothing, but I'd take that any day over Blaze's scandalous getup. Val and Caedmon might have thirty-seven documented instances of public indecency, but every person here deserved to be ticketed.

So. Much. Skin.

"Silence! Settle onto your mats!" Zaph shouted, starting our class. "Assume your favorite yoga pose."

I had this one down. I sat cross-legged on my mat and waited. Boom. Sukhasana.

"When I release the animals, you will hold your pose

until one chooses you. This will be your partner for the duration of the session."

Everyone around us adopted whatever pose they wanted, most choosing something simple like mine that we could easily hold for a while — how long would it take us to be chosen? Nobody knew — but a few overachievers took more drastic positions. Peg Fernsby had her legs spread in a triangle with her head hanging down between them, waving her butt in the air. Another ticketable offense, in my opinion.

Kit held a plank position with Nimue under him, staring lovingly into each other's eyes.

"You two make me sick," I hissed, and they laughed.

"No talking! It will disturb them!"

The back door to a stock trailer rattled open, and, with a cacophony of hums and grunts, a herd of alpacas descended on the green. I didn't dare move, only shifting my eyes as the animals meandered between the rows of people. Unlike the cute, cuddly dwarf goats Zaph normally used during yoga, alpacas weighed upwards of 100 pounds. There would be no mini goat jumping on your back while you were in cat-cow. At least, I hoped not. Though with Zaph involved, anything was fair game.

One stopped behind me, breath huffing as it sniffed along my head, then began nibbling on my hair. "I've never had alpaca meat before, but I'm willing to try anything once. Try me, Kuzco."

Whether in answer to my words or just a typical alpaca trait, the beast had the audacity to leave a huge wad of spit in my hair. I clenched my teeth, the opposite of calm, but tried to remember the bigger picture.

Zaph called for us to shift positions and I pushed to my

feet, shooting death glares in the alpaca's direction. Just as I rose into a sun salutation, a shrill voice cut through the air.

"I already shut you down!" Pascar said, holding up a copy of the same form she'd been handing out faster than Mo gave out candy on Halloween.

Zaph cowered slightly, eyes downcast as he moved away from Pascar, though Archie stepped in front of him, silently staring down Pascar with unnerving focus. Fortunately, Blaze stepped forward, stretching his arms over his head as he jutted his hips slightly forward, making sure everyone saw how indecent his outfit was. I choked, turning my head as he ripped the paper from Pascar's hand, holding it exaggeratedly close to his face. His finger trailed over the words, eyes squinted in scrutiny until he handed it back, smacking it into Pascar's chest. "Interesting. I don't see anything about *alpacas* in your warning. It says *goats*, and these lovely creatures are just here to trim the grass while we get a little exercise. Do you have something against well-kept lawns or stretching?"

Smoke practically billowed out of Pascar's ears as she fumed, staring down Blaze, who only cocked his head and grinned. Beside me, Petra's yoga mat caught fire at the corner.

"Shit." She lurched forward, patting out the flames quickly before Pascar could notice. "He's so hot."

I rolled my eyes, but our plan was off to a good start.

Pascar narrowed her eyes, then pulled out her clipboard from the in-between, and hastily made an adjustment to the paper before shoving it back under Blaze's nose.

"There. No ungulates of *any* kind. Pack these beasts up and be gone within the hour!"

She turned on her heel and stomped back up the steps into Town Hall.

Blaze turned around to face the crowd, still beaming. "You heard her, folks. No uvulas of any kind!"

Honestly, yoga being over for today was a relief. And we had a plan for Phase Two ready to go.

Chapter Nineteen

DEVANNA

THE REST of the day we all behaved, at least, as much as the residents of Deadlights Cove knew how to. Blaze insisted the slow and steady approach would work in the long run, wearing Pascar down like the twins in the *Parent Trap*. While I wanted to rip the bandage off and run her off as fast as possible, I happened to know firsthand just how much Blaze's shenanigans could drive someone crazy. So I decided to trust him, for now.

The next morning, I took my coffee out to the front step, eager to see the work he'd done overnight. Even knowing what Blaze had planned, I couldn't help but laugh.

Across the green stood the gazebo, as always. From a distance, it looked like flames licked up the sides — reds, turning to oranges and yellows. As I wandered closer, I could make out exactly what caused the gradient effect.

Paint or actual flames would have been much too easy and bland for the flavor of chaos Blaze liked to wield. But the red, orange, and yellow Beanie Babies stacked tightly, one on top of the other, was right on-brand. Hundreds, if not thousands, of the little stuffed animals covered the structure.

Several humans already stood on the grass, snapping pictures as they laughed at the gazebo, leaning in to touch the mural ode to a millennial childhood.

"I've seen so many Beanie Babies in this town," a tourist commented to me, ignoring my permanent resting bitch face. "They're all over the fudge shop too. Is this a local artist? I've never seen anything like it before."

"Yep," I said, a small smile tugging at my lips as I sipped my coffee. "It's kind of a thing here."

"I love it." The man shook his head with a laugh. "God, remember when we all thought these would sell for a fortune?"

"Only an idiot would think they were a good investment," I said, then moved to walk away. "You should check out the harbor. I heard there are more of these murals hidden around."

His eyes lit with excitement, turning to his friends to tell them about the scavenger hunt for more Beanie Babies.

If Blaze had worked his magic, there were six of these "murals", and before Pascar could do anything about it, humans flocked the town, laughing and snapping pictures. Both Beanie Babies and Deadlights Cove were trending on social media by the end of the day as a fuming Pascar stood in front of the gazebo, removing them by hand. With so many humans present, even she couldn't use her magic on them.

"You should have seen her face!" Val said with a wide smile as he sat on a stool in my basement.

Blaze sighed contentedly, resting his elbow on the bar top, chin cradled in his hand. "This might be my proudest moment to date. The only thing I can do is top myself tomorrow."

"Stiff competition," I smirked, though I could admit the Beanie Babies were a stroke of genius. "However will you do it?"

"Ye of little faith," Blaze said, pushing off and wiping down the counter. "This was the pre-season. A warmup. I'm just getting started."

Over the next few days, we adhered to the letter of the law regarding Pascar's yoga requirements.

No ungulates? No problem. We didn't need two-toed creatures to have a yoga class. The next day, we had chickens. The fox-shifters had taken one look at them and excused themselves before there could be any carnage.

Pascar added, "No farm creatures of any kind," to the list.

Every day, Blaze had a solution to her ever-expanding list of excluded animals. After chickens, we each got our own parakeet. The chirping drew her from her office pretty quickly, and she declared no birds.

Bearded dragons got all land-based reptiles, mammals, insects, and birds banned. She probably thought at that point that we'd be out of options, but boy, was she wrong.

Overnight, Blaze and some others set up a huge above-ground pool in the square, and we did underwater tai-chi with baby sea turtles and baby harbor seals.

Since the Beanie Babies sculptures had put Deadlights Cove on social media's radar, human tourists now made it a point to come watch our classes — Zaph had immediately shot down any of them who tried to join, saying the class was by invitation only — and they were delighted by our aquatic take on the exercise class.

At that, Pascar threatened to throw Zaph and Blaze in jail for antagonizing her, and banned all exercise of any form with any living creatures from the square for all time.

With all the added visitors, Blaze had gotten permission from Val and Caedmon to repurpose their van into a Scally-wag-on, and set up on the beach every afternoon, serving drinks and snacks to locals and tourists alike. Anytime Pascar was on her way, the warning got out *Telephone*-style, and he'd quickly pack up and drive away.

Val and Caedmon, meanwhile, decided to try to help out in Immortali-Tea, since Nadir was overrun with customers. They were slightly affronted when they found out about Kit's secret espresso machine, but then set to work running a black market coffee business, donning disguises just in case Pascar ever spied them through the swinging kitchen doors.

"Have you guys come up with your plan yet?" I asked, hopping up onto the countertop while I waited for Val to finish my pour-over.

"Well, we don't want *everyone* to *know* yet," Caedmon said pointedly, pumping his bushy white eyebrows in emphasis to indicate our little secret.

"Sure." I waved a hand, once again struggling to keep

my cool. But I wouldn't interrogate them, no matter how much I wanted to know more. I would. Not. Interrogate. Them.

"But," Val continued, and I realized I was leaning forward to hang on his every word when I nearly slipped off the stainless steel. "We've actually already begun."

"*Oh?*"

The guys dropped into silence as Nadir came to grab a tray of danishes, waiting until he passed back up front before continuing.

"Well, since we can manipulate shadows, we've been making her think her room at the Last Resort is haunted," Val said casually, though he kept his voice low because of the shifters out front.

My eyes popped open, and my hands gripped the counter so hard the counter creaked. "Shadows, you say?" My voice came out about two octaves too high. I cleared my throat.

"And we've been flying past her window, too, but then every time she looks, there's nothing there," Caedmon added. "Only shadows." They high fived.

I tried not to faint. "Um. *Fly?*"

They shared a glance. "We can summon wings."

I wheezed.

"Mhm," Val said, beaming at Caedmon. "You should see my male all cloaked in shadow and gliding in the moonlight." Caedmon's pale cheeks pinked.

"Anyway," Val continued, finally passing over my coffee. "She hasn't gotten any sleep in five days now. She'll crack soon."

That gave me another idea, so I hopped off the counter, thanking the guys for my coffee, and pulled out my phone.

While the others set up, we stationed Akil, Kit's youngest brother, outside Pascar's window to keep us updated. She had to be exhausted, so we wanted to wait for the opportune moment.

Glamoured from view — for now — a handful of the rest of us set up a giant outdoor movie with the biggest speakers we could find.

"And you all said it was silly of me to buy the cotton candy machine when I could rent one," Blaze snickered, whipping up a whole tray of cotton candy sticks. "I knew it would pay for itself."

By the time Akil let us know that Pascar was sound asleep, we were ready.

"I do love when the whole town comes together like this," Mo said, settling into her beach chair. Blaze handed her a rather large drink with a magenta umbrella that matched her kimono. "Thank you, dear."

When we were all settled into our seats with our snacks and beverages like we did this all the time, Zaph lifted the glamour from around us, and Blaze started the movie.

The blaring trumpets of the *Star Wars* main theme rattled the windows of the Last Resort, and I couldn't help but smile. Akil gave us a thumbs up from under Pascar's window, indicating she'd woken up again, before he ran over and slid onto a picnic blanket.

Her window sash slammed open, and Pascar stuck her

head out, her hair ruffled and wild from sleep, dark circles under her eyes.

"What is this?" she screeched. "Who orchestrated this? You need a permit for public gatherings!"

"Oh, we have one," Mo assured her, popping up and pulling a paper from her pocket. Pascar's face turned purple as she read the paper that Darius had indeed signed earlier today. Mo patted her arm. "Are you quite all right? You look like you could use some sleep, but if you want to join us —"

Pascar sneered, but pulled her head back into her room and slammed the window shut.

We waited again, and once she'd fallen back asleep, the fight began.

"The *Phantom Menace?*" Peg Fernsby shrieked, right on cue. "What is this garbage?"

"To fully understand the nuances of the saga as a whole —"

"What are you calling *garbage?!*"

I pressed my lips together as everyone took a side, arguing the pros and cons of Jar Jar Binks. In my opinion, there were no pros. Before long, everyone assembled was arguing and bickering, throwing popcorn and candy and, once in a while, throwing a glass against the wall outside Pascar's room for good measure.

With a crack of thunder, Pascar appeared on the back step to the motel. Her hair was a mess, her wings barely glamoured, and her eyes wild with rage.

"What is the meaning of this?" she seethed. "Some of us are trying to *sleep.*"

While Pascar argued with us, Akil, Cole, and Casey

slipped into the motel, sent to wreak havoc on her motel room.

Finally, Mo ushered her back inside, patting her back and promising this time we would definitely keep the noise down.

The frustrated curses that came from Pascar's room a minute later told us the foxes had been successful in destroying her room.

Blaze turned the volume down, but most of us stayed, enjoying the summer evening as the movie played. Times like these were when I loved Deadlights Cove the most. Fireflies drifted in the cool breeze blowing through the surrounding trees while stars twinkled into view overhead. The scenery couldn't be beat, but the people around me… this was my family. Lys nudged my shoulder where he sat next to me, Maisie in his lap, and I couldn't help but smile at him.

This town — these people — were worth protecting and I'd do anything in my power to keep them safe and happy.

Just as the final credits rolled, sobs sounded from Pascar's windows.

"Right about now she should be deep in a nightmare. Hopefully something truly terrible like an unalphabetized library or a pantry full of empty boxes," Mo said casually as she slurped the last of her drink. "It's been a long time since I've used the darker side of my Aura magic. I forgot how fun this is."

I laughed with a shake of my head right as Winston strolled out from the forest, nose to the ground as he sniffed out every piece of scattered candy like a bloodhound. With each strawberry-flavored Starburst, Winston let out a bellow that sounded like he was in the midst of mating season.

There was enough candy here to keep him occupied for *hours*.

After the movie, we decided it was time to launch the Grand Finale. Blaze could hardly keep the flames off his fingertips, he was so excited.

Like we'd done every morning, the town gathered in the square, ready for yoga. I looked around at the large crowd, a mix of humans and supes wondering how Blaze planned to top the chaos he'd already caused, but noted that all of the local demons were absent, and there was no sign any animals would join us.

As Zaph ordered us to take our first positions, my brow scrunched in confusion, wondering what the plan was. This was… almost normal.

Just as I closed my eyes, placing my hands in front of my chest, the ground began to shake. My eyes snapped back open, glancing around at the crowd, searching for the source of the disturbance.

"What is that?" a tourist called, gripping her husband's arm in alarm as she looked around the square. "I didn't know there were earthquakes in Maine?"

The rumbling grew louder, and with a snap, the official Deadlights Cove sign in front of Town Hall — which had been fixed for the Summit — slipped off one of its chains, once again hanging askew as it had for countless years before.

"Ahh," Caedmon sighed in relief, putting a hand to his chest. "It just looks *right* again."

Kai, the librarian, hurried out of Town Hall, looking back at it in alarm as Darius and the rest of the police force also evacuated the building, clouds of steam or smoke now billowing out of every opening.

"What's that smell?" Lys said, and I sniffed the air as Petra beside me started snickering, her eyes flickering with a hint of the fire she now carried. She really was spending too much time with Blaze.

"Just wait," she said, nodding towards the Town Hall.

"I think it's —"

With a shattering crash, all the windows in Town Hall blew out, glass shards flying everywhere, and enlarged popcorn the size of grapefruit started to pour out of the building, crashing onto the ground in a tidal wave of buttery mess.

A shriek sounded a moment before Pascar ran out of the building, her hair in disarray and burn marks and butter spotting her grey sheath dress. She looked even worse than last night, her eyes blood-shot and heavily shadowed from lack of sleep, her dress rumpled and frayed from the foxes' destruction.

"Oh, my God," a tourist said with a laugh, phone in hand filming the whole thing. "This is better than *Real Genius*. Where the hell do you get popcorn like that? Do they have it for sale at Pop Nox?"

"This is some A-Plus marketing," another agreed with a nod. "Someone needs to send this to the Guinness Book of World Records."

"It's amazing what science can do these days. GMOs and what not."

"What's that following that lady?"

I squinted to see what they were referring to at the same time as Pascar turned and screamed again. Rolling behind her in what could only be described as a giant aquatic hamster ball, Belphie the goblin shark was swimming towards her, his cold dead eyes set on her as he pushed his magic ball forward.

"Is that a baby fucking whale, Jay?"

"I think it's sick or something!"

"That thing looks dead. We gotta save it!"

"Holy shit. Look at that fuckin' thing!"

"Where do you buy a fish hamster ball like that?"

In her attempt to evade Belphie's relentless pursuit, Pascar failed to notice the pile of goat and alpaca droppings to the side of the Town Hall sign, and went tripping into it.

"Oh, wow, that's unfortunate."

"The animals had some digestive upset after not being allowed to partake in their usual regimen," Blaze called to her as he strode past, having emerged mysteriously from within the building, utterly unscathed. "You might want to shower sooner than later."

"Having a bit of a problem with the pipes over at the motel, though," Castor added, arms crossed over his chest as he observed Pascar, who was now frantically trying to extricate herself from the pile of green poop goo, only she kept slipping and falling back in. "So it might be a few days."

We all held our breath as Pascar finally scrambled to her feet, goop dripping off her usually pristine self. She seethed at us like some bog hag, and electricity crackled in the air from her magic.

"Deadlights Cove is closed to all visitors," she spat — literally, a glob of shit came out with it. Then, imbuing the word with a frisson of magic, she ordered the humans present, "*Go.*"

The humans' eyes glazed over like they were in a trance and, unable to resist the force of her magic, they all quietly and quickly got into their cars and left.

"Ezra and the rest of the Council will be hearing about this —"

"What, about how you can't handle one little town?" someone jeered from the assembled crowd, which Pascar ignored.

"— And believe me when I say I know just who the ring-leaders are here."

With a thundering *crack* that shook the town, Pascar disappeared, and rampant applause followed in her wake.

Chapter Twenty

DEVANNA

WITH PASCAR FINALLY GONE, things returned back to normal in the Cove. Darius and the wolves put "Road Closed" barriers blocking access in and out of town for visitors after Pascar had banished the remaining humans. Scallywags reopened, the van could sell coffee again, Town Hall was fixed back up, Blaze's demon friends repaired the lighthouse, and everyone was more relaxed — or, as relaxed as we could be looking over our shoulder for an evil demon invasion at any moment. We knew it was only a matter of time before we heard from the Council about this, but for now, we had no angel overlord ticketing our every move, and that was a relief.

Maisie had texted me earlier to confirm we were still on for another training session tonight, and I'd spent the day prepping my gym. With the rise of threats to our community, I hated the thought of any of us vulnerable. Self-defense wasn't just about magic — there were times that wasn't an option. For some reason, men never expected women to fight back, the idiots.

Joan Jett's *Bad Reputation* blared through the speakers as I snapped the last of the rubber carpet mats into place. I dusted off my hands, looking over the space. Blaze's guys had helped me hang a mirror wall on the far end of the room when they cleared out the tables and chairs from Mini-Wags. I'd decided to keep the bar and sign for myself.

My punching bag still hung in the corner, but now there was also a treadmill to the right and a variety of weapons hung on the walls. I also had jump ropes, free weights, and resistance bands.

A voice called from above, and I hopped up the steps, fighting back a smile that threatened to take over my face as I thought through my plans for tonight's class.

I skidded to a halt when the foyer came into view, counting not two, but *six* women standing there.

"Please don't get mad," Nimue said as my eyes squinted in disapproval at her, Aurora, and Ruby. "Petra told Mo about how great you were at our last lesson, and Mo thought it would be a good idea if Ruby, Aurora, and I joined you."

Aurora looked as sweet as ever in a floral sundress, standing arm in arm with Ruby — her opposite in every way. The teen was back to her usual goth-punk self in a black mini skirt, fishnets, and Doc Martens, but since she'd been *demon possessed* a few weeks ago, I was a little surprised to see her here.

"Are you sure you're up for this? None of us will think less of you to take some time."

Ruby nodded, determination lighting her eyes. "I need training now more than ever. I *never* want to lose control of myself again."

She tilted her chin up, and I could see there'd be no getting rid of her.

"And I brought snacks!" Aurora smiled as she held up a large bag of popcorn. "We've been working on a new recipe, so I thought maybe we could try it after our lessons and you can tell me what you think." She shook the bag, rattling the pieces. "Honey blueberry."

I snatched the bag from her hand and put it to the side — I'd *definitely* be trying that later — as I eyed the unfamiliar blonde standing next to Maisie. "And who are you?"

"Riona," the girl said with a small wave.

"My little sister," Maisie explained. "There's no real reason for her to be here since she hasn't Linked with anyone and knows how to use her sea nymph powers just fine. She has always been a tag-along."

"Listen," Riona said, stepping forward, her chin up in a defiant way I couldn't help but respect. "Sure, your witchy lessons don't apply to me *yet*, but someday I'll be more than just a sea nymph, and I want to be as prepared as possible. Plus, like, girl power, and all."

I chewed on my lip, thinking through how I could adjust my plans to include someone whose magic I had no familiarity with, but threw my hands up.

Taking that as a sign of acceptance, Riona beamed. I wasn't a completely heartless bitch. She could stay.

The door opened and closed again, and I sighed heavily, looking up at the ceiling. "Now what?"

"Sorry I'm late," Selene said, and I snapped my head back down, staring at my friend.

"What are you doing here?" I asked, brow scrunched in confusion. "Why aren't you working in Boston?"

"Well, with everything going on, Ryker has gone into feral mode and won't let me out of his sight," Selene said with an annoyed huff. "He's here in case there's more trouble from the Council coming, and his overprotectiveness has gone into overdrive. It would be infuriating if it wasn't so damn sexy. Something is wrong with me."

"No." I shook my head. "That practice means everything to you. You're not giving up your dreams for a male, no matter how big his wingspan is."

"Yeah!" Riona said, fist in the air. No one else said anything, and Riona slowly lowered her fist. "Sorry."

I pointed at her and she shrunk back. "No more apologizing for stupid shit. Do men walk around apologizing for being too loud or interrupting women? No. They just bulldoze over us, expecting us to make ourselves smaller to appease their tiny little… *egos*. Take up space. Be passionate. Be loud."

I paced in front of them, fists clenched tightly. "Goddess forbid we don't bow down to their every whim, they call us bitches and whores. Even before our supernatural world was threatened by these dumb shits, we, as women, were threatened. Fuck that."

"Cheers to that," Petra said, jaw clenched tightly. "Even the term 'witch' is villainized, and you ladies are some of the best women I've ever met."

"So, what's the plan then?" Nimue said, eyes sparkling with mischief. "I know you have one. Ready to share that big witch energy with the rest of us?"

"Basement, now," I barked, feeling like a drill sergeant and loving the thrill it gave me when they hopped to it. Nimue made a pit stop at the bathroom first, unable to comply with orders, and Petra checked at her phone before following the others.

"Not going to apologize," Petra said as she walked past, chin held high.

I bit back a laugh, shaking my head as I followed the rest of them downstairs.

"This is pretty impressive, Dev," Selene said, inspecting the equipment setup. Selene was by far the fittest of the group here, but her witch powers were sporadic and inconsistent. The rest of them... Well. There was room for improvement.

"Everyone stretch," I said, pointing at the floor. "Stamina matters when defending yourself, magically *or* physically. All of you have work to do on one or the other. Maybe both."

When Petra's face fell slightly, staring at the wall, a twinge of guilt went through me for my harsh words, but following my own rule, I didn't apologize. It was the truth. What Petra didn't know was that even though my words might have hurt, no way in hell would I leave her behind. She was a scholar, and I held a wealth of knowledge I could share with her.

"My hips are so sore," Nimue said, stretching her legs out to the side in a wide V.

"No one wants to hear about your crazy sex life." I held up a hand to stop whatever she was about to say. "We know. Kit is a *literal* animal."

Nimue blushed, and I rolled my eyes.

Maisie held one leg up behind her, stretching her quad until she slowly began to tip over. "You're working on balance first. You're a landlubber now. Get used to it."

Riona snickered, and I pointed at her. "Not anticipating you're much better. Selene, walk them through some yoga poses to get them started."

Selene saluted, pulling three mats down from the wall and spreading them across the far side of the room.

"Nimue, get Ruby and Aurora started on the treadmill," I said as I pulled Petra up from her feet, tugging her towards the boxing gloves and punching bag. "You're with me, Pet."

"I have enough nicknames, please don't," Petra said, resting bitch face firmly in place. I nodded as I grabbed a pair of gloves and handed them to her.

"Fair. Thanks for telling me."

Petra studied me, then nodded. "What are we doing first?"

"I'm going to teach you how to fight with your hands, so when we add your magic in, you're that much more deadly. Eventually, you're going to fight Nimue for practice."

"Uh." Nimue bit her lip, turning our way slowly. "About that."

I squinted at my best friend, at her awkward, hesitant smile, and the blush rising in her freckled cheeks. "Nims, whatever you're trying to keep secret from me, spill it right now."

Nimue scanned the room, snagging on Maisie and Riona whom she didn't know well, before she turned back to me. "Please don't be mad," she said, and instantly my guard was up. "I'm…" she wrung her hands, staring at her feet as she let a deep sigh go, "I'm pregnant."

"What?" Selene shrieked, a bright smile on her face. "Oh my Goddess, Nimue, that's so exciting!"

Petra stared at them wide-eyed while Ruby, Aurora, and

Selene hugged her and Maisie and Riona offered their congratulations. Nimue smiled, happiness radiating from her while I stood frozen in place. Nimue had been my best friend for as long as I could remember, my chosen family when my own let me down time and time again. The thought of how drastically her life had already changed in the past year, and was still changing, was jarring. And now, a baby?

Why did it feel like I was being abandoned all over again?

Her smile faded as she stepped away from the girls over to me. "Please say something."

Shaking myself, I asked, "How far along are you?"

"Seven weeks," she whispered. "I've wanted to tell you, but with everything going on lately, Kit wanted us to keep it secret for a bit longer. Plus, I wasn't sure how you'd react. I know kids aren't your favorite, and I'm not just having one, but *two*."

I reared back in confusion at her words. "You were worried about how *I'd* react? It's your life, Nimue. You get to live it how you want, no caveats. As long as you don't plan on leaving me as their sole guardian, forcing me to raise two Pokémon in case of your untimely demise, then my opinion doesn't matter at all."

"Goddess, Dev," Selene said, gaping at me. "Don't even put that thought out into the universe."

Nim chuckled, and I thought back over my words. "Okay, that I might be sorry for. I'll kill you if you die on me, Nimue."

"Not planning on it." Nimue smiled, tension leaving her shoulders as she looped her arms around my shoulders and tugged me into her chest. I was not a hugger, but, for Nimue, I always made an exception. "I hate keeping secrets from you," she whispered, the words meant only for me, and I loved her for that. "You have no idea how many times I've picked up my phone to call you and tell you. You're my person, Devvie. You always have been, and always will be."

I squeezed her tightly, her words sparking a twinge of guilt about my own secret I was keeping from her. "I'm happy when you're happy."

Nimue pulled back, tears gathered in her eyes, and swiped them away. "Pregnancy hormones are no joke," she said through a sniffle and a laugh.

"Does Mo know yet?" Ruby asked, moving into the circle where we all stood. It hadn't escaped my notice that she'd hung back a bit today, watching and observing, but she'd been through a lot lately, and I was giving her space.

"No," Nimue said, wiping the last of her tears. "Can you even imagine? She's going to lose it." I made a mental note to buy earplugs before then, knowing we'd never hear the end of Mo's excited rambling about grandchildren.

"This is all surreal," Nim said, hand on her belly. "It's still early, but Kit could smell it on me right away, saying my scent changed now that I'm carrying. I keep thinking about that morning at Mo's house when she said Selene would be the first one of us to have a baby. Guess she was wrong, huh?"

Nimue laughed, but when I looked at Selene, her face was damn near blanched, which was hard to do for darker-skinned girls like us. The whites showed all the way around her irises, her chest heaving before she sprinted up the steps. I turned back to the rest of the girls.

"If you think I'm taking it easy on any of you in light of this news, you'd be wrong," I said, swirling my hand above my head. "Back to work!"

After everyone had a task set for them, I followed Selene upstairs and found her in the kitchen, cheeks full of crackers. I raised an accusatory eyebrow.

"I got snacky all of a sudden."

Uh-huh. A likely tale. "Something you'd like to tell me, Dr. Flores?"

She swallowed, then took a big gulp of orange juice. "Okay, you caught me. But the only reason I didn't tell you is because Ryker is losing his mind. He's terrified the baby will be shifted during birth and the wings will kill me."

"Oh, please," I scoffed, waving a hand through the air as I leaned back against the counter next to her. "There are spells for that. It'll be fine. He should be more worried you'll hatch an egg."

Selene's eyes popped out of their sockets, and I threw my hands up. "Kidding! That's not how that works." Probably. "You'll be fine."

Selene nodded, blinking her eyes slowly back to their usual size. "I know, but try telling him that. The male invented the word 'overprotective.' Anyway, he doesn't want anyone to know yet until I literally can't hide it anymore. Something about jinxing it."

"I thought you had an IUD?" I asked, getting a little too personal with the doctor.

"I did." Selene nodded, shoving another cracker into her mouth. "But then we Linked, and dragon magic apparently isn't compatible with a human IUD. Burned right through it. I probably got pregnant the night we Linked." She laughed, the sound almost manic, but I let her talk. "Nimue sounds ecstatic about her news which only makes me feel worse because I *panicked* when I found out. It wasn't pretty. What if I'm a terrible mother? Dragon babies are extremely rare — there's a reason there are only five left on earth. And *me?* I don't know anything about dragons. How am I supposed to raise one? What if it's not even a dragon and I already failed? And have you *seen* Ryker? This baby is going to destroy my body." Another cracker. "But none of my insecurities matter because I'm Fertile Myrtle and Starvin' Marvin, all in one tiny package."

I chuckled, brushing crumbs off the counter into my hand. "As long as you don't turn into Bitchy Witchy next, I think you'll be fine." I eyed her as she polished off the crackers and tossed the box in the recycling. "And those fears all seem valid. But when has being afraid of something ever held us back?"

"You?" Selene raised a brow. "Never. Me? Almost daily."

"Whatever." I waved her off, my mind immediately snagging on the t-shirt that didn't belong to me stored in my top drawer. I was pretty afraid of evaluating whatever emotion had me feeling sentimental about it. "You've been mothering Nimue and I for decades. I think you'll be great."

Tears filled Selene's eyes and she pulled me into a hug. "I'm so lucky you found your way to us, Dev. Joined our weird little family."

I patted her back, letting my chin fall to her shoulder as I soaked in the warmth of her words. It was hard for me to explain how much Selene and Nimue's friendship had meant to me when we were kids. As we'd grown, that circle had expanded to include Blaze, Lys, and some of the skulk boys. But for an abandoned only-child, this was the dream.

Needing to pull myself out of an emotional tailspin I felt myself moving towards, I cleared my throat. "Mo's going to figure this out when she hears about Nimue, and then it'll be all over town. She's never been wrong about a prediction and she said you would be first."

Selene let go, turning to the fridge, then emerged with a jar of pickles like a cliche. "I think Ryker's plan is to whisk me away to one of his many remote residences before then."

I snorted. "Yeah, right. I'd like to see him try to get you out of Mo's clutches at that point. He'd have to have a death wish. If she doesn't put you under house arrest at her place, she'll at least pop by his house once a day."

Selene laughed, then bit her lip, pausing between pickles. "I'm afraid to be excited. But I'm a little excited."

My heart warmed at that, joy for my friend squeezing tight in my chest. Or maybe it was expanding, bursting out like an inflating balloon. Even if motherhood wasn't something I'd ever been interested in, seeing Selene happy after some of the things she'd been through almost made me tear up.

"I'm happy for you, Leens."

"Thanks, Dev."

"And, just so we're clear, I'll allot both you and Nims two extra hugs for the year, because pregnancy hormones, and a bonus one for the day you give birth. On the house."

Selene chuckled as we headed back downstairs to keep training. "Gracious of you."

The girls trickled out a little later that night, Maisie and Riona leaving with Ruby and Aurora while Nimue and Selene talked about all things baby in my living room, gushing over ultrasound pictures together. Petra lingered behind, side-eyeing me as she sipped her water.

"Whatever you want to ask me, just spit it out, P."

Petra paused, screwing the top back on her water before turning to me. "Explain to me witchy birth control. I'm staring at the two of them and having thoughts of demon sperm destroying any and all barriers, and I'm trying not to spiral."

I laughed, turning to look at her. "What, no epilogue babies in your future?"

"Four-legged ones, maybe. But no, I've never seen that path for myself. And have you met Blaze? While I'm sure he'd be an excellent father, I do not have it in me to raise one of him."

"That may be the smartest thing I've ever heard you say," I said, pouring two fingers of whiskey into a glass for myself. "But now that you're at least part witch-part demon, I can help you out. And yes, it's more fool-proof than human medicine."

"Excellent," she said, snagging the whiskey from my hand and taking a large sip. She shuddered at the taste, sticking her tongue out as it burned its way down her throat.

"Can I get you something else to drink instead?" I asked, one eyebrow raised.

Seemingly shocked I wasn't pushing her out the door —

I was a little shocked myself — Petra nodded, then pulled back a stool, taking a seat at the counter. "Have any cider?"

"Blaze left my fridge stocked, so probably," I said, feeling closer with Petra than I had in the year since she'd arrived. Twisting the top off a cider, I handed it over, clinking my glass with her bottle and taking the stool next to hers.

My little friend group was expanding, and I didn't hate it.

I didn't hate it at all.

Selene and Petra left arm-in-arm a little while later and Nimue patted the couch cushion next to her. The moment I sat down, she slid over, resting her head in my lap as she reclined, hand on her belly. Instantly, I let my hand fall to her silky brown hair, running it through the long strands as I'd done hundreds of times before.

"Don't ever tell Kit I said this," Nimue started, her black eyes looking up at me with a hesitant smile, "because I love him dearly and he is my mate, my husband, my everything. But he's not my soulmate. You stole that title long before he ever could."

"Don't say shit like that to me," I said as my eyes burned. I blinked back the tears that threatened to fall at her words, but Nimue just chuckled.

"What? That you're beautiful and hilarious and loyal and so smart, it's frightening? Don't say those things?"

I pulled the pillow out from behind my back and slapped her with it, making Nimue's chuckles turn into full belly laughs I couldn't help but join in on.

"Goddess, I've missed you lately," I said. Nimue's face fell, her smile gone as she reached over and squeezed my hand. Part of me regretted my words, but… I did miss her. So much had changed lately. I'd thought Nimue moving back to town meant we'd fall right back into our bond, doing everything together, but that hadn't been the case.

She had a whole life now outside of our friendship, a whole new family through her marriage, and I was happy for her, even if I mourned the way we used to be.

"I miss you too, Dev," she whispered. "And I'm sorry. I need to be better about being here for you. About prioritizing time for just us like we used to."

"I'd love that," I squeezed her hand, "but I also understand, especially with the babies on the way."

Nimue laughed. "Well, lucky for all of us, these kids are going to have half the town lining up for babysitting."

"True."

"I strongly suspect Mo will make them mini matching kimonos. Actually, she's insinuated as much every time she's not-so-subtly hinted about her future grandbabies."

"Say the word and I'll make sure they magically disappear every time she drops new ones off."

"Enough about me," Nimue said, pushing to sit back up on the couch. "I've let you keep your secrets for long enough. Spill it."

I shrugged innocently. "Spill what?"

Nimue grabbed the pillow I'd hit her with and slapped me in the face with it. "Don't pull that crap with me. I want to know why Orion was arrested wearing one of your shirts. As your best friend, I have every right to this insider knowledge."

"I might have given him it instead of his own shirt."

She grinned then shook her head. "How very devious of you. I'm so proud. But why were you there when he was getting dressed, hm?"

With a sigh, I slumped on the couch, tilting my head back to look at the rafters above me. Admitting it out loud made everything feel very real, opposite of how I'd tricked my mind into remembering that night. "It was after we hate-fucked." Nimue gasped dramatically, but we both knew she'd already guessed as much. "And before you say anything, *no*, it's never happening again."

"Okay, well," Nimue said, pausing so long I tilted my head to side-eye her. "How was it? I've always wondered if he's that uptight behind closed doors or if he's a total freak, hidden beneath all those button downs. He seems like the type that might have a sex dungeon. But, then again, so do you, and I've never seen one around here so maybe I'm wrong."

I couldn't help but chuckle. "Just a gym dungeon. So far."

Nimue waved a hand. "You're still renovating. There's time. Back to the deets."

I bit my lip, for the first time ever debating how much, if anything, I should share with my best friend. Hell, I didn't even know how I felt about the whole thing. Maybe I'd be better off if I just pretended nothing ever happened between Orion and I. But it had, and I kept sniffing that damn shirt every time I opened my drawer. I wanted to forget. I *needed* to forget. But... I couldn't.

"He's just as much a condescending control freak in bed, I can tell you that," I said before I'd even made up my mind to say anything. My heart raced at the memory, clenching in a way I didn't approve of.

"So it was bad?" Nimue scrunched her nose, and I could have reached across the couch to boop it, she looked so cute. How had we ever become friends, her and I? Maybe opposites *did* attract.

With a frustrated sigh, I said, "He's impossible. Demanding. Domineering. Contradictory at the strangest times — it makes him so unpredictable. And Nims — he has *tattoos*. What the hell?"

"Oh," Nimue laughed. "You liked it. I get it now."

"No!" But she was still laughing and it spiked my anger, a flush rising to my cheeks. Not because she was laughing at me, but because dammit, maybe I had liked it. Just a little. "You don't get it. I mean, the *sex* was — it was — but, it doesn't matter, because the *male*?" I coughed. "Forget it, you know?"

Nimue grinned. "Wow. You're all flustered. I don't think I've ever seen you flustered over a male before."

"I'm not flustered. I'm annoyed. And anyways, it doesn't matter. He's gone."

"Uh huh," Nimue laughed again and I smacked her with the pillow to shut her up. She snatched it from my hands and launched it across the room, far out of reach. "You have feelings for him, don't you?"

"I don't have feelings. Period." Nimue was probably too in love with her husband to remember that some of us could separate sex from feelings. Because I definitely did *not* have feelings for Orion, unless loathing counted as a feeling. Anything else was purely physical, and now, it was in the past.

"Okay," Nimue said as she stood, stretching her arms above her head before she circled the couch. She stopped behind me, lacing her arms around my neck and pulled me tight, planting a kiss on my cheek. "I know you love me. That counts as feelings."

I squeezed her forearm around my neck, leaning my head into hers. "Just the one."

She laughed again, but let go as she moved towards the door. "I love you too, Devvie."

I smiled, my heart feeling lighter than it had in weeks at my best friend's words. "I know you do."

The door clicked behind her as she left and I looked around my house, the space large and empty without my friends here. But I liked being alone. I'd always been alone. Why did I suddenly *feel* lonely?

I flicked a hand in the air, turning the lights off throughout the house as I moved to my bedroom and pulled open the top drawer. Instead of lifting it to my nose as I'd done a dozen times, I pulled my own clothes off and slid Orion's shirt over my head, crawling into bed.

Chapter Twenty-One

ORION

I LOST count of what day it was, of how long I'd been here. In the beginning, I counted days by the meals that showed up, the kitchen clearing momentarily of clutter whether I'd cleaned it or not. Apparently, even angel hell had standards when it came to food. They wanted to torture me, not *kill* me with salmonella. At least, I hoped.

Somewhere after day nine or maybe ten, I stopped keeping track. I gave up on endlessly cleaning, letting the magical clutter pile up everywhere. No matter how many times I tidied the space, it was back the next time I entered the room. So I sat, staring at the TV with no remote, focusing on my breathing. Ignoring the way my skin itched.

With nothing to occupy my time, I'd turned over every possible outcome in my mind several thousand times.

Best case scenario: re-credentialing, which could take anywhere from three months to ten years, depending on how vindictive the Council was feeling at the time of sentencing, and then they'd give me my Mayorship back.

The worst case scenario made bile rise in my throat. I'd

never set foot on Earth again, and be deemed unworthy of representing our species to the other supernaturals and humans.

And *shit*, I wanted to get back to Earth. It was all I'd ever wanted, all I'd worked for for centuries.

When I was a youth, I had posters of human meals, human movies, and human architecture up in my room. I had a book of the 10 Man-Made Wonders of the World and practically memorized it — in awe of the things humans could do, even without magic. I knew from the moment I entered training that I wanted to be assigned to Earth in some capacity — in *any* capacity. I'd finally attained my dream, leading a town of supernaturals, and I'd tried my absolute best to run it according to Council standards.

After spending the last few weeks in the Council's equivalent of Angel Hell, the very real possibility was settling in that I might never see it again. The damn khaki shorts and boat shoes I still wore proved how bad I'd become at following their many rules.

I pinched the bridge of my nose, tension coiling between my eyes, and tilted my head back. It was impossible to get comfortable on this furniture with my wings, no matter how I shifted them.

They couldn't break me like this. I'd lived in Deadlights Cove for almost 30 years. I'd witnessed goats destroying the gazebo, elderly nudity far more often than any one person should be subject to — I'd lived with Sabazios fucking Rosewood. I could survive this, too.

As if sensing my new resolve, the TV flicked on, static filling the screen until the sound of laughter started, then a picture appeared.

I tilted my head, confused by the *Friends* episode. While it wasn't my favorite show, this didn't feel like torture. Leaning forward, my elbows rested on my knees until I jerked upright.

Janice.

Oh God, that laugh. My body convulsed as I pushed to my feet, moving to the far side of the studio. I cleared trash from the floor, making a path to the bed as I threw myself down on the mattress. It was miserably uncomfortable, but anything was better than listening to Janice on repeat. I smashed my singular pillow down over my head, but the TV volume went up, refusing to be drowned out by cotton.

For the first time, doubt crept into me. I wasn't sure how much more of this I could take.

Little did I know, it was about to get a whole lot worse.

A dissonant clang sounded, something I hadn't heard before in my time here, and I lifted my head off the lumpy mattress a moment before the exterior door to my studio opened.

"Well, I don't know why I'm surprised to see that this is what it has come to with you, Orion. This is what you get for cavorting with that half-breed demon you insist is a 'friend.'"

I lurched to my feet as *my mother* swept into the room, eyeing the trash around me in distaste. Her pristine white wings shimmered, each feather perfectly coated in an opalescent sheen I knew was all the trend with upper level angels. She tiptoed around a puddle of unidentifiable goo, crinkling her nose as she lifted the hem of her impeccable ballet-pink satin skirt.

"Mother." My pulse sky-rocketed as I staggered forward,

not even sure what to do first. Clean everything? Beg for forgiveness? Ask what the hell she was even doing here? "How — why — "

"Close your mouth if you're done stuttering, and try again when you've made up your mind." With a graceful sweep of her thin, pale arm, the trash in the room disappeared, and she perched on the edge of a clean wooden seat she conjured from nowhere. "Do you have any idea what this" — she gestured vaguely to the state of my life — "has done to us? Your father and I? Imagine our humiliation when we were informed the Moretti's second son had been moved to Omega." She pulled out a silk handkerchief, blotting her face.

"Is he coming too?" I cast a worried eye towards the door.

"Oh, please, Orion. You know your father's constitution could never bear this place. Your brother has been consoling him around the clock since we heard the news, only stopping to attend to his many important duties."

I pursed my lips, knowing it would come to this sooner or later. Ezra, my brother, the perfect son. The one who had risen through the ranks to become one of the pre-eminent angels in our world, second only to the Premier himself. The son who had correctly taken no interest in humans, in Earth, in anything so lowly as all that. Unlike me.

"Now, I've read your file, of course — Ezra was able to acquire it for me easily, what with all his connections — and I'm afraid there's very little any of us can do." She gave me a pointed look which very strongly implied all of this, as usual, was my fault. As if she would even try to get me out of this, which I knew, given my dear brother's position, would have been easy for her to do if she wanted to. She gave an exaggerated sigh. "Why you *insist* on throwing your life away with those humans and mortals is beyond me. Where did we go wrong, Orion? What drove you to this madness? Your brother never harbored any of these… urges."

I counted backwards from ten to stop myself from saying something I'd regret. I wished I could say her attitude was uncommon among angels, but that would be a lie. Most angels viewed humans as worthless at best, pests at worst, and most other supernaturals weren't viewed much better. Shifters and witches, as "mortals," were often seen as lesser, since their powers were severely limited by comparison and barely marked them as worth being considered supernaturals at all. Demons were the only real competition, in most angels' eyes, since their powers were nearly on par with our own. But, of course, with their incessant need to balk rules and general refusal to adhere to most institutionalized policy, they were typically reviled.

Where had she and my father gone wrong? Where had they gone *right* would have been an easier question to answer: nowhere. For the most part, they'd left me to my own devices, focusing their attention, money, tutors, and affection on my older brother. I had tutors and nannies as well, of course, but most of my free time had been spent in libraries, reading, while Ezra was pampered and networked with other future leaders of our world.

So I read. And I learned about Earth, and all its fascinating history.

But I knew my mother didn't want to hear about all of that, that she didn't really care.

"Is there a reason you came to visit me, Mother?" I tried to keep the exasperation out of my tone, but I didn't quite succeed, judging by the hurt expression that flashed across her face. Another carefully curated mask.

"Can't a mother visit her son — who hasn't come home to visit in 25 years — when he's placed in holding on Omega?" She placed a hand over the empty chasm where her heart would be, if she had one, before she dropped the act. "Though, now that you mention it, there is something."

I pressed my eyes closed, then nodded as I reopened them.

"This whole business is hurting your brother's career. You've tarnished the Moretti family name." I highly doubted that, but I silenced my scoff. "So if you could make an announcement on Aethergram that this defiant behavior was all of your own accord, or maybe due to some temporary insanity, and that you fully intend to make amends to the Council, whatever it takes, with a personal apology to your brother, that would be best."

I leveled a stare at her. "Aethergram? You think I have access to —"

She pulled a phone — *my* phone — out of her slim, white leather clutch. "I have temporary approval for you to use this to post a single announcement, then I have to turn it back in."

I sighed as she slid the phone over to me. Why didn't she just do this herself, since clearly getting into my phone would be easy work for someone with her power?

This was why. She wanted me to have to press *Share*. She wanted me to be the one to post these words, even if she'd no doubt already drafted what she wanted me to say verbatim. She wanted me to feel this deep-seated humiliation.

I swiped open my phone, not at all surprised to see that everything except Aethergram had been blocked. Since no one I cared about was on Aethergram, which was an angel-only social media platform, I wasn't worried about anyone back home seeing this.

But it still stung as I typed out my mother's dictation, just as she intended.

As I hit *Share*, I was certain that Ezra had purposefully orchestrated her visit, just to add that certain extra flair to angel hell for me.

Thanks again, brother.

Chapter Twenty-Two

DEVANNA

I SAT on my favorite barstool in Scallywags three weeks after Orion had been removed from office, listening to the raucous conversations that filled the bar. The threat of Nergal and Errakal still hung over us, but until they showed their hand, there wasn't much we could do but carry on with our lives. Tonight, everyone was light and happy, still reliving the utter chaos we'd caused to drive Pascar out of town yesterday, embracing the feeling of success and distraction it afforded us.

"The look on Pascar's face when she saw Belphie?" Val said, mimicking her scream like Kevin from *Home Alone* before he slapped his hand down on the counter with a laugh. "That was a stroke of genius. Belphie is *hideous*."

"Don't let Endymion hear you talking about his baby that way," Blaze chuckled. "His attachment to that creature is almost as intense as your love for Edward Cullen."

"Love blinds you, I suppose," Caedmon said with a sigh. "I still don't understand why Bella looked twice at Edward

Cullen when Jacob was *right there*, growling and flinging his luscious hair around."

"You're aware of how completely toxic those relationships were, right?" I said, unable to contain my opinion on *Twilight* a second longer. "And don't get me started on the vampire c-section. That was the dumbest thing I've ever seen in my life, and I've lived *here* for most of it. I've seen a lot of dumb shit."

Val and Caedmon gasped in unison, moving away from me with hurt expressions, but someone needed to say it. Now that I knew they were vampires — something I still had approximately ten thousand questions about — I understood their obsession, but I never understood why everyone glamorized that series.

"Your claws are showing," Blaze murmured, wiping down the counter. "That was mean, even for you."

"Should I hiss at you then? Give you the whole picture of an angry cat?"

"Fine, just be a Devvie Downer today," Blaze said as Morgaine dropped into the seat next to me. I eyed her, but didn't say anything. While she'd always taken care of me when I needed it growing up, Nimue's mom and I weren't the closest. Mo loved to overstep, meddling in our lives when she thought we needed a good shove in the right direction, and there was nothing I hated more than someone trying to manipulate me, whatever their intentions.

"Dark and Stormy, dear," Mo said, smiling brightly at Blaze. "And make it special for me. You know how I like it."

By that, she meant damn-near deadly for anyone but her.

The elderly-yet-ageless witch had raised both Blaze and Nimue, which made more sense after discovering the witch was from the original Coven of witches that Linked with a demon. I was willing to bet Mo had inherited more than a drop of demon blood, encouraging her many mischievous ways.

"What is it you want to say?" I asked after she sat quietly for a minute, smiling at the other patrons.

"Me?" Mo blinked wide eyes behind her enormous turquoise glasses, the picture of innocence. "What ever could you mean? I can't join in on the fun in town?"

I didn't buy it. Not even a little. "You sat next to me, and you never do anything unintentionally."

Mo chuckled, sipping at the drink Blaze passed to her. "I always find your blunt words refreshing, Devanna," she said, shocking me with the compliment after I'd just been scolded for them moments before. "No one ever has to wonder how you feel. If you don't say it with your words, your face says it for you."

"Thanks, I think."

She patted my hand on the bar, fingers circling my wrist gently before I yanked my hand free of hers. "You're welcome, dear."

Turning her attention to Blaze, she asked, "Has anyone heard anything about the mayoral position yet? Or if Orion has had his sentencing?"

"Not that I know of." Blaze shrugged, his mouth a grim line. How the two males had become friends, I still didn't understand. Blaze and Orion were polar opposites.

"After the chaos we caused, I can't help but be a little concerned about what might come next. After Pascar's attitude towards us, I'm starting to wonder if our stickler Orion wasn't half-bad."

"I saw on Aethergram he's been taken down to Omega," Zaphiel said from a table behind me. I swiveled around to see him shudder, the white feathers in his unglamoured wings shivering with the motion.

"Oh dear," Mo said, sipping at her drink casually, as if I couldn't see the giant wooden spoon in her hand, stirring the metaphorical pot.

Blaze scrubbed a hand through his dark hair with an exhale. "That bad? Shit."

"Yeah," Zaph said.

"What's Omega?" Maybe I was part cat — curiosity got the best of me.

"The farthest an angel can fall from grace before the Iron Keep. No one knows for sure." Zaphiel dropped his voice to a whisper as he moved to the bar, leaning on the counter. "It's rumored to be a correctional facility for angels."

"Correctional facility?" Blaze scrunched his nose in confusion. "Unless they're removing the sticks up every angel's ass, what are they *correcting?*"

"I don't know," Zaph said, tucking his wings tight behind him, maybe to stop them from shaking. "No one who comes back from Omega talks about what happens down there. It's not only the end of your career, but some angels go insane."

Some unknown emotion stirred in me, and I didn't like it. "Orion's been gone for three weeks."

"Yeah," Zaph nodded. "He's probably lost it by now, if his last post is anything to go by."

I reared back. "Post?"

"Yeah. He posted on Aethergram a few days ago."

All of us stared at him until he sighed and pulled his phone out.

"Aethergram is angel social media," he explained as he swiped through his phone, then set it on the counter and flipped it around for us to look. "Going to warn you — it's not great."

Blaze, Mo, and I leaned forward to look at the screen. It looked like a typical social media platform, and my gaze zeroed in on Orion's post.

It is with deep regret and shame I share today that I, former Mayor of Deadlights Cove, Maine, am currently awaiting trial for several infractions. My actions were my own mistakes, and should not reflect on my family, who were not involved. Perhaps if I had listened to their advice earlier, I would not be in this disgraceful position. I can only hope they forgive me in the future and perhaps, after making amends, give me a second chance, though I do not deserve it. Until then, I will accept any sentence the Council sees fit. - Officer Orion, Former Mayor

My blood pressure rose with every word I read, my face heating with rage. "But he didn't do anything wrong," I barked. The last thing I wanted was to be sympathetic to the mayor, but nobody deserved to be punished like this when most of the things they'd accused him of were out of his control. And what was all this about his family? He'd never mentioned anyone in all the time I'd known him, as far as I knew.

"That's up to the Council to decide," Zaphiel said with a shrug, returning to his table. "Orion knew what he was getting himself into when he didn't follow the exact letter of the law."

"That's bullshit," I spat, pushing back from the counter and dropping to my feet.

"Terrible," Mo agreed. "It's too bad we can't do anything about it. Sounds like the male might need to be rescued. But breaking into Headquarters is an almost impossible task. It's too risky, too difficult. Maybe Blaze could have done it, but now with Petra here, he can't risk the consequences of being caught. Of being imprisoned himself."

Blaze opened his mouth to answer, but Mo patted him on the cheek, sliding her hand over his mouth as I clenched my fists at my side, anger coursing through me.

Who the hell had said angels could rule our lives like this? Who had given them the power to decide our fates without knowing the full picture? To hold us for weeks before we'd had a fair trial?

This was unfair, an injustice, and it couldn't go on, no matter who it was that was being punished.

I didn't care about Orion, not in the least. It wasn't about him. I'd be this outraged for anyone in a position like this.

"I'll do it."

"Oh," Mo said, clapping her hands together over her heart. "How brave of you."

"You can't—" Zaph started until I walked up to him, grabbed him by the joint in his wing the same moment I flicked open my switchblade, and pressed the tip into the base of his first primary feather. He hissed and shifted back, which only made my knife cut a shallow slice down the quill, and he glared down at me.

Angels and their feathers. They made themselves such easy targets being so precious about them.

"I wouldn't finish that sentence if you'd like to keep these. Don't tell me what I can and can't do."

Zaph nodded slightly, and I flipped my blade off his wing, letting him take a step back.

"Tell me everything I need to know about Headquarters."

Blaze followed me out of the bar a half-hour later, a tentative plan forming in my mind.

"So, what's your angle?" he said, jogging to catch up with me. Blaze was well over a head taller than me, but I didn't have any time to waste. "Bust in, guns blazing? Show those seagulls who's *really* boss? Light up HQ like the Fourth of July, and blow a hole in their realm as you leave? Maybe have a bomb go off in the shape of a giant middle finger as your parting gift?"

I scoffed. "No, to literally all of that."

The bright smile on his face fell, turning into a look of exasperation. "Well, this is much less exciting then. I can't lie — I'm pretty bummed to miss out on the show."

"No show." I shook my head as I wrenched open my front door. "In and out, as quickly as I can. That's the plan."

"And you're doing this because?" Blaze crossed his arms, one eyebrow lifted as he studied me. "I saw what he was wearing, Devvie. I know what you did this summer."

"You know nothing," I snapped as I flicked on the lights

in the living room. The front door opened and closed behind us, and I tipped my head back, teeth clenched as I stared at the ceiling. "Does *no one* knock in this town?"

"Considering I'm saving your ass, I could do without the attitude," Ryker's deep voice cut through the air. Now, him, I was actually glad to see.

Even in my spacious living room, Ryker was still a giant in his human form, an ancient Viking come back to life — or, more accurately, still alive. His blond hair was tied back in a messy knot as usual, the sides shaved close to his scalp, tattoos covering nearly every inch of skin his fitted black shirt and jeans left exposed. His bright green eyes maybe had a slightly more feral gleam than usual, actually, but knowing about Selene's condition, I didn't blame him. He effortlessly swung a huge black duffle bag onto my coffee table with an audible *thunk*.

Blaze and I hurried over to inspect the bag. "Tell me you brought fun things for me to play with and you'll be my third favorite dragon in the world."

"Third?" Blaze asked absently, and I met Ryker's sharp glare, fighting back a chuckle.

"I'm counting Selene twice because she's that special."

Blaze nodded like that made sense, and Ryker eased his searing gaze off me.

Yanking back the zipper, Ryker pulled free a large cylindrical canister Blaze and I eyed with excitement. Ryker was a supernatural bounty hunter and had more weapons than any one person should own in their lifetime, though who knew how many lifetimes he'd been accumulating them. I envied him just a smidge for his collection.

He pulled a large roll of paper out of the canister instead of the rocket launcher or bazooka I'd hoped for, and my shoulders slumped slightly. While Blaze's idea to go in, guns blazing, wasn't a smart one, I wouldn't mind ruffling a few feathers on my way in and out.

Ryker rolled the paper out across the coffee table and I leaned closer, studying the blueprints. "I'm going to take a wild guess and say the angels aren't aware you have this."

The dragon shifter grunted, which was his general sound that could mean anything from *yes* to *fuck you*, but in this instance, I took it for agreement.

His large, tattooed finger trailed across the page, settling on several points. "This is how you get in," he said, pointing at a section labeled *Lobby*.

"Right through the front door, I like it." Blaze rubbed his hands together, sparks skittering over them as a wide grin took over his face. "Then we shoot 'em up?"

"Zaphiel is going to handcuff you," Ryker said, ignoring Blaze completely. "The angels are such sticklers for the rules, the thought of someone attempting to break and enter into their facility hasn't even occurred to them. Their defenses are an utter joke once you're inside, but getting there is the difficult part. The only way in and out of their realm is with an angel. Zaph is your way in."

"Will he do it?" Blaze asked. "He's not the brightest of angels, but he's still an angel."

"You leave that part to me." I waved him off, pointing back at the papers. "Show me how to get to Omega."

Ryker outlined our path for me, showing me how to get to where they were rumored to be holding Orion, explaining that the Lobby was the only place angels could enter and exit Headquarters. That would be the hardest part — getting back to the Lobby after freeing Orion.

I sat back in my chair, thinking through my plan of attack. While I'd never done anything like this before, I'd never backed down from a challenge, and I wasn't about to start now.

"Now, the question is, how are you getting out if this doesn't work?" Ryker said, his head tilted to the side as he studied me. "Zaphiel is going to duck out the moment he can, and only angels can get you back out."

"Easy," I said, a smug smile taking over my face. "It's going to work, then Orion is going to get us home and owe me a lifetime of favors for saving his sorry ass."

That was all there was to it. I refused to fail, at this or anything.

"Have you seen any sign of Nergal or Kal out there?" Blaze asked, switching gears from my suicide mission and flopping onto the couch. "We've been trying to figure out why he showed up to give us his villain speech and then just vamoosed."

Ryker took a seat in one of my purple velvet armchairs and kicked a boot up on the coffee table. "I don't know if you've ever met someone who's been in the Iron Keep before, but it's not a vacation. He hasn't had access to his magic in the seven years he's been in there, and that takes its toll, even to a demon as powerful as he is. From what I've heard of his stunt here at the Lighthouse, he probably drained himself. My guess is he's holed up somewhere, biding his time until his power replenishes fully."

"What about Kal?" I asked. Sitting and waiting for impending doom wasn't my forte.

"He's been in and out of Vegas," Ryker answered with a flat stare in Blaze's direction who cringed in response. "I talked to a few buddies who have been trailing him, but he's gone by the time anyone goes to apprehend him again."

"That can't be good."

"What's so bad about Vegas?"

"Vegas is like Demon Disney World," Blaze said. "Inhibitions low, urges high, no rain. There's a huge community out there."

"And Kal and his cronies are done being subtle," Ryker continued. "The PRICs and their affiliates — like me — have had our hands full trying to keep humans safe and in the dark about their presence. Any idea what he's after here in Deadlights Cove?"

"No, and Mo is being cagey about it," Blaze answered. I pulled my lips into my mouth, trying to stay quiet even as rage boiled in me for what Nergal had planned for Blaze. "I've been scouring my house for anything my mother left behind after she died for more information on him, but I can't pinpoint anything helpful or with any sort of magical signature."

"We need to talk to Morgaine," Ryker said, crossing his arms over his thick chest, black tee stretching across his muscles. "I'll take over our defenses now that I'm here in town, but I need to know what it is they're hiding."

"Divide and conquer," I said with a nod. "You work on Demon Daddy Defenses and I'll get the prickly sonofabitch back for us."

"I'm a little surprised you're willing to help him," Ryker said, a smirk playing on his lips.

"Oh, haven't you heard? Orion was arrested wearing —"

I launched a throw pillow at him, hitting Blaze square in the face as he chuckled. "No time for stories. Let's get to work."

Chapter Twenty-Three

DEVANNA

MY FEET SLAMMED down on the white tiles of PRIC Headquarters as my vision swam, stomach churning wildly. "Holy hell," I said, nearly doubling over since I couldn't grip my stomach with my hands cuffed together behind my back. Not a comfortable sensation on its own — at least, not in public — but especially so after the mind-bending sensation of inter-dimensional travel it took to reach the angel realm. It was at least twenty times worse than demon flickering.

"Can I help you?" a woman's voice said from our right, and I straightened, hoping if I was going to vomit I could aim it at the angel walking our way.

"Associate Zaphiel Leoni," the angel gripping my arm said, his voice shaking only slightly as he said the words we'd recited multiple times. "Bringing in Devanna Bailey, Witch of the Deadlights Cove Coven lead by Ostara Theroux. With 102 infractions filed against her, Ms. Bailey is due for a trial in front of the Council."

The tall female angel, her silver hair pulled into a severe

bun at the top of her head, studied the tablet in her hand, tapping rapidly before looking back up at us. "I don't have her name on file for a trial, but you're correct. She should have been on the register. Take her to a holding cell to await. Floor Kappa."

Zaphiel shoved me forward, under the giant unironic *Lobby* sign. "Ow." I glared at him.

"Sorry," he whispered, hand trembling as he gripped my arm again. "I've never done anything like this before. Trying not to piss myself."

"Wouldn't want that, Zaphiel *Leoni*," I said, barely holding in a smirk. "How did I not know your last name? Is that an angel thing?" Zaph eyed me, but said nothing. "Wait. What's Orion's last name? Do you all sound like you're part of the Italian mafia?"

Zaph avoided eye contact as he pushed me down a long hallway and into an atrium, muttering, "I'm not at liberty to say."

A domed ceiling arched overhead, showing several levels of what looked to be a large office building. Angels flew from one floor to the next, landing on platforms as they carried about their business. As Ryker had predicted, not one person stopped us, which was a damn shame. I was ready to use the gear I'd brought with‹ me all conveniently located in the fanny pack Zaphiel had slung over his shoulders, which no one bothered to check either. This was a joke.

"There's never been an angel who went rogue, ready to light this place up?" I whispered, eyeing the pristine white walls, the boring as shit grey decor, and the stuffy wardrobe on every single angel here. "How do you all not go utterly insane?"

"Never," Zaph said, shoving me towards an elevator hidden in the wall. "Well, not never, I guess. There was this one angel, but nobody talks about him, ever. Now, please stop talking to me. I highly doubt most angels are this chatty with their captives. My skin is itching from this much deceit, and I need to get out of here before they realize I was part of your plan."

"Not to worry," I said. "If I'm caught and they put me in one of those truth bubbles you angels love so much, I can answer confidently and truthfully that I forced you into this, and you had no choice. Once they hear I threatened to saw off your wings with a blunt blade, no one will judge you."

"Somehow that doesn't make me feel any better about this."

The elevator doors slid open, letting us in. Greek letters were written on the panel and Zaph leaned forward, hitting the Kappa button.

"Stick with the plan," I reassured him as the doors slid closed. I scanned the ceiling for hidden cameras or anything of the sort, but couldn't spot any. With a heavenly *ding*, the doors slid open and a long, empty hallway stretched before us. Now or never.

I wasted no time, throwing my weight into Zaph until he crashed to the ground. I slipped my hands free, thankful he hadn't tightened the cuffs, and gripped his throat, cutting off his air supply. His body slumped sooner than it should have, but the male had been more than a little nervous leading up to this point. I wasn't sure whether he was faking it or had simply passed out from distress, but I grabbed his limp hand, raising it to the panel as I pushed the Omega button. The doors slid closed once more.

"Thanks, buddy."

He didn't open his eyes, but I didn't miss when his left hand moved, a tiny thumbs up.

The elevator dropped quickly as I yanked my pack from Zaph's shoulders, slinging it over my own. The doors slid open again, and I tiptoed out into the empty hallway, eyes peeled for angels.

Ryker hadn't been able to confirm if there were hidden cameras, but I knew time was of the essence. We needed to get out of here as quickly as possible. Moving into a jog, I ran past rooms, listening to the muffled screams and cries of distress coming from within. What the hell were these angels doing to their own kind?

Pulling a feather loose from my pack, I crushed it in my hand, willing my power to lead me to a door farther down the hallway. I paused in front of one when a frisson of static resonated within my power, listening to the silence from within. My magic had never steered me wrong, so hopefully it didn't this time either. Pulling tools from my pack I'd spelled to the likes of Mary Poppins' carpet bag, I got to work, magic-infused crow bar yanking on the metal as it began to separate from the wall.

"Stupid angels with their ultra white modern decor —"

Pushing my magic into the tools, the door gave way, swinging open to reveal a cramped studio apartment. The stench of rotting food and stale trash hit me as Orion blinked at my abrupt entrance where he sat on a small couch, surrounded by trash littering the floor.

I scowled back. While I was sure my sudden appearance

was a shock, the fact that he sat there dumbstruck annoyed me, as did everything the male did. Why was I rescuing him again?

"Well, you're welcome."

Chapter Twenty-Four

ORION

I TAPPED my fingers against my leg, a nervous habit I was usually better at repressing, and wished I hadn't stopped tracking the passage of time. Usually, I would have my atomic watch, but considering my state of dress when Ezra had arrested me, I didn't have it with me.

Trash had continued to build up since my mother's thoughtful visit, but I'd stopped caring about cleaning it up. It would only come back.

Suddenly, a new sound reached my ears, and I frowned. Except for my mother, no one had come to visit or even inform me when my hearing would be held. Even when she had visited, she'd just magicked the door open.

This sounded like someone trying to claw their way through the metal.

With an ear-splitting screech, the door finally gave way, and to my complete astonishment, Devanna crashed into my cell.

For a long minute, I could only blink at her, too stunned to speak. What the hell was she doing here?

She scowled back at me, and swung her crowbar over her shoulder. "Well, you're welcome."

"What are you doing here?"

"Saving your sorry ass," Dev said as she slipped the crowbar back into the small bag around her shoulders, nowhere near large enough to hold the tool.

I shook my head, sure this was one of the Council's next forms of torture, but even as I blinked, Devanna stood there, hands on her hips, staring back.

"Can we hurry? No thanks to you, the Cove is even more of a shit show than when you were in charge and Nergal is probably coming back any day now. You know they put *Pascar* in as mayor?" She made a gagging sound in the back of her throat. "But we took care of that bitch. She ran out of town faster than the Cullens ran bases playing baseball, never to return. Oh, my Goddess," she smacked herself on the forehead, "What have those two va— uh, old geezers done to me. I never should have agreed to that movie night." Devanna cleared her throat, and my brows lowered, trying to follow what she was saying. "Anyway — Blaze was in rare form."

I could only imagine what that meant. Deadlights Cove was not exactly tame on a good day, let alone when the townsfolk were *intentionally* causing chaos. Blaze may have liked to joke about being arrested by the PRICs, but he'd never done anything bad enough to earn serious time in jail. I had to hope he hadn't done anything too stupid this time, either.

"Devanna." I wasn't sure my brows could lower any further, and yet they did. "How did you even —"

"It's amazing what a few well-placed bribes—"

I pursed my lips.

"—Okay, *threats*, can get done these days. I told Zaph if he didn't bring me here, I'd pluck his feathers one at a time while he spun over hot coals like the chickenshit he is."

"I see. And where is Zaphiel now?"

"Long gone, probably." Devanna rolled her eyes, but I wasn't surprised by the news. Zaph hated Headquarters, and for good reason. Angels could have a bit of a *survival-of-the-fittest* mentality, and those with lower amounts of power were frequently the subjects of jokes. Not to mention he would face serious consequences for transporting an unapproved visitor.

I leaned forward, elbows on my knees, shifting my stiff wings again. "And your plan is…"

"Look, I hate this as much as you do." She gestured to my current predicament, hand waving over the dirty cell I'd been trapped in for weeks, which I very much doubted she hated as much as I did. "But the drama in Deadlights Cove is far from over, and after Pascar, I can't help but think you might be the least terrible option for our town. You and I both know the PRICs won't leave us alone without *any* angel, and frankly, you're the only one that seems remotely tolerable, even if you are still a giant pain in our asses 99% of the time."

"How flattering."

I received another glare for that.

"*So,* I'm here to bust your ass out of jail. Again, *you're welcome.*" She threw her hands up, turning to pace and muttering under her breath. "Goddess, do I have to do *everyone's* jobs for them?"

Before I had half a moment to process that, the door

moved again, and Ezra, the Chancellor of the Council and lead inquisitor, strode into the room, looking not at all surprised to find Devanna here with me.

"Funny," he said, not bothering with introductions as the door swung shut behind him, leaving the three of us locked in the small studio. "Intake paperwork shows you should be held on the Kappa floor, not here on Omega, Ms. Bailey. But," he glanced between us as a sinister smile spread over his face. "You know what? This is better. You will be confined to this room with Officer Orion until his hearing."

"Which will be when?" I asked.

"Currently, your hearing is 137th in line."

My heart dropped to my stomach. "A *hundred*—"

"Oh, no. Fuck that. I'm going to need to speak with your manager. *Premier!*" Dev shouted, banging on the white walls. "Don't think I won't be as obnoxious as possible for as long as it takes to get an answer. You can't even *imagine* the shit I'm capable of. Just ask Orion. I've been holding a grudge for ten years over the smallest, tiniest thing he probably doesn't even remember, and I've made his life *hell* ever since."

My mouth hung slightly ajar, shock coursing through me as I tried to recall what could have happened ten years ago to make her so angry, but Devanna barreled on through her tirade.

"Ezra, you little piece of shit, you're going to get us out of here, and back to Deadlights Cove. Now. We have a town to protect."

Ezra smirked, his eyes darting between me on the couch and Devanna pacing in front of me. From the look on his face, I could tell what was coming next, having been on the receiving end of Ezra's ire my whole life.

He made for the door. "How unfortunate. There's been a schedule change. You're now 742nd. Enjoy your stay."

With that, he swept out the door, slamming it shut behind him with an ominous clang before Devanna could wedge her crowbar in to stop it.

A laugh stuttered out of me without my permission, the sound bouncing off the walls. Once it started, I couldn't stop, my body shaking violently as I laughed, and laughed, and laughed.

"I see you're finally having that nervy B you've been edging for three months now," Devanna said as she dropped onto the couch to my left. "Goddess, I'm starting to sound like Blaze. Who says nervy B?"

I had no answer for her.

Never, not even in my wildest dreams, could I have guessed that I'd be sitting in a holding cell on Omega next to Devanna, the one female who hated me most, while I awaited my sentencing.

"This has to be the worst day of my life."

"You and me both, Lucifer. You and me both."

I pinched the bridge of my nose. "Please tell me you have a plan. Other than waiting for our hearing. I assume your razor-thin patience won't tolerate staying here that long."

"I'm not stupid, you know," Devanna said, her tone already argumentative. It was a talent of mine to be able to piss her off so quickly.

"I never said you were. In fact, I think you're one of the most gifted witches I've ever met."

She reared back, an incredulous sound coming from her throat before her eyes turned to slits. "But?"

"But nothing." I shook my head. "I didn't say friendliest or kindest. Those would have been lies."

She mumbled something under her breath, and pushed to her feet as she wandered around the room, kicking a crumpled soda can. "What's with all the trash? And really, *Friends*? I always pictured you more of a History Channel guy. You let yourself go this badly here?"

"It's magicked." I sighed. "Even if I clean up, it reappears within minutes. And while I don't hate *Friends*, no one likes Janice. It only plays the 19 episodes she's in on repeat."

As if on command, Janice's laugh boomed from the TV and Devanna shuddered. "Okay, that is cruel and unusual punishment, even for you. Good thing I have a Plan B."

She reached into the pack around her shoulders, which must have been bewitched Tardis-style, because the tool kit she pulled free shouldn't have fit inside it. She moved to the door, neck craning as she studied it. I always forgot how small Devanna was until I watched her from afar — her personality more than made up for her tiny stature.

Devanna was fierce as a hellcat; she could be your worst enemy or your best friend — I'd seen her as both towards many people in town. Her loyalty and protectiveness over Nimue, Selene, and Blaze — even Lysander and Petra now. How she'd had zero hesitation in going after Nergal at the Lighthouse or Ezra here.

And yet, she was here. For *me*. Somewhere in all those barbed insults she'd thrown at me for the past decade, was it possible she'd decided to include me in her sacred inner circle?

She came for me. The words were as shocking to me as they were to her. Never would I have imagined that *anyone* would come to rescue me. Imagined I mattered enough for anyone to care what my fate held. I'd made each of my decisions on my own, leading me to this very place I more than deserved to be, no matter how terrible it was.

And of all people, *she* was the one who'd come. With her Tardis fanny pack and a stadium-sized amount of confidence in herself and this ridiculous plan that she should *not* have been carrying, and yet, she was.

My mind immediately went back to the last time I'd seen her, the way she'd fit so perfectly with me. That night had been different than any other experience I'd ever had. I'd told myself it was just because of how much we loathed each other, how we'd had years of animosity to work out.

Had I been lying to myself?

For that one night, I'd been able to forget all my other responsibilities. I'd thought I was taking something for myself for once, but really, I'd given myself to her — and it had freed something in me I hadn't known had been trapped.

I couldn't stop myself as I rose to my feet, standing behind her. The heat of her body reached mine, and her light jasmine scent brought images of that night rushing back in a visceral shock. In an out-of-body experience, my hands circled her waist, resting on her hips as I pulled her back into me.

Her breath stuttered, hands stilling on the tools as she tilted her head back, eyes meeting mine.

"You came for me," I said, repeating to her the words that wouldn't stop echoing in my mind.

"Don't think this means I like you," she sniped back, but her heart raced as my hand glided across her neck, her pulse thundering beneath my fingertips as I pulled her hair to the side. Her next words were barely a whisper, her whole body holding stock still like a deer in the headlights. "I still hate you."

"I can tell," I said, feeling my lips tip up. I hadn't smiled in weeks, let alone much before I arrived in this hell, but the sight of a defiant Devanna standing before me, freeing me from this prison… I was lucky to have her on my side.

But Devanna wasn't some timid deer hiding in the forest, frozen in fear of being seen. No, she was a panther — waiting for the opportune moment to pounce.

She spun, putting her back to the door as she looked up at me, her finger tracking over the logo you could still faintly see even with the shirt inside-out. "I didn't know Ezra was waiting for you when I gave you this instead of your shirt."

I cocked a brow. "Is that an apology?"

"No." She shook her head, blue hair swishing around her shoulders. "Just a fact."

"Your timing was impeccable, I will say that." I shivered as her hand flattened on my chest, settling warmly over my beating heart. "Karma most certainly is a witch."

She smirked, malice sparkling in her dark brown eyes. "I found out an interesting bit of information from Zaph today."

"And what's that?"

"Zaphiel has a last name. Is the same true for you, Orion?"

I chuckled, the sound foreign to me as I let my eyes drift

away from hers, settling on the door frame above her head. "Wouldn't you like to know."

"Yes." Her fingers bent to scrape her nails across my skin, just the hint of a threat. I fought back a shiver at the touch, trying to focus on anything but the memory of her body wrapped around mine. "I would. It's the least you can do to repay me for saving your sorry ass."

"The last time I checked, you haven't saved me yet. Now you're stuck here too, so that plan didn't quite work, did it?"

Her nails dug into my skin, raking downwards against my chest until I seized her wrist. "I was working on it until you started humping me from behind like a horny dog."

A laugh rose out of me, shocking us both. "Clearly your memory is going, as you know exactly what me humping you from behind feels like. You came for me then too, didn't you, Devanna?"

Her scent changed, lust crackling in the air between us. My hand rested on the side of her neck, thumb tracing over her jaw as I leaned down, looming over her. Her lips parted slightly, tongue darting out to wet them, and I couldn't help but stare at her mouth. Hovering an inch from her, I whispered, "I thought you had a plan to get us out of here. Unless the idea of being trapped with me is making your mind wander to ways we could pass the time together."

She shoved hard at my chest, forcing me back several steps as she went back to working on the door. Muttering furiously — something that sounded remarkably like "As if," and "Worst mistake of my life", but it was half-hearted at best — she yanked a small screwdriver out of her bag, jamming it into the gap in the door.

"I don't think that's going to work." I shoved my hands

in my pockets to stop myself from reaching out for her again. I couldn't take my eyes off her, noticing the way her black tank top hugged her curves, her tight black leggings amplifying the ass that had featured in many of my dreams lately. Magic hummed in the air, and I jerked my gaze away from her back to see what she was doing. "You shouldn't have access to your magic within these walls."

"*I* don't have access to it, but Ryker was right — the PRIC's security is seriously lacking. They didn't even search Zaph when he sauntered in wearing my bag of tools, all spelled individually to contain my magic, even when I don't have access to it."

She wiggled a tool above her hand, and I noticed the crystal shimmering in its handle.

"Earning my title as the most gifted witch you know."

Already, I regretted the compliment I'd paid her, even if it was true. Desperation clawed at me as I watched her work, itching to take charge, but she needed to be the one to do this if the tools were spelled to work by her magic. I warred with myself, unsure if she could really get us out of here, and worried about what would happen if she did.

If I ran, I'd no longer be awaiting trial, pending a return to Earth. If I ran, I'd be a fugitive, and the Omega Level would seem like a beach vacation compared to what awaited me in the Iron Keep.

Just then, a loud pop sounded, and Devanna swung towards me, a dark smirk on her face.

"Hereby changing my name to Ethan Hunt. I just made this *Mission: Impossible* my bitch."

She sauntered out into the hall, glancing to the left and the right. Of course, there were no guards here since a breakout was unheard of for the exact reasons why I stood rooted in place, panic seizing me. No way could it be this easy.

She stretched out a hand for me, then furrowed her brow when I didn't rush towards her, ready to break free of this hell hole.

Devanna opened and closed her hand impatiently as sweat beaded on my brow. It was one thing to flaunt the Code by not reporting the many instances the residents of Deadlights Cove broke laws like they were going out of style. It was another thing to break it so openly, running from the fate awaiting me.

But my town needed me, and I couldn't help them fight Nergal from here. Their safety was more important than the rules.

Devanna stomped, her eyes wide as she waited another moment, then sighed heavily, moving towards me and grabbing my hand. She dragged me out into the hall, our powers zapping back into our skin across the threshold.

The moment my foot stepped out of the cell and into the hall, the lights went out, red flashing alarms casting over the darkness in the hallway as a loud siren wailed. My heart leapt in shock, looking back at the door behind me, but it had already swung closed.

What had I done?

Chapter Twenty-Five

DEVANNA

"WELL, THAT DOESN'T SOUND GOOD," I said as I grabbed Orion's hand and dragged him down the hall towards the elevator. Panic threatened to climb up my throat, but I banished it, determined to see this plan through. "We need to get up to the Lobby so you can get us out of here."

My arm jerked backwards when Orion stopped when we were several feet from the doors, his substantial size acting like an anchor weighing me down. "I can't go with you. I can't put you at risk. I need to go back to my cell."

I laughed, the sound crazed as I planted my feet, hands on my hips. "Listen, Lucifer," I spat, anger rising in me quickly that I'd come all this way and he wanted to go *back*. "I get that you're a goody-two-shoes and you think you're a big deal. But this whole alarm system, blackout lights thing tells me this isn't about your little jailbreak. Even *you* can't think you're that important."

When he didn't argue back, I shook my head. "My mistake. Your ego knows no bounds."

Orion opened his mouth to retort, but the elevator doors slid open to reveal Malachi, the Premier leader of the PRICs. I'd never met the male, but I'd seen his picture splashed on supe news plenty in recent years. Unlike most angels, Malachi's wings and hair were a shade darker, the white-and-grey ombre peppered with darker shades. His steely eyes landed on Orion, who was practically wheezing in his effort to breathe normally behind me.

Orion cleared his throat, inexplicably putting an arm out in front of me, almost as though to shield me, but that was a stupid thought. "Premier —"

"Get out of here before I shut all entry into and out of Headquarters down," Malachi said, shocking the shit out of both of us.

Orion's arm dropped as he recovered faster than I did. "What's happening, sir?"

"Seraphina was framed," Malachi said, placing his hands on the door to our right. "It wasn't her that let the prisoners out of the Iron Keep."

I didn't know who Seraphina was, but the news shocked Orion. Before I had time to ask, a stumbling, bedraggled angel I didn't recognize launched free of the cell Malachi had opened, his wings a charcoal grey so dark, they were nearly black. I looked him over in surprise as I realized this was the first angel I'd ever seen with anything other than silver hair — his shaggy hair was as dark as his wings. The angel straightened up when he saw Malachi, his sapphire blue eyes — another odd color for an angel — closing off as they met Malachi's more typical grey. I looked between the two males, noticing they bore a similar shape to their tense jaws, though Malachi looked a few decades older.

"Massimo," Malachi said, almost reaching out to him before stopping himself. He dropped his hand, shooting a glance at us before returning to the dark angel, Massimo, and clearing his throat. "We've been betrayed. I need you to —"

Massimo met Malachi's eyes with a dark, heavy look, then ran a hand through his hair and stepped out of his cell. A crackle of electricity indicated his magic returning, and after he shook himself out, closing his eyes for a breath, he straightened up again. In the blink of an eye, his entire posture changed, transforming him into a different person. With a sinister grin, he gave Malachi a mocking salute, and took off towards the elevators.

Malachi moved on without a backwards glance, heading for another cell, so I turned back to Orion.

"Don't make me slap you again," I said, standing toe to toe with him. My words snapped him out of his stupor, his jaw ticking. "Get me out of here, Orion."

"Who framed her?" Orion called out to Malachi, grabbing my hand possessively. Just as Orion placed his hand on the wall to call the elevator for us, an explosion rocked the floor. I fell, catching my balance on the wall as Orion's body covered me completely, shielding me from the fire and debris raining down in the hallway. My ears rang from the noise as I blinked rapidly to clear my vision.

Malachi stood in the middle of the hallway as flames spread behind him down the hall. Twelve doors down from where we stood, a hole was blown in the wall. Twelve doors down, where Orion and I had been only minutes before.

"Your brother," Malachi said. Orion's jaw slacked in shock. "Ezra's been working with Nergal all along."

The elevator opened, and Malachi shoved us into the car with the other angel, Massimo. "Go. Get out of here. I don't know what they're planning on Earth, but you have to stop him, Orion."

Orion's jaw ticked, but he nodded, and the doors slid shut behind us.

"Brother?" I sounded more than a little incredulous, but I kept my voice low in front of the unknown angel. After what Zaph had said about Omega Level driving angels insane, I didn't know if one wrong move would send him into a meltdown. "Since when do you have a brother? I suddenly feel like I know nothing about you."

He didn't answer me, focusing on Massimo. "Max, once we get to the lobby, get to Timber Creek and make sure none of Nergal's demons are trying to use the wellspring again."

Massimo, or Max, nodded, his gaze raking over me curiously, though he didn't ask what a witch was doing here. The doors slid open, revealing the hallway leading to the lobby. Angels flew through the atrium, lightning crackling and pieces of stone cracking off the walls as they battled in mid-air.

I threw my arm over my head, crouching as Orion tugged me through the space and to the lobby. "What's going on?"

"Ezra must be leading a coup," Orion answered as he stopped and picked me up, launching into the air. I tried to muffle my startled screech into a cough, but the slight twitch at the corner of Orion's lips made it clear I hadn't quite succeeded. My arms circled his neck as he flew low to the ground at a breakneck speed. "He's had a chip on his shoulder his whole life, though hell if I know why he'd want to side with Nergal. He's even more anal-retentive about following the Code than the Premier himself."

"Are you saying *you're* the fun brother?"

Orion grunted an acknowledgment as he touched down inside the Lobby, and immediately, we vanished.

Inter-dimensional travel once in a day was bad enough, but twice? Hand over my mouth, I braced the other on a wall, eyes squeezed shut tight as I focused on slowly inhaling and exhaling, willing the world to stop spinning and my stomach to settle.

A gentle trickle of coolness started at the back of my neck, and the overwhelming vertigo and nausea lifted as the magic spread through me.

Opening my eyes, I realized Orion had brought us to the side of Town Hall. His jaw and shoulders were still tense as he watched me, grey eyes full of something that might have been concern, if we were different people to each other. His hand rested on the back of my neck as his magic washed over me, his white wings cocooning us against the brick of the building.

"Um, thanks." I cleared my throat. He nodded, his hand on me a moment longer before he blinked, dropping it and stepping away, folding his wings tight on his back. "Now what?"

Orion sighed, head tilted skyward in a way that exposed the long line of his neck. And dammit, why was his neck sexy? Why did I want to lick his Adam's apple, to ride this high I was on and throw caution to the wind? "Now we wait and see what happens next. If Ezra's staging a coup, working with Nergal, I can only imagine —"

"Yeah, about that." He flinched, and his eyes narrowed as they locked on mine. "You have some explaining to do about your family history."

"Oh, you did it."

We turned to see Ryker, standing a few feet away. "Faster than I thought, too." He glanced behind us. "Did you leave Zaph behind?"

Orion shifted towards Ryker. "There's a coup happening. Ezra has been working with Nergal and he's trying to overthrow Malachi from within."

Ryker tensed. "That can't be good, but I can't say I'm surprised either. He's always been a prick."

"Nergal's not here, then? No sign of him?"

Crossing his arms, Ryker shook his head. "Not yet. The last intelligence I had said he was in Vegas, but it's been quiet."

"If Nergal wants enough power to overthrow the Council, he needs to either use the wellspring, or lift the binding on his power. The wellspring will be guarded, and as far as he knows, the Cove isn't, since he'll expect me to still be in holding. That makes this town the easier target, if he can figure out what object Willa used to bind his powers and get past the spell keeping him out."

"So you're saying we should get ready." Ryker's green eyes flitted between his round, human pupils, to the narrow, slitted ones of his dragon before shifting back, as excited as I'd ever seen the male. "Get out the big guns."

Orion nodded, and when Ryker huffed in confirmation,

sparks shot out of his mouth, accompanied by a trail of smoke.

"But the most important thing is to keep everyone protected," Orion added, one eyebrow raised.

Ryker shrugged. "Of course."

I had a feeling that Ryker's idea of protection would be something like my own — the best defense being a good offense, and all that — but chose to keep that to myself.

"I should log into my computer, send a town-wide alert —"

"No," Ryker cut in, shaking his head. "When was the last time you looked in a mirror, Orion? You need a shower. And probably a couple nights' sleep, but take what you can get." He eyed Orion's shirt, noticing the inside-out imprint of the logo before his gaze flicked over to me. "A change of clothes. I'll handle getting the town prepared for this." He clapped Orion on the shoulder. "For today, take care of yourself for once."

With that, Ryker turned and marched back up into Town Hall, pulling his phone out of his pocket as he went. As he pulled open the door to step inside, I heard him greeting Blaze.

"You really do need a shower," I commented, crossing my arms.

Orion sighed, physically wilting in exhaustion in front of me. "There was a shower… there, but it was covered in black mold, and it hardly seemed worth it anyway. The trash just kept coming back." A hollow, haunted look crept into his face, and once again, I felt that uncomfortable twinge in my chest. He took a step and blinked, swaying on his feet.

My hands were around his arm before I knew I moved, steadying him. "Whoa, there. What's wrong with you?"

He stared down at where my hands were, blinking again. "I'm just — I haven't traveled like that in a while, and before a half-hour ago, I haven't had access to my magic in weeks. It's catching up with me, is all. I just need to lie down." He stepped away, staggering slightly, and I caught up with him again.

"You won't make it all the way back to your place like this."

"Well, call Blaze, then. He can —"

"He's busy getting the town ready for whatever shit is about to go down," I snapped. I threw his arm over my shoulders, trying to prop him up even though he was twice my size, and he all but slumped onto me as he simultaneously tried to push away. "It's ten yards to my place. You can shower, you can crash. Regroup. Stop being a stubborn ass and let's go."

"Bossy," he muttered, but gave in, allowing me to steer us across the street and down my front path.

"Men always pronounce *assertive* wrong when they're talking about women."

Chapter Twenty-Six

DEVANNA

ORION INSISTED ON SHOWERING FIRST, and I was relieved. Though it wasn't his fault, the reek of trash had infected his pores, and getting it out of his skin would improve his morale.

While he was in the bathroom, I hunted through my merch for clothes that would fit him, coming up with a pair of grey moon phase sweats and the plainest shirt I could find — a black, bleach-splotched one with snakes and crystals. He could get his own clothes once he rested a bit. Placing the clothes just outside the bathroom door, I stopped to listen for a minute, just to make sure he hadn't dropped in exhaustion while he was in there.

The water stopped running, which I took as my cue he was still alive, so I backed away, making for the kitchen. Had they fed him regularly? He wasn't wasting away, so it was likely, but when was the last time? Did traveling like that take a lot of energy, like using my magic did for me?

Why was I so obsessed with his physical condition? It

wasn't my job to take care of him. He was a grown male. He could take care of himself.

But isn't it sometimes nice, when you've been through something traumatic, to have someone take care of you for a little while?

Damn my conscience for its logic.

Fine, a sandwich. I could make him something simple to eat without it getting weird. I wanted one anyway, so it was barely doing anything special for him.

I was eating my sandwich and scrolling on my phone up in the bell tower — ostensibly checking my work social media, but mostly just keeping my hands and mind busy — when I heard the bathroom door crack open downstairs. Minutes later, footsteps sounded on the stairs and Orion appeared, plate in hand.

I kept my eyes glued to my screen, willing myself not to notice the droplets of water clinging to the ends of his silver hair as he raked a hand through it, causing them to slide down his bare, tattooed chest. The sweatpants were inside out, the print hidden, but who would even notice after seeing how low they rode on his hips? He approached where I sat, feet dangling out the window with my sandwich next to me.

"Is this for me?" He pointed to the sandwich I'd left on a plate on the end of the island.

No, I left that downstairs in the kitchen for me but came all the way up here. I rolled my eyes in my head, but managed just to shrug in front of him. "If you want it."

Images from the last time we'd been in the tower together raced through my mind, and I wasn't reading anything on my screen anymore, every sense attuned to his half-naked presence. The barely-there sound of his breathing, the scent of my soap and shampoo on his skin, the slight static of his magic in the air. The static intensified as he closed the distance between us, sinking down right next to me, his own legs hanging off the side as well.

I swiped over to my sales app, scrolling through the new orders that had come in since I'd last checked, and decidedly ignored the male next to me as we ate in silence.

With the crickets chirping down in the graveyard, a soft breeze drifting idly through the tower, and Bagheera sitting on top of a tombstone down below, tail flicking as he watched the fireflies, it was almost nice. Peaceful.

If we were any other two people, anyway.

"So, Ezra's your brother."

Orion let out a long-suffering sigh, staring out into the night, and nodded.

"He seems like a delight."

"Not the word I'd choose to describe him."

I hummed noncommittally, sensing he didn't want to talk more about his family, and after what I knew of Ezra, I probably wouldn't want to talk about him either.

We sat in companionable silence, a strange sensation when it came to Orion and I, but then again, we were in uncharted waters. I'd put myself at risk to save him, something that now felt like an almost out-of-body experience.

Taking a bite of my sandwich, I let my eyes drift towards him momentarily, noting how tense he still looked, even now.

Could I blame him?

Just about everything in his life was in upheaval. Now that I understood just how shitty his family was, I wondered for the first time who Orion turned to when he needed someone. Needed support. Needed to fall apart and be put back together.

Blaze, obviously, but they didn't have that type of relationship.

While I was all but orphaned at a young age and had all of the emotional baggage to show for it, I'd never truly been alone. I'd chosen my family right here in Deadlights Cove and been welcomed with open arms, whether I'd wanted it or not.

But could the same be said of Orion?

I wasn't sure, and that made my stomach turn.

"You seemed surprised about his betrayal," I tried again, not even sure what was prompting me to try getting Orion to open up. I could try to convince myself it was because he just looked so tightly wound — even for him — but I was pretty sure there was more to it than that.

"Ezra was always the perfect one of the Moretti brothers." Orion shrugged and a muscle in his jaw flexed, but I didn't miss the last name drop. I'd been spot-on with my guess that angels sounded like they were all in the mafia, but I kept my mouth shut for now. "For him to turn on the angels like this… My parents are probably mortified."

"Your *parents*?" Okay, I knew, logically, that Orion had to have come from somewhere, but maybe a tiny part of me had just assumed he'd just popped into existence, fully grown in a suit and tie.

"They put everything they had into making sure Ezra had every advantage academically, socially, financially to have the career of his dreams — or their dreams. No one needed me. I was the spare — there were no expectations on my life at all."

There was a hint of bitterness in his tone, and suddenly I had a thousand questions I'd never even contemplated about the male beside me. I knew angels could be assholes — obviously — but it almost sounded like Orion had been neglected, if not outright scorned, by his own family.

I'd always pictured him as the silver spoon type.

"How did you end up here?" I couldn't contain my questions anymore, not as his words tugged on my heart in a way I wasn't fond of.

He turned to me, his grey eyes holding a hint of sadness that nearly broke me. "Earth was about as far away as I could get. Everyone needs an escape. This was mine. All I wanted was to get away, to make a name for myself outside of my family's circle of influence. To help others who didn't have the means to help themselves, if I could."

I broke our stare, turning to look back out the window as I felt the depth of his words. No matter how long I'd hated the male, I… didn't. Not anymore.

Maybe I hadn't in a long time.

Needing to steer the subject away from more revelations into Orion's not-so-terrible character, I said, "So what's going to happen to you now? Will they make you go back?"

Orion sighed, his chin dropping down onto his chest as his wings flared behind him. "I don't know. I ran from my sentencing, so that can't be good. But with the Council in upheaval and Malachi letting not just me free… I don't know what to expect."

I nodded, leaving it at that. I picked up my phone, scrolling through my orders once more, but hardly saw the words on the screen.

When we'd both finished our sandwiches, Orion stood,

stacked my plate with his, and left them both on the floor by the top of the stairs. Then he was beside me, his hand landing on top of mine as he forced my phone face down on the floor, bringing my focus to him.

I swiveled to face him, tilting my head up in inquiry.

"I wanted to say thank you," he said.

"It was just a sandwich."

He shook his head, lips twitching in that way I'd come to realize was sometimes as close as he let himself get to laughter. "Not for that. For coming to get me." His eyes held mine. "You risked a lot, flouting the laws like that, and with Nergal out there and the town at risk, there is nowhere else I'd rather be."

The moment stretched between us, and my mouth went dry with the intensity of his gaze.

"I didn't want the town subjected to someone even worse than Pascar."

His hand still rested on top of mine, warm and firm. I struggled not to let mine twitch underneath his, fought the urge to turn my wrist over and thread our fingers together.

A ridiculous impulse.

A hum of disbelief sounded in his throat as he pulled me to my feet. I didn't know why I let him push me up against the wall. I didn't know why I didn't push him away.

"Zaph told us about the Omega Level, and it sounded inhumane —"

"I'm not human, so what does that matter?" For dramatic effect, his wings stretched out before relaxing again.

"I just meant, for *any* being —" I let out an involuntary

gasp as Orion lifted my leg, wrapping it around his waist as he stepped between my legs.

His large hand wrapped around my neck, his thumb forcing my chin up to meet his eyes, and my heart stopped as heat flooded my core.

I didn't want to admit how much I liked that, but my body held all the evidence. I swallowed heavily, the movement emphasizing the weight of his hand on my throat even if he wasn't tightening it.

He brought his lips down to my ear, his voice low as he murmured, "When will you stop lying to me, Devanna?"

When my heart started again, my pulse rushing in my ears was all I could hear.

"I'm not —"

He *tsk*ed softly, and his lips found the soft skin behind my ear. "*Liar.*"

He sank his weight into me, and it took everything in me to stifle the whimper in my throat as he pressed himself against me.

"I don't know what you're talking —"

"Until you can be honest with me, maybe it's best if you don't say anything at all."

He pulled away just enough for me to glare at him, and a split-second before the retort in my mind left my mouth, his lips crashed into mine for the first time.

Holy shit. Orion was kissing me.

While we'd done *plenty* on our night together a few weeks ago, kissing had never happened.

No, this wasn't a kiss. Orion had me pinned in place, and he took my mouth in a plundering.

He *devoured* me.

Even though his hand wasn't cutting off my airway, I was breathless, and he didn't let up. My palms went to his bare chest, raking my nails down him hard enough to draw a growl from his throat, but he only leaned into it, encouraging me to keep going.

I trailed down to the waistband of his sweatpants, searching for the drawstring, when suddenly my hands were pressed to the wall beside my head, held there with no small force of magic.

"That's not what this is about," he breathed into my mouth. He started tugging down my leggings instead, sinking to his knees in front of me. He helped me step out of them, pressing a kiss to the seam of my hip that made my knees weak.

"Are you sure?" Damn, it was embarrassing how breathless I sounded. "It kind of seems like it is. Not that I'm complaining, exactly, but we sort of said that was a one-time thing last time. One night, I guess, since it was definitely more than one time."

Quickly stripping me out of the rest of my clothes, his eyes flashed with lightning as they met mine.

"Can't believe I still don't have that tie."

My mind barely had a minute to register his words before he threw my leg over his shoulder and pressed his face between my legs. One arm formed a band across my hips, pressing me against the wall, and the other rubbed small, gentle circles over my ass. I threw my head back as he laved his tongue over me in tantalizingly slow, gentle strokes.

I tried to urge him faster, but his arm across my hips was firm, not letting me buck into him.

I looked down at this giant of a male on his knees before

me, white wings glinting in the moonlight streaming through the arched windows of the bell tower. I hated that I wanted to run my fingers through his silky, silver hair. That I wanted to strip him out of his clothes as he had done to me. That I'd loved his mouth on mine; that I loved it even more where it was now.

My skin flushed with anger as my breathing grew more rapid in time with his tongue. How dare he make me feel this way about him?

How could I have let him?

What was happening here?

That weird feeling in my chest twinged again, and I tried to shove it aside and focus only on the sensations coursing through my body.

This was a thank-you orgasm, and well deserved. That was all. I'd earned it, and I'd enjoy it, and then I'd send him on his way.

His eyes, dark with desire, flicked up to mine a second before he slid two fingers into me, and I looked away as ecstasy lit my nerves. I pressed my eyes shut to stem the prickles forming there, emotions flooding me in an unfamiliar way.

They were only tears of rage. Those were the only kind I knew.

I was mad he'd been treated so unfairly, especially now that I knew just how long this had been going on. I was pissed our town would be under attack any day. I was furious with my friends for moving on with their lives around me while I stood stuck, afraid to let myself be attached to anyone. But, more than any of those things, I was terrified of the way my heart clenched as I looked down at this male who deserved so much better than what he'd had.

But I couldn't give it to him. Not like this.

I couldn't be what he needed, couldn't let him in, couldn't let him see just how broken I was, too.

Letting anyone in only set you up to let each other down.

"Get out," I barely managed to whisper, needing this to stop.

Orion's eyes were steady on me as he rose from his knees, but I turned away, unable to look at him as I pulled on my clothes. I refused to acknowledge the hurt and confusion on his face.

For whatever reason, after a moment's hesitation, this once he listened to me. After a frustrated exhale, he dropped from the bell tower's open window, and I heard the rustle of his wings snapping open, carrying him away, but I didn't turn to look.

My feet pounded on the stairs as I ran down the tower, heading straight for the basement.

ORION

I LANDED on the Cottage's deck with a hard thud, my magic crackling over my skin as I fought to contain it. The French doors burst open in front of me, and slammed shut hard enough to rattle the glass after I walked through.

Blaze and Petra looked up from where they were seated at the kitchen island eating, mouths hanging open in surprise. Ignoring them both, I went straight for the freezer and pulled out the first bottle of alcohol I could find.

Slurping the last of his noodles loudly, Blaze said, "My *my*, O, what urges we're having this evening!"

"Back off," I tossed over my shoulder. I was sure his demon senses would be going haywire with all the impulses flaring off me, but I didn't want to hear it.

"Since when does he have tattoos?" Petra murmured to Blaze, reading the room a bit better than her male since she didn't target that at me directly.

Shit, I'd forgotten to grab a shirt before I dropped off the bell tower. Too late now.

"Dev got you out of jail, then?" Blaze trailed me through the hall towards my wing of the house.

"I assume that's rhetorical."

He chuckled, immune by now to my tones. "Pretty chivalrous of her, though, right?" His elbow nudged my side. "Almost *romantic* —"

His words cut off with a yelp when I wrenched his arm behind his back by the wrist, slamming him face-first into the wall.

"I said *back off.*"

"What the hell, O? What's going on?"

I shoved him away, and quickly slammed the door to my room shut behind me, heading straight for my patio, unable to stay inside.

What *was* going on? I took a long swig of the bottle I'd grabbed before I set it down on the balcony railing, then pulled myself up on top of it.

I didn't know what was going on. That was the problem.

The moment Devanna's blue hair had popped through the door on Omega, something awoke inside me. I couldn't look at her now and not see the force she was, fighting for the underdog, throwing herself in harm's way for anyone who needed it.

That she chose *me* to save… I'd never forget it.

Something changed, and I didn't want to go back to how things had been before. So I'd tried to let her in, to share my story with her, something I hadn't done with anyone else in my life. Even Blaze didn't know how messed up my life was before I'd arrived in Deadlights Cove, and sharing with her had felt cathartic. I didn't have the words to tell her how much her coming to my aid meant to me, so I'd thought I could show her.

But she'd slammed the metaphorical door on me, pushing me away, and shit… That hurt.

I launched back off into the night, heading out over the dark water, needing to keep moving.

Why couldn't that witch just *admit* what we both knew was the truth? We were more alike than either of us cared to admit.

I kept replaying the picture of her in my mind, her eyes glistening with rage and unshed tears mere moments after I'd worshipped her body.

Had she not wanted that? Had I read *everything* wrong?

But this was Devanna. She never did something she didn't want a day in her life. She didn't know the meaning of the phrase *back down*. If she hadn't wanted it, I *knew* she would have told me.

Probably would have kicked me where it counted, too.

The night air rushed around me as I flew over the ocean. Out to sea was safer, fewer chances of encountering humans who might realize I was a little large for the average seabird.

I knew I should be at home, resting, but flying was addictive, and I hadn't been able to stretch my wings in all the weeks I'd been kept on Omega.

What had I done wrong? And how could I fix it?

Turning over the night's events in my mind, trying to figure out what the hell had happened, I barely noticed my surroundings, simply flying out into the night.

"Orion, you're back!"

I whipped my head around so fast, I lost my updraft and

dropped 20 feet before I regained my balance. My wings snapped out again, and I leveled out, scanning around for who had spoken.

"Who —"

"Oh, our mistake," a voice chuckled from the darkness, and a minute later, shadows dissolved a few feet above me to reveal, of all people, Val and Caedmon gliding along in mid-air.

"What the hell —"

My jaw was on the seafloor. I'd never known what type of supernaturals these two were, but seeing them *flying*, manipulating *shadows*, with black, leathery *wings* that contrasted heavily with their bright Hawaiian shirt vibes never would have crossed my mind.

"It's hard to resist the open air on nights like this, isn't it?" Val said, rotating his wings to fly closer. I fought not to pull away from him, confused by what I was seeing.

"What *are* you?" I asked, the question leaving me before I could find a more dignified way to pose it.

The males exchanged a look, then chuckled. "You really didn't know? We thought for sure, you, of all people, would have figured it out by now."

I blinked, trying to clear my eyes, thinking surely I must be hallucinating as Val and Caedmon hovered in mid-air, as close as their wings would allow.

"Vampires," Caedmon said so nonchalantly I forgot to move my wings, sinking yet again towards the water below me.

"This town is trying to kill me," I muttered.

"We'd appreciate it if you kept it to yourself, though," Val added. "Not many supes know about our kind."

"How is that even *possible*?"

"We can hide all trace of our species," Caedmon responded to my rhetorical question. "Has to do with the shadows."

The muscles in my shoulders twitched with fatigue, and I lost a few feet of air again.

"Hey, something wrong there?" Val grasped my arm in concern, and I blinked.

I was too tired to process an entirely new supernatural species right now.

"He's about to crap out, V," came Caedmon's voice as I shook my head, trying to wake myself up. "Let's get you home, Mayor."

Next thing I knew, I was being gently escorted, and sometimes held up on either side, by two flying *vampires* back towards the Cottage.

What in the actual fuck was my life.

A couple hundred yards from the house, they cloaked themselves in shadow again, seeing me off with a wave and then taking off back out to sea.

I touched down on my patio, stumbling a few steps before catching my balance.

"You all right?"

Petra stood from where she'd been sitting on a deck chair, her brows furrowed.

"Just tired," I said, and she nodded.

"Good. Then I can yell at you."

I blinked.

"I don't know what you went through up in angel jail or whatever, but what the hell was that, attacking Blaze earlier?"

With a sigh, I made my way off the patio and into my room, Petra following at my heels. "I couldn't deal with his needling. Not tonight."

She scoffed. "He was *worried* about you. You idiot."

I stopped, shocked by Petra's tone. The last time I'd heard her raise her voice at anyone had been that first day in my office when Blaze had thrown his popcorn everywhere. "Pardon?"

"He was freaking out all night that you and Dev — his two best friends in the world — would end up in the Keep, and then you turn up back here all silent and broody and he tries to see if you're all right and —"

"He was just fucking with me. Like he always does."

The look Petra shot me was pure disbelief, and suddenly, I felt about twenty years old again.

"You'd think he'd tease you and come after you if he didn't care about you?" She shook her head, her long red hair swishing around her. "What's it going to take for you to realize he loves you? That this whole town does, for that matter."

With that mind-boggling pronouncement, Petra strode from my room, leaving me alone in the dark.

Chapter Twenty-Eight

DEVANNA

THE LIGHTS FLICKED ON OVERHEAD, and a training staff was in my hand before I could think. I flipped it twice before I spun, slamming it with all my weight into the practice dummy.

Turn after turn, I slapped the wood into the dummy, blood rushing through my ears like static that only reminded me of Orion's stupid beautiful magic.

I was so *angry*. Rage thrummed in me, powerful enough to charge a hundred crystals with magic, and I pushed it all into my hits, denting and ripping the fabric of the dummy.

A hand landed on my shoulder, and I whipped around with my staff. An *Oof* sounded before I managed to blink out of my trance.

"Dev?"

Blaze stood in front of me, his brows drawn in uncharacteristic concern. His hands landed on my elbows, steadying me and holding my staff from hitting him again all at once.

I turned from him, back to the dummy. "Go away, Blaze."

"What's going on? Orion just came home looking —"

"Go away."

But he was a demon, so of course he didn't listen. He moved around to the other side of the dummy so I'd have to look at him as I began smacking into it again.

A drop of weakness welled in the corner of my eye, and Blaze's blew wide.

"Holy shit."

I leveled the staff at him, lining it up with his liver as the singular tear escaped and rolled down my cheek. "One more word and I'll run you through with all I've got."

Blaze grimaced, the order physically paining him, and I rolled my eyes. He grasped the end of the staff and gently pried it from my hands, dropping it on the floor to his right.

"Come on, then."

Hands held up in a *come at me* motion, I tilted my head.

"Don't you think you'll feel better beating up something with a pulse than this dummy?" His eyes flashed in a taunt, and with a kick, he sent it crashing to the ground. "Come on. You know you've dreamt of it for years."

I met Blaze's black eyes, seeing more understanding there than I wanted to admit. I clenched my teeth against the swelling feeling in my chest as I took a step aside from the dummy and took a running lunge towards one of my best friends.

Even though he could have easily overpowered me, he didn't. Like a trooper, Blaze gave as good as he got but no better, giving me an outlet that I needed more than I could ever admit.

Hit after hit, he blocked, flickering just out of reach, letting me land a punch every once in a while. He swung back, keeping me on my toes, but neither of us ever landed a hit hard enough to do any real damage. Still, he pushed to focus my mind on staying out of his reach. Sweat dripped off my body with the exertion, my heart pounding against my ribs as we moved.

When I finally ran out of steam, we slumped on our backs on the exercise mats, staring up at my cobwebbed ceiling. My knuckles stung along with my torso where Blaze had landed several hits, but the pain felt good. Felt real. I understood this pain so much better than the one in my heart.

"That bad, huh?" He nudged my foot with his.

I couldn't even answer, but the hand that reached out, squeezing mine, told me he understood all the same.

"Thanks for saving him."

I nodded, words lost to me as I willed my heart back into submission.

Blaze leaned over, hooking his arm behind my neck as he pulled my head towards him and kissed my forehead. Before I could pull away, he ran his knuckles across the top of my head. "Love you, Devvie," he said, then flickered out before I could respond.

With a deep sigh, I pushed myself to my feet and up to my room.

"Yoo-hoo! Devvie dear!"

I groaned and shoved my pillow down over my face,

pressing it into my ears. Did no one respect a locked door in this town? I needed to look into warding this place ASAP.

I heard steps out in the main space of the house, then clattering from the kitchen.

"Where's your — oh, found it! I'm making coffee for good witches who get out of bed to greet their house guest!"

"*Uninvited* house guest," I muttered as I tossed my pillow aside. Pulling myself to my feet, I allowed one tiny whimper of pain for the soreness radiating through every single muscle after my bout with Blaze last night — muscles I didn't even know I had screaming in protest.

I pulled a robe over my tank top and shorts, and shook my hair out of my sleep cap before I headed out to face the music.

There was only one reason Morgaine was here so bright and early when the town was all but on lockdown, waiting for news of Nergal.

"Ah! *There* you are," Mo tossed over her shoulder as she puttered around my kitchen, making herself right at home. Her bright orange hibiscus print kimono fluttered around her as she moved, fuschia clogs clacking over the hardwood floor as she gathered supplies from the pantry.

I inspected her coffee-making set up, begrudgingly admitted to myself she'd done it to my standards, and slumped onto a stool at the island to wait for it to brew. I took my coffee seriously, and black.

"You know, you really should ward this place sooner than later. Any supe could just waltz right in!"

"You don't say," I deadpanned.

"Anyway, I brought you a housewarming gift," she

continued as though she hadn't heard me, and gestured to a cardboard box on the island.

I contained my sigh as I flipped open the lid and pulled out a crystal ball the size of a cantaloupe, clouds of white and grey swirling within it.

"Isn't this a little cliche?"

"This isn't a typical crystal ball, dear." As I held it, the clouds changed from white to red. "It will show your aura, or the overall aura in a room with more than one person, since I know you're unable to see them on your own." She threw a glance at me over her shoulder where she was somehow already making pancakes on the stove. "Hmm. Red."

I pulled out the stand that was also in the box and set the ball on top of it, looking around to decide where to put it.

And then I froze, eyes glued to the far wall of my living room. Hanging on the wall behind my couch was the brightest, boldest, largest floral painting I'd ever seen. Neon pinks and oranges contrasted against the blue background, as bright as my hair. While it wasn't my taste, it wasn't the floral that was wrong with the painting. It was the black and white intertwined figures painted within the flowers, looking a hell of a lot like kamasutra poses.

"Mo. What is that?"

"Hmm?" She slid a stack of placation pancakes over to me, and took an exaggeratedly long time to follow my stare across the room. "Oh, that. Just another gift from little old Mo. Willa used to love to come to this church to paint, probably to hide from toddler Blaze, and who could blame her. I was looking through the collection I stored for her and thought you needed a little pop of color in here. It's so dark with all this black."

I tore my gaze away from the painting, the glaringly contrasting colors seared into my retinas as I attacked my pancakes, narrowing my eyes at the rainbow of sprinkles she'd added to them. These were *celebration* pancakes. What the hell did she think we were celebrating here?

"How are your pancakes, dear?" She took a long drink from her giant coffee mug that was basically a bowl, blinking innocently from behind her teal-framed glasses.

I set my fork down. "I know why you're here."

She fluttered a hand over her chest, looking around the room as if there were anyone else here I could be referring to. I leveled a stare at her to drop the pretense, and she lifted a shoulder.

"I may have heard a rumor or two through the grapevine about a certain… canoodling."

I nearly spat out the sip of coffee I'd taken. "Gross. Get out."

"But that's not why I'm here anyway." I stared, knowing her better than that. "Well, not entirely. Do you remember the first time we met?"

I paused at her words, trying to think back to my earliest memories of Deadlights Cove. "The beach?"

Mo smiled, reaching across the counter as her hand circled my wrist. "Yes. How could anyone forget?"

I chuckled at the memory, pulling my hand free from Mo's grip as I leaned back on my stool.

"I'd taken Nimue to the beach to wade with me — her very first Wine and Wade Wednesday! No wine for her though, of course. But even at four, her demon blood was so strong, she couldn't stand being in the water long. So she sat on the beach, pouting with her toes just out of reach of the water." Mo's face wrinkled as she smiled fondly at the memory. "You dropped down next to Nimue without knowing anything about her, handed her a shovel, and ordered her to start digging a hole."

I remembered the day clearly, and emotions surfaced in me thinking back on that day, the way Nimue's friendship had changed my life for good.

"Bucket after bucket, you carried up to her on the beach while she dug, never getting her wet — as if you understood exactly what she wanted, but couldn't have. So you made it happen for her." Mo sniffled. I looked up to see the tear track down Mo's cheek as she smiled at me. "My baby couldn't be in the ocean, so you made her her own, right there on the beach. Just for her. And you didn't even know her name."

Shoving my hands into my eyes, I pushed back the emotions that threatened to break free. "What is the point in reliving this story, Mo? I'm sure you have one."

"Of course I do," Mo said, her arms wrapping around me as she pulled me into a hug and kissed my forehead. "You are so easy to love, Devanna, just as you are. Your intelligence. Your honesty. Your bravery. Your undying devotion to those you give your heart to. You're extraordinary in every possible way, shining so bright even when you try to hide yourself away."

My hands drifted up to squeeze on her arms around me as my heart clenched.

"It's okay to let other people in." Mo brushed my hair back from my face, but never let go of her grip on me. "You have enough love to go around. And those of us that are lucky enough to be on the receiving end of it understand that *we* are the lucky ones. I'm positive that Nimue, Blaze, Lysander, Selene, even Petra would tell you the same."

I sucked in a breath, my heart both breaking and reforming at her words as I let her go. She dropped her arms from around me and walked to the painting.

"Now," she said as she put her hands on her hips, her head tilted up to look at the kaleidoscope of color. "Don't even *think* about taking this down. Not only would it be a personal insult to me, Mama Mo, who has looked out for you for your entire life, but you need it."

Confused by her comment, I took a shaky breath and let it out slowly to steady myself, then hopped off my stool, moving to her side. "Is *need* the right word?"

"Yes, it is." Mo's tone brooked no argument. "Willa painted it."

"Shouldn't Blaze have it, then? Why did you bring it here?"

"Althea insisted on it," Mo said, eyes twinkling with mischief as they so often did.

"... Althea. The one whose tombstone is just outside. Who died a century ago."

"The very one." Mo smiled, grabbed her bag from the couch, and moved towards the door. "You remind me a lot of her, you know. Althea loved harder than anyone, and was the best friend I've ever known."

"So you've been communing with the dead now?" I asked, a brow raised in question. "I wasn't aware that necromancy was in your wheelhouse."

Mo laughed, head thrown back as a broad smile split her

face. "Oh, sweet girl. All of this has been in motion for longer than you've been alive." Mo paused, hand on the door as she turned back to me. "Althea was the strongest Seer I've ever met. You are exactly where you were meant to be, in this life, in this town, in this church. This is only the beginning for you, and I am so happy I get to be here to see your story unfold."

Chapter Twenty-Nine

DEVANNA

SHORTLY AFTER MORGAINE LEFT, I grabbed a ladder and placed it in front of the painting. Even though I'd been around witches my whole life and believed in divination, I was also well aware of how Mo loved to manipulate a situation.

Hell. In hindsight, I could see just how well she played me like a fiddle into freeing Orion, bringing me right to my current predicament.

To hell with fate.

I decided my journey in life, not some dead witch buried in my front yard. And not a meddling old woman either, no matter how much her words meant to me.

The second my fingertips settled on the edges of the painting, power zapped me. I snapped my hands back, shaking the burning buzz from my fingers as I eyed the painting. It wasn't unheard of for objects to be spelled as items of power, but a painting?

And why had she given it to me?

I climbed back down the ladder and pulled my phone from my pocket.

"What's up?" Lysander answered after the second ring.

"Can you come check out this painting Mo gave me?" I didn't bother explaining more than that over the phone as I stared up at the bright, swirling colors on the canvas.

"Sure?" The single word held a dozen questions.

"Great. See you in a few." I hung up and shook my head. Just what I needed — more mysteries.

By the time I'd cleaned up the breakfast dishes, a knock on my door sounded before it opened.

"You rang?" Lys said as he pushed the door closed behind him. He let out a low whistle of appreciation as he took in my home. "Whoa, Wednesday. You've really over-hauled the place."

"Thanks." I smiled, then moved to the living room to point out the painting on the wall. "Look at this."

Lys followed me, then jerked his head back, blinking rapidly as he stared at it. I rolled my eyes as he pushed the sunglasses from the top of his head down onto his nose. "It's bright."

"Well aware," I deadpanned. "I tried to take it down and it shocked the shit out of me."

"What?" Lys asked, flipping his sunglasses back up on his head as he turned to look at me. "Why?"

"No clue. Figured you could look at the magic on it for me."

Lys hummed in thought, tilting his head as he looked at the painting. His magic didn't work like mine, not needing spells, and containing a much larger well of power to pull from. "It's not Mo's magic, I can tell you that."

"She said Willa Rosewood painted it," I said, turning my focus back to the painting. "Blaze's mom."

"Makes sense, I guess," Lys said, moving up the ladder to hover his hand above the canvas. "It's definitely a witch spell."

"Why would she spell a painting and then do nothing with it for a hundred years?"

Lys closed his eyes, breathing deeply as his palm floated over the painting. The air around the painting shimmered, dust and static eddying as Lys worked until he dropped his hand to the side.

"It's a protection spell." His brow creased as he climbed back down the ladder to my side. "A ward. A pretty huge one, actually. This is an insane amount of power to have locked in a painting like this. If I had to guess, it's casting a radius all the way out to the street from here, encompassing the church and most of the property."

"Why?" I asked, not following this logic. "I mean, sure. It makes sense to put a ward on your house, but why would it need to go out into the yard and not just the house itself?"

"Well," Lys said, his hand scrubbing over the dark stubble on his light brown cheeks. "Your yard isn't just any yard, is it?"

Several beats of silence went by as we processed that before I turned and walked outside, stopping in the yard in front of the church. Closest to the door — facing the wall of my living room — were three headstones.

Henry Rosewood
Althea Rosewood

Willa Rosewood

"What is it with you three?" I scowled down at the headstones. "I don't want anything to do with your drama."

Lys clapped me on the back, squeezing my shoulder lovingly. "I wouldn't worry too much about it. Maybe it'll keep out unwanted visitors."

"You walked right in."

He laughed, walking across the street towards the green. "You called *me*. I was very much wanted."

"You're the worst."

Lys shot me a smirk. "Neither you nor I believe that."

I worked in the shop for a while once Lys left, confirming there was nothing we could do about the painting, but business was slow, and my mind was elsewhere. Maisie had texted earlier asking if they could come over tonight, and I was slightly surprised by how much I was looking forward to seeing the girls.

Maisie, Riona, Ruby, Selene, and Petra came in together, talking and laughing as they followed me down into the basement.

"You know what to do," I said, then realized with a frown not everyone was here. "Where's Nimue?"

"She's at the Cottage," Petra said as she started up the treadmill in the corner. "She arrived a little bit ago with Kit and Nadir. There are a whole bunch of them meeting over there about town safety — Ryker, Ostara, Lys, Mo, Darius."

Confusion tinted with a touch of annoyance seeped into me as I fought to control my breathing. "Why are they meeting at the house? Have they heard something about Nergal? Is he about to make a move? Why aren't they telling the rest of us what the hell is going on?"

And after I saved Orion's sorry ass too, he was just going to leave me out of this? I didn't care if I'd hurt Orion's feelings by kicking him out of the tower — I was there the day Nergal attacked at the lighthouse. I knew better than most of them how powerful he was.

Selene stepped up to my side and placed a gentle hand on my back. "Now that Orion's back, he and Ryker have been talking. Making a plan. They'll tell us what we need to know when it's time."

I shrugged out of her hold, anger making me clench my fists at my side. How long had these secret meetings been going on? "So, they just get to decide for us? No town meeting about this? They get to tell us what to do without involving the rest of us? What," I scoffed, "are they planning on sending the *weak females* away for our own safety until the threat has passed?"

Petra stopped the treadmill, sensing the shift in the room as I clenched my teeth together. Selene's eyes darted to Petra, then Maisie, before meeting mine again.

"Unbelievable," I said, breathing deeply even though my heart was racing. "They are, aren't they?"

"Not the women, particularly," Selene said, sounding nervous, and I hated myself for making her feel bad. Of course she should leave. "Just those of us who would be safer elsewhere. Anyone who wants to leave, they're creating an evacuation plan to get us out of harm's way."

A small part of me understood maybe there was a chance I was acting irrationally. While wildly frustrating, the males of Deadlights Cove had never treated women as lesser at anything, but I refused to be left out. This was my town to protect as much as it was anyone else's — this was my home, my family, and I didn't just want to be involved, I *needed* to be.

"Well, I, for one, am not leaving," Maisie said, and I turned her way, tipping my chin up in solidarity.

"Me neither," Riona said.

"This is my home, too," Ruby said, linking hands with Riona. "I'm not leaving. I won't abandon the town when it needs us most."

Selene said nothing, but the hand on her belly told me her answer, and I couldn't even begin to blame her. In fact, I was glad she was leaving.

"What about you, Petra?" I said, a raised brow in her direction.

She breathed deeply, eyes darting to the punching bag and back to me. "I need time to think about it."

No Doubt's *Just a Girl* came on the stereo at the perfect time, mirroring my emotions. A slow grin spread over my face as I ran my tongue over my teeth and moved towards the stairs.

I'd had it up to *here*.

Chapter Thirty

ORION

BLAZE STOPPED in his tracks at the kitchen island, brow furrowed in suspicion as he eyed the peace offering I'd left there earlier. I set down my coffee, turning to him on my stool.

"What's this?"

He picked up the paintball gun, dangling it on one finger like it was a trap.

"Haven't you been trying to get me to play for twenty years?"

"Hmm." Blaze flipped the gun in his hands. "Do we all get to take a shot at you? Oh, I'm sorry, should I shove myself against the wall, since that's how we talk to each other now?"

"I apologize for that," I said, and slowly Blaze set the gun down and met my eye. "I shouldn't have — I wasn't quite myself." Why was this so hard? I cleared my throat. "I shouldn't have taken my frustration out on you."

"You weren't half as bad as Dev." Blaze rotated his

shoulder in a stretch then meandered over to the coffee maker and proceeded to assemble a disgusting concoction of milk and caramel that could barely pass as coffee. "Damn, that tiny witch can pack a punch."

"You saw her?"

"Well, when you had your conniption and took off, I had to go see if she was all right." He leaned back against the counter, taking a giant sip of his candy coffee and giving an exaggerated *ahh.*

"And was she?"

"Nuh-uh." Blaze wagged a finger at me. "This isn't high school. Ask her later yourself."

"I doubt she wants to see me."

Blaze scoffed as Ryker let himself in the French doors. "You guys are two idiotic peas in a pod."

"Who are the idiots?" Ryker crossed his arms, looking between us.

"No one —"

"O and Dev." Blaze waved a hand towards me. "They can't get their shit together to admit they want to be together."

"It's not that simple." I glowered at him.

Ryker shrugged. "If you want her and she wants you, what the hell else matters?"

"Yeah, it's not like you poisoned her and then skedad- dled. It could be *way* worse."

Ryker leaned over and smacked the bottom of Blaze's coffee, sending the liquid flying into the air and up his nose. Not wanting to deal with the mess — or a tantrum — I twirled a finger and directed the coffee back into his cup as Blaze spluttered, coffee dripping off his chin.

"I don't know," I replied honestly, shaking my head. "I mean, she came all the way to Headquarters to save me. That's not something you do for someone you don't care about. Everything was going fine, and then it was like a switch flipped and she changed her mind. Something is holding her back."

"Oh."

I turned to Blaze, waiting for him to expand, and he sighed.

"It's her history to share if she wants to. But if you want her, you'll have to show her you mean it, and you're not going anywhere."

"This is what you want?" Ryker crossed his arms over his chest. "You two have been at each other's throats for a decade."

"Well aware," I deadpanned, then ran a hand through my hair, yanking on it in frustration. "It doesn't make sense."

"Sure it does." Blaze bumped me with his shoulder. "You're both the most loyal people I know. If anyone deserves happiness, it's you two. It makes me happy to think of you with someone who won't put up with your shit. You need her as much as she needs you."

"Even if any of that is true, this isn't the time to deal with it. We have a demon army coming after us any day now."

"These things rarely happen at a convenient time," Ryker commented. "Don't put yourself dead last, even if it's the end of the world as we know it."

I met his steady gaze as he echoed my own words from months before.

"Probably especially then," Blaze put in helpfully.

"After the way we parted, I doubt she'll even speak to me."

Ryker grunted, but it had a pensive tone to it. "A bunch of idiots once told me I needed to make a grand gesture."

"Like what?" I asked, trying to think through what I could do that would make a difference to Devanna.

"Weapons are probably a bad idea." Blaze tapped his chin. "I'm not positive she wouldn't use them on you first."

Ryker chuckled, then cocked his head to the side. "Angels usually pair for life, don't they?"

"Usually, but she doesn't know about angel traditions. And I doubt she has much respect for angel culture anyway."

"That's not what I mean. Devanna won't want your words — she doesn't trust them. You need to *show* her this isn't a fling. Stake your claim the way angels do."

Blaze sat up straighter, curiosity lighting in his eyes as he looked back and forth between us. "Wait a minute, how do I not know this? What does that mean?"

I pushed off the counter, paintball forgotten, clearing my throat as I left the kitchen and headed towards my room. Maybe Ryker wasn't wrong. Maybe I needed to claim her. Maybe this was an answer to more than one problem concerning Devanna. But to do what Ryker suggested… I desperately wanted it.

Fuck.

Hopefully she wouldn't kill me for this later.

I sat at the kitchen counter, forehead propped in my hand as I listened to Ryker discuss the plans to increase our security around the town, strengthening barriers. We'd been going over this for hours, and I was exhausted.

I hadn't exactly slept well after Devanna's rejection, Val and Caedmon's big reveal, then getting yelled at by Petra.

"I'll talk to Ronan," Lys said, pointing at the ocean on the map. "We can work on strengthening the barriers around town from the sea. Funnel any attacks on the town from land, forcing them to come at us exactly where we want them."

"Darius and I have a plan for the shifters," Kit said, his hands slung protectively around Nimue in his lap, and exchanged a nod with Darius. "Together we can block access through our lands in case the protection spell falls."

"Considering the main threat here is my father, a full-fledged, scary-as-hell demon, water isn't a huge threat," Blaze said, crossing his arms as he leaned on the counter behind him.

"Sure." Lys stepped away from the map. "But considering *I* was the most recent victim to your brother's evil plans via Inessa, let's err on the side of better to be safe than sorry. What if something like that happens again to one of our girls? How would you feel if we left the waters unprotected and Petra was taken? How well can she swim? Does your witchy-demon energy give her the ability to breathe underwater for hours?"

Blaze stood, his fingertips sparking into flame as fury emanated from him in a way I'd never seen.

"Boys." Mo shook her head where she sat at the kitchen

table behind us. "Really. You'd think with two heads you'd be the smarter sex, but that's far from the truth. The only thing you're good for is a good deep d—"

"Oh," Blaze cringed, then gagged as he cut her off. "Mo. Gross."

"Enough." I cut my hand through the air before anyone could say more, a wave of magic silencing all of them. "Lysander, talk to Ronan. Get him on board. Inessa is still very much a problem for him, but he needs to be prepared to help however he can. His people aren't safe here any more than we are. Same with the shifters, Kit, Darius. Handle it."

Lys nodded, his jaw ticking as he looked at the other males in the room.

"I heard from Max out in Timber Creek yesterday. There was an attempt —" Ryker started when movement outside caught my attention. I pushed back from the bar stool and moved towards the French doors to peer out into the darkened yard.

The others turned with me, just as Devanna's blue hair popped up at the edge of the lawn, moving towards the house at a fast clip.

"Ooh," Blaze drew out the sound knowingly, shooting me a grim smirk. "I was wondering how long it would take her to come yell at you."

With a flick of Devanna's hand, the doors flew open, missing me by mere inches.

"Care to tell me when you were planning on informing the rest of us of your plan?" Devanna hissed as she marched up onto the porch, a hand on her hip as she stopped, chin tipped up.

"*Finally*," Mo said, glancing at her watch. "About damn time someone with sense walked into the room. And I've just remembered the rest of us all have somewhere else we need to be. Pip pip, boys."

"What?" Blaze frowned at Mo, but she was already up and out of her seat, ushering Blaze, Lys, Darius, Kit, Nimue, Ostara, and Ryker out the door, winking at me as she swept it closed behind her and Blaze exclaimed, "This is *my* house!"

"You don't think the rest of the town deserves to know what we all need to do to defend ourselves?" Dev crossed her arms over her chest. "I was there at the lighthouse. I saw how powerful Nergal is. I know what we're up against. I want in on the planning."

I sighed, turning away from her to face what Blaze was calling our "serial killer board," i.e. Petra's whiteboard, over which we'd taped a map of the town and added notes and scribblings, marking out weaknesses and magical protections. I felt like we were missing something, but I couldn't put my finger on it, and we'd been over it a thousand times.

"Hey, asshole." A sharp nail poked my shoulder repeatedly, and I let out a grunt of annoyance. "Answer me."

"We don't need to incite mass panic," I gritted out. "If word gets out how bad this is going to be..." I ran a hand through my hair. "Best case scenario? People freak out. People do not make logical, reasoned decisions when they're freaking out. Worst case scenario? They accidentally break our own protection spells when they mass exit."

"So get them out. It's clear Nergal is coming here to *town*," Dev gestured at the board. "They'll probably be safer *anywhere else*."

I shook my head. "It's not that simple. They can't just go out into the human world right now. With the Council in upheaval, I don't trust anyone. Nergal has succeeded in causing mass panic for the supernatural world — nowhere is safe right now. I got a call this morning from West Larkin that he's already hearing reports of supes being captured by humans. I'm sure one or more of Nergal's people are behind that, giving them tips on how to find us."

Dev's jaw went slack. Apparently, she hadn't heard those rumors yet.

"Now, if you just came over to give me shit about what a terrible fuck-up of a mayor I am, you can go. Mission accomplished. I have other things to worry about and I don't need you slowing me down."

Dev groaned in frustration, looking like she was seconds away from strangling me. "I'm here to *help*, you idiot! This is my town too. If you could learn how to delegate for *once* and see past your own reputation, maybe you wouldn't be so burnt out all the damn time."

"Listen here." I stepped into her space, forcing her to tilt her head back to maintain eye contact. "This has never, not *once*, been about my reputation, or my career. The *only* thing that has ever mattered to me is keeping this town and these people safe. Safe from other supernaturals, safe from humans, safe from each other if need be, and even safe from the PRICs."

My magic simmered with static between us, so much so that Devanna's hair began to lift. She was breathing hard, chest heaving, but I wasn't done yet.

"Now, Ryker and Kit are sending Selene and Nimue to Alaska until all this blows over, one way or the other. There's another dragon there Ryker trusts." I met her eye, willing her to understand my words. "But I know the males were counting on *you* being there to protect the girls, while they need to be here."

Her jaw worked as she let that sink in, no doubt picturing Selene and Nimue cooped up all alone. I knew she wouldn't want to leave her friends without all the help she could give.

But then she tipped her chin up, narrowing her eyes. "And who is going to protect *you*, then, Orion?"

I scoffed to cover up my confusion at her words, trying to understand what she really meant. "I don't need protecting, Devanna."

"Sure." She laughed. "I should have known you'd be arrogant, even now."

I sighed, leaning back, fisting my hands so I didn't reach out and shake some sense into her. "Do you not understand how dangerous this is? We could be signing our own death certificates by staying in this town. After seeing how powerful Nergal was at the lighthouse — and need I remind you that his power is currently *bound,* so that wasn't even him at full-force — you should be terrified of what's coming."

She crossed her arms, jaw tense, but never broke my stare. "I'm not leaving. I won't leave you here to fight this battle for the rest of us. If you think you and a few of your *buds* can take on this battle alone, you're stupider than I thought. And, up until this very minute, I didn't think you were stupid at all. Judgmental, yes. A pain in my ass, absolutely. But stupid? Far from it."

I scrubbed a hand down my face in frustration. Why was she always so damn stubborn? "I can't," I paused, tipping my head back to look at the ceiling. "I can't be worried about you while I'm trying to protect everyone else."

Several beats of silence went by before she hissed, "I'm not weak."

I dropped my head back down, meeting her stare as I boxed her in against the kitchen counter. I knew I shouldn't have, that she'd rejected me last night, sending me away. But I needed her to get this across to her, loud and clear, whatever her feelings for me. "Never once have I said you were." Her brown eyes danced between mine, and I hoped she could see the sincerity written on my face. "Judgmental, yes. A pain in my ass, absolutely. But weak?" I leaned over her, my lips ghosting across the shell of her ear. "Far from it."

This close, it was impossible to miss the way she sucked in a breath, holding it. I moved back, meeting her eyes once more as I hovered above her.

"Well if you don't think I'm weak, why would you be worried about me?"

"Because you already haunt all my dreams, all my night-mares, and I shudder to think how your ghost would haunt my waking hours too." Lifting my hand, I laid it across her neck, thumb tracing along her jaw as I felt the way her heart raced. "You may hate me more than any other male, but I won't forget that *you* were the one who came to save me in my darkest hour. The image of a beautiful hellcat standing outside my cell, ready to free me, is burned into my mind, there everytime I close my eyes."

"I don't *hate* you."

I chuckled, unable to hold in my amusement at her words. "You were pretty full of hatred last night, and I have more than ten years of evidence to go with it."

"Hate is a strong word." Her face was still guarded, but as her eyes darted down to my mouth, her tongue darted out to lick her lips. "I'm not blind to a few of your admirable qualities."

"Such as?" I arched a brow. This witch was going to give me whiplash.

Her eyes snapped back up to mine. "If I told you, I'd have to kill you."

"I bet I could get it out of you." The image of her bound and at my mercy flickered through my vision, but a second later I remembered the dire circumstances we were all in. The imminent doom hovering over us. I took a step back, forcing myself to pull my mind away from that fantasy. "You should go. Think about going with Selene and Nimue. There's nothing else we can do tonight."

"Yeah? And you're telling me you're just going to go relax for the night?" Devanna scoffed. "No, you're going to keep planning and strategizing and obsessing. So, I'm not leaving."

I cocked my head to the side, eyes roving her body, noticing the way her chest heaved, her pulse pounded in her neck, her scent changed under my appraisal.

"And there's nothing to think about. I'm not leaving town, either." She stepped towards me. "You can't make me. This town means everything to me, and it's just as much mine to protect as it is yours."

"Anyone who stays has a deathwish, Devanna."

"I'm not afraid. Not of you, or them, or death. I'd never forgive myself for abandoning you."

"You should be," I said, leaning down until my face

hovered mere inches from hers as her words rang through my head. Abandoning *me,* not the town.

"Afraid?" she asked, one eyebrow raised in challenge. "Of you, or them?"

I breathed deeply, pulling in her light jasmine scent as my mind focused on the woman in front of me. "Both."

"Either I'm staying here to help you plan, or you come up with some other way to occupy our time, but I'm not leaving you here alone tonight." Her eyes met mine in defiance.

I growled in frustration. "Make up your damn mind. If you're staying here with me, you know exactly what I want. But if we do this in my house, you can't exactly kick me out after, and I'm not letting you just run away either. In case you haven't figured it out yet, I don't want just your body. I want *you.* I don't do things half-way — you're in or you're out, Devanna. I'm not touching you again until you decide."

"I'm here, aren't I?"

"Not good enough."

Grabbing my neck, she pulled my face down to hers in a searing kiss. Her arms looped around my neck instantly and I bent down, grabbing her ass. As soon as my fingers dug in, her legs wound around my waist while she held on, her body molding against mine perfectly, just like I remembered. Not wasting even a second, I carried her out of the kitchen and towards my room.

"Thank the Goddess," she said between kisses. "You don't have to make everything so dramatic all the time."

"Shut up," I growled, grabbing her tighter as we moved down the hallway to my wing of the house. Frantic energy overtook both of us, forcing me to stop, pinning her against the wall several times as we clawed at each other's clothes, needing to feel skin.

She pulled back from the kiss as we walked through the doorway to my room, brow furrowed as she unlaced her ankles from around my waist, dropped to the floor, and looked around the space. "Damn. I was hoping for a sex dungeon."

My nostrils flared as I fisted her hair, tugging her back and twisting her around. My other hand rose to her jaw, pulling her face to look at me. "You think I need leather and chains to restrain you? Scarves to blind you?" My voice dropping to a whisper, I said, "You have no idea how many times I've thought about bending you to my will. Punishing you for that bratty behavior. Making you submit to me."

She slapped my hand away from her jaw, eyes flashing, and I dropped my hand from her hair. "As if you even have that in you."

I chuckled, because despite the front Devanna put up, I could sense, in more ways than one, just how much she hoped I did have that in me. "You want that, don't you, hellcat? Though I doubt you could handle me."

Devanna huffed a laugh. "You think you can do anything someone hasn't done before?" She shook her head slowly, eyes glinting, somehow oblivious to the burning fury her words ignited in me as I imagined anyone else doing the things I wanted to do with her. "Do. Your. Worst."

My blood heated as I fought to maintain control of the situation. "I don't think you understand what you're agreeing to." I scraped my teeth along her neck. "If you submit to me, you'll submit completely. You know I don't do anything by halves. So I'll do anything I want with this little body. Mark you. Restrain you. Gag you. Spank you. Force you to your knees." I bit down on her neck, and she shivered as her head tipped back, her hands digging into my back where she held on. "I intend to own you. And once I own you, you're mine, Devanna."

She took a moment to steady her breathing, then met my gaze. "Anything you can do, I can do better."

I wasn't completely sure what she meant by that, but she reached down, lifting the hem of her shirt slowly as she tossed it to the side. A dark smile crept over my face as I took half a step back, licking my lips as I assessed her. The purple sports bra she wore pushed her breasts together, leaving a trail I wanted to lick my way down. Her tight shorts left nothing and everything to the imagination, and I wanted them gone. I reached out with a flick of my power, and smirked as she gasped when it locked her hands behind her back. I hadn't even lifted a finger.

"Pick a safe word," I said before I lost myself to the haze taking over my body. "Say it if you change your mind and you don't want this anymore, and everything will stop."

"Popcorn," Devanna answered without hesitation. Her eyes danced with mirth at the word choice, knowing how much I hated it.

"Anything I can do, you can do better, huh? Prove it," I stepped towards her as I unbuckled my belt. "On your knees."

Her chest rose and fell, eyes lit with defiance as she ground her teeth together. I smiled, knowing this was coming.

Devanna wouldn't submit to anyone.

She was too proud, too strong, too independent.

I let go of my belt and moved to step away from her, to leave the way to the door open. But then I stopped in my tracks when Devanna dropped to her knees, just as I'd been on mine last night for her, and her chin tipped up as she waited for my next command.

Fuck.

Chapter Thirty-One

DEVANNA

MY HEART THUNDERED in my chest as I sank to my knees on the rug in Orion's room, staring up at him as his magic held my hands behind me.

Even in his business casual attire, I could see how unhinged he was becoming, desperate desire overriding our common sense.

He stepped back, and unbuttoned the cuffs of his shirt before slowly rolling up his sleeves. I watched the movement, unable to look away from how undeniably sexy he was like this, hair disheveled from running his hands through it, wings ruffled, clothes askew from how desperately he needed me.

He ripped his belt free from his pants and closed the distance between us, hand gripping my jaw tightly as he tipped my face up. "Open your mouth."

I did as he said, shocking both of us as I stuck out my tongue. He slid his thumb in, running it along my tongue. "Suck."

In an out of body experience, I followed his orders, lips

closing over his thumb. A slow, satisfied exhale left him as he adjusted his pants, which already looked to be growing too tight, and we hadn't even done anything yet. Need coursed through me as I wondered why I was giving in so easily. I'd never felt sexual tension like this, but it wasn't the power that oozed off Orion that did it for me. I could *feel* how desperately Orion needed this. Needed to be in control when every other part of his life was spinning out of it.

Someday, it would be my turn to boss him around, but today I was willing to be what he needed to be. To put that look of pure bliss on his face. To give him control of my body. To use me as he needed it. He tipped his head back in ecstasy as I traced his thumb with my tongue.

Knowing I was the one who could make him come unraveled like this was a power in itself, and I loved it.

Maybe I needed this too, though I'd never give him the satisfaction of admitting as much.

Pulling his thumb free, he unzipped his pants, pulled out his cock, and fisted himself, giving himself a few lazy strokes as I tried my best not to drool. His fingers laced through my hair, bringing me closer and I followed his silent command. I licked his length, then pulled him deep into my mouth as his grip tightened, holding my head in place as he worked himself in and out of my mouth at his own pace, but I wanted more.

Orion groaned as I pulled him deeper. "Do you know how many times I wished I could shut you up like this, with my cock shoved down your throat?" Orion said, hand tightening on my hair as I fought not to gag on him. He pulled back, letting me breathe, then pushed forward again. Heat surged in me at his words, my belly tightening as my eyes fluttered closed. "Look at me, Devanna. Open your throat and swallow around me."

I couldn't help my own moan as I did as he said, and he groaned, the sound like a surge of electricity in my veins. I fidgeted against the magic binding my hands, desperate for friction myself as he worked himself in my throat.

"*Yes*," he hissed before he pulled out of my mouth and yanked me up to stand. With a flick of his magic, the rest of my clothes fell from my body, leaving me naked before him.

"By my accounting" — he slowly unbuttoned his shirt and dropped it to the floor, revealing the many tattoos that painted a collage of a life I knew next to nothing about — "and yes, I have been keeping track" — pushed his pants and boxers to the ground, stepping free of them — "you've been a brat to me exactly 138 times in the past ten years. We'll take off the 8 for what you just did, so that brings us to 130." He came closer again, trailing a finger from the hollow of my throat down my chest, between my ribs, and I shivered at the faint touch. He clocked my reaction with a smirk. "I have lots of ideas for how you can pay for the rest of them, but we won't have time for everything tonight. You've racked up quite the tally."

I pulled on my hands, needing to touch him, but the magical restraints didn't budge.

"Ah ah." Orion circled behind me as he leaned down over my shoulder, hands gripping my hips and sliding up until he cupped my breasts, and I arched into his hands before he pinched hard. I gasped, head tilted back on his chest from his harsh touch. "Submission means no fighting me, Devanna. I get what I want."

"Then do it already," I ground out as I shifted on my feet, needing more. Needing him to take me.

His hand slid around my throat, squeezing lightly as his other hand slid down my body between my legs and circled at my apex. *Finally*. I couldn't help the whimper that left me as he gave me some relief. "Don't try to tell me what to do, hellcat." His fingers slid inside me, pushing deep as his teeth bit down on my shoulder. My knees buckled, but he held me pinned to him as he worked his hand in and out of me. "And when you're in *my* room" — My body hummed under his touch, spinning quickly towards ecstasy— "Under *my* control" — Just as I teetered on the edge, he pulled his fingers free, pushed me down over the arm of the couch and slapped my ass hard — "You'll refer to me as *sir*."

I gasped at the sting, and his hand came down on me several times more in rapid succession. I should have been outraged. Should have fought back. Should have screamed at him, but my body had a mind of its own, pushing back into his hands, the sting of his palm teetering that edge between pain and pleasure that left me craving more.

And *sir*? He was one of those? Why wasn't I telling him to go fuck himself? Why was the idea of calling him that already making me even wetter?

His warm hand smoothed over my ass, giving us both a break. I started to twist around, wanting to see his face, but he *tsk*ed a breath before his magic pinned me down.

"I have you exactly where I want you." His body brushed up against mine as I turned to look over my shoulder. He smiled as his fingers dug into my ass then slid down between my legs again, teasing me. "I'll take off a point for each slap, so you're down to 125. How many more do you think you can take?"

I tried to scoff, but it came out breathier than I intended. "You'll break before I do. *Sir.*" I pushed back against his hips pointedly, and he couldn't stifle his groan as his shaft brushed up against me.

My head dropped forward, knees giving out as need overrode my senses. "Don't make me beg, Orion."

"You have no idea how much I want to hear that, but we can save it for next time."

With one smooth thrust, he slid home.

My mouth dropped open as he pushed in and out of me, using my body just how he needed it. His hand cracked down on my ass several more times, always followed by a smoothing touch, easing the sting. I was appalled by how much I loved it, how fast he had me spinning out of control.

"Don't you dare come," Orion growled as my body clenched around him. "Hold it."

"I can't. I need—"

He pulled free, and I gasped at the emptiness, wanting to let the frustrated growl escape.

Suddenly, the magic binding my hands disappeared and he spun me around, grabbing my ass as he lifted me into the air. My hands looped around his neck, lightly tracing a finger over his sensitive wings, which earned me another slap as he hissed a curse. The next moment, he dropped me onto his bed.

"You are my weakness in so many ways," Orion said as he put his knee on the bed and climbed over my body, dropping down onto his elbows. He kissed me far more tenderly than I expected after the way he'd ravaged my body so far, and fuck me, I liked it just as much as his rough touch. He smoothed a few strands of hair out of my face, his eyes dropping to my neck before meeting my gaze again. "Tell me you trust me. Tell me you're mine, not just for tonight but forever. It's all or nothing, Devanna."

My heart lurched at his words, at the softness in his features as he looked down at me, the depth of emotion I saw shining in his grey eyes. I turned my head to the side, squeezing my eyes shut as his words rang in my head.

But forever was a concept that didn't exist in my world. I couldn't fathom what that looked like, even if I desperately wanted it.

"You won't want me for forever," I managed to get out, closing off that part of my heart that wanted to accept what he was saying. I blinked hard before I met his eyes again. "I'll never be able to be what you want, what you're looking for."

A low growl started up in Orion's chest as he shot me a stern look. "Don't presume to know what I want."

"I'll never be easy to love," I snapped at him, anger overpowering any other emotion I felt, as it so often did. "I might have submitted to you tonight, but don't for one second think that would ever apply outside the bedroom. I'll never be compliant, or soft, or dainty, or whatever angel females are like."

Orion reared back, his face crinkling in confusion. "I'd never want you to be. Why would I? I want you exactly as the hellcat you are."

It was the fierce determination in his gaze that did it, that finally convinced me. That, and my absolute belief that

Orion was incapable of lying, to me or to anyone. No matter if his truths would hurt their listener or not.

"Okay," I whispered, nodding slightly as I let my eyes fall, unable to look at him as I gave in to the tidal wave of emotions that pulled me out to sea.

Orion's hand slid under my jaw, lifting my face tenderly towards his as he placed a soft kiss on my lips. "Look at me, Devanna."

I pulled in a deep breath, then opened my eyes. A smile spread across his face as his thumb traced the edge of my jaw, holding me in place. "Say you're mine."

I nodded silently.

"I need to hear the words, Devanna. I won't force this on you. We can stop right now and walk away. Go back to hating each other, or you can tell me you're mine. I won't have it any other way."

I nodded again, knowing he meant it. Even though we both needed release, he would walk away. Would leave me alone if I denied him. But I didn't want to. Not anymore.

I'd known, maybe for years, that it was more than hate I felt for him, more often than not. Or at least, not *just* hate. It was impossible not to admire Orion's dedication to the town, his loyalty to his friends, how he so selflessly gave every part of himself to everyone around him, even when it drove him to a mental breakdown like he'd been teetering on for months now.

And, really, what I hated most was that I didn't hate him. Orion held an immense power he could wield against me if I ever gave in to this admiration, to this feeling that was swallowing me whole.

"Don't break me," I whispered, hating how fragile I sounded.

He kissed me softly, once, then again. "I wouldn't dream of it."

"I'm yours." And just like that, I gave in. Dove headfirst into the face of my fears.

The fear of being alone forever, of being abandoned again was the one thing that held me back, but I trusted Orion. He'd take the protection of my heart as seriously as he took everything.

He kissed me again, harder this time as his tongue traced my lips, insisting I open for him. My hips shifted, opening as I waited for him to close the space between us, needing to feel him once more.

Orion's knees pushed my hips wider as he sank back into me, his energy humming under my skin as he moved. Rather than the bruising, brutal pace of before, this was different. My hands rested on his back as I held him close to me, needing to touch him everywhere.

He broke our kiss, sliding his mouth down my jaw to my neck. "I want to mark you, Devanna. It's an angel thing. A declaration for all to know you're mine."

It wasn't phrased as a question, but I knew he was asking for permission. I tilted my head away, giving him more access to my neck in invitation. "Do it."

His teeth sank into me as he sucked hard, bruising the skin at my neck and just barely breaking my skin. I gasped, the pain quickly turning to pleasure as his hips moved against mine, pushing deeper.

His mouth pulled away from my neck, as he turned his

head, leaning down into me. "Mark me. I'm yours, Devanna."

My body tensed at his words, and I slid my hands up to his head, pulling him towards my mouth as I bit down as he'd done seconds before. He growled in frustration, urging me to bite harder, only letting up when I tasted a drop of iron.

His sea salt and sandalwood scent overwhelmed me as I licked over where I'd just bitten him, feeling the way his body shuddered along with mine. Electricity skittered over my body, humming beneath my skin as he groaned, hips slamming into me harder.

"Come with me."

My body had no choice but to obey his command, flying over the edge as I arched into him with a moan.

Orion's head dropped down to my chest, his body slumping against me as we both struggled to breathe.

I'd never felt like this before — sated, satisfied, *whole.*

Orion had ruined me, and with or without the promises we'd made tonight, I knew I'd never be able to walk away from him.

This was it.

He was where I belonged.

Chapter Thirty-Two

ORION

I ADDED a handful of shredded cheddar into the bowl of egg mixture, whisked to combine, and poured the whole mix into the pan. I knew Devanna was a late riser, but I'd been up for hours already.

The little bubble we'd been in last night had been a nice distraction, but I couldn't shake the feeling that this was the calm before the storm.

Absently I rubbed my shoulder, feeling where Devanna had bitten me last night. Luckily, my shirt covered it, but I could feel the change in me from the exchange. She'd claimed me just as much as I'd claimed her. I only hoped she'd forgive me when she realized exactly what she'd agreed to in the heat of the moment. Even knowing how permanent this was, I couldn't find it in me to regret it. Hopefully, she'd feel the same when she understood what this meant for both of us.

"You know, it's kind of rude to leave a woman to wake up alone."

I half turned from where I stood at the coffee pot, planning to pour her a mug, and choked on nothing.

Devanna stood in the doorway dressed in nothing but one of my dress shirts, the crisp white of it a stunning contrast to her darker skin, and just barely buttoned enough to cover her up. Her bright blue hair was tied up in a messy ponytail, paired with her black glasses, and this disheveled morning-after version of Devanna was the sexiest thing I'd ever seen.

I was still blinking like an idiot when a gleeful cackle started up from the other side of the room.

"Oh, shit, *Dev!*" Blaze slapped his thigh. "Again?"

"You can shut your mouth," she snapped at him, but it lacked heat.

"Jesus, I'm so torn. I want details and yet, I'm afraid to ask." Blaze pushed me out of the way, pouring both of them a mug before joining her at the island.

"A lady doesn't kiss and tell."

"Oh, is Nimmie here?"

Blaze ducked the coaster Devanna threw at him, and I bit my lip to hide my laugh.

Devanna scoffed. "You couldn't handle my details."

"Please." Blaze rolled his eyes. "Not *your* details. I already know all your details, remember? You have no secrets from me, little Devvie. I meant—" He jerked his head pointedly in my direction as though I wasn't standing right there, watching this bizarre exchange.

Devanna tried to smirk again, but she met my eye over the rim of her mug. If I wasn't standing right there, would she be spilling everything we'd done last night? Shit, I didn't know how I felt about Blaze, my closest friend, hearing some of those details. I rubbed the back of my neck before returning my attention to the omelets.

"Wait." There was a clatter as Blaze set his mug down. "Are you two being… bashful? What is this?"

"None of your business, for one."

"Hilarious. Now, spill it. I figured once you two had scratched the itch, buttered each other's biscuits, did some squats in the cucumber patch, rode the bony express, that'd be it. One and done, so to speak. But this doesn't feel like…"

"Jesus, Blaze," Dev said, squinting in his direction. "Where do you even come up with this shit?"

"I can keep going." Blaze winked. "Jammed the clam. Stuffin' the muff—"

I held up a hand, power sizzling out of me as Blaze's mouth froze, unable to go on. His black eyes lit with amusement as Dev shook her head.

"We're…" I leaned back against the counter, crossing my arms as I stalled. Would Devanna balk at making things official? Labels? Did she still want any of that now in the bright light of day, or had it all been just in the heat of the moment?

"Orion and I —" Devanna started, but then stalled out, too.

"*Orion and I?*" Blaze practically screeched, his eyebrows reaching his hairline.

"Listen here, hyena, whatever we are or are not is none of your business, so back off," Devanna interrupted Blaze's laughter, but he continued beaming at us.

Suddenly he appeared right beside me, pulling me forward until his arms were wrapped around both of us —

Devanna still on the other side of the counter, leaning over it awkwardly — in an unwelcome group hug.

"My two best friends," he cooed, planting wet, loud kisses on both of our cheeks in turn. "Yes, yes — a thousand times yes. I'll be your best male / male of honor combo package. Or maybe one of those grown-men flower girls I keep seeing. I can do it all. Name the date."

"Oh, my Goddess," Devanna ripped herself from his arms. "You're as bad as Mo, you realize that?"

She settled back in the barstool across the counter from me as I slid an omelet and fresh orange juice towards her. She smiled at me, and the sight was so breathtaking I could hardly breathe.

Blaze took the stool to her left and I passed him an omelet as well, knowing the chances of him leaving us alone were slim to none.

The little moan that escaped Devanna as she slid the fork from her mouth went straight to my dick, reminding me of everything we'd done last night.

Devanna nodded to herself as she took another bite. "If I'd known you could cook like this, I might have given in a hell of a lot sooner."

I grinned at her, wanting to reach across the counter and pull her mouth to mine for another kiss even though I'd stolen hundreds last night, but held back in Blaze's presence.

"Was that" — Blaze paused, eyes shifting between Devanna and I — "Did you just *compliment* him?" He shook himself like a wet dog, then took a bite of his omelet. "That's gonna take some getting used to."

"Momentary lapse in judgment," Devanna said. "Probably won't happen again."

I smirked at her words, remembering how she'd stroked my ego last night every time she'd cried out under my ministrations. "I can think of a few ways to make you compliment me again."

"Shit, this is weird," Blaze muttered as he gulped his orange juice. "Quick, Dev, say something bitchy."

"Okay, when you drive your Mustang without Petra, you look just like any other middle-aged dude having a life crisis."

"Damn, Dev! I meant to O!"

Dev shrugged. "You should have been more specific, then."

Seeing Dev's attitude turned on someone other than me was more amusing than I anticipated, and the urge to kiss her only grew. Needing to rein myself in, I subtly adjusted my pants and changed the subject.

"We need to get the girls out of town today, and anyone else who plans on leaving."

Devanna's gaze rose to mine, an intensity shining through as she said, "Which doesn't include me."

"If you insist." I nodded, jaw tense.

"Phew." Blaze sighed. "This is more like it. I'm not sure how much of this lovey-dovey shit I can take from you two. You have to ease us into this change."

Turning my back to both of them, I dropped the skillet in the sink and flipped on the faucet. "I've been wondering why Nergal didn't make a move on the town while I was gone. It's odd that he'd attack the lighthouse, threaten us all, then disappear as he terrorized the rest of the country for weeks."

"Ryker said he suspects Nergal will need time to recover

from attacking the lighthouse after so long in the Keep, though who knows how long he needs before he shows up again."

"The moon," Dev interrupted Blaze. "There's a supermoon next week. If he's working with witches, they'll want to use it for extra power"

I nodded, pride simmering in me that she drew the same conclusion as me.

"Shit." Dev pushed back from the counter and turned to the hallway to my rooms, understanding just how quickly we needed to move.

The next full moon — the super moon — was in four days.

"I think I know what Nergal is after."

The three of us whipped around to see Petra standing in the entryway to the kitchen, her red hair up in a messy bun and still in a matching set of pajamas with flame emojis and red Mustangs all over them. Blaze took in the sight like he wanted to devour her, but she held up a small black notebook to stop his thoughts in his tracks.

"This is Willa's diary." She moved forward to set it on the kitchen island and open it to a specific entry. "Some of it was written in Haexeti, the demon language, so it took me longer to translate it. In this entry from October 1874, your mother wrote how worried she was getting about Nergal's thirst for power and chaos." Petra glanced up at Blaze at that, but Blaze had no illusions about his father, so he nodded at her to continue as he stood and moved to her, wrapping an arm around her waist and resting his chin on her shoulder to read along. "You were born shortly after, and her notes all switch to jumbled half-thoughts on ways she could possibly suppress his power, to bind his magic, as well as keep him away from the Cove."

Petra didn't mention anything about Nergal's desire to use Blaze to increase his power, whether it wasn't in Willa's diary or she was also protecting Blaze from that knowledge.

"She wanted to keep him away from me too."

All three of us whipped our heads up, staring at Blaze, who shrugged nonchalantly.

"He wanted to sacrifice me for this big demon spell once upon a time."

Dev and I shared a perplexed look as Petra's jaw dropped open.

Not sure if I should reveal we'd known something about that, I asked instead, "What makes you say that?"

"Oh, Willa brought home this creepy looking demon spell book one day. When she saw me, she tried to hide in her bag so I wouldn't see it — so, obviously, I went and stole it later that night once she was asleep. I didn't *really* know Haexeti back then, but for a forbidden spell book, you better believe I worked my ass off to figure out what was in there she didn't want me to know about. Anyway, the bookmarked page was all about sacrificing a child in a spell to grant the demon an incredible amount of power." He scoffed. "I knew enough about my father even at that age to put the pieces together."

We all gaped at him, struggling to come to terms with the news that Blaze had known about this all this time.

"So, your whole life, you've known your own father wanted to murder you?" Petra spoke for all of us, her words stilted and low.

"Yeah," Blaze chuckled. *Chuckled.* "And he's failed for a

hundred and forty-eight years. Isn't that hilarious? He thinks *I'm* the fuck-up?"

A strained silence followed before Petra finally broke it, bringing us back to the matter at hand.

"Okay, well, obviously he didn't succeed at *that* spell. But Willa still worried about him, even a decade later. Here, she says, '*I worry about him losing himself to this impulse, his desire for more taking control. For his own sake, and for our children, I may need to gather the Coven and have them assist me in tempering his power before it's too late. My black obsidian crystal might be strong enough to be the vessel. I can only hope it could trap enough of his power to make a difference.*'"

Petra looked up over her shoulder at Blaze, who tugged the journal closer and read it over again.

"Do you know what crystal she referred to?" Dev asked, and Blaze shook his head.

"She was a witch." He shrugged helplessly. "There were always tons of crystals lying around."

"Is there anything in there to suggest she actually did it? Actually bound his magic to a crystal?" I asked.

"No," Petra sighed. "Mo told me about the night Willa tried to confront him, but no one knows if the spell actually worked. Unfortunately, she died not long after this, so it's possible, even if she intended to, she never got the chance."

"But we know Nergal is looking for something in town," Dev mulled it over. "Which suggests he, at least, believes that she did. Right?"

I nodded slowly. "I would say so, yes."

"So, whether or not she ever charged that crystal with his powers, we need to find it before he does."

Blaze huffed a laugh. "Find a single crystal in this town?

That's like finding a needle in an Olympic-size pool of other needles. Any suggestions on how to do that?"

"Lys and I can handle it." Dev waved a hand. "Knowing it's probably a black obsidian helps narrow it down."

"And I'll keep reading through her journals," Petra added. "See if there's anything else I can find about whether she actually completed the spell or where she might have put the crystal."

Blaze clapped his hands together, rubbing his palms. "Perfect. That leaves setting border traps to —"

"—Ryker," I cut in abruptly, and Blaze frowned. "I don't want you anywhere near the border in case Nergal tries to grab you or possess you or God only knows what else. You can help me coordinate getting people out if they want to leave, and then figuring out who's left."

Four days. We had four days, and not nearly enough people, to get ready for a demon horde.

If we were going to survive this, we needed backup.

Chapter Thirty-Three

DEVANNA

WHILE THE REST of the town was a flurry of activity, Lys and I spent the day in the Cottage's basement, then attic, searching through Willa and Althea's old crystal collection. A few of the rarer ones might have made their way into my pockets as well, but so far, there hadn't been a single black obsidian in sight.

We'd tried a few locator spells to track it down as well, but each one directed us either to my shop — where I sold them — my house — where, of course, I had a handful — or to Ostara's, who had her own collection as head witch of our Coven.

"So, you and Orion seemed different," Lys said, and my hands stilled on the box I was looking through, scowling up at him.

"Really?" My eyes narrowed behind my glasses, not bothering to hide my annoyance at the probing statement. "I thought it smelled like chum in here, but just chalked it up to how much time you've spent underwater lately. Didn't realize you were fishing in the attic."

Lys chuckled as he picked up a box and moved it aside. "Do you know how delightful it feels to give you even an ounce of the shit you dish out to everyone else? It might be my favorite past-time."

"I hate you."

"Okay, so we're lying today, then. So I should tell you that you and Orion are definitely *not* the main topic of conversation around town today."

I clenched my teeth to keep from saying anything, from spitting the venom that sat so readily on the end of my tongue. "How did you even—" I paused, cutting myself off with a shake of my head. In the hours that had passed since I'd left Orion this morning, everything seemed almost unreal. As if last night was a dream and couldn't possibly be reality. What we'd done, the things he'd said… how much had been real, and how much just a distraction? "It doesn't—"

"Stop whatever shit you're about to say, Dev," Lys said, dropping to sit on the floor as he stared at me, tattooed arms resting on his knees. "The only thing everyone is saying is that they want you both to be happy, no matter what that looks like."

"But that's the thing." I turned to him, needing to say what made me so mad about this whole thing. "Who decided that I needed to be with *anyone* to be happy? That I was unhappy before? That I couldn't be happy on my own? That I have to fit into everyone else's picture-perfect view of what my life *should* look like?"

"No one." Lys's hands went up, palms out. And dammit, like he always did, that took the wind right out of my sails. How can you argue with someone who so readily agrees with you? "But Dev, I wish you could see yourself through the eyes of those who love you. You are one hell of a force to be reckoned with, exactly as you are. *Allowing* people to love you doesn't make you less. To lean on others doesn't make you weak. To let others fight beside you, *with* you, doesn't mean you're not capable of fighting for yourself. You don't *need* any of us, which makes the fact that you want us that much bigger, more important."

I wiped the dust from my eyes, pulling a stack of books out of the box in front of me as I listened to his words, not sure I believed them even though Mo had said pretty much the same thing. But, unfortunately, Lys loved the sound of his own voice so he kept talking.

"Being with Maisie has made me realize you don't have to change for the people who love you, to be something you're not. If they really love you, then they'll accept you just as you are. There is no better feeling."

I scoffed, hating the way my chest tightened at his words. "And what on earth would make you think Orion, of all people, is capable of accepting me just as I am, Lys? We have been at each other's throats for *years*. And that's just supposed to, what? Stop? Change? Am I supposed to be nice now?"

A bitter laugh escaped me, thinking through last night, how vulnerable he'd made me feel. In the moment I'd felt needed, but I understood exactly what he wanted from me and gave it to him. But in the light of day, I couldn't see how this would ever work.

How I could be myself and still be loved, especially by someone as truly *good* as Orion? Sure, the male was a dick, but not a single thing he did was for himself. He was selfless to a fault in everything he did, and I equal parts loved and hated him for it.

"Sometimes it blows my mind that you can wear such thick glasses and still be so blind, Four Eyes." Lys laughed and the dig was enough to draw me out of my spiraling thoughts. "But who am I to talk? Maisie was right here all along and I missed it, missed out on years I could have had with her."

"Even dimes are hard to see when your head is stuck so far up your own ass."

"Same could be said about the way Orion has been quietly taking care of you for years, boo-boo," Lys said as he pushed to his feet, grabbing another box and turning his back to me.

I stood with my hands on my hips, staring at his back as my brow furrowed, trying to understand what that meant.

"Maybe she got rid of it." Lys wiped his sweat-covered brow with the back of his hand as he slumped onto an old trunk an hour later.

I collapsed onto a crate. We'd been moving boxes and old furniture for hours to access all the nooks and crannies of the old Cottage attic, and I was exhausted and covered in sweat, dust, and cobwebs.

"I doubt that," I said, fanning myself. Did it have to be a thousand degrees the day we needed to go digging through this sauna of an attic? "If it was big enough to hold a demon's magic, I'm guessing it was huge. Not the type of crystal you just toss out."

Lys sighed, knowing I was right. "What do you want to do, then? I'd say we could try targeting her magical signature, but the spell would probably just pick it up on Blaze, or any number of random things in town she might have spelled."

He had a point there.

"Let's regroup tomorrow," I suggested, standing with several gratifying *pops* from various sore joints. I needed a shower and a whiskey, not necessarily in that order. Maybe even at the same time.

"I'll look through some grimoires, see if I can come up with other ideas," Lys agreed, and stood with a groan himself before climbing down the ladder out of the attic.

I'd just slid the ladder up and closed the hatch to the attic when my phone buzzed, and I pulled it out to read the text.

MORGAINE

Town game night! Tonight at Mini-Wags!

I did a double-take to my phone. Mini-Wags was closed for business since Umbridge left and regular Scallywags opened again — and what the hell was Mo thinking, inviting the entire town over to my basement without even asking? Forget the fact that this was *not* the time for town games; we were all stressed and preparing for a damn siege, for crying out loud. Before I could even swipe open my phone to shoot off an irate text back to tell Mo to invite everyone to her own damn house if she wanted a party, another message came in.

MORGAINE

Everyone is stressed and needs to relax.
Scallywags is closed with Blaze out of town.

Attendance mandatory.

"Of course it is," I muttered under my breath, making my way outside and heading home to shower. I knew Morgaine would just invite herself in again, so I didn't worry about setting anything up for her event. At least I'd get that whiskey.

Freshly showered, I pulled on black bike shorts, an oversized tee, and black platform sandals, feeling the magic in my hands float over my hair as it instantly dried and curled the way I liked it. Of all the things magic was capable of, this was one of my favorites.

I opened the door to the basement, expecting to hear voices, but there was nothing. The lights weren't even on.

8pm. Definitely people should have showed up by now.

Bagheera blinked at me from one of the stools at the kitchen island, and I shrugged.

"More whiskey for me," I said and pulled down my Knob Creek to pour myself a tumbler. Somehow talking to Bagheera had become a regular thing lately, but I liked his company, even if we avoided each other most of the time.

I was mid-pour when I heard a muffled thump of a footstep at the front door, then a reluctant knock.

"Oh, *now* you're knocking?" I called out to Mo. "Just let yourself in like usual — Oh."

Orion frowned at me from the front door he'd opened, a board game in his hand. He was back to looking like his usual buttoned-up self, his grey dress shirt tucked into navy blue chinos, his silver hair neatly combed. It gave me the distinct urge to ruffle his hair, to pull his shirt until it wrinkled.

"You're not Mo." I narrowed my eyes. "Is that *Doctor Who* Risk?"

He lowered the box slightly. "I was hoping if I provided an alternative, we could avoid the usual Bendy Bobcat Bagel chaos, or whatever Blaze calls that stupid game."

I shook my head, stepping aside to let him in and motioned for him to head towards the basement. "A little surprised Mo isn't here already, setting up something equally absurd."

Orion didn't respond, just moved towards the basement steps and I followed behind him. Why did I have to notice how well his shirt hugged his broad shoulders? I squeezed my eyes shut, trying to think of anything other than the sight of those same arms, caging me in, holding me down, wringing pleasure from my body in a way I could never forget. But how was I supposed to move on to whatever this was between us now?

Seemingly unbothered by the same thoughts twisting my insides into knots, Orion flicked a hand in front of him and the basement lights surged, complete with the spinning disco ball hanging over the dance floor Blaze had insisted Mini-Wags needed, then had left behind when he'd cleared out the furniture. As the neon sign on the brick wall hummed to life, Orion paused, taking in the other side of the room, his gaze lingering on the punching bag before sliding to my wall of weapons.

"What?" I crossed my arms.

He set the board game on the mini bar and shrugged. "I guess I expected a sex dungeon."

My jaw dropped slightly, chest weirdly tight at hearing my own words repeated back to me. "Did you just crack a joke? Should we record the date, celebrate this first milestone?"

He glanced over his shoulder at me, his grey eyes that same deadpan expression I knew so well.

"Besides, it's not like I'd keep any of that out in the open where any meddling Mo could find it."

For a second, his wings tensed, then he must have sensed I was kidding — mostly — and let out a huff of a laugh. We stood in awkward silence for another minute, then Orion went behind the bar and helped himself to a beer from the mini-fridge. He leaned muscled forearms across the bar top as he took a long sip, pressing the bottle to his lips, his steel grey eyes never leaving me.

I downed my whiskey and went for another when my phone buzzed with an incoming call from my mother. I set it on the bartop, watching it ring out.

Orion cleared his throat. "Are you going to get that?" His gaze dropped down to my screen, seeing the name of the caller, and his brow furrowed.

"I talked to them last month."

I could see more questions in his eyes, so I flipped over the phone. Not that that hid anything from him.

"Blaze mentioned —" Orion's words cut off when I shot him a glare.

"Yeah?" I stiffened, immediately on guard. "What'd that Judas say?"

Orion's hands went up, but he didn't step back. "Just — something he said implied you might have some family issues. Or maybe I inferred the family part."

I scoffed, backing off and returning to my drink. Was I supposed to share all my feelings and shit with him now? The thought made my skin crawl — I wasn't a *sharer*. Not with him, not with anybody.

But wasn't that what people did when they… *cared* for someone?

"Look, I don't need *them*, and I don't know how to do this," I blurted after a long swallow of my whiskey.

Orion quirked an eyebrow, and I gestured between us. We needed to confront this head-on, or I was going to explode.

"Blaze was right. This is awkward, right? Do I have to be nice to you now? Because I don't know if I can do that."

"Nice?" Orion chuckled. "After all these years? Why start now?"

A little of the tension I hadn't realized I was holding in my shoulders loosened, and I nodded. "Okay. Good."

Orion checked his watch, his lips pressing into a line. "I'm beginning to think no one else is going to show."

"Then why —" I didn't have to finish my sentence before the pieces fell into place. No doubt, as Lys said, the whole town had been talking about Orion and I being whatever we were now, and Mo had decided she wanted to force us to spend some more time together. I cleared my throat. "Well, good. I didn't want this place turned back into a speakeasy anyway."

"Still," Orion started, and I tilted my head. "Morgaine might have been right about everyone needing to relax a little." He inclined his head towards his board game, and I snorted.

"There's no way in hell I'm playing that."

"Then what do you usually do to relax?"

"Try to figure out how to piss you off."

He scowled, and I let it sit for a minute before I laughed, then gestured around the room.

"Honestly? I work out. Nothing is more relaxing than punching something with everything you got."

A glint entered Orion's eyes at my words, and his lips curled slowly into a smirk. "Oh really?"

He set his beer down with a *clink*, then strolled around the mini bar in a way that had my adrenaline spiking. Suddenly, I felt like I'd just poked the bear and was about to get my ass handed to me.

Chapter Thirty-Four

ORION

HOW I COULD IGNITE Devanna's body with just a few words, just a look, was intoxicating. She wanted to relax by punching something? Well, that could be arranged.

I may have had an ulterior motive for enticing her to fight me, but I kept it to myself.

Dev set her glass down as I started unbuttoning my shirt, and I nodded towards her ridiculous sandals.

"You'll probably want to ditch those."

She indicated my slacks. "You'll probably want to ditch *those.*"

"Already trying to get my pants off, hellcat?"

Rolling her eyes, she slipped her sandals off then started for the stairs. "I'll grab you some shorts."

I peeled off my shirt, folding it before placing it on the counter of the bar as I watched her ass moving up the stairs. Her slip about not needing her parents revealed more than she probably thought, but if she wanted to push that aside and focus on something physical for now — well, that was a coping mechanism I could understand.

Music pounded through the basement not long later, sweat dripping down us as we sparred. As expected — to me, anyway — Dev's reflexes were quicker, her punches harder than they would have been yesterday. I hid my grin and spun out of her way as she launched herself at me, then swept her feet out from under her, watching as her body dropped to the mat.

She wasn't faster than me. Yet.

I stopped for a sip of water as she pulled herself back to her feet, wiping her forehead with the bottom of her shirt, exposing a strip of skin above her waistband that I did my best to ignore.

"Had enough?" I asked casually, knowing it would rile her up.

Fire lit in her dark eyes just like I knew it would. "Just warming up, Lucifer."

She hissed a word, holding her hand up in the air as the bo staff flew off the mount on the wall and landed in her hand. A quizzical expression flitted across her face momentarily, but her eyes flicked back to me when I stepped closer.

"The moon is already boosting your powers," I said, not hiding my smirk this time. "Too bad it's still not enough to beat me."

Instantly, she moved, hands swinging wide as the staff whooshed through the air. I stepped back, electricity crackling through my fingers as I sliced down through the air, breaking the wood in two.

Instead of stopping, Dev threw the pieces in her hands

to the side and sprinted towards me at a speed I paused at, wondering what she was planning. Before I could move out of the way, she leaped, her legs scissoring around my neck as she twisted hard to the side, sending me flying to the mat beneath her. Thankfully, I turned before I landed on my wings, but the wasted second was enough for her to climb on top of me. She rested her forearm across my neck — not pressing down, but making a point — before her lips curled back into a smile and she snarled, "Yield."

I leaned up, wrapping a hand around the back of her neck and pulling her face down into mine. Heat seared my body as the kiss lingered, hard and unrelenting, until I wove a leg around hers, flipping her to her back beneath me. "Not in my vocabulary."

Her small dark hands shoved against my pale chest as she forced me off her, and rolled quickly to her feet. My breath caught as she grabbed the hem of her shirt and pulled it over her head, leaving her in just her tight shorts and a sports bra, just like last night. "If you're going to use all that naked skin to distract me, two can play that game. Also, why am I not surprised that with all of the ink painting your chest and back, all of it is black and white? A compass, a skull, a lighthouse... as unoriginal as your J. Crew wardrobe."

She leaned over in an exaggerated manner as she set her shirt down on the floor, all but waving her ass in the air, and I chuckled.

"You'll have to do better than that." I flexed my wings to hide the flicker of arousal her body caused in me, but this wasn't the time. Not yet. I heard my phone vibrate from inside my slacks pocket, and walked over to read the message.

Devanna walked around the bar to the fridge and pulled out an ice cube, running it over her neck, her chest, while making satisfying moans in a way that would have probably worked a minute before I'd opened my phone.

Now, I could only stare at the text.

MALACHI

Attack in Timber Creek. No backup headed your way. Good luck.

I read his words over again, then another time as I felt the blood leave my face.

No backup.

Vaguely, I was aware of Dev saying my name, but the sound in my ears started to go muffled until all I could hear was my own pulse pounding in them.

No backup.

In every one of Ryker's and my plans, we'd counted on Malachi sending us assistance from Headquarters. I knew with the upheaval we wouldn't have as many as I'd like, but *none?*

Fuck.

Who were our fighters? I started to tick off the ones I knew we could count on from the wolf pack, the fox skulk, the bears, the sea nymphs — would sea nymphs be any help to us on land?

I tried to blink away the pinpricks of darkness creeping into my vision.

Ryker. The demons.

Who among the witches could actually fight?

My heart was pounding.

How strong a ward could the Coven make around the town?

Would Nergal be stupid enough to fall for any traps we'd have time to set?

Shit, there wasn't enough *air* down here in this basement. My lungs heaved, straining for oxygen.

No backup.

The words echoed in my mind, images flashing of all the ways our town was about to be destroyed.

The gazebo in flames. Kits and wolf pups running for their lives. Witches huddled and bleeding and screaming. Even though I understood the extent of the problems elsewhere and that there weren't enough fighters to go around, I couldn't help but think that this was all because of me. If I'd done better, tried harder, protected this town better, we wouldn't be in this position.

Fuck, fuck, fuck.

"Hey —"

A hand landed on my arm, and I reacted before I could blink, closing my hand around a throat and forcing my assailant's back up against the wall behind the bar. Sparks shot from the overhead lights as my magic flared.

Then a hand slapped me, hard, and I hissed at the smarting pain in my cheek.

"Snap out of it! What the hell's gotten into you —"

I blinked, and looked down at the figure I'd subdued. Not an assailant, just Devanna.

No, not *just* anything. My Devanna.

I loosened my grip, horror creeping in on me that I'd hurt her. I tried to take a shaky breath as static skittered over my bare arms and Dev scrambled to regain her footing.

But she didn't back down, didn't cower in fear like she should have. She took a step *towards* me.

"What's going on?" she demanded, concern taking over her features where anger should have been. Why wasn't she furious with me? Why wasn't she kicking my ass for throwing her around like that? I wordlessly handed her my phone, the text still open.

Realization dawned over her face as my hands started shaking, the hum of electricity in the air ratcheting up as my power threatened to explode into the room.

"No backup?" she breathed. "None at all? They're just abandoning us without question? But —"

She looked up, as though she could see all the residents of the town, how unprepared we were for an attack like what was surely coming.

It had been decades since there was any kind of supernatural uprising on this scale. Centuries since demons had banded together. But the stories about them were still the stuff of nightmares. Still studied in training as cautionary tales, as justification for the way the Council operated.

No one, not even the most anarchist supes, would want a repeat of the days before the Council was formed, before the worst demons were contained or put down.

Blood pounded in my ears, my wings twitched, hands clenched into fists. The light bulb directly above me sparked and shattered, glass shooting out.

This was going to be a bloodbath, and it was all my fault.

This whole town, all these people — I'd failed them.

"Look at me."

Dev's voice cut through my frantic thoughts, and I brought my gaze to meet hers. With a wave of her hand, the glass pieces lifted and she gathered them into a ball, then flung it to the side.

"You need to get it together. This is not the time for you to fall apart." She poked a finger into my chest, and static zapped between us. "This town is counting on you to protect them, to lead them."

I scoffed. "Then they're idiots. I can't do—"

Another slap came, this one hard enough to snap my head to the side.

"Those are my friends you're shit-talking, including you, and I won't take that," Dev hissed, rage crackling like lightning in her eyes.

But for that split second of surprise, my panic had lessened. The more Dev pushed me, the more I could focus on anything but fear, could ground myself here in the moment, could think clearly.

I stepped into her space. "Again."

She cocked her head, brow furrowing as she tried to work out what I meant.

I grabbed her wrist, aiming to bring her palm back up, but in a burst of strength, she spun me around, swept my feet from under me, and had me pinned on the ground with my arm behind my back.

The buzz of static in the room lessened noticeably.

I finally took a half-way full breath.

Dev was silent a minute before I heard a soft, "Oh."

Then she cackled.

Chapter Thirty-Five

DEVANNA

WELL, if it wasn't my lucky day.

Orion wanted to be, *needed* to be controlled, dominated right now? I could hardly hold back my cackle of glee. Okay, I didn't even try to hold it back.

"And they say dreams don't come true," I murmured as I leaned my knee between Orion's white wings, though not pressing down. "You want this?"

Cheek pressed into the cool basement floor, Orion nodded.

I *tsk*ed. Oh, this was going to be too fun. "I don't think I heard you."

Orion licked his lips, his eyes pressed shut. He was still shaking, his fight-or-flight response engaged, but if he thought this might help, I was happy to oblige. *More than* happy.

Goddess, Orion metaphorically on his knees? For *me*? A shiver of anticipation went through me. Vindication on so, *so* many levels.

And on the other hand, I could understand where he was coming from. The rug had just been pulled out from under him. We were on our own, about to face an unknown number of demons, and had limited fighters. There was a decent chance our town wouldn't survive. He needed to regain some control by giving *up* some control. And damn, I didn't mind helping out there.

Still, I needed to hear him actually say he wanted this. Both because of the satisfaction it would give me to hear it, but also to be sure we were on the same page.

I brought my lips to his ear. "Use your words."

"You know what I want," he grunted. There was a pause, while he waited for me to acknowledge his request, before he added, more softly, "Please."

Hearing him beg sent heat pooling low in my abdomen, but that would have to wait.

"Careful what you wish for, *sir*." I climbed off him slowly, taking quick inventory of what was available here in the basement as he exhaled heavily. I couldn't help but smile at his visceral reaction to the word even when I was the one giving the orders. "Remember our safe word?"

Orion's gaze snapped to mine, that same deadpan expression he so often wore as he said, "Popcorn."

My smile turned into a full grin. "Sit on the chair."

I moved to the side of the room to grab a few items while Orion settled on the simple wooden chair, then I came up behind him.

"Give me your wrists."

Without hesitation, Orion held his arms behind him, and I tied them together with the jump rope I'd grabbed, firm but not tight. My adrenaline spiked at having Orion at my mercy like this, in a way I'd never expected him to want, to allow. A spark shot between our hands, so it seemed he was getting as turned on as I was.

Who knew.

I stood, trying to calm my breath, wanting to savor this rare opportunity since I had no idea when he'd ask for this again, if ever. Even if this role reversal was a one time thing, I couldn't bring myself to care. I loved the way he had commanded my body, pulled pleasure from me, and I wanted to return the favor more than anything.

I held the bandana I'd also retrieved in front of him so he could see it.

"Yes or no?"

It took him a minute to understand, but then he shook his head. "I want to see you."

Goddess, I loved the sound of that, the way his eyes raked over my body. I needed to get air conditioning installed down here. Why was it a million degrees in a basement?

I tucked the bandana in the waistband of my shorts, and placed a finger tip on his wing joint. He shuddered instantly, his feathers twitching.

"Dev —"

"Oh, are your wings sensitive?" I traced my nail down the bones of his wing, his shoulders shuddering as I went, slowing even more torturously right at the tip before I finally lifted my hand away. He let out a breath that could have been relief or disappointment.

Moving around to face him, I saw the expected bulge in

the front of his shorts, and smirked. Lightning flashed in his eyes, but he still looked better than before — focused, instead of panicked.

Planting my feet on either side of his, I leaned down over him and tilted his face up with a finger under his strong jaw. "The real question is, do you want to be a good boy, or just my fuck toy?" I searched his eyes, still trying to read what he needed from this, but if I had to guess, even he didn't know. He needed *me* to be in control and give him what he needed, but that would've been a lot easier if this wasn't his first time switching roles.

He licked his lips again. "Whatever I am, it's yours, Devanna." His steel grey eyes bored into mine, and it felt like a channel opened between us, like wires had been strung between our hearts and the circuit finally closed, power streaming between us, through us. Shared. I drifted closer, unable to stop myself, drawn in like a magnetic field pulled us together, until our cheeks pressed together, his stubble scraping my skin. His head turned until his lips pressed against me instead, and he breathed, "I'm yours. Take what you want."

Hearing those words, from Orion especially, spiked my heart rate. Heat flushed up my neck, and I pulled back, pressing a hand to his chest as I focused on him, pushing my own clenching heart to the back of my mind. He felt almost cold to the touch as my palms pressed to his chest, his panic riding just under the surface, but his heart thudded rapidly, just like my own.

I took a deep breath to center myself, then stepped back, trailing my hand down his chest, his chiseled abs, to toy at the waistband of his sweats as I dropped to my knees. He wanted this, wanted the physical distraction, and I was somewhat surprised to realize there was nothing I wanted more than to be the one to make him feel better.

"I think I'm going to torture you a little, then." I smirked, laying my hand over the bulge in his shorts with pressure that was way too light. Orion huffed and tried to push his hips up into my hand, trying to get more friction, but I pulled my hand away.

"You'll take what I give you and no more," I chided, standing and stepping away.

Slowly, so slowly, I pulled off my shorts, Orion's pupils widening as I discarded the rest of my clothes. From the freezer, I grabbed a cup of ice before returning to him at the chair. Standing right in front of him, I trailed an ice cube over myself again, but this time, I had his full attention. Pausing at my nipple, I swirled it there until it hardened, and Orion swallowed audibly.

"Come here," he growled, but I only chuckled.

I lifted the mostly melted ice cube to his lips. "Open up." He let me place the ice on his tongue, his eyes closing momentarily like he was savoring the barest taste of my skin left on it.

"Raise your hips." My hands dropped to his shorts, and he grunted again.

"Finally," he muttered as I started working them down, his cock springing up once it was freed. I tossed the shorts aside and grabbed another ice cube, popping it straight into my mouth.

I licked a cold trail on his chest, his abs, and he shivered at the chill of it. When I dropped down between his knees again, he shifted on the chair, starting to get frustrated with his restraints and how slow I was going. I rested my hands on his thighs and pressed a chilled kiss to the inside of his knee, waiting for the ice cube to finish melting.

"I need your mouth on me," he growled, and I could see the truth of that leaking and twitching in front of my face.

I hummed in acknowledgment of his words. "Excuse me, sir. Don't forget who's in charge here." I rose on my knees just enough to flick his nipple, and while he grunted about that, I quickly dropped back down and swirled my cold tongue around his tip.

He let out a hiss, his hips jerking, but I took my time, enjoying the contrast of the warmth of his skin against the cold of my mouth. The longer I toyed with him, the heavier his breathing became, until it became just a constant, low growl.

"*Devanna* — fuck —"

At precisely that moment, I flicked my gaze up to his and pulled him deep into my mouth. A breath left him in a whoosh of air, his wings flexing in a way that sent a breeze through the room, and together we found a rhythm. His hips moved with my mouth, and the frantic magic that had been coursing off him calmed, replaced by something else.

An energy of a wholly different kind.

I reached between my legs, needing relief of my own, and another groan left Orion as he saw what I was doing. He grew even harder in my mouth, and just when he began to slam his hips harder into me, I pulled off him with a gasp, his cock slapping wetly against his abs.

"*Devanna*," he hissed, but I was already rising to my feet, straddling his waist, and lining him up with me.

322

I sank down slowly, or tried to, but Orion had other plans, and slammed up into me from beneath.

"Hey, you said take what *I* want," I reminded him, though when he moved his hips again, the gasp that left me might have contradicted my complaint. "I'm in control this time."

"Well, you were terrible at it," he growled.

I laughed. "Your giant hard-on begged to differ."

Orion licked his lips. "Giant, huh?"

I rolled my eyes. "Next time I'm gagging you. I see the appeal now."

"Shut up and ride me, hellcat."

"No backseat driving."

After that, we were a blur of sweat and friction, both of us chasing relief, riding the high of our fear, of this role reversal, of the adrenaline from our sparring. Orion's lips trailed the juncture of my neck and my shoulder where he'd bitten me last night, the nerves there tingling right before he sank his teeth into my skin again. I cried out, the increase in sensation enough to send me hurtling over the edge, and I rode out my pleasure as Orion found his release as well.

We stayed there, breathing hard, sweat dripping down both of us, until slowly Orion's teeth lifted from my neck, his lips pressing there instead.

I pressed my own to the edge of his jaw. "Good boy."

With a snap of magic, the rope binding his hands snapped, and his arms came around my back, his hands rubbing gently up and down my spine.

My own hands cupped his jaw, searching his eyes to try to decipher how he was feeling. *I* couldn't stop myself from leaning forward, placing a kiss on his lips that was far more tender than everything that had just happened between us, the only way I knew to show him how much I cared about him. "Better?"

He let out a shaky breath, but nodded, his forehead dropping to lean against mine.

"Good. Now let's get ready to kick some demon ass."

Chapter Thirty-Six

ORION

OVER THE NEXT THREE DAYS, I worked tirelessly, coordinating efforts to fortify the town however we could. Kit, Darius, and Winona, head of the bear shifters, had the shifters working on setting physical traps at all entry and exit points, blocking any access for other shifters Nergal might bring to accompany him. While I wished I could be out there to set them myself, I was one person and I had to trust that they could take on this task. After all, there was nothing the foxes loved more than mischief. Kit could handle this. I had to trust that he could.

Meanwhile, Ronan led the sea nymphs in a coordinated effort along the shoreline and in the waters around town. Thankfully, the male was as serious as I was about the threat Inessa posed, the reminders of the destruction she'd caused a bitter chip on his shoulder.

Ostara lead the witches in their effort to solidify any part of the spell that kept Nergal out, working in shifts as they cast the immense spell, save for Lysander and Devanna, who were still working on locating the missing crystal mentioned in Blaze's mother's journal. With the FBI occupied else-where, I reinstated the glamour, running any lingering humans out of town. No one was allowed in or out without my permission.

Blaze escorted Nimue and Selene out of town, as well as any other residents who wanted to flee. No one would be required to stay and fight what would most likely be a losing battle. None of us were under any illusions here. The odds were terrible.

I called in every favor I had, hoping Malachi was wrong and more help could be spared for us, but the entire super-natural community was in upheaval. No one was willing to abandon their own towns and people in the same way I wasn't willing to leave, either. Ryker called in a few of his bounty hunter contacts, but most of them had already committed to other towns.

Glancing at the scattered plans and maps on my desk, I dropped my head into my hands, wondering where it had all gone wrong. What I could have done differently. How I could have been better. Trying to fight against the anxiety threatening to swallow me whole, I drew in a steadying breath. With only one night between us and the super moon, we were well and truly out of time.

The smell of burnt popcorn wafted up through the hallway of Town Hall right before Blaze turned the corner, leaning casually against the door jamb as he munched on popcorn, one ankle crossed over the other.

"You look terrible," Blaze said as he tossed a piece of popcorn into the air and caught it in his mouth, not a care in the world.

"I can always count on you to make me feel better."

"On that happy note," Blaze paused, turning to look out the window behind me before he cleared his throat. "Thought you'd like to know that everyone in town is losing their shit."

I frowned, following his gaze as I looked at the town below me, but everything seemed normal, albeit quiet. "What do you mean?"

"Well, Nox has been pacing in front of his store for the last hour, looking at the gazebo as if it's a bonfire just waiting to be lit."

"And that's different from any other day, how?"

Blaze chuckled, then pointed a finger at me. "Not wrong. Although I'll say my desire to throw your electric car into the ocean is a bit out of my usual range. Normally I'd settle for changing your horn to *Move Bitch* and call it a day, solely to annoy you, not destroy property."

I crossed my arms, one eyebrow raised. "What's the saying about tigers and stripes? Pretty sure you haven't outgrown destructive habits yet either, Blaze."

Blaze grabbed a handful of popcorn and tossed it in the air, catching only two in his mouth as the other dozen pieces rained down on the floor around him or got stuck in his dark hair. "Annoying you *is* my favorite pastime. But that's not my point."

"Then what is?"

Blaze squeezed his eyes shut, pinching the bridge of his nose in a gesture I'd only ever seen him make when he dressed as me for Halloween, but somehow, I didn't think whatever he was about to say was another one of his practical jokes. "Eva Watford streaked through town earlier, tits bouncing as she sprinted into the ocean. I suddenly understand the term 'knockers' because those things were swinging harder than Rocky Balboa. The fact that she didn't take herself out is a *miracle*. If ever you needed confirmation that a horde is gathering, that should be it. Until now, I didn't think that woman had an impulsive bone in her body."

I flinched, both at the visual and at the thought of a horde of demons gathering nearby. Part of me had still hoped I was wrong, that Nergal wasn't headed here, but it didn't seem we were going to be that lucky. "Why didn't you lead with that?"

Blaze shuddered, popcorn flying out of the red- and white-striped box with the jerky movement. "Trust me, it's not an image I wish to replay in my mind, let alone plant in yours. You can't say I've never done anything nice for you, O. I tried to spare you."

I grabbed my phone and quickly dialed Ryker's number.

"What now?" Blaze asked, the barest hint of concern etched in his face. My heart lurched for the hundredth time today at the thought of any harm coming to Blaze or any of the people I loved here. Deadlights Cove had become my family, one I'd chosen in place of my own shitty one. Whatever happened tomorrow, I knew I'd put my life on the line for every single resident here.

The ringing stopped as Ryker grunted on the other end of the line. "They're nearby."

"On it," Ryker said and the line went dead.

I slid my phone back into my pocket, then moved around the desk towards the door, loosening my tie and rolling up my sleeves as I walked past Blaze and out into the hallway.

"Well, brother," I said, clapping him on the shoulder as he fell in line with me. "I'm feeling a bit impulsive myself."

Blaze's jaw dropped before a wide grin took over his face, his hands rubbing together in excitement. "What do you want to do?"

"Destroy your brother and mine. Your father too, while I'm at it. Watch Ryker set all of them on fire, leaving nothing but ashes to remind us they ever existed. Then watch as a kraken devours *those* ashes whole. Sounds like a good plan to me, don't you think?"

A high-pitched giggle emitted from my best friend moments before he leaned over and grabbed my face, pulling me towards him as he laid a wet kiss on my cheek. "Sorry. Blame the horde — I couldn't help myself. Petty Orion is my favorite Orion."

Blaze flickered out of sight shortly after we exited the building, and I strolled through town on my own, hands in my pockets. No matter how much time I had left, it would never be enough. While I'd lived well over 200 years before I'd arrived in Deadlights Cove, none of it mattered in comparison to the memories I'd made right here in town.

As I reached the grass in the square, I stopped, pulling my loafers off my feet as I curled my toes into the thick summer grass, feeling the earth beneath me. My body moved of its own volition, pulling me towards the gazebo I'd looked at so many times but had never once stopped to sit in, to just... be.

Every moment I'd spent here had been with a sole

driving purpose — to protect the residents and keep our supernatural world hidden. The latter had exploded so far past my control, I had to let it go, even if it felt like cutting off a wing. But the former? I knew, without hesitation, I'd do anything in my power to keep these people safe. I understood the pledge I'd made to the Council when I took this position — to lead, to enforce, to protect. While the organization I'd pledged it to now seemed questionable, that oath still meant everything to me.

I leaned back on the hard wooden bench, staring at the teeth marks from an errant goat and didn't have even the smallest urge to fix it. If my bare feet, loosened tie, and rolled sleeves hadn't been indicators the horde was, in fact, near, not fixing an imperfection would have sold me.

But nothing about my life in Deadlights Cove had been perfect, and yet… it was.

With that thought in mind, I turned to look at the church across the green. Light shone from the windows I'd replaced all those weeks ago when Devanna had passed out in the cemetery, exhausted from working so hard to refinish the exterior. In the setting sun, the black church with the warm lights was a bit like the woman who called it home. Hard, foreboding exterior hiding an inside that was so stunning it was hard to look at directly. A study in contrasts, just like she was.

I rubbed a hand across my neck, feeling the way my skin tingled in the same spot I'd bitten her, the connection we shared. Just as I closed my eyes, tipping it back against the post behind me, a loud *meow* sounded from my right.

"What do you want, Bagheera?" I asked, not bothering

to open my eyes. He'd either maul me or he wouldn't — I was past caring.

He meowed again, but it was the deep huff that followed it that pulled my eyelids open. Standing with his front two hooves in the gazebo, Winston, a giant bull moose, stood not three feet in front of me, his enormous face hovering over mine.

I pushed upright, leaning back against the railing as I fought to put distance between me and the animal. Whether I wanted to or not, I couldn't help but eye the antlers that had somehow squeezed into the opening of the gazebo, and were now scraping against the wooden roof.

Ma-roww, the cat said again, and Winston ducked his head, lowering it so his exhaled breath huffed against my feathers. Even though I knew the moose was spelled to be gentle to our residents, I couldn't escape the sliver of fear that shot through my spine being this close to a thousand-pound animal.

But fear and I were longtime friends, and nothing was as fear-inducing as the thought of letting my people down tomorrow. Chalk it up to the horde, I pushed to my feet, my eyes even with the moose's lowered head, and slowly lifted my arm to run it along the side of Winston's face.

"I'm glad you're one of us, you big weirdo," I said, feeling his smooth fur between my fingers. "You'll protect us too, won't you?"

Movement near his antlers caught my eye, right in time to see the black ball of fur wedged between his antlers unfurl into a small, angry cat glaring at me.

I chuckled, shaking my head as I dropped my hand and swung my legs over the railing, retreating away from the moose. Seeing his huge butt sticking out of the gazebo was amusing, but I didn't feel sorry for the animal. He'd chosen his weird life here, just as I had, but we Covians looked out for each other. With a flick of my hand, I magicked the gazebo to twice its size, giving the moose plenty of room to escape, then strolled across the green towards the church.

If this was my last night here, I wanted to spend it with Devanna — as unlikely of a pairing as Winston and Bagheera, but I wasn't going to question it.

Not today, not ever.

Chapter Thirty-Seven

DEVANNA

THE WORLD WENT silent seconds before the first explosion.

BOOM.

Orion and I jolted upright as the aftershock shook the bell behind us, unintentionally sounding a town-wide alarm with its clanging. I covered my ears, waiting for the ringing to pass, and we scanned the town.

Orion had showed up last night after sunset, his expression shockingly relaxed for what was coming, but the nearness of the demon horde had everyone acting off-kilter. Impulsivity on me looked a little different — I'd climbed Orion like a tree, clinging like a desperate koala that refused to let go. I didn't even want sex, just to be held and adored. What was wrong with me?

We'd fallen into a restless sleep up here in the tower a few hours ago, both of us struggling to sleep even as we acted unnaturally. At least from the bell tower we could keep an eye out and be ready to take action quickly.

Now, we scrambled to our feet as Town Hall went up in

flames. A choked sound came from Orion and I wordlessly gripped his hand as the windows blew out, glass shards flying into the street.

It was still dark, the middle of the night, so no one should have been in the building, but this was a clear signal from Nergal.

How had they gotten in?

"Remember, buildings can be rebuilt, Orion," I said as I squeezed his hand, grounding him here in the present so he didn't spiral again. The last few days with him had been eye-opening. I knew Orion carried the weight of the town on his shoulders, but I never fully understood how much he blamed himself for the terrible things that happened to us. While Orion was insanely powerful, no one was *that* powerful. "No one is in there. No one is hurt. But you can make sure the fucker who wants to destroy this town pays for everything he's ever done wrong."

The next second, all the streetlights blew out, sparks flying from them as they were fried with a burst of magic.

As the darkness settled over us, only the supermoon shining high in the sky, Orion nodded, a killing calm sinking over his features that was such a turn-on, I squirmed next to him.

It was starting. I hurried to pick up my bo staff, feeling steadier with the wood in my palm.

Orion's phone buzzed, and a text from Ryker came in.

RYKER

Breech in the barrier but Ostara is closing it again now. Darius reports ten bypassed his traps. Ronan is already engaged at sea,

can't see how many. Heading your way.

"Let's go." Orion grabbed me, leaping out of the bell tower before I could protest, and we soared over the town, hunting demons.

Smoke rose from several points around town, not just the blazing fire that simmered in the remains of Town Hall, but Orion had ensured everyone in town was as prepared as we could be. If Nergal was coming here for power, then he would head to the nexus points. That, and wherever the missing black crystal was that Willa had hidden, if there had ever been one to begin with. Even after days of searching, Lys and I had come up blank.

Orion shifted, wind blowing through my hair as we flew over the town. A few shapes moved out of the woods behind the Town Hall, probably the ones who had blown it up, and began to move towards the center of town.

"Put me down and let's get them," I called to Orion over the rushing wind around us. He nodded and swung us around to land behind the black-clad figures.

One of them saw us and turned, hurling a ball of flame at Orion just as we touched down. Orion shoved me out of the way and threw his hands up, his magic whirling the flame to the side and extinguishing it.

"Officer Orion," the demon said, his lips curling back in a vicious grin that matched the snarling wolf behind him.

Knowing Nergal had drawn more followers than just demons to his cause was one thing — seeing it was an entirely separate realization. "Thrilled to meet you so quickly."

One of the other demons had already set fire to the gazebo and was moving over to the row of buildings that housed Scallywags and my shop. Another one doubled back to join his friend against Orion.

Orion didn't waste time with pleasantries, shooting lightning straight at him, and within seconds, the three of them were a blur of fire and lightning, smoke and swirling air and magic.

But that fucker running for the shops was *not* about to get away.

I left them to it and took off after the third. He pulled his arm back, a ball of flame gathering there that he intended to throw right at my shop.

"Hey, Azula," I called to stay his hand. He turned to see who was shouting at him, and I seized my moment.

I swung my staff directly into his face, and, thanks to a little modification Orion had helped me with last night, the lightning of angel magic blasted through him with the hit. He was lifted off his feet, the supermoon fueling my power, and skidded across the pavement as his ball of fire flickered out.

But I wasn't dumb enough to think one little hit would keep a demon down for long. With a snarl, he launched back to his feet and charged towards me. I braced, ready to feint and strike again, when he blinked out of existence.

Next thing I knew, searing fire wrapped around my throat as he reappeared behind me, his magic strangling me.

I tried to twist my staff around to hit him again, but he yanked it out of my hands and tossed it aside.

"I'd heard of angels and demons Linking with mortals, but didn't think I'd see one so soon," he scoffed. I tried helplessly to loosen his hold on my neck, but his bonds were magical, not physical, so there was nothing to grasp. Even if I could have spoken, I wouldn't have bothered to correct his assumption. Let him think I was Linked with someone and not just carrying a charged weapon — maybe it would give me an edge at some point.

As my lungs struggled for air, I felt my power coiling within me, magic sparking and flaring easily with the power of the full moon. With all my strength, I spun in his magical grasp, and shoved that concentrated blast of magic towards him.

A bolt of lightning shot from me, searing a hole of scorched flesh straight through his chest.

He crumpled to the ground as smoke drifted from my palms.

"Damn, Devvie." Blaze materialized beside me with a laugh, his eyes bright with glee amidst the chaos around us. "What the hell?"

What the hell, indeed, but this wasn't the time. It was probably latent magic from my staff.

"He was going to blast Scallywags," I said instead, and fire lit in Blaze's black eyes.

"Oh, hell no." Blaze shot to stand over the demon, palm held downward. A stream of demon fire shot from him, incinerating the body until only ash remained.

"Think you missed a spot." I pointed at the pile, no signs that a supernatural had stood there minutes before.

His eyebrows raised, but a shot of unnecessary fire flew from him again. "Extra crispy. Just the way I like it." Before I could react, his gaze shifted to something behind me, his eyes expanding.

I spun to see dozens of demons, witches, and shifters emerging from the shadows and into the moonlight.

"Dev?" Blaze was right behind me all of a sudden, his voice quiet. "Last chance. I got Petey to Alaska with Selene and Nim last night. I can still get you out of here, too."

I shook my head, reaching behind me to squeeze his arm as my eyes found Orion fighting amongst the fray. Already his white wings were dirty, tarnished with ash and blood, but the ferocity in his gaze as he battled for our town was something I could feel burning in my own heart, too. "I'm not leaving you."

We shared one last look as he nodded in understanding, and then all hell broke loose.

I ran for my staff again as fireballs shot over the square, everything going up in flames.

A shriek came from the sky as Ryker soared overhead, targeting his green dragon flame on Nergal's forces. Screams rang out from those caught by the dragon fire — no supe could stand against it.

Lys stood on the far side of the green, the ocean at his back as he wielded water and the other elements in equal measures, sweeping up any who approached in a torrent of wind I couldn't help but be impressed by.

I quickly lost sight of my friends as Nergal's forces swarmed us. A witch came at me, raising what was probably a poisoned dagger, but one sharp hit with my staff knocked them out with the shock of the lightning. After this was over,

I needed Orion to supercharge all of my weapons — this was fun.

As the next demon approached, two figures leapt out of the alleyway behind me, launching themselves at my assailant. Before I had time to register what was happening, two clouds of shadow enveloped it, snarls and screams coming from within the swirling darkness. A moment later, two grey heads of hair appeared, detaching the demon's neck as they threw him to the ground. The shadows pulled back further to reveal matching Hawaiian shirts, and Val and Caedmon gave me a salute, their elongated canines dripping with blood.

"I'll just…" I stuttered, a shocked laugh escaping me, "leave this one to you."

Nox flickered back and forth on the opposite side of the street, drawing attention to himself as Aurora stood behind him, a spell brewing between her hands as she prepared to launch it. Pride swept through me at the sight, knowing I'd helped her get there with her power. Before worry could take over, I threw myself into the fight, swinging my staff wide as electricity crackled on the end.

While this was my first battle, I'd trained to fight for years and this felt natural to me. My heart pumped, pulse racing, but my breathing was even as I disarmed and put down as many enemies as I could.

As I surveyed the town, the fighting around me, I couldn't help but think this was all a distraction. Most of the faces I didn't recognize were fighting, but not to kill. So what was the point? What were they waiting for? Where was Nergal?

I ducked a hit, but was pushed from the side and fell,

Chapter Thirty-Eight

ORION

AS SOON AS ENOUGH OF our people arrived to deal with Nergal's minions, I shot into the air. Blaze and Devanna were battling in front of their shops with Zaphiel backing them up, and as much as it hurt me not to drop back to their sides to help them, I knew they were fully capable of defending themselves. Lightning flared as it crackled out of Devanna's staff and I couldn't hold back my smile. She might hate me for it later, but I didn't hold one ounce of regret for what I'd done.

Turning away from her, I could feel the edges of my glamour around the town under attack from all points and needed to see what was happening.

Wind rushed past my ears, and with a hard beat of my wings, I caught an updraft and soared higher. The second I cleared the crest of the southern hill, I saw smoke. My best guess was the nexus at the Haunted Meadow had been blasted.

I cursed under my breath, banking sharply and twisting west.

Screams reached me from the town square behind me, and my heart clenched. Were those our people? How many would I let down tonight?

I didn't have time to stop and go back. I had to do everything I could to keep the glamour up, to keep everything happening within our town limits hidden from the human world. I had to trust that our people were capable of more than I'd ever given them credit for, Devanna included. The glamour wasn't fully down yet, still holding some of his forces at bay and we needed to slow them however we could. The closer I flew to the border, the stronger the lure of demon magic pulled at me, my impulses ratcheting up.

I hadn't been alive during the last major demon battles, but I was starting to understand, on a new level, the danger Nergal posed to our society. With this many demons at once, chaos was a force all its own, a wildfire devouring everything in its path, nothing but death and destruction in its wake.

Finally, the Hanging Tree came into view, and I shot down to land beside it.

In the woods to the west — the same spot Ryker had broken up Kal's attempt at human sacrifice last year — Nergal's witches chanted, a pentagram of crystals and burning herbs between them. Snarls and screams pierced the air as shifters clashed nearby — ours trying to reach their witches, theirs fending them off.

I joined the fray, throwing up a shield around myself as I charged my palms with lightning, preparing to throw it into the witches' pentagram.

"Heads up!"

I jumped out of the way right as a roar sounded when one of Nergal's bears threw a fox into the Hanging Tree.

With how much blood covered its fur, I couldn't tell who it was, but my stomach leapt to my throat all the same.

Planting my feet, I aimed my magic toward the witches and threw my lightning with all my might.

White streaks lit the forest a split second before the clap of thunder, then an aftershock that threw all of us to the ground.

A grunt escaped me as my shoulder hit the forest floor hard. I scrambled quickly back to my feet, letting out a relieved breath when I saw the scorched ashes where the witches' spell had been moments before.

"Orion!" A voice yelled, and I turned, the blood draining from my face.

The blast hadn't been solely from my magic. The witches had completed their spell just in time.

The Hanging Tree was cracked down the full length of its trunk. As the magic in this nexus point crumbled just like the Haunted Meadow had, I felt my energy deplete, lowering significantly the way it would for everyone here.

I couldn't stop to help the wounded here, even though it killed me to abandon them. Under the trees, shifters and witches continued to fight, and the best thing I could do was head for the next nexus.

This was what I'd missed. Nergal didn't care about his own forces, whether they lived or died. If he destroyed all of our nexus points in town, it would leave every supe in the area near powerless. Except for him.

But not today. I wouldn't let him.

Three more to protect.

"I'm sorry," I murmured under my breath, then shot back into the air.

The old schoolhouse was gone. Flying over it, all that was left was a stone foundation and piles of ash.

In the air, Ryker flew towards the lighthouse, a huge black dragon soaring through the sky casting a formidable shadow over the scene below. He had no doubt realized the same thing I had about the nexus points, so I turned south-east to the one in Ronan's territory.

As I neared the ocean, the water was frothing, the waves taller than usual. Possibly due to the unnatural storm winds, probably amplified by undersea fighting.

A giant tentacle whipped out of the sea, tossing a tiger shark against the cliffs where it thumped and fell, motion-less, back into the sea.

Shit, was that Ronan? Or Inessa? They could both take kraken form.

Maisie's teal mermaid tail breached the water, followed by a column of swirling water propelled by a white-tailed mermaid, the two of them wielding it together. It followed the momentum started by the first one, hurtling towards the cliffs. At the last second, it solidified into ice, shattering upon impact to reveal a sea-nymph had been encased inside. Now, lifeless.

I circled the scene, searching for the nexus under the roiling waves.

Seabirds clamored above water, shrieking and cawing, eager for the feast they thought the churning waves promised. Tentacles whipped around, nymphs in seal, dolphin, and shark forms clashed and thrashed and breached.

Red stained the water.

The birds dove.

I didn't have time to deal with the prickles in my eyes.

Finally, I caught sight of a particular rock shape under the surface, and tucked my wings tight to my back to shoot downwards.

Under the water, it would be much harder for Nergal's witches to undo the glamour, but judging by the swarm of nymphs down there, he'd come up with a backup plan.

Likely, to blast it to all hell.

Panic clawed at me as I realized Nergal's nymphs were herding Ronan's closer to the nexus, hoping to take out as many as they could in one fell sweep. I needed to get a message to Ronan to pull his people away —

I soared just above the waves, trying to spot someone I knew for sure to be one of ours. A large hammerhead balanced right under the surface, then, in a split second, changed into a giant mer with rich orange scales as he shoved a glowing trident through a shark he'd been battling.

Xuma. Perfect.

"Get your people away from the nexus!" I shouted at him over the howling wind and rush of waves as I shot by him.

I didn't pause to see if he heard me, but when I turned back around, he'd disappeared beneath the waves. A moment later, nymphs started pulling back from the nexus.

I beat my wings, soaring higher, then banked and returned, coiling my magic. I aimed, then shot a bolt of lightning right for Nergal's nymphs who'd been working on the nexus.

Water blasted and sprayed straight up out of the ocean, a tsunami wave radiating out from the point of impact that jostled the other nymphs.

I held my breath, waiting to see if I'd done enough.

A controlled wave dragged half a dozen nymph bodies in various forms from the nexus, pushing them onto the rocky shore behind me like beached whales.

I exhaled and turned to see a giant, inky blue kraken as the source of the wave. One giant eye rose above the surface, its wavy, W-shaped pupil meeting my gaze with a look I felt in my soul. Somehow despair and gratitude in one.

I nodded to Ronan as he slipped back underwater, his people more than capable of handling the remaining nymphs.

As I took off for Turner Lighthouse, my muscles beginning to strain with how much flying and magic I'd done today, a giant whirlpool of water rose into the air.

I flew higher, and below me, the whirlpool was ringed on all sides by Ronan's nymphs, working together against the second kraken, Inessa, caught in the relentless current.

With an almighty chorus of roars, the nymphs acted as one, wrenching each tentacle in a different direction, shredding the kraken into dozens of pieces.

Inessa, now no more than ink on the water.

But there wasn't time to celebrate the nymphs' victory.

The Lighthouse was in flames again.

Green flames swirled around the Lighthouse as I

approached, Ryker twisting his giant dragon form around it in chase of an all-too-familiar angel.

Ezra.

Even knowing he'd been working with Nergal, it was still a shock to see him here, actively fighting against us.

But now wasn't the time to process the trauma he'd given me. A fury I'd never known took over, pushing me forward, and I was ready to tear the male to pieces for what he'd done, not just to me, but to my whole town — my *family*.

Much smaller than the dragon, Ezra made tighter turns as he circled the lighthouse, toying with Ryker, keeping him distracted.

Because the real threat to the nexus was at the base of the lighthouse.

Errakal poured fire at the lighthouse, ringing it in demon fire and, based on the chanting, throwing some witch magic in there as well to destroy this nexus.

I touched down at nearly the exact second Blaze flickered into existence beside me.

Blaze's jaw clenched, but without hesitating, he shot forward, tackling Kal. They rolled over the flat rock of the lighthouse promontory until Blaze got Kal underneath him.

"That's — my — favorite — lighthouse —" he growled, accentuating each word with a punch to Kal's face. "And I *just* fixed it!"

Ezra swooped down, knocking Blaze off Kal with enough force to send him rolling to the edge of the promontory. In the next breath, Kal flickered on top of him, Blaze's head hanging off the side of the cliff as Kal wrapped a hand around his throat.

"Still choosing the wrong side of history, little brother," Kal snarled at him. Blaze grappled with Kal's wrist around his neck, trying to push him off.

I shot forward to help him, but Ezra swooped into my path. Lightning shot between his palms in a clear threat as it exploded at my feet.

"What's between brothers stays between brothers, Orion," he admonished with a patronizing smirk. "Isn't that right?"

"Funny enough, Blaze and I bonded over having such shitty brothers. I much prefer him to you."

"So sentimental," Ezra laughed, hovering just above the ground as the flames licked up the lighthouse behind him. Ryker torched other demons in the background, not letting anyone else close to the nexus. Ezra's tone turned mocking as he sneered, "Did I hurt you?"

But I was done letting my brother get to me. I hurled lightning at him, the moon amplifying my power just as it did Devanna's. Stronger. Faster. *More.*

Ezra was momentarily surprised at my show of power, but didn't have long to evaluate me as Ryker swooped down, jaw open as he aimed straight for Ezra.

He pushed off the ground, shooting straight into the air. He floated above the scene, thunder cracking as lightning lit the night sky.

"This nexus will fall and leave you defenseless. The moment Nergal unlocks the rest of his power, this little game is over," he called to me as I flew to clash with him in the sky, Ryker circling us.

"You're a fool to side with Nergal, *brother*," I spat as I landed a blow to his wing, singeing the feathers.

Ezra flinched, but he blinked away the pain and raised his arms to the side as his wings expanded too. "I wouldn't be too sure about that. With Malachi and the Council in charge, I've risen as far as I can. But with Nergal? I don't have to follow anyone's rules — I get to *make* them."

I scoffed. "Do you really think he'd let you have more power than you have now? More than *him*? You were supposed to be the smarter brother."

"There's a new world coming, Orion. Supernaturals should have always been on top, and Nergal has the vision to do it. I wouldn't expect a simpleton like you to understand the sacrifices a leader has to make to create a perfect world. You can't even make this little podunk town follow you."

My gaze slid to the ground, where Kal had Blaze by the throat, feet dangling over the cliff, fire wrapped around his hands where he held him.

That single moment when Blaze's eyes locked with mine was all it took for me to abandon the fight with my brother in the sky.

Ezra wasn't my brother in truth.

Brothers loved each other unconditionally. Defended each other at every turn. Were there for both the best and the worst days, lifting each other up when they needed it.

Blaze was the only true brother I'd ever had, and the only one that mattered.

I turned my back on Ezra, and dove. Lightning blasted from my hand, hitting Kal square in the back. He stiffened with a cry of pain, hand loosening on Blaze's throat for a split-second, but that was all it took for Blaze to flicker to safety. I landed in a crouch, and unleashed another bolt of lightning, hitting Kal again and again with everything I had.

I grit my teeth, my power ebbing at the excessive use and loss of nexus points, but nothing could stop me. "Not today, Satan."

With one final blast that lit the whole cliff in blinding white light, Kal's body slumped to the ground. Smoke curled off him as I stilled, lowering my hands slowly. In my blind rage, I momentarily forgot about the threat Ezra posed.

My whole body stiffened as a jolt went up my spine, the breath sucked out of me as Ezra hit me from behind, but it was short-lived.

A wash of heat hit me right as Ryker swooped, jaws closing over Ezra's body. The blood-curdling scream he emitted was one I'd hear for years in my nightmares, but I couldn't muster even one drop of sorrow over the turn of events.

Watching chunks of ash fall off Kal's slumped body, a moment of clarity hit me.

"Keep him alive!" I called to Ryker as he flew off over the trees, Ezra caught in his sharp teeth.

A disgruntled sound answered from the dragon, but I knew he'd heard me.

"Well, that was fun," Blaze said, drawing the last of the fire from the lighthouse before dropping his hands to his knees in exhaustion. "Although I'd really like it if my family stopped trying to destroy this lighthouse. I'm getting sick of it."

I turned to survey the damage. Waves churned below us,

but the fighting was slowing. "They're not your family. I am."

Blaze clapped me on the back, offered a brief nod, and flickered back to town. With a heavy sigh, I pushed off the ground to follow.

Chapter Thirty-Nine

DEVANNA

THE WORLD SPUN and churned with my stomach as we reappeared. I tried to wrestle myself free of the hands grasping me, but the demon only tightened their hold.

"Let *go* of me —" I jerked an elbow behind me, hoping to make contact with an organ, but there wasn't enough space between me and my assailant to gain momentum.

"Shut up and take down your wards, witch," a gruff voice hissed in my ear.

I blinked, trying to understand what he meant when I realized we were in the woods just behind my church, the sounds of battle from the town square drifting over to us.

I didn't know what this demon wanted with my church, but I'd be damned if I gave it to him.

"Not a chance," I huffed, then gasped in pain as my arm was wrenched back, my shoulder twisting painfully. I ground my teeth, blinking away any moisture in my eyes as metaphorical fire shot up my arm.

Suddenly, the back door to the church opened, and Morgaine strode out, teal glasses perched on her nose as she looked at my captor in a disappointed frown. She crossed her arms, shaking her head.

"It's not her wards you need removed, Nergal," she called. "Willa put a lot of protection on this place. She knew you'd come back some day."

"Morgaine," the demon — Nergal — snarled from behind me. "Thought you'd have kicked the bucket by now."

"Sadly for you, I still have lots to live for. Not only my children you seem hellbent on destroying, but I also made a promise to Althea and Willa that I'd protect the world from *you.*"

Laughter rattled against my back as Nergal pulled me tighter to him. "The *world* doesn't need protecting from me. Only the humans who think they can rule over us. Who foolishly believe they are the most powerful. The world is changing, Morgaine, and I refuse to be swept under the rug like a dirty secret any longer. I want to *free* us. To live a life not in the shadows, but on a throne where I belong. To have the humans cower before us, understanding the mercy I grant them every day when I choose to let them breathe, knowing I could take it all away."

She shook her head. "I'll never understand what Willa saw in you."

"Power, Morgaine. Like you, she didn't follow the rules. Didn't like the way the angels enforced laws on Covens, on marriages between species. I am a law unto myself — those PRICs can't tell me what to do any more than the humans. Not anymore. It's not too late to switch sides, you know."

Her white brows climbed, a broad smile stretching

across her face as she eyed me. "Did you hear him, Devanna? We can still swap sides! How kind of you."

"Except I hate losing," I picked up on her sarcasm, rolling my shoulders back to push against Nergal however I could. "And there's no chance you'll succeed. Not against Orion."

Nergal laughed, leaning into my ear as he hissed, "Careful, witch. Love is what got me into this predicament. I could have ruled on high long ago if I hadn't fallen so foolishly in love, letting it blind me." Turning his attention back to Mo, he said, "Where is it? I feel her magic all over this church, mingled with yours and this one's" — he jostled my arm at that, and I hissed at the pain — "and I know you know where it is."

Mo blinked innocently. "Where *what* is?"

Nergal growled. "We're not playing, witch. You think I won't kill this one?" He shook me in his grip again. "You mortals are no better than humans. You mean nothing to me."

Mo tapped her finger against her chin, seeming *very* calm despite the threat to my life. "Wasn't your wife one of us mortals?"

"And she *betrayed me*."

"You mean she died?"

Nergal spluttered, rendered speechless for a minute, then sparks shot from his hands, searing my skin, as he refocused.

"I won't ask again, Morgaine. Where is it?"

Mo sighed. "Where do you think? The one place she knew she could keep it safe. Forever. Right here in the center of her protection."

Nergal's grip on me loosened for just a breath, but I took

the chance. I ducked and rolled out of his grip and over the wards of the church, running straight for Mo as Nergal let out a frustrated growl from the other side of the barrier.

Unlike at the lighthouse, when Orion had hidden him from my view, now I could see the family resemblance to Blaze. The dark hair, olive skin — but Nergal's eyes held a chaotic frenzy, a simmering rage that Blaze's never had. He paced the line of the ward, running his fingers through his shoulder length hair, sparks shooting out his fingertips. Then he stopped and pointed an accusatory finger at Mo.

"You're a fool if you think I won't get a hold of it," he jeered.

Mo stepped out of the way, beckoning him towards the church. "Well, be my guest, then. Oh, wait, you can't."

Nergal roared, forming a giant javelin of fire out of thin air, and a second later, hurled it across the wards, aimed straight at Mo.

She pulled up a shield of magic, dissipating the javelin into nothingness, and a breath of relief left me right before another, smaller fire arrow shot through her leg.

"Mo!" I shrieked as she sank to one knee with a gasp, then collapsed back on the grass. I patted the fire out as fast as I could. Mo grimaced, but met my eyes pointedly, curling her fingers into the grass. A shimmering rainbow of color swirled out from her hands, dancing across the ground as it wrapped around me, then towards the church behind us, pouring whatever magic she had into a protection spell, like she always did.

"Don't touch my children," Mo growled at Nergal, pushing upright and shoving her hands hard towards him, a blast of magic exploding out from her.

Nergal jerked backwards as it slammed into him, but fury radiated off him in waves, and he launched back.

Another arrow caught Mo in the shoulder, and I heard a shriek of rage that I only later registered came from my lips. The second I knew she could extinguish the rest of the flame herself, I stood, fury boiling through me as I turned to face Nergal.

He thought he was going to come here and mess with *Morgaine?*

Oh, hell, no.

Nergal smirked as I approached the edge of the ward.

"Witches are no match for demons, sweetheart. Go brew your little herbs in your cauldron and leave this fight for someone actually capable of it." He held up his hands, his face twisting into a sneer. "No hard feelings if you back down now, I promise."

Little did he know the words "back down" weren't in my vocabulary.

With the supermoon overhead, power swelled within me like I'd never felt before. I thought of the blood on Orion's white wings, the rage in Blaze's eyes, the shifters risking their lives this very minute, Ryker's roar overhead, and Mo behind me, wounded on the ground — and my magic charged within me. My palms crackled with it, my blue hair lifting, billowing out around me on a phantom wind, thunder rumbling somewhere far above.

I took a low, steadying breath, and with all the focus I could muster, threw all of my power out towards Nergal.

An explosion of light flashed, followed by a piercing crack of thunder, and for a heartbeat, I couldn't tell what I'd done.

As my vision cleared, I saw a crater where Nergal had been.

"Well done, dear," Mo panted as she slumped to the ground, patting my ankle.

I passed out.

Dirt hit me in the face as I shook myself back to consciousness. "What the hell?" I pushed upright, taking in my surroundings — different than when I'd passed out behind the church.

"Oh good," Mo said from my left where she stood knee-deep in the dirt in front of a headstone. *Willa Rosewood.* "You're back. Be a dear and move the rest of this dirt since you're up now? As magnificent as I am, I'll admit my muscles aren't quite what they used to be."

"What..." I paused, taking in the scene around me. "How did we move to the front of the church? And what are you doing?"

"Well," Mo said, her eyes moving towards where Nergal's body peeked out from behind the back of the church near the forest, not quite dead, but struggling. "Trying to make that asshole stay dead."

I pushed to my feet, looking down into the grave she was currently digging up. "Move," I said, jumping down to stand at her side, willing my magic into the ground around us as dirt pulled back to expose a crumbling coffin. "And tell me why I'm digging up a grave."

"Althea always spoke in riddles with her visions, infuriating woman. Half the time nothing made sense, but she was adamant this church was the answer to Nergal's undoing. It's all she talked about after Willa died, saying she took her secrets to the grave, and we needed to protect it."

I worked faster. "You think she meant her literal grave."

"We're out of options, so I certainly hope so."

The moment the lid was exposed, Mo fell to her knees, a gasp of pain leaving her as she pulled at the lid. I turned, looking back over the ground towards where Nergal was attempting to push to his feet. I didn't understand what I'd done to take him down, but whatever power I'd hit him with was intense, something far beyond my own capabilities, and yet it still wasn't enough.

"Hurry, Mo," I said, unable to look away from Nergal as he sluggishly moved, fighting still taking place in the background behind him. "Kind of out of time."

The creaking of hinges had me looking down for a split second, staring at the bones laid within the coffin. While the sight was jarring, knowing this was Blaze's mother, it wasn't what drew my attention.

No, I couldn't look away from the massive black crystal in her bony hands.

Mo leaned over and plucked it from the skeleton's hold, kissing her fingers before she touched the skull. "We'll end it for you," she said in a whisper.

As she examined the crystal, Blaze flickered in, landing right in front of me. Mo's eyes shone with love as she handed it to him. Without missing a beat, Blaze wrapped his fingers around the crystal and stood, looking to where Nergal pushed to his feet just outside the barrier that held him at bay away from the church.

"Do your little lightning trick again, sweetheart," she

said, kissing me on the cheek. "And Blaze will blast him with his own cursed magic at the same time. Finish him."

Not stopping to think through her words, I smiled, feeling the power bubble up in me once more from unknown depths, far more than I'd ever had, and took Blaze's hand as we stepped forward together. "Gladly."

Chapter Forty

ORION

THE MOMENT I touched down in the square, my head turned, looking for her. The fight had all but ended, and relief coursed through me as I saw several of my own people moving about the green. There, in the midst of a pile of bodies I shouldn't have been surprised to see, stood Devanna.

Until the moment I saw her again, I hadn't let myself acknowledge the knot in my stomach formed by worry for her. And she looked like the goddess that she was.

Her windswept blue hair, the smudges of dirt and blood on her face and arms, the sparks that still skittered on her arms —

She was just turning towards me when I all but crashed into her, pulling her face to mine in a searing kiss. One hand tangled in her hair, desperate to tug her closer, the other wrapping around the small of her back. Without hesitation, she gripped my shirt, pulling me in, then coasted her hands up my chest to wrap around my neck.

I pulled back just enough to press our foreheads together, bending down to meet her height.

"About damn time you showed up," Devanna said, voice breathy. "Though it's just like you to miss all the fun."

A shiver of electricity skittered over her skin, and my hands wrapped around her shoulders reflexively, absorbing some of the errant magic.

We'd have to work on that, but later.

"Thank fuck you're all right. Injuries?"

She raised an eyebrow. "I think you took care of that."

Okay, we'd get to that later, too. "What about everyone else? Do you know if anyone —" Shit, the pile of bodies. Were those ours?

Devanna shook her head. "Everyone who was here in the square is accounted for, but we haven't heard back from those at the border or in the woods. The Coven is dealing with any injuries that aren't already healing."

I kissed her forehead, pulling her into my chest again as I ran my hands over her, reassuring myself that her words were true and I'd been able to protect her after all.

"What happened?"

"Hey." Lys clapped me on the shoulder, his expression exhausted, if also full of relief. "You'll never believe it." With a nod, he indicated the graveyard in front of Devanna's church.

I furrowed my brow at him, then at the church, but he only motioned for me to go over there, so I threaded my fingers through Devanna's and we made our way over.

Mo and Blaze sat with their backs against Althea Rosewood's headstone while Mo alternately sipped from what looked like a rum punch and poured it over the grave beneath her.

But my eyes snagged on the giant hole to her right.

"Did you — did you *rob a grave?*" I coughed, leaving Dev only when I was sure the sparks had stopped, and made my way over to Mo.

"Yes, dear, now if you wouldn't mind?" Mo gestured to the mound of dirt. "Be a gentleman and fix it for me. We're all a little worn out here."

I shook my head in confusion, but did as she bade and shifted the dirt back over the grave, reburying Willa Rosewood.

"One of you needs to start talking. Why would you dig up this grave?"

Mo lifted the glass to her lips, taking a sip before she answered, "Well, once Dev blasted Nergal to smithereens —"

"*What?!*"

"— *Almost* to smithereens, I had an epiphany and realized the crystal might be *in* Willa's grave." Mo shrugged. "Althea must have buried it with Willa, inside the protective spell they put on that painting hanging in the church. I have a bone to pick with Althea when I see her in the afterlife for not telling me outright what she meant by *taking her secrets to the grave.* Fortunately, Devanna seems to have an *extraordinary* well of power these days" — Mo shot me a knowing look, clearly already aware of what I'd done, and I pressed my lips together, willing her not to reveal anything to Dev. Not yet. I needed to have that conversation with her in private — "So, while the blast she gave Nergal threw him for a loop, it wasn't quite enough. In a nice twist of karma, Blaze was able to use Nergal's power in the crystal against him. Devanna blasted him at the same time and together, they took him down, then blasted his little minions, too. Lys had the idea that Nergal might have joined threads of their magic, not fully Linked like you — er, are more familiar with," she caught herself, but her eyes said everything. "But just enough that when Dev and Blaze locked on, they were able to hold all their powers in place long enough for the rest of us to swoop in and take care of everything else."

"Teamwork makes the dream work," Dev nodded sagely, bumping knuckles with Blaze, then leaned into me.

I turned, rubbing a hand across my jaw as I looked at the scene around us, taking in the destruction.

Sitting in the middle of a smoking pile that was once Nergal was a small black cat, licking his paw.

"Nergal is dead?" I asked, needing to hear the words aloud. To know it was well and truly over.

Sensing my distress, Dev placed her hands on either side of my face, dark eyes focused on mine. "Yeah baby. He's gone." She smiled. "I'm fine. We're good. Go do what you're best at and look after everyone. Put this town back together."

With a nod, I pulled back, my chest loosening just a little with her encouraging words. For as much as we'd fought over the last ten years, I couldn't help but appreciate what it felt like to be on Devanna's good side — somewhere I hoped I could stay for the rest of my life.

My phone buzzed with an incoming call, and I swiped to answer.

"Darius?"

"Orion." His voice sounded strained. Instantly, I was on the alert.

"Did you —"

He let out a deep sigh that turned into a choking sob. "We — we lost three of the pack. We'll be putting them to rest our way, but I thought you'd want to —"

"When?" A small hand squeezed mine, Devanna hearing the news beside me too, and I squeezed back.

"This evening. Sunset."

"I'll be there," I said, unable to give him any more comfort than that. He told me where to meet them, and we hung up, his grief weighing heavy on me.

"Just got back from chatting with Ronan."

We turned to find Ryker striding over — buck ass naked.

"Goddamn," Dev murmured appreciatively, her eyes raking over his large frame without an ounce of shame. "I didn't realize the tattoos were *everywhere.*" I shot her a scowl that made her chuckle.

"Ryker, my old friend, you're going to give Peg a heart attack," Mo said, holding out her kimono. Peg, from several yards away, had indeed turned bright scarlet at the sight of him, fanning herself profusely. "Or a spontaneous orgasm. Either way, this is neither the time nor the place."

Ryker huffed, smoke drifting from his nostrils, and gruffly wrapped the neon blue garment around his waist. That act alone was enough to tell me how much he'd drained his magic — normally Ryker could summon clothes from the in-between without a problem.

"Ronan has a few injuries among the sea nymphs — apparently his daughter Saoirse was banged up pretty badly after Inessa threw her into the rocks. But Owen, of all people, was there to help out, and it looks like she's going to be all right. A few other serious ones, but they've got them with healers."

A tiny fraction of stress relieved from between my shoulders. Now we just needed to hear from Kit and Winona.

Before long, Winona texted me that they were all clear. Then I dialed Kit.

"Orion," he answered, sounding bone tired.

"How did it go?"

"Mostly injuries," he said on a long exhale. "Akil is… It doesn't look great right now." He cleared his throat, and his voice cracked slightly on his next words. "If there are any witches to spare, we'd really —"

"I'm on my way," Lys called loud enough for Kit to hear over the phone. Apparently everyone was eavesdropping today, but it was for the best. I nodded to him, and he turned, grabbing Nox's arm next to him before the two of them disappeared.

"Thank you," Kit managed before cutting the call.

I exhaled. "Shit."

"Lys will fix him up," Dev stated confidently. "He's the most talented witch of our generation. You're not alone here, Orion."

"She's right, man. We all just love you so much." Blaze, who had just appeared from nowhere, patted me hard on the back. "Oh, who am I kidding? C'mere, you."

Despite my muffled protest, I was wrapped in a giant hug from my cackling friend, who knew I was not a hugger. After several awkward seconds ticked by, Blaze said, "You do realize I'm not letting you go until you hug me back, right?"

I lifted my arms, patting him lightly on the back until

Blaze pulled back with a shit-eating grin on his face. With a shake of my head, I turned, looking over the ruined town.

Eva Watson and Peg Fernsby stood in front of the remains of Town Hall, hands on their hips as they surveyed the damage to the once historic landmark of our town. "It's just a building," I said, repeating Devanna's words from earlier as a mantra, even as my heart clenched at the sight.

"I spelled the books," Mo said with a tip of her rum punch in salute.

"What?" I asked, not following her logic.

"The library," she said, pushing up to stand as Blaze held out an arm to steady her. "Earlier this week, I stopped by and spelled the books to be fireproof. While the rest of the building will need to be redone, the artifacts in the library should all be safe."

"Oh, thank *God*," someone gushed, and turning, I saw Kai, the librarian, gasping in relief, hand to her heart.

"Thank *Mo*," Blaze corrected, throwing an arm around his mother. "Petey would've been devastated."

Scrubbing a hand over my face, I nodded in acknowledgment, glad to hear that something had been saved, even amongst such destruction.

The sound of a slow creak forced me to turn around, watching as the last beams of the gazebo tumbled to the ground, sending ash into the air in a black cloud.

"Anyone else shocked that gazebo lasted this long?" Blaze said, a hint of laughter in his voice. "For the number of times that thing has gone up in flames at the hands of a demon, we really should have spelled it against fire decades ago."

I shot him a flat stare. "Since more than half of those

instances have been at your own hands, I'm thinking you should be the one to rebuild it."

Blaze saluted, standing taller as a smile spread on his face.

"Before Ryker gets the munchies," Dev said, and I turned to her, barely containing a chuckle, "what are we doing with these dead bodies?"

Ryker crossed his arms. "Demons aren't really to my dragon's taste. It's like eating charcoal."

I stepped out of Devanna's hold, moving towards the bodies strewn across the green. "Do we know any of these faces? Recognize anyone?"

Blaze moved with me, using a booted toe to shift bodies. "I recognize a few of the demons here from my last trip to Las Vegas. Errakal loved it there, so I'm not shocked he garnered a following among them. Those demons have been stirring, ready for trouble since the day the PRICs disbanded hordes."

"Same for the witches," Mo said as she limped to our side, hanging on Devanna's arm. "I've seen a few of them over the years. Most of the ones I recognized today were lone witches, outside of Covens, to which the Council has never been friendly."

"These shifters too — this male was a lone wolf I've run into a few times in the Rockies," Ryker added, nodding to the body at his feet.

"The Council will want them all identified," I said. "But for now, we should see to injuries."

The others nodded, moving off to help where they could, but I turned to Dev.

"Let's find somewhere to talk."

She gave me a saccharine smile that was pure warning. "Yes, I think that'd be best."

"So, it wasn't just my staff you magicked." Dev spun to face me from the center of her living room, her voice echoing in the cathedral ceilings.

I cleared my throat, but I wasn't going to deny it. "No."

She narrowed her eyes. "What did you do?"

My gaze dropped to her neck for a split second, but she caught it, and her palm flew up to slap the spot where I'd bitten her.

"You —" Her brows flew up. "Did you *Link* us?"

Lifting my hand to rub across the back of my neck, I turned to look at the hideous painting on the wall that had kept Nergal at bay. "Not… not exactly."

Her eyes squinted as she stepped into my space. "You have exactly one minute to explain to me how you could *not exactly* Link with someone without their knowledge. Or *consent.*"

"We're not Linked." I dropped my hands down to my side as I forced myself to meet her eyes. "At least, not yet."

"Keep talking."

"When we bit each other," I began again, "you got some of my blood. Well, angel blood carries our magic. As long as you have some of that in your system…"

Dev blinked, processing my words. "I can access your magic?"

I tilted my head side to side. "Sort of. It's more like, whatever magic was in that portion of blood is yours now.

You don't have access to *all* my magic or all my powers, the way Linking with me would give you. It's sort of the equivalent of my charging a crystal with my power and then giving that to you to wield. Only, without you having to carry around a crystal. It was the best way I could think of to offer you a little more protection. A bit of a power boost for the field."

Dev was nodding along as she took in the implications. "So, this power boost will fade over time? We'll go back to normal?"

I winced. "Not… quite. Usually, only angels in committed partnerships bloodshare like this, because afterwards, if the balance is uneven, it begins to drain you of the power you gave up." Fury ignited in Dev's eyes, but I hurried on with my solution. "But this doesn't have to change anything. I can either keep you supplied with blood as you need it, or if we do officially Link, that should alleviate any unpleasant symptoms."

Dev threw her hands up. "Great, so, either I keep drinking your blood forever so you don't drain yourself into oblivion, or we essentially have to get married. Excellent solutions, Orion. Really genius plan there." She scoffed, stomping off to pour herself a glass of whiskey and muttering something under her breath that sounded suspiciously like *Stupid freakin' angels*.

"It's not a big deal. A little blood — who cares?"

"Oh, my Goddess, can you even hear yourself?" She spun on me, whiskey sloshing out of her glass. "I'm not a fucking vampire! I don't want to drink your blood!"

I rubbed my neck. "Mix it in something then, you won't even notice."

Devanna shook her head, her blue hair swishing around her shoulders as she took a long sip of her drink, then tipped her head up to the ceiling above her. "I can't do this, Orion."

My heart stuttered at her words, a bone-deep ache taking over as I nodded. I should have seen this coming — I *did* see it coming. "Right." I drew in a breath, brushing a hand through my hair as I turned towards the door.

Her head tipped down as she glared at me again, stilling any movement I made. "Did I say you could leave?"

I jerked back at her words, brow furrowing in confusion. "What do you want me to do here? If you're looking for an apology for me giving you some of my power to protect you, you're going to be waiting a long time. I don't regret what I did, not even a little, because you're standing whole and healthy in front of me after a battle that could have ended terribly for all of us. And somehow, that was all that mattered to me then. It's all that matters to me now. So no, I'm not sorry."

Her brown eyes studied me, jaw working as she listened, but I could feel the storm brewing beneath her skin. I stepped in closer, placing a finger under her chin to tilt her head up towards mine.

"I'm not sorry. And I don't want to leave. In fact, I'd love to stay for as long as you'll let me." Her breath caught in her throat as her eyes flicked back and forth between mine, seeing the honesty in my words. "Can I do better at communicating with you? At making this a partnership between us? Yes. And I will. But Devanna" — I brushed a strand of hair off her cheek and tucked it behind her ear — "I'll always want to protect you, to keep you safe in any way I can, even though I know how little you need me, how capable you are on your own. I can't change that part of me, so don't ask me to."

Her glaring eyes glistened, the tears probably a mixture of frustration and withheld emotions if I knew her well. "I don't know how to do this. To be in a relationship. To fall in love." She shook her head, her eyes dropping to stare at my chin rather than my eyes. "I'm not soft, not emotional. Hell," she scoffed, turning her head to the side, "I'm not even nice. *I* don't even like me most days, so why would you?"

"You think I haven't noticed that you would tear this world apart for your friends? For Nimue, for Blaze, for Lys? You're the most loyal person I've ever met. And fuck being nice — niceness is pleasantries and small talk. Meaningless. You give people passion, kindness, truth they can count on — believe me, that matters way more in the end."

Slowly she turned back towards me, her chin lifting, and I couldn't help but smile.

"I knew exactly what I was doing when I shared my powers with you, Devanna," I said, my voice barely above a whisper as I leaned in, dropping my forehead to hers. "I knew I'd be tying my life to yours forever, and I chose it. Just like I'm choosing it now, because you're worth it. Because you shine brighter than anyone I've ever met. Because my world is dull without you in it and I can't bear the thought of going back to a life without you at my side."

She said nothing, her hands still clenched at her side, not touching me, so I drew in a breath and pulled away. It was the hardest thing I'd ever done, but I stepped back, giving her space to breathe.

"But the choice is yours now. I'll go if you tell me to, and we'll figure… something out, I don't know." I shrugged, pinching the bridge of my nose.

Watching her head tip down to study her feet broke me, but I forced myself to turn and walk towards the door, hearing her unspoken answer loud and clear.

As I pulled open the door, a crackle of electricity shot through the air, slamming it shut again.

"Don't go."

Not daring to hope yet, I turned back, and Devanna launched into my arms.

Chapter Forty-One

DEVANNA

MY FIRST TRIP to angel HQ had been chaotic, at best, but compared to the total shit show it was now? I could hardly believe my eyes.

The place was a total shambles. Apparently, more than just Ezra had revolted, and the angels who'd tried to orchestrate the coup had trashed everything on their way out. Walls were torn down, statues destroyed, papers and trash and rotting food was everywhere. One of the fountains in their pristine atrium had completely blown to rubble, its water flooding the entire level.

Orion's eye had been twitching since we arrived. I fought to stifle my chuckle.

It might do the angels some good to shake things up a little.

"Hey, maybe this time your designer will be someone who knows about colors other than white. Wouldn't that be something?" I elbowed him, but he only grunted. The male was wound tighter than a bow string, being back up here.

Something I'd be happy to fix later tonight.

The thought lent a little bounce into my black leather platform boots, and I added an extra swish to my hips as well, hoping my tight black skirt would scandalize a few closed-minded angels along the way to the Council chambers.

Malachi — the Council Premier — had summoned us, along with a handful of other officials he wanted to speak with, to try to figure out a new way forward.

Passing through the chamber doors, Orion stopped short. West Larkin, the wolf Alpha from Timber Creek who I'd met at the Summit, stood next to the angel we'd seen escaping earlier this summer. Once again, my eyes were drawn to his wings — so much darker than any other angel's.

"Max," Orion said, offering a short nod to the males. "West."

West moved forward, his hand outstretched. Orion took it, shaking briefly, before West dropped his hand and offered me the same greeting.

"West Larkin," he said, a grim smile hidden beneath his brown beard. "We met briefly at the Summit, but it's good to see you again and in one piece, Devanna."

"Likewise," I said, eyeing him tentatively. While I didn't know the male well, everything I'd heard about him had been good. I was more than a little surprised to see a wolf in Angel HQ, but maybe this was a change we needed.

"How did you fare in Colorado?" Orion asked as we walked towards a set of double doors at the end of the hall.

"There was an attack at the wellspring, like we anticipated," he answered, jaw clenching as he glanced at Max and then back at Orion. "More than a few angels showed up."

Max and Orion studied each other, silently communicating some unknown message that was annoying as shit.

"Care to share with the rest of us plebeians?" I said, hands on my hips as I stared up at the men. "What does that mean?"

Shockingly it was Max that answered. "I've been working undercover for the last several years, trying to identify the source of a mole inside the Council. Someone was leaking information to Nergal and his associates for over a decade, all leading to this."

I frowned, my feet stilling as I tried to piece together his words. "So wait, you *knew* this was all going to happen? You knew Nergal would likely escape, that Kal would murder multiple times over in an attempt to gather power and free his father, and you just, what? Let it happen?" Swinging my gaze to Orion, I stilled. "Did you also know about this?"

"No," he answered immediately, the look in his eyes just as flinty as mine. "I didn't. The Council never thought to share that information with me."

I drew in a deep breath, feeling the rage boil under my skin as I tilted my head to one side then the other, preparing for a battle of a different kind. "Open the damn doors, gentlemen. It's time for a new world order."

A half-dozen angels were already seated in the Council chamber, along with a few head witches I vaguely recognized but had never officially met, and a handful of shifters besides West. Then, of course, there was Malachi.

To say the Premier had seen better days would be the understatement of the century.

Most of the other angels had tried to keep up to their usual standards of dress, though there were a few unbuttoned shirts here and there, and one female angel even wore jeans. But Malachi had gone off the deep end. His wrinkled chinos didn't even match the rumpled *t-shirt* he wore, and his hair desperately needed a comb.

"Have a seat." Malachi gestured to the remaining empty chairs, and we settled in. I was pretty sure I'd heard Blaze describe the room as having stadium seating, but now, we were all seated on the same level around a table.

I doubted angels did anything by accident.

"As you are all aware," Malachi began, looking around the room at all of us, "We've entered some... unprecedented times."

To our left, Max covered his mouth for a cough that sounded oddly like, "*Understatement.*"

"For the first time in our recorded history, humans are aware of the existence of supernaturals to some degree," Malachi continued, ignoring Max. "The Council has had insiders in human government for decades, but Ezra was over them. He pushed the FBI into Deadlights Cove for the murder investigation to keep you distracted down there. Now that he's gone, I've instructed our insiders to wipe the FBI files — there will be no trace of the murders there, so no FBI agents will come sniffing around again. We'll have to wipe a lot of memories, but that's what the times have come to."

Orion nodded, relief sweeping through both of us at that. We weren't exactly equipped to deal with a long, drawn-out investigation. Sooner or later, someone in the Cove would break, and then it would get out that we were a supe town. This was definitely for the best.

"Now, so far, we've managed to limit the scope of their knowledge to shifters, encompassing sea nymphs in that category as well, which humans don't know to be a separate species. One of the things we need to discuss today is whether we stick to that story."

He cleared his throat, shifting in his seat for a moment before he continued. "Additionally, it has become clear due to — ah — recent events, that not *everyone* in the supernatural community has been thrilled with our governing system."

"You can say that again," I muttered, but clamped my lips shut tight when Malachi frowned and searched for the source of the words.

"You — *we* — need a diverse governing body," Max stated, crossing his arms and leaning back in his chair. "That was the most common complaint I heard undercover. Having *only* angels on the Council makes every other species feel like their voices aren't heard, or won't be taken seriously. Not to mention setting up supernatural headquarters in a location only *angels* can access? Our people need an accessible government."

With a heavy sigh, Malachi nodded. "Here is what I propose. Each species band together and elect a representative, then those five meet regularly, working together to ensure our supernatural laws are fair for all parties."

"You expect *demons* to be capable of orderly government?" one angel scoffed, making pointed eye contact with her neighbor. "I say there is no demon representative. They can't be trusted with anything, especially not after Nergal started all this with the intent to destroy us. I bet they wouldn't even show to the meetings!"

"If there's no demon representative, then I say no shifters either," another angel chimed in. "What, are we supposed to find a new representative every few decades? Their life-spans are so short. It'll be a waste of time."

Max gave a sharp laugh that was all bitterness. "These are *exactly* the prejudices that make the other species hate us and distrust the Council. You realize that, right?"

"My son has a point," Malachi nodded before the angels could start up again. No one else seemed shocked by this revelation, but I looked at the angel with the dark wings again, seeing the way his shoulders bunched with tension in the room. The Premier's own *son* had been working undercover? How long had everyone here thought *he* was the enemy? For that matter, how long had he been locked up on Omega before Malachi freed him? "*Every* species is going to need to have an equal say. That's the best way to ensure something like this uprising doesn't happen again. It'll probably take decades for the new and improved Council to gain everyone's trust even *with* these reforms."

"There are a lot of shifters who'd like to see all angels behind bars right now," West agreed, then held up his hands. "Not that I'm one of them. But there's been a lot of grumbling about what it would take to make our species feel repaid for taking the fall with humans. The least we can do is ensure we have a real voice in supe law going forward."

"And any angel that disagrees is welcome to fuck right off," Max added, staring down the angels who had voiced their complaints. "Or I'm sure we could find a few newly emptied cells in the Keep to throw you in."

I smirked. Max and I would get along just fine, I was beginning to think.

"I might have phrased it a little more tactfully," Malachi said. "But I'm inclined to agree with Massimo. So, to that end of a more democratic government, all in favor of electing representatives from each species to serve on the Council from now on?"

A witch shot her hand up. "I'd like to request each species have two representatives, ideally from different regions."

Malachi looked around the room at her words, assessing whether the rest of the room agreed with her. Most were nodding, so he acquiesced.

"Two representatives. All in agreement?"

All the shifters and witches' hands shot up straight away, and half of the angels' did too. Slowly, the angels who had voiced complaints lifted their hands in the air, though it was clear they did it with some reservations.

"How long do you all think it will take to make your decisions?"

Each species turned to their other members, discussing amongst themselves, then gave their answers to Malachi.

"Then we'll reconvene for our first modernized Council in three months' time. If any of you have suggestions of where we should hold that meeting, you can send them along to me as well."

That business concluded, Malachi turned to Orion and me.

"For anyone here who may not know, this is Orion

Moretti, Mayor of Deadlights Cove, and Devanna Bailey, local witch. Now, I'm sure we're all dying to hear exactly how you —" Malachi's grey eyes dragged over me, noticing the bite mark on my neck that hadn't faded, before settling on Orion "—your town was able to deal with Nergal and Errakal."

"And Ezra," Max put in helpfully, and Malachi flinched.

"Yes, and Ezra."

Orion launched into the driest possible version of what had happened, how the town had come together to handle Nergal's groupies, then turned to me to explain the whole magic crystal business.

When I explained how Blaze had harnessed the power of a demon through a century-old witch-charged crystal while I helped to incapacitate Nergal's army, jaws hung slack.

Well, the other witches in the room smirked, clearly enjoying, as I was, this moment for our kind, but the other supes were stunned.

"You and Blaze are suffering no ill effects?" an angel asked from the far side of the table.

I lifted a shoulder. "All in a day's work."

I could sense Orion stifling an eye roll, but Max chuckled.

"Sabazios Rosewood and Ryker Odinsson were able to capture Ezra," Orion continued the thread of the story. "Kal is dead by my own hands."

"And you believe Nergal to be dead?" Malachi asked.

"Our head of Coven, Ostara Theroux, performed both an imprint reading and an essence analysis. Both confirmed

Blaze's and my last blast of power incinerated him on the spot."

Orion's wings flexed slightly as he rubbed his jaw, clearly proud of what I'd done.

"Then all that remains is to decide what to do with Ezra Moretti," Malachi continued. "But until our new Council forms, he'll remain incarcerated."

"With better guards, I hope," Max raised an eyebrow.

"You should hire a new head of security altogether," Orion added, to which Max nodded in agreement.

"Any suggestions?"

Orion and I shared a look. I was pretty sure I knew where he was going with this. "On a temporary basis — because he'd never agree to this permanently — I'd recommend Ryker Odinsson. Nothing dragons love more than keeping something protected — no way Ezra will escape under his guard."

"And I'd suggest Nox Hayes to test your security," I said. "He's a young demon, but he got past Ryker's security once. Trust me, there's no one better to find weaknesses in your systems than that kid."

"A *demon*?" the snobbish angel said again, her lip curling.

"Hey, you want a demon-proof jail? You need a demon testing it," I shot at her, and she dropped her gaze.

"Then it's done," Malachi said, pushing back from the table. "Ryker can guard the jail for now, this kid Nox can tell us where its failures are, and we'll be back in three months to make more lasting decisions."

"I'd also like to warn everyone to be on their guard, and you should pass it along to your people," West added before Malachi could stand. "Shifters have already started going missing. Mostly from rural areas, mostly loners, but it's happening. I'm working with a few other Alphas to come up with a task force to track down where they're going and how we can prevent it from happening, but we don't expect it to stop anytime soon."

"Humans?" a witch asked.

"We assume so," West said. "Best case scenario, it's some kind of fringe group who want to study us. Worst case? Well. Let's hope they're not too organized, or this is going to get much worse, very quickly."

His words hung in the air. We weren't all shifters in the room, but we all *knew* shifters, lived among them. Loved them.

If he was right, this was about to affect all of us.

"On that ominous note," Max pushed to his feet and gave a half-hearted salute.

Orion took my hand as the meeting disbanded, and we made our way out of the chambers.

Back in the atrium on our way back to the Lobby, Orion stopped dead in his tracks.

"Mother."

An elegantly tall woman who could have passed as Galadriel's severe older sister stood there, not a stitch out of place in her wrap dress, her hair in a strict ballet bun. Her white wings shone with unnatural shimmer, but she held them with poise, pulling herself even taller as she turned to face us. Glancing between them, she looked only a few years older than Orion himself, but with angel lifespans being nearly immortal, her actual age was anyone's guess.

"Orion." Her tone was clipped, her eyes raking over Orion before flitting over to me.

Orion's jaw tensed for only a moment before he placed his palm on the small of my back. "Mother, this is Devanna Bailey. Devanna, this is my mother, Miriam Moretti."

Anger clawed up my spine at the sight of this female, knowing how she'd treated Orion. Orion's hand slid from my back up to my shoulder, tucking me against him to make our relationship clear, and I pushed down my personal feelings to offer Miriam a polite smile. This wasn't the time to make a scene.

"I am *delighted* to put a face to the name at last," I told her honestly, and the slight tightening at the corner of her eyes showed she might have caught on to my true meaning. Mainly that I knew exactly what to make her voodoo doll look like now. We shook hands, hers cold and bony and lifeless, as expected.

"Are you going to visit Ezra?" Orion asked, tilting his head back towards the elevators.

Miriam's wings twitched ever so slightly at the mention of her eldest son, and her mouth turned to an even sharper frown.

"Your brother is a *disgrace*," she managed to hiss, then covered her mouth with a satin handkerchief, her hand trembling. Taking a shaky breath, she dabbed at the corner of her eye before discretely tucking the cloth back in her clutch. "Your father is waiting to speak with the Premier and see what amends can be made. Orion —" she broke off, her grey eyes, slightly lighter than Orion's, searching his.

She was looking at him like she'd never truly seen him before. And maybe, blinded by her adoration for Ezra as it sounded she'd been, she never had.

After a long moment, she stepped forward, and patted Orion awkwardly on the shoulder, then quickly turned and strode away.

Orion watched her go, her stilettos clicking on the marble, until she turned a corner and was gone from sight. I slipped my hand into his, wanting him to know he had plenty of people in his life who *did* see him, and loved him just the way he was.

"That was a beautiful family moment."

Orion huffed a laugh, and tugged me to continue walking towards the Lobby.

"I think that was the closest to an apology I'll get," he murmured and I squeezed his hand.

"Reunion's over," he sighed. "Time to go rebuild our town."

Chapter Forty-Two

ORION

WE LANDED with a crack of thunder, and, while Devanna doubled over, gasping and trying to blink away the nausea that inter-dimensional travel caused for non-angels, I looked over the town square.

Town Hall was rubble. The gazebo, all but gone. Debris and blood stains littered the streets, the grass, and every-where I turned.

The Cove might never have been the most pristine town in mid-coast Maine, but this was worse than I'd ever seen it. Even the aftermath of the Harvest Festival never looked this bad.

"Oh hey, you're back," a voice called out. Val and Caedmon were sweeping up shards of glass that had been the Town Hall windows, hands raised in a wave.

I waved back, then realized they weren't the only ones already at work.

On the other side of the square, Nadir and Emerson were busy lifting a large new window into place in the Immortali-Tea storefront. Lysander was power washing the blood stains from the sidewalk in front of Scallywags, and Maisie was picking up larger pieces of trash and debris out of the street. Peg Fernsby and Eva Watford were in their gardening gear, picking up broken branches on the square that had been blasted in all the fighting.

Beside me, Devanna squeezed my hand.

"See? You don't have to do it alone. Everyone wants to help out. We'll have this place up and running again in no time."

At that moment, Petra and Nimue came around the corner heading towards Immortali-Tea, carrying a box of new ceramic mugs between them. Devanna let out a shriek and launched into a sprint towards them.

"Are you *insane*, Nims?" she screeched, then skidded to a stop right beside her friend, hip-checking her out of the way to take over her side.

"Oh, my God, I can still carry stuff," Nimue rolled her eyes, but allowed Dev to take over. "I'm *barely* pregnant. You can't even tell yet. You're going to be as bad as Kit."

"*Worse*," Dev seethed, marching past her. Nimue shook her head, but smiled at Dev's back.

I couldn't help a grin of my own. My hellcat was a force of nature, and I was still a little dumbstruck that she'd chosen to add me to her team.

But damn, I was glad to be there.

Zaphiel walked by as I moved to follow Devanna, and I reached out to stop him. His grey eyes met mine, confusion written in his expression when I held out my hand to shake. "I haven't had a chance to thank you for helping rescue me. I won't forget it."

The other angel nodded, a blush rising in his cheeks. "I did what you would have done for any of us, Orion."

I dropped his hand, overcome with emotion at the show of loyalty from everyone here, and patted him on the shoulder before moving on.

Kit came around the corner next with another box for the shop, and I fell in step with him as we followed the girls towards the store.

"How is Akil doing?"

"Thanks to Lys, he'll be okay," Kit said. "One of Nergal's crew threw him into a tree — his spine got mangled pretty badly. His wounds are healed up now, but emotionally?" He shook his head. "It shook him, being that injured. Helpless. Shifters are used to healing almost immediately and, with the nexus points down, he suffered for a while."

My heart was heavy for them, but Kit was an excellent Alpha and brother — I knew he'd take good care of Akil.

"How is Lily handling Julian's passing?" I asked, knowing his sister was close with Darius's Second, one of the wolves who hadn't made it out of the fight.

Kit blew out a breath, running a hand over his mouth. "Their mate bond wasn't complete, and their relationship was always tumultuous, but I can feel her pain through the skulk's ties. She won't talk to any of us. I'm at a loss for what to do other than give her space and hope she comes to me when she's ready to talk."

Devanna walked towards us and grief nearly swallowed me whole, too easy to put myself in Lily's shoes with all of the what-if's today had held. But she was alive, and so was I.

Knowing how hard Kit would be on himself as their leader, I stuck out my hand, needing to show some sort of solidarity I so often wished for. Kit placed his palm in mine, eyeing me quizzically. "You're a good male, Kit. They're in good hands. And when you or Lily or anyone else needs help, you know everyone here in town has your backs. We're not going anywhere."

Kit leveled that steady, amber gaze of his on me and nodded. "Thank you. And you know I've always got your back, too."

Later that night, after a long day of town cleanup and a very satisfying — in more ways than one — shower, Dev and I sat up in the bell tower, looking over the town and enjoying the cool breeze and cooler drinks.

"Are there actually any materials that are demon-fire-proof?" she asked absently, both of us watching Blaze and Nox struggling with the steel frame for the new gazebo.

I took a sip of my beer. "Well, metal's better than wood, at least."

Dev hummed at that, sipping at her whiskey.

We sat in silence for a while, the sky darkening as night fell, and the sounds of summer filled the air in place of light — the waves crashing against the beach, the crickets in the woods, the muttered curses of demons.

It was good to be home.

Dev shifted her weight slightly, and her bare leg ended up pressed against mine. I took it as an invitation to wrap my arm around her, pulling her into my side. Resting my chin on her head, I closed my eyes to breathe in her light jasmine scent.

"Do you ever regret choosing this life for yourself?" Dev asked. "Trying to herd these cats."

Bagheera let out an indignant chirp from Dev's other side.

"Never." I didn't even have to think about it. "This is always where I wanted to be, even with all its ups and downs." Fireflies flitted in and out of view, and Bags bolted upright, then took off running down the bell tower, his tiny paws somehow thundering with each step.

"So, you're planning to stay, then."

I furrowed my brow. "You were there when I told Kit I wasn't going anywhere. Why would I?"

"I don't know. There are a lot of changes going on in Angelville. Maybe you'd want to be a part of that."

"Not a chance. It's more important than ever that I stay here. I couldn't live with myself if anything happened to any of our shifters, or anyone else. It's bad enough we lost Julian and the other two wolves."

"None of that was your fault," Dev reminded me gently. "But I know what you mean. My parents couldn't pay me to leave this town."

"Why would you even ask?"

Dev sat up, putting a little distance between us, and leveled a stare at me. "Are we in a relationship?"

What? How could she ask that? "Yes." Shit, I hoped that was the right answer —

"Good." *Thank fuck.* "Well, I'm not ready to full-on *Link* with you — no offense — but I think maybe Bags and I wouldn't mind a roommate."

I blinked. "What?"

"I know how annoying Blaze is."

"Sure, but —"

"And we can fix the acoustics in the main room for your piano, if you want."

I wrapped a hand over her mouth, the corner of my own tilting up as her eyes flared. "I see I'll need to start carrying a pocket-gag around." Dev rolled her eyes. "Are you asking me to move in with you, hellcat?"

Dev pushed my hand away, then rose up onto her knees to throw one leg over my hips, straddling me. "Seems fitting, doesn't it? Every church needs an angel."

"And a devil," I smirked, hands dropping to her hips.

"And a poltergeist," she added, and from somewhere in the graveyard below, Bagheera yowled.

"We might have different definitions of church."

"My church, my rules."

I narrowed my eyes. "*Our* church, our rules."

"Hmm, I'm not so sure this is a democracy."

"Really?" I chuckled. "After everything we just talked about today at Headquarters?"

"*Especially* after that conversation. Clearly, angels can't be in charge."

I laughed, then pulled her tighter into my chest, placing a kiss on her forehead. "Okay. You can be in charge. For now."

"Yes, sir."

Not ready to say goodbye to the Cove? Good news!! Wild Wild Wolf is a spinoff book, the first in the series in Timber Creek! Ready to know more about West Larkin and his fated mate who wants nothing to do with him? Read it now.

MORGAINE

Epilogue

Five Years Later

"OH, HUSH NOW, DEAR," I cooed to the currently humanoid baby in my arms, bouncing little Ayla gently on my lap as I kissed her dark hair. "You'll be big enough to run around and set fires in no time."

I glanced up just in time to see Phoenix, my five-year-old grandson, scampering around the gazebo, the white tip of his fox tail alight, and Keahi in her miniature opalescent dragon form close on his heels. It was a good thing the gazebo had long since been remade and spelled against fire since my grandbabies were giving it a run for its money.

A light breeze drifted off the ocean, scattering the first autumn leaves of the year across the field. This was always my favorite time of year in the Cove — when the sky turned clear and blue, with that crisp fall scent filling the cool air.

On the far side of the green, my daughter Nimue sat on a picnic blanket with Phoenix's twin, Ember. Older by two minutes, Ember was serious and steady like her father, while

Phoenix was all chaos and restlessness he must have inherited from the demon side. In matching green plaid shirts and pink overalls, Nimue and Ember were attempting to show little Magnus how to make a daisy chain, though his stubby three-year-old fingers weren't quite dextrous enough to do one himself. Selene leaned over, trying to help her son, who turned a scowl on her that looked every bit like his grumpy father, his bright green eyes a stunning contrast to his lightly tan skin and dark curls.

Some days it was hard for me to reconcile that this was my life. Eddie and I had dreamed of having a large family, but it hadn't been in the cards for us. Happy tears gathered in the corners of my eyes as I took in the scene before me, full of not only my children, but my *grand*children. None of them were biologically mine, but when had that ever mattered? I loved them all with a ferocity no magic could compare to. Eddie would have loved them all just as dearly as I did, I was sure of it.

The last five years in Deadlights Cove brought a whirlwind of change. Orion had been reinstated as the mayor shortly after Nergal was taken care of, once and for all. He and Devanna had finished renovations on the church, and then began working on several other of the abandoned properties around town. Since then, Devanna had taken over the Historical Society, sick of the Ladies meddling in their renovation projects. Nobody dared tell her, but she was far more a tyrant than Peg Fernsby and Eva Watford ever were.

Lysander became the leader of the Coven when Ostara retired and moved back to New Orleans, bringing in a new age of younger witches to the town. Maisie ruled the sea nymphs side by side with Ronan, who had no plan to retire anytime soon even though he was enjoying his new role as grandparent as much as I was.

Ryker and Selene lived in Boston, but expanded on Ryker's property here in the Cove as a weekend home, at which they spent more and more time lately with their two children. I still had hopes Selene would want to move home someday, especially with Ryker gone for work as much as he was, but I'd settle for the moments I got to spend with their family in between.

Nimue took to motherhood like a fish to water, the embodiment of calm and patience, even with her three hellion children. Kit had finished their pack home before the twins were born, and luckily there was room for a dozen more children as I could tell from the way Nimue's cheeks glowed, I had another grandchild on the way.

Petra and Blaze traveled the world for a few years, hopping from library to library while she conducted her research on the history of supernatural society, but they'd since resettled in the Cove for good. With Devanna's help, Blaze transformed the old Schoolhouse into a museum, and Petra ran the day-to-day operations while she continued to work on her book. Blaze had made the Poop Deck a permanent feature on the roof at Scallywags, and it quickly became the go-to spot for everyone to hang out after work. Despite the removal of all humans from the Cove, our town was now a supernatural tourist destination since the events here five years ago, so Blaze was busier than ever at the bar as business boomed.

Everyone was happy, and right where they needed to be, including me.

Suddenly, Ayla let out a screech, and with a popping bubble sound, the baby turned into a tiny red fox kit, scrambling out of my arms and shooting across the town square to the gazebo before I could catch her.

These hybrid children were something else.

"Incoming!" I called. Nimue picked her head up, shaking it as Ayla bounced around the outside of the gazebo, yipping and trying to keep up with her older brother and cousin.

While most shifter children didn't typically start shifting between forms until they were two, these half-demon-half-fox-shifters could nearly as soon as they'd opened their eyes, though they had little control over when it happened. It took child-proofing the house to a whole new level. Luckily, none of them had mastered flickering yet, but Goddess help us all when they did.

"O'Connell, no! Those little Vulpix aren't puppies."

Petra held firm to the leash to stop her pitbull mix rescue puppy from running after the foxes, his large brown eyes pleading with her to let him go play. Since the dog was as likely to be accidentally set on fire as to have fun running around, she was right to keep him away until the kids had more control.

I hummed in thought to myself as I sat back on the park bench, taking in my growing family. Maybe little O'Connell needed a special something in his food to help ease along the obedience training. I'd need to consult some books, but I was sure I could come up with something. No matter their species, Grammy Mo took care of her grandbabies.

"He doesn't understand why he can't go play," Petra said

as she took the seat next to me, tying O'Connell's leash to it.

"Someday, he'll be three," I assured her, patting her hand. "And unlike those kits, for your puppy that'll make a big difference. He's doing great, dear."

With a disgruntled grumble, O'Connell lay down, head on his paws, and tried to content himself with just watching. Then his ears pricked up, and he turned his head as Bagheera sauntered past, pausing a few feet in front of him before doubling back to curl up next to the puppy.

"You're a big softie in your old age, you know that?" Devanna shot at the cat, who only stared at her in response. Since Mrs. Farrington's passing, Bagheera and Devanna had become nearly inseparable, though both refused to admit they liked each other, and the cat had become a begrudgingly sweet nanny to all the grandkids.

Petra leaned over, scratching the black cat behind the ears, earning a gentle purr as Bagheera closed his eyes in contentment.

"Wow," Dev snorted at Bagheera, sitting on the bench next to ours. "I thought I was your favorite, you traitor."

"Where are Blaze and Orion?" I asked.

Petra nodded towards the far end of the square, facing the town beach. "Setting up."

Blaze and Orion wrangled a large white sheet, stretching it out on a frame to serve as the backdrop for the movie projector.

As had been the tradition for the past several years since Petra arrived in town, it was outdoor movie night. The scent of fudge and popcorn filled the air as Nox and Aurora laid food out on one of the snack tables in front of Pop Nox.

Nadir, Emerson, and Maisie manned another table with assorted drinks — iced teas, lemonades, and more adult beverages for those who wanted them. Delia, Maisie and Lys's two-year-old daughter, ran circles between them, giggling as she tried to sneak up on Nadir, who of course heard her coming from a mile away but pretended to be shocked every time she "caught" him. Around the square, Lysander, Dillon, Akil, and Ruby set up speakers for the film.

Maisie's sisters helped Kit and a few of the other foxes to arrange blankets and beach chairs around the square, and Val and Caedmon had parked the coffee van on the edge of the square to supply ice for the drinks and a selection of donuts. Winston lingered on the beach nearby, waiting for someone to throw a donut to the bull moose — or for Val and Caedmon to turn their backs long enough for him to steal some. Once the screen was up, Blaze flickered to the side of the van and switched on his cotton candy machine — a town staple at every event.

Selene and Nimue rounded up their kids, moving towards the blankets to settle in for the movie when the deep rumble of a motorcycle engine roared along Ocean Avenue.

"Daddy!" Magnus cried as he leapt to his feet, running towards where Ryker parked his bike. "You're back!"

Ryker bent down, scooping his small son into his arms and up onto his shoulders as he moved through the crowd. Magnus grabbed onto his father's hair, pretending to use the bun tied on the top of his head as a gear shift, encouraging Ryker to walk faster as he made his way to Selene's blanket.

In a smooth move, Ryker flipped Magnus off his shoulders and onto the blanket, then dropped to sit behind Selene, pulling her back into his chest.

"How was Colorado?" Selene asked after Ryker kissed her. "Everything good with the Larkins?"

Ryker grunted, then looked my way. "Timber Creek was the same as always."

I couldn't help but smile, sipping at my whiskey smash, so strong it would surely kill a lesser witch. "Just in time," I grinned, then jerked my head towards the screen where the opening credits of *Shanghai Noon* began playing. "I chose this one just for you."

I was on the receiving end of the same deadpan expression of Ryker's I'd seen so many times over the last millennia, I could read it as well as if I could read his mind.

"Were you alive during the Wild West?" Ember asked as she settled into my lap, watching the train heist gone wrong. I wrapped my arms around her, squeezing my granddaughter tight as memories surged to the forefront of my mind.

"I was," I whispered, kissing her gently on the head. "So was Uncle Ryker."

"Was it as wild as they say?"

I hummed in agreement, visions of saloon fights, runaway trains, and stampeding buffalo swirling in my head. "Yes, dear."

"And no one was wilder than your grammy," Ryker grunted, at which Selene and Nimue both laughed and cringed in turn.

"What was it like?" Ember asked, voice turning sleepy as she snuggled into my chest.

I couldn't help but lean my cheek down on her head,

soaking in the comfort her little body gave me as my heart squeezed, remembering the day I'd met my Eddie, and all of our wonderful days after. Falling in love with a human had been foolish — we'd known from the day we said "I do" that I'd outlive him by a thousand years, but true love was inescapable. We were a once-in-a-lifetime love, and I considered myself the luckiest witch alive that I'd gotten to spend as many years with him as I did, even if it would never be enough.

Maybe that was why I'd dabbled in a little meddling in the lives of those I loved. I knew what it was to find that one person that made everything worth it, that made everything *right*, and all I wanted was for my people to find that, too. Looking around the square, seeing so many of my family had found their person — a sigh of contentment left me. I could see Eddie's grin in my mind's eye; he would have loved this as much as I did.

I pressed a kiss to the top of Ember's soft hair, and murmured, "It was magnificent."

Want more Deadlights Cove?

There's more to come in our little paranormal universe! Join Aimee's newsletter at aimeevancebooks.com to be the first to know!

Deadlights Cove

Smoke Show

Deja Brew

A Very Merry Christmoose (Novella)

Wing and a Miss

Pier Pressure

Karma is a Witch

Foxing Day (Novella)

Timber Creek

Wild Wild Wolf

Love Bites

ALSO BY AIMEE VANCE

Mayhem Hockey Club

Moms of Mayhem

Call of the Norns: A Viking Time Travel Fantasy Trilogy

Fates Illuminated

Fates Promised

Fates Defied

Acknowledgments

Look at us. A finished series.
Who would have thought? Not us!

No one is as shocked as we are that this whole thing happened in a little over a year from start to finish. When we started writing *Smoke Show*, the idea was to create a chaotic supernatural town where everyone could fit in. Along the way, we have truly fallen in love with this world and these characters.

To everyone who has ever picked up one of our books, thank you for reading and diving into this universe we've made. It's been so fun to share it with you! We have so many more stories to tell, and we hope you'll stick around!

To our Ultimate Covies — Amy, Brit, Elle, and Lex: Thank you doesn't seem big enough, but truly. THANK YOU! To Amy, for your enthusiasm and support and helping us start our DC universe wiki. To Brit, for your constant willingness to read our early drafts when we need convincing not to throw it in the trash. This one, especially, you came through for us, the champion in our Karma Support Group. To Elle, for loving Orion the most and finding so many of our typos. And to Lex, for jumping on board to try to wrangle two chaotic creatives who would forget our heads if they weren't attached.

From B: Aimee, who would have thought all those hypothetical "Maybe someday we should co-write something" conversations would turn into this series and a whole fictional universe to explore. Here's to many more series and standalones to come!

To J, thank you for your continued patience and understanding when I have my Do Not Disturb face on while writing, for reading my books so you know what I'm talking about all the time, and for supporting me every step of the way.

From Aimee: B, I feel so lucky to be on this journey with you. We complement each other in ways I didn't even know we would, and it makes all of this so much more fun. I am so glad we're doing this together, and excited about what our future holds. The mountains are calling and we must go!

To Chris and the girls, as always, I love you more than words can express. Thank you for reminding me daily how proud you are of me!

About B. Perkins

B. has been making up stories about magic since she learned how to write words on paper. When not immersed in fictional worlds, she enjoys spending time in nature. She has several degrees in various things, and if all they're good for is to provide background in creating fantasy worlds and systems, then maybe they were worth it.

instagram.com/b.p.writes

About Aimee Vance

Fueled by peach tea and chaos, Aimee Vance writes heartwarming and laugh-out-loud romance stories. She holds a B.S. in Public Relations from Texas Christian University and has always been an avid fantasy reader.

Residing in Texas with her husband, two young daughters, and Labrador Retriever, Aimee loves to transport readers to worlds hidden between the pages where magic and love intertwine. She prefers sassy heroines, grumpy heroes, and enough humor to keep you chuckling with every page.

facebook.com/aimeevancebooks

instagram.com/aimeevancebooks

goodreads.com/aimeevancebooks

amazon.com/author/aimeevancebooks

bookbub.com/authors/aimee-vance